DAWSON'S FALL

ROXANA ROBINSON

DAWSON'S FALL

SARAH CRICHTON BOOKS
Farrar, Straus and Giroux
New York

Sarah Crichton Books
Farrar, Straus and Giroux
175 Varick Street, New York 10014

Frontispiece photograph courtesy of James Cummins Bookseller.

Library of Congress Cataloging-in-Publication Data
Names: Robinson, Roxana, author.
Title: Dawson's fall / Roxana Robinson.
Description: First edition. | New York : Sarah Crichton Books/Farrar, Straus
    and Giroux, 2019. | Includes bibliographical references.
Identifiers: LCCN 2018043948 | ISBN 9780374135218 (hardcover)
Subjects: LCSH: Charleston (S.C.)—Social life and customs—
    19th century—Fiction. | GSAFD: Historical fiction.
Classification: LCC PS3568.O3152 D39 2019 | DDC 813/.54—dc23
LC record available at https://lccn.loc.gov/2018043948

Designed by Richard Oriolo

Our books may be purchased in bulk for promotional, educational, or
business use. Please contact your local bookseller or the Macmillan Corporate
and Premium Sales Department at 1-800-221-7945, extension 5442,
or by e-mail at MacmillanSpecialMarkets@macmillan.com.

www.fsgbooks.com
www.twitter.com/fsgbooks • www.facebook.com/fsgbooks

1   3   5   7   9   10   8   6   4   2

This book is dedicated to the writers, not only those in my family, but all the writers throughout history, those who have set down our stories so that we can remember and understand them, and then rewrite them.

. . . my beloved south's mad and willful march into hell—the voluntary destruction of an entire civilization.

—CHRIS DIXON, *THE SCUTTLEFISH*, JANUARY 3, 2015

PREFACE

Francis Warrington Dawson and Sarah Morgan Dawson are my great-grandparents. I grew up hearing stories about them.

All families have origin myths: we tell our stories to remind ourselves of who we are. The stories are handed down through the generations to reinforce our beliefs about ourselves.

One of my ancestors came here from Wales in the seventeenth century. He wrote this message in the family Bible:

I, David Morgan, Gentleman of Wales, bequeath to my descendants in America, this comfortable certainty; they come neither from Kings nor nobles, but from a long line of brave gentlemen and women with unstained names. [I am] son of Evan, and grandson of David, gentleman of Wales, whose ancestors returned to its mountains rather than be enslaved by William of Normandy, called William the Conqueror.

Principle is important in my family. I wasn't surprised to learn that my Welsh ancestors had moved into the mountains rather than submit to a foreign invader. But I was surprised by the dates: William the Conqueror arrived in England in 1066. This means that the Morgan family had been telling this story, handing it down from generation to generation, for seven hundred years. Clearly it was an important part of who we were.

———•———

WE WERE TAUGHT that principle was more important than money or comfort or peer pressure, that conscience was a reason to act. My parents converted to Quakerism; my brother did community service during the Vietnam War. Our family believed in honoring your conscience.

My mother's family had deep roots in New England. Many of them arrived in that early surge of searchers for a place to practice the religion they chose. Religion played a big part in my mother's family. Many were ministers, and many were outspoken: Lyman Beecher and his son, Henry Ward Beecher, my great-grandfather. Harriet Beecher Stowe was my great-great-great aunt. We spoke out for what we believed in.

My father's side of the family had roots both in New England and in the South. Principle played an important part in that history as well: one ancestor had been put to death by Henry VIII for his loyalty to the Catholic Church.

But the story of my Southern family and their principles was more complicated than that of my New England family because of slavery. I couldn't ignore its presence. All Southern families, regardless of their race, who trace their bloodlines back before the Civil War are affected by the presence of that peculiar institution. They may not mention it, but it helps shape who they are. My great-grandfather Frank fought for the Confederacy, and my great-grandmother Sarah grew up in a privileged household in antebellum Louisiana. Certainly slavery played a part in their lives.

So I wondered about this. How did people of principle navigate the ethical maelstrom of slavery? How could they maintain personal integrity during that dark basilisk reign, or during its terrible aftermath?

Frank and Sarah were both writers, so I could read their thoughts in hundreds of pages of editorials, essays, letters, and journals, both published and unpublished. They wrote about their joys and excitements, grieved over their losses, set down their hopes and fears, and told their own moving and tender and hair-raising stories. But in one sense, even before I read their stories I knew who they were: they had bequeathed their beliefs to me. I was the recipient of the family culture, I was part of it.

I wanted to learn more. I wanted to learn how they had maintained the code of honor of my Welsh ancestors. I wanted to learn and tell their story, a modern version of the one my family had been telling for seven hundred years. How we had climbed up into the steepest, most inaccessible mountain heights rather than give up our principles. If we had.

———·———

HERE IS THAT VERSION. All the facts in it are true as far as I could determine. All the letters and diary entries are real, as are all the other published sources.

As a biographer, I hewed to the facts, even when they made me uncomfortable. The language, words, and attitudes are drawn from published and unpublished material. These are sometimes shockingly racist, reflecting the reality of those shockingly racist times. As a novelist, I wrote this as a living, breathing tale, one that unfolds to span the lifetimes of my great-grandparents. Frank Dawson was born in England and Sarah Dawson died in France, but they are both buried in Charleston, South Carolina, where they spent their happiest years together.

PART I

1.

HE WAKES AS HE IS FALLING.

He feels himself plunging into space, a great wheeling emptiness be-low. He's been on the edge of a cliff, grappling with a man trying to shoot him. Dawson grabs him, wrestling for the gun, but he wrenches away, pull-ing Dawson off-balance. The man presses the gun against Dawson's chest; he hears the great enveloping sound of the shot. Then he feels the sickening shift beneath his feet as he loses his grip on the world.

As he falls Dawson grabs the man's shoulder to save himself, but instead pulls the man over with him. They fall together, still grappling, as though holding on to each other will help. Dawson's body is clenched and tight, muscles still focused on what he just had, solid ground beneath him, but in-stead there is this: the long drop into whistling black.

Dawson sits up, sweating.

He's in the narrow bed in his dressing room. His thrashing has pulled the sheets loose, and his feet are now tangled and trapped. The room is dim and shadowy, the curtains drawn for the night. The patterned wallpaper, the tall mahogany bureau, the brass bedstead are all familiar but irrelevant. He's still in his nightmare, heart hammering. He still feels the terror of pitching into space, the body's last clenching try at holding on to life. He still feels the man's coarse sleeve in his grasp, smells his sour rankness. The sound of the gunshot still explodes in his ears.

He kicks his feet free and gets up. He goes through the connecting door into their bedroom, where his wife lies submerged in the big mahogany bed, nearly hidden by pillows.

She lifts her head and sees his face. "What is it?"

The struggle is still running through him. He takes a breath and shakes his head. In his body, it's still happening. He begins walking up and down the room. This is familiar, too, the mirrored armoire, the high sleigh bed, the dressing table. Also irrelevant in this swift current of feeling.

"What's wrong?" Sarah sits up, the white nightgown crumpled high around her throat.

"I had a dream," says Dawson. "A man had a gun and was going to shoot me. I was trying to stop him. We were on the edge of a cliff." Again he feels himself pitching into emptiness; he can smell the man. "Then he did shoot me, and I fell. I can feel it still."

The dream possesses him. And some other moment flickers into his mind, when he stood somewhere high, behind him emptiness.

"My poor Frank." Sarah's hair is in its nighttime braid, the loosened strands making a fine furred halo around her face.

"What do you think it means?" he asks.

He doesn't really believe in this—the reading of dreams, second sight, premonitions—but Sarah does. She's the seventh child of a seventh child, and believes in another realm of perception. Dawson believes there are kinds of knowledge we don't understand, but he also believes that most people who claim this knowledge are frauds. Sarah is not a fraud. Sometimes her intuitions are uncanny. He's seen it happen; sometimes she's attuned to something he can't explain. Though sometimes she's wrong.

Right now he wants to rid himself of this feeling, the sickening plunge. He hopes that whatever Sarah says will lessen its power.

"Did you know the man?" Sarah leans forward.

"I'd never seen him before."

"A stranger," says Sarah, "trying to harm you. Maybe it's someone who's attacking the newspaper?"

Dawson snorts. "The people attacking the paper are quite open about it," he says. "I know exactly who they are. They don't need to hire anonymous assassins."

The dream begins to recede, which is what he'd hoped for, though not like this. Now he's back in another kind of conflict, the alarms and confusions of daily life.

In daily life Dawson is the editor and part owner of the Charleston *News and Courier*. He and Bartholomew Riordan bought it twenty years ago, first the *News*, then the *Courier*. Dawson was editor in chief, Riordan business manager. Now that Riordan's gone, Dawson runs more or less everything. The paper has always been his voice. He's always written the editorials, always had strong opinions, and he has become a kingmaker. His candidates usually win. He was a representative at the Democratic National Convention; he's a friend of President Cleveland. *The News and Courier* is one of the most influential newspapers in the South. Dawson thinks privately that it's the most influential.

He and Riordan met in Richmond, after the war. They were both Catholic, both hardworking, earnest, principled. They trusted and complemented each other. Riordan was quiet and reserved, Dawson bold and forceful. Their mission was to inform and educate. They believed in integrity. They wanted to rebuild the world: the one they'd known was gone.

Dawson wrote daily editorials. He was fast, informed, and opinionated, never afraid to challenge his readers. Riordan scrawled comments in the margins. *Is this what we want to say?* Sometimes he'd put a query at the head of the whole piece. Sometimes he wrote, *Too strong.* Sometimes just *No.* Sometimes *Yes!* Dawson had relied on his responses; sometimes he changed the piece, sometimes he didn't, but always he listened.

Three years ago Riordan had left for New York and Dawson had hired his old friend J. C. Hemphill as publisher. Hemphill was trustworthy and experienced, but he never disagreed with Dawson and never asked questions. Last fall he'd left. The new publisher makes no comment at all.

Though Dawson doesn't really need Riordan. After twenty years he knows how to run a paper. And he knows Charleston; he loves it. He wants to help Charleston move into the larger world; he wants it to thrive.

Dawson believes in God (he's devout), in education ("A life without Books is death," he wrote to his younger brother), and in telling the truth. He's certain of his convictions. He has a vision of Charleston's future. He wants industry, tourism, railroads, shipping. "Bring the mills to the cotton" is his motto. He is friends with priests, ministers (both black and white), rabbis, policemen. He knows everyone in city politics. He belongs to the exclusive St. Cecilia Society and the populist Hibernian Society. He believes in drawing the community together.

He also believes in the rule of law, and he defends the rights of the freedmen. Once, soon after the war, he'd tried to put Negroes onto the aldermanic ticket. He arranged the first political meeting between colored men and Democrats in Charleston. He'd rented the hall himself, an empty store on Hayne Street, hoping they'd form an alliance. (They hadn't.) When the big earthquake hit Charleston, three years ago, Dawson led the relief efforts, working with both black and white leaders.

His opinions have made him some enemies. He's not a native (he was born in England), and his opinions are not always shared by Southerners. Some of his readers don't want to put the war behind them or give black people political power. Some readers are enraged and accuse Dawson of lying about his rank (captain), his war record (Army of Northern Virginia, Mechanicsville, Gettysburg, served under Longstreet), and his U.S. citizenship (real). He's been challenged to duels, though he's denounced dueling and helped to ban it. He's received death threats, which he ignores. He's opposed to violence on principle. When he gets a threat he won't even change his route to the office.

Dawson doesn't mind all this; he's certain he's right. He has Charleston's best interests at heart. He holds fast, and usually his readers come around. Though when his readers resist too vehemently, or when his candidate loses, Dawson yields and supports the winner. He believes a newspaper should reflect the views of its community. It should lead, but it must also listen.

This has been successful for twenty years, but things have changed, first gradually and now drastically. A group of powerful men, men he used to call his friends, have turned against him. They have founded another newspaper, *The Charleston World*, which is trying to run him out of business. The *World* is a year old, and disturbingly popular. It's cheap, gossipy, and poorly written. Dawson despises it. It's flourishing. It's openly hostile to him, mocking his opinions, stealing his staff, undercutting his price, and taking his subscribers. Dawson has had to let reporters go, cut pages, and borrow money. He knows he'll win in the end, because he has right on his side. He just has to outlast the *World*, keep going until it fails. The thing is that he's running out of money.

The problem is a man called Ben Tillman. He's locked himself onto Dawson like a terrier on an ankle, and Dawson can't shake him loose. At first Tillman was just a struggling plantation owner from upcountry in Edgefield (they're all struggling, the farmers all over the South, now that labor is no longer free). Several years earlier Tillman had started by writing fiery letters to the paper, complaining about The Citadel, a military college for planters' sons. Tillman hated it. He wanted an agricultural college for farmers, instead of an elitist one for rich boys. He was outspoken, energetic, and bold. He simmered with resentment.

Dawson likes controversy. He welcomes new voices and challenging ideas: they make for a good paper. At first Tillman only criticized the school, but his real target was the whole politically powerful Low Country: rich, aristocratic, insular, and exclusionary. Tillman suggested that they meet, and when Dawson agreed, he swore him to secrecy. They met in a remote country inn. There they adopted a strategy: Dawson would support Tillman's agricultural college if Tillman would stop attacking The Citadel. Tillman told Dawson to criticize him a bit, in order to keep the alliance secret. He'd consider the attacks "love licks": a light battering by someone who loves you.

Later Dawson saw that Tillman had been planning his strategy from the start. The secrecy was to protect Tillman from accusations of collusion. It had been Dawson who'd given Tillman prominence, publishing his voice in *The News and Courier*, with one of the largest circulations in the Cotton States. By the time he began his attacks on Dawson, Tillman had a following. Tillman wanted political power, and one way he planned to get it was by bringing down the famous Frank Dawson.

Tillman is now known throughout the South, and his rallies draw big crowds of angry white men. They've all lost the world they once knew, these men. Tillman tells them to blame Dawson, their enemy, the voice of Charleston, heart of the Low Country. Tillman calls him a political manipulator, the Lord High Executioner. Tillman claims that Dawson and a circle of his friends control state politics; he calls Dawson the leader of "Ring Rule." Tillman's a white supremacist, a Fire-Eater. His world has been destroyed by war and emancipation, and he resents this. Tillman wants Redemption, which will obliterate Reconstruction. The Fire-Eaters hate the fact that Negroes are now free. They hate the fact that these men can now vote. They want to put power back in the hands of white people.

Tillman himself was intelligent and articulate. He'd had a classical education, though he'd had to drop out of school because of the war. He resented that, too.

———•—•———

NOW THE EARLIER MOMENT comes back to Dawson, the fear of falling. It was when he faced the crowd at City Hall: he remembers looking out over the brilliance of the torches, the high cavernous darkness beyond. He'd stepped up onto the base of the balustrade, setting his feet between the balusters, gripping the railing. Tillman had introduced him with a sneer. That mocking introduction invited the first catcall from the crowd, which was primed for it.

Gentlemen, Dawson began, but they would not let him finish. *Ring Rule*, they shouted. Each time he spoke there were more catcalls. He kept talking, but he began to realize that they would shout him down. He felt fear enter him, not physical, but some other kind, at being silenced, erased. He felt the crowd's hostility rise toward him, huge and gusty, like a hot wind.

As he began to speak he'd leaned out over the railing, but as the shouts overrode his voice and uncertainty entered him, he lost his sense of balance. For a moment it seemed that if he stepped backward he'd plunge into deep nothingness. It comes back to him now.

———•—•———

HE'LL PUT ALL THIS away from him. Dawson stands in the doorway in his nightshirt and puts a hand on the solid hump of his belly. Light seeps into the room in long fiery shafts through the gaps between the curtains. His body is calming, and its big engines—the heart, the lungs—are slowing. It's morning, light is filling the room and the city. He marshals his own forces—reason, certainty, vitality—against those of fear and darkness.

He's working for Charleston. He doesn't care if public opinion is against him now, it's happened before. He has always prevailed.

Dawson is forty-eight years old, hale and energetic, in his prime. He's five foot nine, a bit portly, actually, though he thinks of himself as strong. Powerful. Blue-eyed and fair-skinned, a broad forehead, straight thick nose, a firm mouth and forceful gaze. Thick wavy brown hair that refuses to lie flat, a long but sparse mustache curling down over his lip. During the war he couldn't raise a mustache, and now he sports a long one, to make up. He gives his belly an affirming pat.

Sarah puts her legs over the side of the bed and slides her white feet into her slippers.

"I had a strange dream, too," she says.

She stands, putting on her thin silk robe. She takes her long braid in both hands, lifts it from inside the robe and drops it outside, down her back. Her hair is thick and honey-colored. The sight of her two-handed gesture, the toppling braid, touches Dawson with its intimacy.

Sarah is in his life. Every day he watches her handling the soft honey-colored braid, putting on her worn slippers. Lifting her chin when she disagrees, pursing her lips when she tries not to laugh. He feels a wave of gratitude.

"Tell me about your dream." He feels protective now.

Sarah goes to the window and pulls back the heavy portieres, and a wide shaft of light enters the room. The sheer inner curtains blur the view of Bull Street, tree-lined. A shrimp woman calls outside, walking slowly, *Raw shrimp, raw shrimp.*

Sarah turns. "My dream was that a woman dressed all in black was scattering burning coals on the floor in the parlor." She's entering the dream again. "You and I were walking on them, in our bare feet. The bottoms of our feet were burning. I could smell the scorched flesh."

"And what does your dream mean?" Dawson asks.

He's only being courteous now; the dreamworld is subsiding. Beyond the railing are high branches, the leaves spring-green, stirring in the early breeze. Mourning doves, invisible, purr to each other their secret messages. From below comes the slow rhythmic clop of hooves, the grinding of cart wheels. The shrimp woman is coming closer. Sarah opens the curtains at the other window and the room is now full of light. Nothing, now, suggests that drop into blackness. He's back in this world.

"It means that a woman will make trouble for us," says Sarah darkly, and turns to face him.

Sarah is small, with delicate bones. High forehead, straight nose, low straight brows. Her skin is very white, her eyes a pale fiery blue. She has the gaze of a visionary.

"Never," says Dawson firmly. "No woman can make trouble for us." They've been married for fifteen years, and he has been in love with her since he first saw her, coming out onto the porch at Hampton's. "Who did she look like?" he asks; Sarah always asks this.

"Sue Covington," Sarah says, broodingly.

This makes him laugh. Sue Covington is an old friend of Sarah's from Louisiana, a tiny energetic woman with snapping eyes and a pointed nose. He can't picture her scattering coals in their parlor.

"My darling chuck-chuck," he says, "I promise that Sue Covington will never come between us."

Now Sarah laughs, too. "I'm glad."

He takes her in his arms. She's small and light. Her shoulder blades shift beneath his hand, her hair smells thick and yeasty. When they draw back she looks up at him, smiling.

Fear has subsided. The little slipper chair where Sarah lays her robe for the night, the silver brush and comb on her dressing table, the wide wash of sun across the patterned carpet: all this is now more real than the shadowy terrors of the night.

"Have the children left yet?" he asks.

"Hélène's taken them to school," Sarah says.

Marie-Hélène Burdayron is the Swiss girl who lives with them. Ethel is fourteen, Warrington, ten. Sarah and the children spent two years in Europe, because Dawson wanted them to have fluency in French and a good Catholic education. Sarah wouldn't let them go alone. When she came back, Sarah brought home the French-speaking girl. They call her Hélène, and they love her. Hélène has meals with the family; she's treated almost as a daughter. She lost her own mother when she was a teenager. The children go now to a local school; Hélène takes them each morning and picks them up.

"Ethel came in earlier. She was upset because she couldn't find her schoolbooks," Sarah says. "You were asleep, but you still had something to say about it."

She teases him about talking in his sleep. He enjoys her teasing; she's the only one who does it. At the paper he's stern. Now that Riordan has gone he has no one to laugh at him.

"You asked me what was the matter," she says. "You said she'd be late for school. But you were completely asleep."

"Well, it's true," Dawson says, laughing, defending his vulnerable sleeping self. "She would be."

"You're right," she says. "Even in your sleep you're right."

He laughs again; she is his boon companion.

Dawson lives in two worlds. The world at the newspaper is noisy, vigorous, fractious, demanding. When he's there his energy goes outward. He writes letters and editorials and comments and checks, makes decisions, responds to readers, job seekers, politicians, landowners, churchmen. The mayor and the councilmen. He has boundless energy, and he relishes all this.

His other world is here, where the household moves smoothly around him. Sarah makes sure of this. She makes sure that the children get to school, the garden flourishes, the meals are prompt and hot. This is his private kingdom, these his adored subjects. The children: Ethel, with her fine limp hair and pointed nose, her ethereal blue gaze, high-strung and melodramatic. Warrington, frail and hollow-chested, bookish, anxious. Dawson plays games with them, teaches them songs, takes them to the theater and to the opera. He's taught Warrington to sail. They all have dinner together every afternoon; Dawson asks them about their day, asks their opinions.

The Dawson house stands on a little rise, in the middle of two lots. Unlike most Charleston houses it faces the street: this is why Sarah loves it.

It's three stories high, handsome white stucco, with white columns along the front of what Sarah would call the galerie, Charlestonians the verandah or the piazza, and the rest of the world the porch.

It was Sarah who'd bought the house, ten years ago, with the last of her family inheritance. It has high ceilings, bay windows, a pair of vast cloudy mirrors set in the parlor walls. They'd put in all the modern things: gas lights, running water, telephones. The bedrooms are on the third floor. Hélène lives up there with them, in a room reached through Warrington's.

Now Sarah's little French clock strikes a tiny silvery chime: eight thirty, time to enter the day. Dawson goes back to his dressing room.

He usually sleeps here, though he may be drawn to the larger bed by ardor. In the evenings he works here, reading or writing, until midnight or later. Sarah sits with him, reading or sewing, in the red plush armchair. Often they discuss what he is working on. Sarah has a formidable memory; he calls her his encyclopedia. She's well-read and opinionated. While Dawson was courting her (which took him a full year) he persuaded her to write for the paper. She was reluctant: she disliked public scrutiny, and it was unseemly to write for money. Dawson reminded her that George Eliot wrote for money. But Sarah didn't think her writing was any good. She said she'd throw each page on the floor as she wrote it, and if he wished to pick them up he was welcome. This made Dawson laugh. He said he'd be glad to pick them up.

She wrote under a pen name. That first piece was about the taxes in Louisiana, and how they were ruining the landowners. His readers loved it, and everyone began trying to guess her identity. She wrote lively pieces about social issues, and gained a following. But she never liked the deadlines, and she hated the attention. After they were married she stopped.

In the mornings the children have usually left for school when Dawson comes down. He has breakfast with Sarah and they go to the office together. When they take the buggy he drives down and she drives back. If she's going shopping afterward they take the big phaeton, and then Isaac drives. When Frank comes home for dinner sometimes Sarah drives down to pick him up, and sometimes he takes the tram, which comes up Rutledge Avenue to the corner of Bull Street. Most of Charleston has dinner at three, but the Dawsons have it at four, because it suits Frank better. They all sit down together, Frank and Sarah, the children and Hélène. Afterward Dawson naps or works until six or six thirty, then goes back to the office. At ten he comes home for a late supper with Sarah.

This room is part dressing room, part study. It holds a desk and bookcases, his armoire, the narrow brass bed, the red plush chair where he sits to put on his socks, the marble washstand. On the bedside table is Trollope's *He Knew He Was Right.* He likes to read novels before going to sleep, likes shifting his mind into someone else's world, letting his own drop away. A life without books is death.

He's just begun this book and wishes he could talk about it with Courtenay, who is the most well-read man he knows, and one of his oldest friends in Charleston. Before the war William Ashmead Courtenay and his brother ran a bookstore and publishing business; he'd introduced Dawson to many Southern writers, in print and in person. Then Courtenay went into politics and became mayor, so he and Dawson became political allies as well as literary colleagues. But now Dawson can't ask Courtenay about this book: they are no longer friends. In fact, it seems they are enemies, over a misunderstanding that has become fixed, apparently irrevocable.

Courtenay was mayor three years ago, on November 10, the twentieth anniversary of Dawson's arrival in Charleston. Dawson was alone that day; Sarah and the children were in Europe. A heavy wooden case arrived from the mayor's office. The case was lined with purple satin, swathing an ornate silver tea set, chased with flowery designs. A handwritten letter thanked Dawson for his services to the city. It was signed by Courtenay and twenty officials. Dawson read and reread the card from his friend.

That Christmas he spent at the office, since his family was away. He'd sent presents to his family, and had given presents to everyone at the paper; he'd even bought presents for the children of his best reporter, Carlyle McKinley. He gave most of the staff the day off so they could spend it with their families. It was a dreary day, and to keep himself busy he went to City Hall. Reading the minutes, he found some planned tax increases. Property owners had been devastated by the earthquake, and he knew they couldn't afford any raises. Dawson was aware that the city had considered this, and he was on the watch. When he saw the plans he wrote a stern warning about them in the paper. Courtenay wrote Dawson a furious note, saying the figures were not official and should never have been made public. But Courtenay was famously tetchy, and if the tax figures were not real, why were they written in the margins of the agenda? It was Dawson's job to keep an eye on these things. He was doing his duty by reporting them.

It took him some time to realize that he'd lost Courtenay's friendship. They saw each other often, at meetings and receptions. Courtenay had often dropped by his office to talk about books and news. But after this, whenever they saw each other they never seemed to be in the same part of the room. Finally, in a crush at the Hibernian Society, Dawson made his way through the crowd. By the time he reached him the mayor's back was turned, but Dawson put his hand on Courtenay's shoulder, and when he turned around Dawson spoke.

"My dear chap, I've missed you," he said. "I haven't seen you in weeks. When are you coming by to talk books?"

Courtenay spoke without smiling. "I'm busy just now. I don't know when I'll have the time."

His face was cold and fixed. It was his look, not his words, that gave Dawson a shock, like opening the door onto a wind-blown spate of rain. For a moment Dawson stared at him, trying to make Courtenay's gaze into the one he'd always known. But Courtenay's face wouldn't change.

That was the last time they'd spoken. Courtenay, his good friend of twenty years, has become his enemy. He's a backer of the hated *World*. There are three of them: Courtenay, William Huger, and Francis Rodgers. They'd all been his friends once; now they're all his enemies. Politics means shifting alliances, and Dawson's used to riding the waves, letting the crest of someone's rage wash under him, dissipating in the open ocean. But this rage is growing, not abating.

He's become used to anger and threats, though they're different here. In England people disagree, but they don't shoot each other. Here in the South they shoot each other. Dawson rejects violence on principle. He owns a pistol but won't carry it. He keeps it in the drawer of his night table in case of burglars. The only time he's ever used it was to shoot his poor dog, Nellie, when she got rabies. Actually, now he can't even find it.

On the washstand are his toilet things, cleaned and laid out by the maid: the ivory-handled straight razor, the badger-hair brush dried to a soft point, the wooden pot of shaving cream. Bay Rum with its long testimonials, the fragrant amber oval of Pears soap. The local chemist sends to London for these; they're what his father used. It occurs to him that he may not be able to afford them now. It is an odd idea.

He doesn't want Sarah to know how bad things are. Last fall, he had to ask for money from Rudolf Siegling, president of his board. Siegling, who's also head of the Bank of Charleston, gave it grudgingly. That loan should have been enough to tide them over until things improved, but they've gotten worse. The circulation has continued to fall: in one day they lost six hundred subscribers.

His former friends are backing the *World*, but the most powerful opposition comes from Tillman. Up in Edgefield the planters resent having to pay wages to men whom they used to own. These men used to work their fields for nothing. It galls the farmers to pay them. Now they've had to watch the Negroes take over government posts, which is against the natural order of things.

Tillman resents this. And he resents Charleston, the rich Low Country, with its dark loamy soil, the long-grain rice plantations, the English aristocratic tradition. Its disproportionate political power. Tillman feels snubbed, and he resents that. The voice of the Low Country is *The News and Courier*, and the voice of *The News and Courier* is Frank Dawson. He resents Dawson.

The circulation of the *World* is now larger than *The News and Courier*'s. When he thinks of this Dawson feels a small icy charge, like a cold bullet, in his chest. Last week Dawson asked Siegling again for money; he refused. Dawson used his own shares as collateral for personal loans. At one time the paper made $30,000 a year, but now it's losing so much money he's had to cut it down from sixteen pages to eight, and fire some of his staff.

He has always been able to make things work. When things have been bad he has worked harder. He paid off his father's debts, sent his sister to school, supported his brother's charitable ventures, lent money to his brother-in-law. He had helped keep the Raines family solvent; the family who had been so generous to him during the war, and who had fallen on such hard times after it. But now, no matter what he does, things get worse. Morale is sliding: three of his staff members have left him for the *World*.

Dawson feels a sharp tiny clench in his gut. He moves his head back and forth to ease it, though this doesn't help. He sets the jug in the sink and turns on the cold water for his bath. He takes off his nightshirt and waits for the jug to fill.

He's seen his doctor about the clench in his gut. Bellinger said it might be an ulcer. Dawson had no interest in having an ulcer, and shook his head at the word.

"It's no good shaking your head, Dawson." Amos Bellinger has a gingery beard and dry pale hands. He is the family doctor, and a friend. "What do you mean, no?"

"I haven't time for an ulcer," said Dawson. "Give me something I can take drops for and which will dry up nicely and go away. I can't take the time for this."

"I should have asked before I made the diagnosis what you might have time for," said Bellinger. "You don't have to take the time to worry about the ulcer, Dawson. It will be there whether you worry about it or not. You don't take any exercise, you know."

"I mean to," Dawson said, "but I haven't time. I used to ride down to the office. I used to do those setting-up exercises."

He's not fat. He feels a private admiration for his solid heft, and thinks himself strong and fit. He thinks of the phrase "rude health." His skin is pink and glowing after his cold bath. During the war they rode through the mountains in icy rain. They slept on the ground, heads pillowed on their saddles. They ate stale corn pone, bacon green with mold. The thought invigorates Dawson. He's still that person. He could do it all again.

"Everyone used to do those exercises," said Bellinger. "It's the ones who still do them who get the benefit."

Dawson smiled and shook his head. The war was something you always owned. If you fought, it was part of you, and nothing could take that from you.

Bellinger was writing something. It would be something Dawson didn't want to read: about eating certain things, drinking certain things, not eating and drinking others. This was not the way he saw himself, as someone with an ulcer. Someone whose life was becoming circumscribed.

Bellinger wore pince-nez. When he'd finished writing he took them off and swiveled his chair around to face Dawson. He rubbed at the little oval indentations the pince-nez left in his pale skin.

"I want you to pay attention to this," he said. "I told Martin Robertson to use this diet and he did not. You see the result."

"I'm not going to die," Dawson said, testy, "and I wish you'd be a bit more discreet. I don't want to know about your patients."

Bellinger shrugged. Robertson was dead; discretion was useless to him.

Amos Bellinger has been his family doctor for years, and except for the indiscretions he's very good. Dawson thinks he has saved Sarah's life, or anyway her health. At nineteen she was in a terrible carriage accident, and for a time she was paralyzed from the waist down. She has been frail ever since, and suffers from intermittent pain in her spine. Dawson depends on Bellinger to keep her healthy.

Bellinger held out the paper. "Now it's up to you, Dawson."

Dawson took the paper with distaste. He felt like Gulliver, surrounded by miniature adversaries, attacked by a swarm of gnats. He has also had intermittent pains in his chest, but he refused to discuss those with Bellinger. He had his life to lead.

Now Dawson sits down to put on his socks. As he sinks into his chair he hears a rich crunching sound. He stands and picks up the seat cushion. Beneath it is his hinged, three-paneled shaving mirror, folded shut. He opens it: the glass is shattered. Bright shards scatter onto the chair, the carpet. He holds it for a moment, angry but impatient. Who put it there? Some big pieces are still intact, one large enough for him to use for shaving. He won't tell Sarah, who'll see more bad luck. Those dreams were bad enough. He wants to move on, into his day.

You choose your own luck, you make it into what you want. Dawson has made his own way since the age of nineteen. You make your own way. Afterward it seems inevitable, as though it could only have happened in this way. But it's you who have chosen your path, and it's always been leading you here.

2.

ALONE IN HIS BEDROOM, he could hear her on the floor below. The rest of the house was silent. The nurse had taken the baby out. The maids had gone now, and his father was not there. He could hear her moving about, shifting in a way that made him listen. He was lying on the floor, making a fort out of books, and when he heard her he put his head down, ear against the carpet. His parents' room was right below his. The bed creaked, then creaked again, sharply. He thought he heard her make a sound, breathing or gasping.

When he stood outside her closed door, listening, he heard her take a quick sharp breath, as though surprised. He knocked. There was no answer. He knocked again, then opened the door.

His mother was bending over the bed, leaning on both arms. Her head was lowered, and when she turned she was looking at him from underneath her arms. Her upside down face was red and strange. Her huge frightening belly hung over the bed, looming and dark under her crumpled nightgown.

She raised her head and tried to smile at him. "Pet."

"Mamma, are you ill?"

His mother was panting, he could hear the breaths. She straightened, pushing herself up off the bed. She turned toward him and put one hand on her belly. Her face looked swollen, and her hair hung down her back in a tangled scrawl.

"I'm not—" she said. "Not feeling well." She had a broad forehead and wide-open blue eyes. Her eyes were very bright, and her face was oddly pink and shiny.

He came in. "Shall I fetch the doctor?"

He was ten years old. His name then was Austin.

She opened her mouth oddly, then closed it. She set her hands on the small of her back. "There's no money," she said. "Nothing to pay him with." She tried to smile again.

"Father would have some," he said.

For a moment she said nothing. "I don't know where your father is."

"There must be something," he said.

She shook her head. "I can't think what." She arched her back, then straightened. "Don't worry. I'll feel better in a little while."

Her face crumpled, and she turned and leaned over the bed again. She swung her head back and forth, like a cow in pain. A tangled hank of her hair fell off her shoulder, swaying as she moved.

Austin backed out, closing the door. In his father's dressing room he opened the wardrobe; the coats hung like a row of men. He rifled through the pockets, scrabbling for coins. He went through the bureau, then the drawers and cubbyholes of his desk. He hurried downstairs. The dining room, with its dark table and chairs, the sideboard, would have nothing. Nor the sitting room, the hall. He went down another flight to the kitchen and scullery.

It was early afternoon, quiet. The only light in the kitchen came from the high window onto the areaway. A big white porcelain bowl stood on the long deal table, but Mrs. Fitch, with her puckered mouth and drooping gray bun, was not there. Austin knew about the jar that held the housekeeping money. He pushed a chair over to the cupboard and climbed onto it. He took down the heavy pottery jar. Empty.

The scullery was dim, with a sharp damp smell. On the slanting wooden drainboard stood a tarnished copper pot. He picked it up: if it were broken he could sell it to the scrapman. It was not, but now the thought was in his head. He wondered if he should sell it anyway. At what point should he sell anything at hand to pay for a doctor? He thought of his mother's rasping breaths, her tangled hair swinging as she moved. He looked around. Beneath the table was a crowd of squat brown bottles. He picked one up: it was empty, still fuming secretly with port.

He carried the bottles out the back and placed them in the wheelbarrow. When he set off, the metal wheel jounced on the cobbles. The scrapman's shop was in an alley toward Oxford Street. He came outside. He had dirty white side-whiskers, and wore an old black jacket missing the middle button. He put his hands in his pockets and looked at the bottles.

"Good afternoon, sir," said Austin. "I'd like to sell these."

The man picked one up.

"You and your friends have a party?" The dealer grinned, unfriendly.

Austin smiled, trying not to show his impatience. He would say nothing against his father.

The dealer hefted the bottle consideringly, as though he'd pay by the ounce.

The offer was for more than Austin had hoped. He folded the bills and stuffed them into his pocket. He clattered the empty wheelbarrow through the streets and up the back alley.

At the doctor's house he rang the bell and a maid let him in. Dr. Brock was in his office, she said.

Dr. Brock was at his desk, writing. He was bald, with a lean withered face and bushy dark whiskers. The air was thick, and smelled of candle smoke.

"Good afternoon, Doctor," Austin said. "My mother, Mrs. Mary Reeks, is very ill. Could you please come at once?"

The doctor stopped writing but did not put down the pen. He looked at Austin over his glasses.

"Has she a fever?" he asked.

Austin, who didn't know, nodded. He thought of her pink face.

When her son left, Mary Reeks felt suddenly hot, as if she'd been blown full of heat with a bellows. Her hair hung loose and lank around her face, but she couldn't lift her arms to put it up. She couldn't do anything. She lay down, stood up. Standing was no better and she lay down again, feverish and frightened. She closed her eyes. When she heard Austin coming up the stairs she tried to make her face smooth itself out, though she could feel it was crumpled. She was trying not to cry.

He burst into the room, his cheeks pink with cold. Behind him she saw the bald head of the doctor, slowly mounting the stairs. Then she did cry.

———·———

THERESA MAY, the last child, was born the next morning. The baby, Joey, was not quite two years old.

They still lived in the tall house on Duke Street, though half the servants were gone and most of the money. Joseph Austin Reeks had lost his fortune trying to corner the wheat market with a friend. He had not quite understood how it would work, but the friend had told him they couldn't fail, and urged him to sign the letter. His wife, Mary, who did not understand how to corner the wheat market, understood from Joseph's face what had happened. They were ruined.

The Reeks (pronounced Ricks) family was Catholic and proud of it: they could trace themselves straight back to the Battle of Barnet, 1471. Their loyalty to the Church had never wavered. They were proud of the connection (collateral, but still) to Bishop Fisher, who'd been executed by Henry VIII for staying true to his beliefs. "He may have a bishop's hat," said the king, pleased with his gallows humor, "but he won't have a head to put it on." They were proud of the bishop for holding fast to principle.

The Reeks sons had always gone to St. Omer, a Jesuit university founded in Brittany in the seventeenth century, when Catholic education was illegal in England. Before St. Omer the Reeks boys went to boarding school at St. Mary's, now run by the famous Dr. Crookall. Austin was at the top of his class at St. Mary's, and was expected to go on to St. Omer, where his father had been first in his class. Austin was expected to go on even though the family money was gone: Austin had a patron. This was his aunt Dawson.

Elizabeth Perkins was twelve years older than her sister Mary, Austin's mother. Their mother had died when Mary was small, and Elizabeth had brought up her little sister. Late, at twenty-seven, Elizabeth had married handsome William Dawson, a wealthy army officer. Mary lived with them until they went out to India, where William became a captain in the cavalry.

Mary had married young. Every month Elizabeth wrote to her sister, who read the letters out loud at the breakfast table.

When the Dawsons came home on leave they stayed with the Reekses at Duke Street. The Dawsons had no children, and made favorites of Mary's. They brought them ebony elephants, ivory figurines, brass bells. Dashing Uncle Dawson had a pitted face and wore a uniform. He carried a long curved sword, and told stories about the army.

When Mary told her about the wheat market, Elizabeth understood. "Austin must have an education," she wrote back. "I'll pay for his tuition and William will adopt him. He must have a proper start in life." She said she would pay for St. Mary's and his Grand Tour of Europe. She would pay for St. Omer, and then she would buy him a charge to a solicitor's practice. Austin would go into the law and save the family fortunes.

Mary read this to Joseph. She was elated, but knew better than to show it. She spoke in a subdued voice, and didn't look at him. Even so, Joseph felt it as a rebuke.

"Very kind of her. Please give her my thanks," he said stiffly.

Mary wrote back. "Dearest Lizzie, I cannot say how grateful we both are for your generosity. Joseph particularly wants you to know that."

Captain Dawson was stationed in Delhi. He was to retire soon, at sixty, but just before his birthday the Sepoy Mutiny took place. Dawson led his troops in a charge. His good horse, Pompey, was shot in the throat, and Dawson was cut to pieces with long knives. Afterward, Aunt Dawson returned to London. She was done with India, she said. She had given it her life and it had taken her husband's. She bought a tall handsome house near Grosvenor Square, and the Reekses visited often. Mary told the children it was their job to cheer her up. They brought her cakes and sang songs. They all sang and played the piano in that family; Mary and Elizabeth had been brought up with music.

Aunt Dawson was small and plump, with tiny hands and feet. Her fine gray hair was drawn into a small bun, and on her bosom was a gold locket with a tiny photograph of her husband. She wore rustling black dresses and always a cashmere shawl: England had creeping damp, she said. She said she might never be warm again.

Austin was a favorite, and she always asked what he was studying. She did not have Latin or Greek, but she had read Gibbon, and Boswell, and Shakespeare. Often she would recite a quotation from one of the plays, and ask if he knew the source. She offered again to adopt him, though Austin declined again, not wanting to dishonor his father.

————•————

THE TELEGRAM reached him at Dieppe. He was on his way home by then. He and his friend Albert Plaisir had spent six months with a tutor, exploring the grandeur of Europe. The telegram said: AUNT DAWSON HAS HAD A STROKE. COME AT ONCE. He took the next ferry.

————•————

HE ARRIVED AT the house off Grosvenor Square in the evening. Travers opened the front door, her face gloomy and decorous. Behind her was the heavy gilt mirror, reflecting them as pale ghosts.

"Good evening, Master Reeks." Her voice was hushed.

He came inside: here was the glass chandelier, the mahogany table, the Turkey carpet. The faintly spicy smell. The big drawing room was dark, but light came from the little sitting room down the hall.

"Good evening, Travers." His own voice was quiet. "I've come to see my aunt."

"Yes, sir," said Travers, but, oddly, she didn't move.

"Who is it, Travers?" A woman came out of the little sitting room.

"Master Reeks, madam," Travers said.

The woman came toward him. She was portly and powerful, with ferocious black eyes. "Good evening," she said, bowing watchfully. "I'm Jane Gunnell, your cousin." Her lips pressed tightly together at the end of each sentence, as though to keep anything from escaping. She was a cousin on his uncle's side, not his aunt's.

Austin bowed. "I'm sorry to hear about my aunt. I was on the continent. I came as soon as I could." He turned to Travers. "Could you take me up, Travers?"

But Travers looked at Mrs. Gunnell.

"I'll take Mr. Reeks up," Mrs. Gunnell said.

She led the way up the carpeted stairs. Her long black dress was tight and strained around her thick waist, and her boots creaked.

His aunt's room was large and square. A big four-poster bed faced the door. In a corner sat a nurse in a white apron, and by the bedside sat a young man, who stood when Austin entered.

"Reeks," he said familiarly. He had a high bulging forehead and small blue eyes. "David Gunnell."

"Good evening, Gunnell. This is very sad." He turned to the nurse. "How is my aunt?"

Mrs. Gunnell answered. "Not well."

Austin turned to her. "How did it happen?"

Mrs. Gunnell told him, though she hadn't been there. A fit, she said, a sudden effusion of blood in the brain.

Austin said, "What does the doctor say?"

"We are following his direction," said Mrs. Gunnell stiffly.

"Have you been here long?" Austin asked David. He tried to remember the last time he had seen him.

"I came on Tuesday," Gunnell said. "Fortunately I reached my aunt while she was still conscious." She was not, actually, his aunt. "My parents arrived on Wednesday. That evening she fell into this sleep."

Austin turned toward her, but Gunnell was blocking his way. Austin waited. For a moment Gunnell didn't move, but Austin stood firm, and Gunnell stepped aside.

The bed had a high headboard and carved posts. Aunt Dawson's head was tiny on the broad white pillows. Her face was shrunken, her eyes closed. Her hollowed cheeks were furred like a peach with an old woman's down. Her hair was drawn back under her lace cap, a few strands loose on the pillow.

Austin spoke quietly. "Aunt Dawson, it's me, Austin."

There was no movement.

On the ferry he'd stood leaning on the rail, watching the moonlight on the dark swells and feeling the steady throb of the engine. He'd thought of himself as a courier, surging through the night, bringing life and hope, but he was too late. The white bedspread barely swelled as her small chest rose and fell. She was already absent.

Austin took her hand, limp on the counterpane. He whispered a prayer. When he turned, Mrs. Gunnell's eyes were on him.

He spent the night in a chair, beside Gunnell. The air was close, and the fire hissed. He slept fitfully, his head nodding and jerking. Early next morning Travers came in with tea. Austin's mouth felt like flannel, and tasted bad.

Near noon, Aunt Dawson's breathing grew loud and slow. It was percussive, like pebbles on a washboard. At the bottom of one breath she paused.

Two days later the entire Reeks family, in their best clothes, gathered in her parlor to hear the lawyer announce that everything in the estate of Elizabeth Perkins Dawson was to go to her dear cousin, David Gunnell. The will revoked in their entirety all earlier wills. It was dated five days before her death.

Austin John Reeks was eighteen years old, in possession of half a gentleman's education, and without prospects.

3.

April 30, 1861. Baton Rouge, Louisiana

SARAH FOWLER MORGAN, nineteen years old, woke as it was starting to turn light. The air was cool and damp, and she heard the quick pattering rhythm of rain on the leaves outside.

Across the room, in the mirror on the armoire, was the reflection of her high bed, shrouded in netting. At the windows the tall white curtains shifted slowly in the rainy breeze, belling, collapsing. The shadows, the sound of rain, and the dim pearly light filled the room with something like sadness. Sarah felt the sadness like a waft of air. It was too early to get up, and the rain meant the trip would be postponed. She turned over, settled her face into the pillow, blocking out the morning, and slept again.

———•———

THE MORGANS WERE Southern by then, though like most Southerners they'd come from somewhere else. Sarah's great-great-grandfather, David, had come from Wales in the seventeenth century. The Morgans were bold, opinionated, and principled. They believed they could succeed at whatever they set out to do, and for the most part they did. They settled in Philadelphia, becoming successful merchants, doctors, and lawyers. Sarah's great-uncle John Morgan founded the first medical school in the country; her grandfather, George, became an Indian agent and a wealthy merchant. He was a friend to the Lenape chief White Eyes, and godfather to his son, George Morgan White Eyes. When the chief and his wife were murdered as troublemakers (he wanted treaties) by the American militia, George took in his godson and sent him to Princeton. George tried to found an interracial colony west of the Mississippi, and he nearly succeeded.

Thomas Gibbes Morgan, George's grandson and Sarah's father, was born in Princeton, New Jersey, where he went to the university and became a lawyer. But he, too, was an adventurer, and in the 1820s he and his brother Morris set off down the Mississippi. They stopped in Baton Rouge, then settled there. They both married planters' daughters, and practiced law. They became Southern.

In Pennsylvania the Morgans had called dark-skinned people friends and kin. In Louisiana they called dark-skinned people servants. Judge Morgan and his family didn't use the word "slaves," though they owned nine of them.

———•———

THOMAS GIBBES MORGAN had two wives and nine children. His first wife died after giving birth to their son Philip Hicky, who was called "Brother" within the family. Later Thomas met Sarah Fowler. This was in the visiting room at the convent of St. Michaels, Order of the Sacred Heart. Her parents had died when she was a child, and the orphaned Sally had been given to the Church at the age of nine. She was the youngest in the family, and it was said that the others were reluctant to share the inheritance. In her will, Sally's mother had assigned her a "curator," the planter George Mather. He visited Sally in the small stone windowless room at the convent. At first she was so small her feet did not reach the floor beneath the chair. She was a meek, quiet child, and on visits she kept her hands folded in her lap. The Church wanted to keep her. When she was older the Mother Superior told Mather how pleased they were that Sally was going to take the veil. She smiled beatifically and tucked her hands inside her sleeves. But when Mather saw Sally and congratulated her, she put her hand over her mouth and began to weep. Eyes shut, she asked if he could get her out.

It was not easy: the family had assigned her to the Church without recourse. But Mather found a young lawyer to take on her case. By the time he got her out she was eighteen, with dark blue eyes and high arching eyebrows. Thomas Gibbes Morgan and Sarah Fowler were married from the Mather plantation, Belle Alliance, in 1830. It was a Protestant ceremony: Thomas was Episcopalian, and Sally said she would never again set foot in a Catholic church. They had eight children, four sons: Thomas Gibbes, Jr. (called Gibbes), George (Mather, after her savior), Henry (called Hal or Harry), and James (called Jem or Jimmy), and four daughters: Lavinia, Lilly, Miriam, and Sarah.

Thomas Gibbes Morgan became a distinguished figure in Baton Rouge. He was a judge, with a large private law practice. He was a scholar as well, and edited two books on Louisiana law, in both French and English. All the children were educated. The sons went into law and medicine; the daughters were well-read and married well. The Morgans lived on Church Street, in a big plain white house with pillars. It had a two-story porch, which in Louisiana was called a galerie. They all spoke French; everyone did in Baton Rouge.

Louisiana was Creole then. At that time the word meant a child of European parents, born in a New World colony. Later the word came to mean mixed, but then it meant pure. Pure blood was important.

Louisiana was under Spanish rule during both the French and American Revolutions. It had never rebelled against a monarchy; Creole culture was formal and aristocratic. Sarah grew up with Creole rules and Morgan principles.

————

THAT RAINY MORNING, when Sarah woke early, three of her brothers were also awake, downriver in New Orleans, in Philip Hicky Morgan's house on Camp Street. It was raining there, too, glistening on the cobblestones.

The war was scattering the family. George was in Pensacola, Gibbes in Virginia. Jem was coming home from Annapolis. Hal (Sarah's favorite) had just arrived from studying medicine in France. Hal was twenty-five, and about to join the army as a surgeon. The family had given him a coming-home party in Baton Rouge, and after that he'd gone down to New Orleans. He'd told Sarah he was going to consult Brother about setting up his practice there after the war, though that was not the real reason.

The war, the war: the idea had been spreading across the South like a prairie fire, flaring in gusts of outrage, guttering down into moderate discussions, rising into towering columns of heat and fury. Southerners resented interference by the North. They talked about their rights. They didn't mention slavery.

The night before, Brother and his wife (called Sister in the family) had sat with guests in the dining room. The tall windows overlooked the street, and the big mirrors reflected the light from the crystal chandelier. The women wore low necklines and the men wore starched white shirts. The servants moved quietly around the table, carrying the yellow Sevres platters.

Philip Hicky was six foot four and powerful, with big hands and feet. He was broad-faced, with a strong nose and deep-set blue eyes. Like his father he was a lawyer and judge. Like his father he supported the Union. The other two guests—John Bouligny, a congressman, and Michel Heriat, editor of the newspaper—were split on the subject.

The talk was war. South Carolina had seceded, and now so had Louisiana.

"The best outcome would be a quick victory for the North," said Philip Hicky, "then for them to be magnanimous to the South."

"The North can't win quickly. The South will never surrender," said Heriat. He was a French Creole, the editor of *L'Abeille de Nouvelle Orleans*. He was small and intense, with dark eyes. "It's a matter of honor."

"Wars aren't fought for honor," said Philip Hicky. "It's always something else. Money. Land."

"We have the land," Bouligny said.

"They have the banks," Philip Hicky said.

"It's culture," said Heriat. "The North and South are separate countries. They can't unite."

"The whole point of our government is the union," said Philip Hicky.

The week before, he'd given a speech against secession. It was in a city park; he stood on a platform above the crowd as it was growing dark.

"War would be a catastrophe," Philip Hicky had warned. "If we fire a single shot against the Union, in five years your former slaves will be your political masters."

As he spoke the evening sky was turning dark, sinking into night. Behind him something jerked into view: a straw man was hauled slowly into the air by a rope flung over a telegraph pole. Pinned to its chest was a placard: "PH Morgan—Traitor." The body hung, dangling over the crowd, while a bright flaming chunk of wood was held to its foot. The straw blazed suddenly against the dark sky. The smoke bloomed upward, pale and opaque, reddening in the light from the flames below.

"But your view is not popular," said Heriat. "As you saw. The people want war. Anyway, England will join us."

"Why will it?" asked Philip Hicky. "They banned slavery years ago. They won't get involved."

"They need our cotton," said Heriat.

"Not enough to go to war," said Philip Hicky. "They're too wise. And they'll have it anyway."

"If we win," said Heriat, "we'll be a great country. The Confederate States of America."

"The north has the mills," Bouligny said. "The factories."

"We'll trade with them," Heriat said. "Just as we trade with England."

Philip Hicky shook his head. "It wouldn't be that simple. And I don't think we'd win." He changed the subject, turning to Jem.

"Young Jem," he said, "tell us what happened at Annapolis."

Jem was fifteen. He told them how during morning convocation someone had come in to say that South Carolina had fired on Fort Sumter, then seceded. They were dismissed, and went out into the yard. The Southern boys all said they'd resign to fight for the South, and so had Jem.

"You did the right thing," said Hal. "It's a matter of honor."

"C'est important, l'honneur," said Heriat.

——— · ———

IN LATE APRIL it was still cool in the evenings in New Orleans. The tall windows stood open and the breeze carried moist air from Lake Pontchartrain. New Orleans was lush with foliage, trees and flowers, shrubs and vines.

Wisteria clambered up wrought-iron balconies, along roofs and trellises, throwing out a dense coverlet of green. Great magnolias, with their dark glossy leaves and velvety white blossoms, towered over the gardens. On the outskirts of the city, near Bayou Metairie, stood the grove of live oaks. They were huge and ancient, with vast green crowns that shadowed the ground below. Nothing grew beneath them. The great limbs swooped low, lying heavily along the ground, like immense serpents.

After the guests had gone, the three brothers stood in the front hall. The candles guttered, the smoke turning thin and black.

"And so to bed," said Philip Hicky.

"Young Jem, come sleep with me," Hal said. "I've hardly seen you, and tomorrow we go in different directions."

"I'm not going anywhere," Jemmie said. "Just home. I'm the only Morgan the Confederacy doesn't want."

"They'll want you," said Hal. "Wait a bit."

"It'll be over by then," Jemmie said. "I can't get older any faster."

"Anyway, come and talk to me tonight." They all made a pet of Jemmie.

"You go up, Hal," Brother said. "Wait a moment, Jem."

Hal started up, the wide stairs creaking under his boots. His candle cast flaring shadows behind him until he vanished at the landing.

Brother turned to Jem. "Don't keep your brother up. He has a duel at dawn, at the Oaks."

"Dawn," Jemmie said, transfixed by the word "duel." "With who?"

"Mr. James Sparks, from Baton Rouge. It's illegal there, they had to come here."

"But what happened?" asked Jemmie.

Brother shook his head. "Off you go. Don't keep him up."

When Jem came in, the room was dark and Hal was already in bed. Jem set down his candle and began to undress. He wanted to hear about Sparks, but Hal spoke.

"Tell me more about Annapolis," Hal said.

Jem began unbuttoning his jacket. "We all went down to the office and gave in our resignations. The secretary wrote down our names and then we had to sign next to them. We felt like patriots. Then we packed our trunks and set out for the station. I was heading across the grounds, and my captain came up to me. He was kind and I liked him. He took me by the hand and asked if I didn't want to reconsider. I said I'd already resigned, but he said that if I wanted to change my mind, he could still fix it. But once I went through the gate I could never come back. I said thank you, but it was too late. He just nodded, but I felt I was letting him down."

"You did the right thing," Hal said. "You'd have been miserable fighting for the Union, the rest of us for the South."

"Not Brother," said Jem. He sat down to pull off his boots. "Or Lavinia's husband, Drum."

"Then if you support the Union," Hal said, "you should have stayed."

"I don't support it," said Jem. "And it's too late now." He set his boots down side by side.

"It's too late," Hal agreed, and Jem wondered if he were thinking about the duel.

Jem padded across the room in his stockings. He climbed into bed and blew out the candle. He wondered what weapons Hal had chosen, what distance. He remembered young Mr. Sparks, with his high shiny forehead and small sneering mouth. He'd come to Hal's party and stalked about, too important to talk.

"You must be glad to be going home," said Hal. "You must have missed it. In France I used to think of it. Everything. The evenings singing in the parlor, Miriam at the piano."

"But you're home now," Jem said.

"Yes," Hal said.

Jem wondered if he were afraid. He thought of the live oaks, their low twisting branches. He pictured Hal, his arm raised, holding a dueling pistol. A loud shattering sound, Mr. Sparks falling.

The street was silent. Branches scraped in a small nocturnal wind; something scurried in the wall. Jem lay awake, keeping watch. Footsteps passed in the street, coming close, then dying away.

He awoke to the door opening. Hal was slipping out, carrying his boots. Jem leaped out of bed. He pulled on his trousers, grabbed his coat and boots, and hurried after his brother.

Outside it was raining lightly. At the curb stood two bays pulling a gleaming carriage, green with black trim. Hal was opening the door; inside were Bouligny and Heriat.

Jem ran down the steps, carrying his boots. He waved to the driver, who waited until Jem climbed up on the box to lift the reins. The big bays moved forward, their backs wet and glistening. Jem pulled on his coat and boots, then hugged himself against the cold.

In Bayou Metairie they stopped beneath a huge tree, near a knot of men. It was raining steadily now. Hal got out, followed by Heriat and Bouligny. Jem climbed down but stayed in the shadows; he didn't dare step forward.

Heriat asked, "Vous êtes bien prêt?" *Are you ready?*

Hal nodded, and they moved off toward the others. The light from the lantern shone upward, reflecting off the canopy overhead. The rain drummed on the leaves, dripping through the branches. Jem followed, at first at a distance, then closer. Bouligny heard him and turned around. His face turned stern.

"This is against the code," he said. "No family members within two hundred yards. You can't stay."

"Yes, sir," Jem said, and moved back.

Bouligny frowned, then turned and went on.

As soon as he turned away, Jem slid behind a tree. After a moment he slipped on toward the duel.

Hal and the others stood beneath the long snaking branches of the tree. The lanterns cast wild shadows on their faces. Jem came closer, keeping behind the trees. The rain was coming down harder now.

The lanterns were set down, making a bright cave of light. The duelers took off their jackets, handing them to their seconds. The white shirts shone against the gloom. The seconds handed each dueler a shotgun. The rain on the leaves was loud. Hal broke open his gun, checked the chamber, then closed it. He raised his hand to push back his sodden hair; the rain was coming down in his eyes. James Sparks faced him, his shotgun held at a slant. They stood very straight. A voice called out and they turned, striding away from each other. The voice counted the paces: fifteen.

They turned, and faced each other again. The lanterns shone on their faces, glistening in the rain. They raised the guns to their shoulders, and their white sleeves caught the light.

It was pouring now, rain sliding through the branches and leaves in sheets, coursing down the hanging moss. Jem could hear nothing but the thunder of the rain.

———•———

GRIEF CAN RISE UP and overwhelm a family the way a rogue wave overwhelms a ship. Looming, enormous, curved, green, and shining, it towers overhead, too large to consider or understand. It is suddenly upon you, exploding, erupting, engulfing you within its glassy depths.

———•———

SARAH WOKE AGAIN later, rain still pattering on the leaves. The roads would be mud; the trip called off. They'd planned to visit Linwood, her sister-in-law Lydia's father's plantation, but it was twenty miles away, in East Feliciana Parish.

Sarah got out of bed. The floorboards were cool against her bare feet, and a shiver rippled up her back. She poured water into the basin and sluiced it onto her face and neck. Her skin tightened in the cold and she rubbed the towel hard against her cheeks, her closed eyes.

She unraveled her night braid, her fingers flicking quickly in and out, then brushed the thick rope of hair. She twisted it up into a chignon. She held it with one hand while she took hairpins from the crystal dish and drove them in, one by one, to hold it firm. Something from that early-morning sadness stayed with her.

She and Miriam were the only children left at home now. The other girls were married: Lavinia to a Union officer, Richard Drum (they lived in California), and Lilly to a French Creole planter, Charlie Lanoue. The boys had left: Gibbes had married Lydia Carter, and lived next door. George had been here, studying law. Hal had been in Paris, Jem at Annapolis.

The others were at the table when Sarah came down. Her father was reading the paper; he read all the papers, from Baton Rouge and New Orleans, in French and in English.

"Good morning." He looked at her over the top of his glasses with his powerful blue gaze. Sarah was his favorite. She knew this.

Sarah's mother was struggling with her melon. "Don't try this, Zay," she told Sarah. "It's like green stone." She set down her spoon. She was also Sarah, called Sally.

Miriam looked up at Sarah. They were close as twins.

"What's the matter, Zadie?" Miriam asked. "Are you sad?"

Sarah shook her head, though she did feel sad.

The feeling clung. After breakfast she and Miriam went over to Lydia's, where they sewed until noon. Sarah was making shirts for Hal. Lydia's little pop-eyed dog lay on the rug, his legs straight out behind him. Sarah wondered how the shirt (she was sewing the long side seam) would reach Hal, once he was in the army. How would the mail find their boys? The rain continued all morning, flooding down the windowpanes. After sewing, Lilly's children arrived, and Sarah and Miriam gave them lessons. Geography, and a French dictée. Sarah still felt clouded by something, but as they went home for dinner she asked Miriam the time. The church bell rang as Miriam answered: three. Sarah declared that from that moment on she'd be herself.

After dinner they all went walking near the State House, Sarah and Miriam; their best friends, the Brunot girls; and some others. Sarah was with a cousin, Henry Walsh. The rain had stopped, but the trees were still wet, and spattering drops cascaded suddenly from the branches. A fine mist rose from the gravel walks.

"Gibbes looked so handsome," Henry said, "with his hair cut short."

"It made him look more like Hal," said Sarah. "Hal's the handsomest in the family." He was on her mind.

When it started to rain again Miriam went back with the Brunot girls, but Sarah went home. The house was empty, and she went into the parlor and took up her guitar. She wanted to play the song Hal had brought back. It was a melancholy march about a young man setting off to war, "Partant pour la Syrie." Hal said in Paris everyone was singing it.

Partant pour la Syrie
Le jeune et beau Dunois
Venait prier Marie
De bénir ses exploits.

Faites, Reine immortelle,
Lui dit-il en partant,
Que j'aime la plus belle
Et sois le plus vaillant.

Leaving for Syria
The young and handsome Dunois
Prays to the Virgin Mary
To bless his exploits.
Please, immortal Queen,
He said as he was leaving,
Let me love the most beautiful woman
And be the most valiant man.

It was sentimental, but the melody lifted it into poignancy. As she sang Sarah's parents appeared in the doorway, with Lydia. Her mother said she was going upstairs; Lydia was going home. Her father stood behind them, his face troubled. When they were gone Sarah began singing again. She heard Hal's voice in her mind. When she reached the end of the verse she heard her mother begin to scream.

She thought of her father's troubled face: he must be ill. She threw down the guitar and ran after them. Halfway up the stairs she heard her mother's voice again. This time it was a low keening, a sound so dark and frightening Sarah turned and fled downstairs and out the front door. In the street she heard herself calling Gibbes, though he was gone.

Lydia came running after her, catching her by the arm. "Zadie, I'll tell you," she said, but Sarah pulled away.

"Father," Sarah called, and ran back inside. She started up the stairs again, Lydia behind her.

"Let me tell you," Lydia said, but Sarah wouldn't stop. She ran down the hall and burst into her parents' bedroom. It looked lit by lightning. Her mother lay on her back on the floor. Her father knelt over her, holding her hands. Her mother's face was white. As Sarah came in her mother looked up.

"Hal is dead," she cried, in a strange low voice. "You loved him, Sarah."

Sarah laughed. "No, he's not," she said. "Father, tell her he's not."

For a moment her father didn't look up. When he raised his face it was glistening. "It's true, my darling. Our Harry's dead."

It was the sheen on his cheek that made her know it. Everything inside her stopped—her heart, her blood, her brain—before that vast green wave, rising up and breaking over her, so high that she couldn't turn from it; there was nowhere to turn.

———•———

A FAMILY'S DECLINE can be slow and imperceptible or sudden and precipitous. It was Hal's death which taught the Morgans that what they had always taken for granted was not theirs. They did not possess it. Fortune, healthy children, a stable life. Whatever you have you think is yours. You believe you're entitled to it. But you will come to learn that you are entitled to nothing.

———•———

WHEN THE DARKNESS left her Sarah could see the room again. Her mother was still keening, low and terrible. Her eyes were shut. Sarah knelt beside her and tried to draw her mother up, but her mother wouldn't move. Sarah hardly knew what she was doing; later she was downstairs. People came to the door. Sarah saw their faces but could make no sense of what they said. She was in the street again, running to find Miriam, at Lilly's. People were there, too, in the parlor. They were silent, with stricken faces. They all seemed strangers. When she found Miriam she put her arms around her, asking and telling. They couldn't make sense of it. They went upstairs. Lilly had fainted when she'd heard and had been put to bed. When they came in she was sitting up, but when she saw them she fainted again, dropping against the pillow as though she had no bones.

None of them could make sense of it. None of them could understand how they could be alive and in the same world with this great smothering void.

4.

1862. Baton Rouge

SARAH MORGAN'S DIARY

January 26, 1862

Three months ago today, how hard it would have been to believe, if any one had fortold what my situation was to be in three short weeks from then! Even as late as the eighth of November, what would have been my horror if I had known that in six days more, father would be laid by Harry's side! That evening he looked so well and was so cheerful, and felt better than he had been for two weeks; I little thought of what was coming. How well I remember that same day, at our reading club at Mrs Brunot's, I stopped reading to tell the girls of the desk father had that morning given me, and I went on to talk of his care and love, for my comfort and me, until—I don't know why, unless it was the premonition of his coming death— I lost all control, and burst out crying, though I tried to laugh it off. At that hour, one week after, I was standing at the head of his grave, looking down at his coffin with dry eyes.

When we came home from reading, we found father with a severe attack of Asthma, but he had it so often, that we thought this too would pass off . . . but it was not to be; he never again drew a free breath. At night, he grew so much worse, that Dr Woods was sent for at his request, as Dr Enders could not be found. O how hard I prayed God that he might be relieved! It seemed as though my prayer was answered, and for an hour and a half, he seemed to suffer less . . . About nine at night, he told me to go to Lilly, and let Charlie stay with him all night. I kissed him good night as he sat in his arm chair under the chandelier in the parlor, and went away confident that I would find him well in the morning.

I woke . . . early the 9th, but dreaded to move for fear that something, which I vaguely felt hovering over me should be true, but Lilly called to me to dress quickly and go home with her, for father had been insensible ever since I had left. At the corner, as we were hurrying here, we met Dr Enders, who laid his hand on Lilly's arm and said "If you go to see your father, you must be prepared for what ever may happen." I waited long enough to hear her ask if he was dying, and his answer "I believe so" and then I was off, and never knew how I reached the parlor.

Father was lying on matresses on the left of the mantle as I entered, or rather he was sitting up, propped with pillows, for he was too sick to be carried up stairs. His hands were moving as though he were writing, and his eyes, though staring, had not a ray of light in them. Dr Woods, Miriam and mother were supporting him, and someone told me he had not an hour to live. I went to my room then, and asked God to spare him a little while longer; it was dreadful to have him go without a goodbye, our dear father we all loved so. When I came down, I felt he would not die just yet. He was still the same, and until two, we watched for some change. Then he began to expectorate, and Dr Woods told me if he could throw off the phlegm from his lungs, his reason would return.

It was a sad way of keeping Brother's birthday, sitting by what was to be father's death bed. But he grew better towards evening, and they said he was perfectly conscious, and almost out of danger. Mother did not believe them; she said if he was conscious he would want to know what he was doing on the floor in the parlor instead of being in his bed. He seemed to know that he had not full possession of his reason for once when I was sitting by him he asked for his spectacles; I brought them and he said "Where is my paper, dear?" I told him he had not been reading, and he gave me back his spectacles saying "Take them, darling; my mind wanders."

That was Saturday; but Sunday, he was much better, and perfectly himself, as I knew the moment I entered the room, for he put out his hand and said "How is my little daughter today?" We thought him out of danger now, for he talked with every one, and seemed almost well. About twelve, Brother and Jimmy came from New Orleans, for we had telegraphed the day before for them. Jimmy had a violent chill a few moments after he came in, and as I was the least fatigued, I undertook to nurse him. After I got him to lie down on our bed, I had to sit by him the greater part of the time and soothe his head when the fever came on, and hold his hand. He is the most affectionate boy I ever saw. All the time he was sick, he could not rest unless he had his arms around somebody's neck, or somebody's hand in his. I sat by him until night, only looking in the parlor every hour or so to see how father was, and then Miriam and I changed patients; she laid down by Jimmy and went asleep, and I went down to sit up all night with father.

I found him still better, and talking of law business with Brother, so I read until Brother went over to Gibbes' house, where his bed had been prepared. As soon as he had gone, father was seized with Pleurisy, and suffered dreadfully until the next morning. Dr Woods, mother and I sat up with him, the former trying every thing to relieve him. He was very kind to father; as tender with him as though he was a woman; and half the time, would anticipate me when I would get up to put a wet cloth on father's head, and lay it as tenderly on his forehead as though he were his son. I shall always remember him gratefully for that. Father would beg me to go to bed; he was afraid it would make me sick he said; he was always so uneasy about me, my dear father! O father! how your little daughter misses you now! It was almost four when I at last consented to lie down in the dining room but I soon fell asleep, and knew nothing more until sunrise when they told me that father had suffered a great deal after I left.

. . . When the Dr pronounced father out of danger, Brother decided to go home . . . Brother's good bye was "The Doctor says you will be all right in a day or two; good bye, Pa," as he leaned over him. Father followed him with his eyes to the door, and he never saw him again.

The greater part of the day I was busy with Jimmy who was still unable to leave his bed, but now and then I would steal down and comb father's head with his little comb—the one I gave him when I was eleven years old, that he ever after used. Better and stronger he still grew, and O how happy I felt. Tuesday he was well enough to sit up in his large chair, and read . . . while I combed his silver hair. How little I realized what was so soon to happen! The next day I was sitting by Jimmy rubbing his hands, when Dr Woods came up to see him. He sat there a long while laughing with me, and I went down to see father with him. Charlie was hastily putting up a bedstead where the matresses had laid, to my great surprise, for I had hoped they would have been able to take father upstairs that day, he was so well. Instead of making any remark, I turned to father and told him some joke Dr Woods and I had just been laughing about. He smiled at me, but the gastly, wan look startled me; there was something in his face which had not been there an hour ago.

A sick, deathly sensation crept over me. I heard him whisper—for he could never talk above a whisper after that Monday—I heard him whisper to Charlie to help Dr Woods lift him in his bed, and I could hear no more. I ran out of the room with that heart sick feeling. One week or ten days before when I expressed my fear that with his attack of Rheumatism he could not walk up stairs without pain, and had better have a bed brought down, he said to me "My dear, if they ever again make me a bed in the parlor, I shall give myself up for lost. I shall expect never to leave it again." They were putting him in it then; what if his prediction should be realized?

I fought against the idea, and tried to talk cheerfully to Jimmy, and had almost succeeded in persuading myself that I was foolishly uneasy when Miriam passed by and put a piece of paper in my hands. On it was "I do not think there is vitality sufficient to recover from this attack." The words stamped themselves on my memory; they meant that we were soon to be fatherless; Dr Woods' name was signed; he wanted us to be prepared. It was kindly meant, but how cold. They chilled me, those icy words.

I heard Jimmy ask what was the matter, but I could not speak with that choking ball in my throat, and that stiff tongue. I felt my way into the little end room, I could not see. And then I knelt and prayed the dear Lord to spare our father, if it might be, if he could be the same that he had always been. But if he was ever to suffer this worse than death again—if his great noble soul was to be weakened, or deprived of its strength on which we so much relied—for I remembered how terribly he had suffered—then, I said, let God take him now, that he may never know this pain again; father would not wish to live without that clear judgement and understanding that has placed him above other men. If God will spare him to us with renewed health, and unimpaired faculties, Well! If not—God grant us strength to bear it. But I could not bear it patiently; my heart failed me when I thought of father's leaving me here; until then, I had hoped to die first. I gave [way to tears] in spite of my endeavor to be quiet, so I promised myself that this would be my day, since I could not conquer, but tomorrow should be Miriam's and mother's; I would be calm for their sake. And I kept that promise.

Poor mother! . . . Wonderfully she bore up, never showing what she felt until he lay dying before her. Jimmy guessed what was to happen, and dressed himself and lay down on the sofa, where he could be near father in the parlor, and Miriam took turns in sitting on the bed near him, with me, brushing away the flies and combing his head. It was about four o'clock in the evening. Lilly and I were alone in the room with him, when he whispered something to us that we could not understand. He cast such an imploring look first at one, then the other, but Lilly put her ear to his lips, and said we had not heard. This time he whispered "Have I committed any mortal sin? I believe in the Resurrection and the Life." Then he looked at each again for an answer, but Lilly cried and kissed him. Since he had been taken sick, every one had been coming to inquire about him, and even now they were still sending, and I had to leave the room to answer the same sad thing to each one—"very low." And then I would have to stay away until I could wipe my eyes and be quiet enough to stand by him.

Sunset came; all without was so quiet and calm; not a breath stirring. I walked up and down the balcony, where I could see him through the open windows. Within, it was more deathly calm than without. Though there were so many there, not a word was spoken, not a hand moved, and the gas, just lighted, was shining on the white coverlid that rose and fell at every painful breath, and father's pale face and silvery hair looked so deathlike that [I thought] my heart would fail me. Several times during the day, I had caught sight of my self in the mirror, and hardly knowing the face that stared so despairingly back at mine, I would whisper "Hush!" to the quivering lips I saw, as though it were a living creature, and would say to the shadow reflected there "It means that tomorrow you will be an orphan," and would vaguely wonder why it trembled so. I felt as sorry for that shadow as though it were living—and yet, I was not sorry for myself; I tried to forget my own identity.

O how still that room was, with the single sound of that dreadful breathing! It made the silence more intense. Among all those living souls, the noblest there was going: floating out to the Great Beyond. Our hearts sickened and turned cold, his never failed; he knew God was just, and he "Believed in the Resurrection and the Life." It was about eight at night, when he beckoned to Jimmy, and drawing him near, he kissed him repeatedly and said "God bless you my boy! Good-night." Poor little Jimmy burst into tears and ran out of the room. He watched him out, and after waiting awhile, and unable to talk, he put his arms around mother and kissed her good bye, then me, then Miriam. O dear father! can I ever forget that last good bye? It said everything that a last kiss can say; and when I turned away, I felt as though my last and best friend was gone.

How kind Charlie was! All those days he never left his side for more than a moment or two, and only for one or two nights, when Cousin Will [Sarah's cousin William Waller] or Dr Woods sat up with father did he leave him. No son could have been more devoted. I do not know what would have become of us, without Charlie.

I had determined to sit up all night by father, but half an hour after he had kissed me good bye, they said I must go out while they changed his blisters. I waited with aunt Caro [the widow of Morris Morgan] and aunt Adèle [the widow of Henry Waller Fowler] in the dining room, but after a while . . . Charlie said I must go to bed; Lilly was lonesome up stairs, and the Doctors found father much better, they would call me if he needed me. I do not know how it happened, but presently I found myself lying on the bed near Lilly, and slept for some time, when Miriam woke me to say father was still better, and I must take my clothes off and go back to bed. I had not the energy to resist, and did as I was told, though every half hour I would wake up, to hear Charlie tell Lilly how father was, and directly fall asleep again. It was always "His pulse has gained" "He is stronger" "Dr Enders finds him much better," until I persuaded myself that he would get well. I kept repeating "O live father! live for your children!" and would fall asleep praying that father might be spared.

The last thing I heard, was that he was still better; it was then half past four. I fell into a heavy sleep, and did not wake until I felt someone trying to raise me up, and kissing me, to wake me. It must have been a few moments after seven then. I half way opened my eyes, and saw it was Tiche, but had not the energy to say anything, though I had not seen her for several weeks, she having come up from New Orleans while I was asleep. I heard her say "Run to Master," and then she was gone.

Half way dreaming, I got up, and slowly put on my shoes and stockings. Then I deliberately commenced to comb my hair, but just then, Margret came in and said "Never mind your hair; Master is dying; run!" In another instant, I was standing by him. I remember to have heard them carry Lilly out of the room, while she was crying; but I saw nothing until I reached his bed. Someone was holding mother, as she stood at the head, wringing her hands and afraid of touching him. Poor mother! how she was crying! Miriam had thrown herself by his side, on the other side of the bed, with her face buried in one of his pillows sobbing aloud, but no one was touching him. So I went to him as he lay on the edge of the bed, and put my left hand in his, while I laid my right on his fore head. The hand of death would not have been colder than mine; but I remembered my promise "To day is mine, tomorrow, Miriam's and mother's," and did not shed a tear.

Father lay motionless, save for that deep drawn breath, each of which seemed to be the last, with his eyes perfectly blue and unclouded fixed on the parlor door, as though waiting for some one to enter. Only four times can I distinctly remember having seen him breathe after I came in the room. What a long, long interval there was between each! It may have been only a few moments that I stood there, but to me it seemed hours. Presently I bent over him to see him breathe again, but mother cried "Shut his eyes!" and closed them with her own hands. I kissed him as he lay so motionless, and turned away, for I knew father was dead. Jimmy was crying aloud in a chair at the foot of the bed, but I dared not go to him; one word, one touch would have unnerved me, and I had my promise to keep. So I went to my room, and hurried on my clothes, for all this [happened] while I had been standing in my nightgown.

. . . When I came back, every one had disappeared, except aunt Adèle who was brushing away the flies. I took her place, and she left me alone with dead father. It seemed impossible that he should be dead, he looked so warm and lifelike, and then I held my breath to hear him breathe again. From that hour, the idea that he would presently come to, never forsook me until I saw his coffin lid screwed. People wondered at my self control, but I could never have kept my promise so faithfully, if it had not been for that wild thought.

. . . Then the next morning before sunrise, I was sitting by father again, looking at his grand head. It looked so magnificent, there was some thing so majestic in the form, that I could not cover it up. Brother came and stood by me; he too was trying to control himself; but I knew all he was suffering, by what I suffered myself. Presently came the men with an iron coffin, and set it down almost at my feet, with a dull, hollow clang, that went to my very heart; and they said Miriam and I must go out; but we would not, and stayed by, and saw him put in it. When they brought the lid, we kissed him good bye—poor Sis! I kissed him for her too—and Brother cried, but did not touch him; and even I had to turn to the window, for the tears would come. And we watched them cement the iron lid, and screw it down, and then I took my old place at his head, and held the handle nearest me, though I could no longer see his dear face again.

5.

November 1861. Isleworth, outside London

IN THE EVENING the sleet struck steadily against the windowpanes. The family sat at the dining room table. Joseph's back was to the window, Mary's to the door. She wore a shawl against the draught, though not one of her sister's thick cashmere paisleys, which had all gone to the Gunnells. Austin faced his brother, Joey, and his sister, Theresa. The room was lit by two candles on the table. Darkness pooled in the corners.

Joseph was complaining about his boots. "I might as well wear carpet slippers," he said. "These do nothing to keep out the wet." Joseph had heavy eyebrows and a forceful manner. "It's the tanning. It's not done properly nowadays."

Joseph's boots leaked not because they were poorly tanned but because they were old. The leaking vexed him; everything did. Ten years later he still couldn't believe the money was gone. He was still rummaging about for a way for it to return. He wanted everything—leaving the big house on Duke Street for this small one in undistinguished Isleworth, letting the servants go, selling his mother's pretty French desk—to reverse itself. He wanted the servants to come back, for Mary to lose the pinch in her forehead, for his sons to be back in schools where they belonged.

Joey was at a Church school, on scholarship, as though he came from a poor family, instead of an old and distinguished one connected to a bishop decapitated by a king. Joey would have no choice but to become a priest: the Church would only educate him if they could keep him, and there was no money for any other sort of education. There was no shame in becoming a priest, but there was shame in having no choice because of poverty, and Joseph resented this.

What Joseph wanted was to have his life return to normal. He wanted to live in a large, comfortable, well-lit house, not to live like this, with a single resentful servant and problems each month about bills. This one simple thing was all he wanted, but it never happened. Each time he thought of it the money was gone. It was always gone. He had spoken to lawyers, but they looked dubious and spoke in tongues.

He leaned back, making his chair creak.

"Wet boots will give you a chill," he declared, looking reprovingly around the table. Young Joey leaned carefully toward his soup plate. He was narrow and quick and clever, with his mother's fair hair and blue eyes. Tessie eyed her father watchfully. She was shy, with a high pale forehead, white-blond hair, and nearly invisible eyebrows. When she saw her father's gaze on her she looked anxious and locked her ankles together tightly under the table.

"We'll make sure your boots are dried out tonight," Mary said. "We'll set them by the fire to toast."

What she offered Joseph was comfort, and a twist of the compass. She saw things ninety degrees differently, if not one hundred and eighty. She took pleasure in her days; going about the house she sang. Under her breath as she stood counting sheets, out loud as she came down the stairs. She took pity on her husband (though she'd never have told him), not because he had lost the money, but because he was unhappy in the world. He was still struggling to make up the money, trying to find a position. It was harder for him than for her.

She smiled at him as though this were nothing. But Joseph knew who would crouch down by the ashes with his damp boots, tug out the smelly leather tongues. It was his wife. It should be a servant, and he should have new boots, made of properly tanned leather.

Austin cleared his throat; he'd heard this before, and changed the subject. He was twenty-one, open-faced and enthusiastic. He was not quite tall, but carried himself as though he were. He had his father's dark blue eyes, strong nose, and thick brown hair, with a troublesome wave. He saw the world as his mother did. He enjoyed his days, liked hard work, and trusted people. He was confident that he'd succeed at what he tried. He worked on Fleet Street, and heard all the news.

"What do you think about the *Trent*?" he asked. This was a British mail packet that had been seized in the Bahamas by a Union ship. They'd taken custody of two Confederate agents, on their way to England to raise support for the South.

"Not very much," Joseph said.

"That seizure is against international maritime law," Austin said.

"What of it? We're not going to war over two Americans on a mail ship."

"The Americans can't tell our ships whom they can carry."

"Those men were planning to rouse support from a foreign government against their own country," said Joseph. "That's sedition. The Americans had every right to seize them."

"They can't seize our ships. We have every right to go to war over it."

"You know nothing of war," said his father.

"I know something of principle," said Austin loftily.

Joseph shook his head. "War is an abomination."

"The Union has invaded its own Southern states," Austin said. "It's disgraceful. The Confederate states are very brave."

Tessie drew a quiet breath. She was eleven. Her dress was becoming too tight, and she was careful not to breathe too deeply or too quickly. She could feel the fabric's fragility, how it might suddenly yield and split. But it was irresistible. She inhaled surreptitiously, filling her bodice with air, stopping before her lungs were full.

"And why do you think so?" asked Mary, who had lost track.

"Because they are standing up to the Union," Austin said. "I'm thinking of going over to fight with them." He knew his father would disapprove.

Joseph set down his spoon. "Going to fight? With the Americans?"

Mary looked at Austin, the pinch in her forehead deepening.

"Why not? I'm free at the moment."

"Having no job is no reason to risk your life," said Joseph severely.

"An idea is reason enough," said Austin. "I sympathize with them. They're like the English barons standing up to the king. It's like the battle of Runnymede. It's a matter of principle."

"It's a matter of rubbish," said Joseph. "We want their cotton for our mills. We're protecting our trade."

"These states are fighting for their independence," said Austin grandly.

"The Americans already have their independence," Joseph said. "They don't seem to know what to do with it. Why on earth would you tangle yourself up in a foreign war?"

"To fight oppression," said Austin, adding, "and it would be an adventure. Plaisir's joined the Foreign Legion. He's gone off to fight the Moors."

"You can't have government without some form of oppression," said Joseph. "You give up some rights in exchange for some benefits. But none of this is your affair." There was too much here to answer. And he couldn't even address the idea of adventure. He did not want to lose his son. Of course it would be an adventure.

"Anyway there's a blockade," he said, changing tack. "There's no way to reach the South. How would you get there?"

"Join the Confederate navy," said Austin. "They have a ship in Southampton right now. That would get me to America and give me a job once I arrive."

"You can't join the Confederate navy," said Joseph. "You're not an American citizen. Also you know nothing about ships or sailing."

"That would be true of every sailor, at some point," Austin said cheerfully. "I can learn."

Nothing deterred him. It was infuriating.

"You're going to America?" asked Joey.

"Only for a few months, young Joey," Austin said.

"You should stay here and go on with your journalism," Joseph said, though he disapproved of journalism. "You could go on writing plays."

"They weren't a great success," said Austin, "and I can be a journalist again when I come back."

"But why would they have you?"

"An American friend introduced me to an agent for the Confederate navy. I've written the captain."

Joseph stared. "You've written to the captain? And how do you have an American friend?"

"I have. And I met him at the paper," Austin said. "He's from a place called Arkansas. His name is Smith."

"And who is this captain?" asked Joseph.

"Captain Robert Pegram," Austin said. "I have an appointment to see him."

Tessie took a cautious breath. She could feel the bodice trembling.

"America?" said his mother. She could not do without him. He held up his corner of the family tent, while Joseph's dragged heavily.

"Don't worry." He smiled at her. "I'll be all right."

"You can't say that," said his father. "This is a war. You have no idea you'll be all right." He tore a piece of bread apart. Crust scattered like shot.

"But I think I will be," Austin said, still smiling.

"I don't want you to go," Joseph said. He leaned back in his chair, which creaked loudly.

"Please don't forbid me. I'm twenty-one, and of age. I don't want to oppose you."

"The Confederate navy sails the high seas, seizing Union ships and burning them. That's not warfare, it's piracy. If you're caught you'll be hanged as a pirate. You'll disgrace the family name. You have no right to do this, I forbid it."

"I promise you I won't disgrace the family name," Austin said.

"It won't be up to you," Joseph said. "You won't have a choice."

"I won't disgrace the name," said Austin. "I won't use it."

"What do you mean?"

"I'll use a nom de guerre. If I'm hanged I'll disgrace only myself."

"Ridiculous," Joseph said. "What name?"

"Dawson," said Austin.

"Dawson!" said Joseph, outraged. "After your aunt who left you nothing?"

"After my uncle," said Austin. "A brave officer who offered to adopt me. Also my aunt, who paid for my education, and did quite a lot for me."

"She could easily have done more," said Joseph, scowling thunder-ously.

"Except she died, sir," Austin said.

"I do *not* want you to do this," said his father.

"Dawson?" his mother repeated. "Dawson what?"

"I'll use Francis, from my name-saint. And I'll use Warren, your cousins' name, for the middle."

"You'll do no such thing," his father said.

"Then Warrington. Francis Warrington Dawson."

Tessie took a deep breath and felt the bodice tear deliciously, swiftly, a smooth liquid opening, running along her side.

———

IN SOUTHAMPTON, Austin had himself rowed out to the *Nashville*. When they reached the ship he handed up the letter to the officer on duty. He waited as the dinghy rode the swells, knocking against the ship's side. Austin stared up at the curving side, looming over him. Someone called down permission to board, and Austin clambered up the long rope ladder, which yielded and swung beneath his weight. At the top stood a young officer. Austin held out his hand.

"Frank Dawson," he said, wondering if they might become friends. But the officer was on duty, and ignored his hand.

"Come this way, sir," he said.

Captain Pegram's cabin was small and immaculate, gleaming brass and polished mahogany. Captain Pegram sat at his desk, and looked up as he came in. He was tall, with heavy brows and a nose like a knife. His manner was courteous.

"Please sit down, Mr. Dawson," Pegram said. "I understand that you'd like to join our navy."

"I would, sir." He explained his sympathy for the Confederacy.

"Very generous, but it's not possible," Pegram said. "You haven't graduated from our naval academy, so I can't take you as a midshipman. And I can't take you as a passenger because the *Nashville* belongs to the Confederate navy. I'm sorry."

"Then how can I come, sir?" asked Austin.

"You can't," Pegram said. "All I could offer is a place before the mast as a member of the crew. Which you wouldn't accept."

"I accept, sir," Austin said.

Captain Pegram made a noise and shook his head. He was sure Dawson was lying about his age; he hadn't even a mustache. And he was a gentleman; he couldn't go below with the crew, who were not.

"I don't think you understand," Pegram said.

"I do," Dawson said. "Just send word when you need me."

Pegram bowed. "When we need you we'll send word."

Dawson gave the salute he had practiced in front of the mirror. Pegram made the little noise again. It came from inside his nose.

At home Austin told his family he was a member of the crew. He bought a sea chest and had his name painted on it in white. His friend Smith said he'd need a bowie knife.

"Do gentlemen carry knives in America?" Austin asked.

Smith nodded. "Everyone has one."

"But why?"

"Protection," Smith said.

"But from what? Bears? Wolves?"

"Everything," Smith said. "Other citizens."

He demonstrated in the air how to use it, miming slicing a rifle barrel in two, throwing the phantom blade unerringly into the heart of an attacker. "Indispensable," he said.

Austin nodded politely. "I had no idea how dangerous it was there."

He ordered the knife from a surgical instrument maker. It was a heavy, savage thing, with a blade three inches wide, fifteen inches long. The edge was steel, bright and deadly, very sharp. Dawson didn't like handling it; he couldn't imagine using it.

———•—•———

HE LEFT FOR Southampton four days after Christmas.

It was bitterly cold. Austin dragged out his sea chest and the family came into the street to wait. Austin wore the inverness cape his father had given him. He walked back and forth in front of the house, and each time he turned, the cape rippled about his shoulders. It was spitting snow, and the cobblestones gleamed with damp. Mary pulled Tessie close in front of her and wrapped her shawl around them both. They stood against the white-washed wall of the house.

"You're sure you must leave so soon," Mary said.

"I must." Austin didn't think Captain Pegram would send for him, and he wanted to be on the ship when she sailed.

"You must write every week," Mary said. She was secretly proud.

"I'll write as often as I can, Mamma," Austin said. "I'll tell you everything." He smiled at her, wanting to be off. The bowie knife lay at the bottom of the chest.

Joseph stood in the doorway, the hall behind him dark.

"Well," his father said, as though it were a whole sentence. He was secretly angry (his son was directly opposing him), secretly jealous (he himself had never had such an adventure), secretly fearful (he did not want to lose his son), and secretly proud (Austin had galloped over impediments as though they didn't exist).

"Bring me a doll," Tessie commanded. She leaned back into her mother's body. Her high forehead gleamed in the soft light.

"Remember everything," Joey said. "Tell us everything when you come home."

At the corner a big white heavy-footed horse appeared, drawing a high-wheeled cart. Austin turned to his family. The moment had come. He shook hands with his father, who frowned. He hugged Joey and kissed Tessie. His mother put her two hands on either side of his face and held it hard.

"Write," she said.

He nodded. "Yes."

The cape swayed around his shoulders; his breath made pale clouds. His cheeks were bright with cold and excitement.

The cart drew up before the door. The driver was small and gray-haired. He held a blanket wrapped around his shoulders. The horse stretched his neck and tossed his head, mouthing at his bit. He had feathery fetlocks and a thick winter coat, and on his pale sides were dark streaks where the snow melted as it hit his warm flanks. Austin shouldered his sea chest and set it in the cart, then climbed up on the bench. Everyone called goodbye; the driver waited for a moment, then shook the reins. He spoke to the horse, who moved off slowly, his big hooves slipping on the wet stones.

Austin turned to wave. They were all watching. His father stood outlined in the dark doorway; his mother and Tessie were bold against the pale stone, both wrapped in the same shawl. Joey stood in the street, his hand lifted.

Tessie shouted, "Goodbye, Francis!"

It was the first time. He felt a leap inside his chest: it was real.

"Goodbye, Tessie," he called. "Goodbye, everyone."

He raised his hand in a showy salute, snapping his hand to his forehead. He had no idea how to do it. They all waved and called, and Joey saluted back.

The carter flicked the whip on the horse's wet-streaked haunches. The horse flattened his ears, jerked his head, then moved into a ponderous jog.

6.

ON THE DECK of the *Nashville* the same young officer was on duty. Gary or Cary? When Dawson asked permission to board, he called down that Captain Pegram was in London.

"I'm expected," Dawson called up. "I'm a member of the crew. Frank Dawson. Captain Pegram told me to come."

The dinghy knocked against the wooden side. The officer vanished, then returned. "Permission granted."

The bosun took Dawson down to the fo'c'sle, which was dim and low-ceilinged and stinking. In the center was a table, run through by the foot of the mast. Around the walls hung filthy gray hammocks. Two men sat on a bench, splicing rope. They were much older than Dawson. One man was missing his front teeth; the other had a gold ring in one ear. They both wore jerseys and ragged pants.

"Frank Dawson." Dawson held out his hand. They stared at him without moving. The earring man moved his tongue slowly along his open lips.

The *Nashville*—a two-masted, brig-rigged, side-paddle-wheel steamer—had been a mail ship, and was being fitted here for war. During the fitting there was little work for the men, who were given shore leave. Dawson went off with the midshipmen. They were his age, and from similar backgrounds. They were pleasant and courteous, and when Dawson introduced himself they gave their own names and shook hands. One of them learned that Dawson was fluent in French, and asked for tutoring. Later another learned that Dawson could read music, and asked for lessons in harmony.

But though Dawson spent time ashore with the midshipmen, on board he ate and slept and worked with the crew. There was one other educated man below with him, a midshipman called Lusson. They behaved as they had been brought up to do, which set them apart. They used knives and forks, napkins. Courtesy. They washed themselves. The crew hacked pieces from the communal meat, stuffing huge gouts into their mouths. They licked grease from their knives, staring at Dawson. They didn't wash. They fought and swore, gossiped and lied.

The crew hated Dawson for everything he did: for speaking four languages and reading music, and for eating so carefully with his fork and knife, for wiping his mouth with his handkerchief. They hated him for becoming friends with the officers: he had got above himself. One afternoon when he came back from standing watch he found his sea chest had been broken open. They had stolen some of his things. A small pocketknife from his father. A prayer card Tess had given him, in an ivory case. When he reported the theft the bosun told him he should have had a better lock. Or brought less valuable things.

In early February the ship was ready, and one cold gray morning they hoisted anchor and set off, floating into the Atlantic on a rising tide. For the first time Dawson was ordered into the rigging. He clambered up the mast, the wind buffeting at his body, the ship surging beneath him. When he reached the spar, the mast slowly tilted away from him. Beneath his feet was the shifting rope, below was the glittering water. He held the mast with one hand, trying to furl the sail with the other. He was in a new element, the tingling emptiness of the ether. It was exhilarating. Later he learned to shuffle easily along the line, working the heavy canvas with both hands, leaning against the spar for balance. He liked working aloft in the spinning air, but he liked best the night watch, standing alone at the bowsprit as the moon spilled herself across the water. Listening to the intimate creakings of the ship, the soft rush of the waves beneath her. It seemed like another language, one he could almost speak.

One morning Captain Pegram came out on deck and saw Dawson kneeling on it with a scrub brush. Pegram frowned: he'd forgotten about the English boy. Later he asked for a report on him. It was a good one: Dawson was a hard worker. He was told that the crew had broken into Dawson's trunk. Pegram didn't want a gentleman below with the crew, it was bad for morale. The next morning the master-at-arms appeared in the fo'c'sle and ordered Dawson and Lusson to move to a small cabin on an upper deck. Paradise, Dawson wrote to his mother: bunks instead of hammocks, and a safe place for their trunks. But the greatest luxury was privacy. Now they could talk.

H. W. Lusson was twenty-one years old and from Richmond, Virginia. He had a high bulbous forehead and an enviably thick mustache. Dawson asked him questions constantly; he wanted to know everything about his destination.

"Tell me about where you live," Dawson said. "City or country?"

Lusson was sitting on his bunk, struggling with both hands to take off his boot. "Country," he said. "On a cotton plantation."

Dawson had gone to school in Berkshire, among smooth furrowed hillsides and thick hedgerows. Isleworth was full of walled orchards, rows of fruit trees. He couldn't imagine cotton fields. "How do you grow cotton? Is it a plant or a tree?"

"A plant. We plant in the spring, pick in the fall." Lusson got one boot off, and took hold of the other. Dawson could smell the rich blossoming scent of wet feet. The leather shrank in wet weather, and stuck to the skin. "We don't do it ourselves. We have field hands."

"Negroes," Dawson said. The word was strange, charged. He'd rarely seen black people in England, and had never spoken to one. Though in Paris, among the flood of students at the Sorbonne, he'd seen a young man the color of polished ebony, dressed like the others, and speaking rapid French. They were all laughing together, like friends.

"We call them servants," Lusson said, tugging.

Dawson didn't want to say the other word. England had banned it. It was barbaric. "Where do they live?"

"On the plantation. There are rows of cabins."

In England the farm workers had their own cottages in the countryside. Dawson pulled off his second boot and flexed his white toes.

"And what are they like?" he asked. "Negroes."

"Different," said Lusson. His foot came free, pale and damp. "Not like us."

"But how?" Dawson persisted, uncomfortable.

"Like another species," he said. "God made them inferior to us."

Dawson thought of the student at the Sorbonne. But that was France, maybe the Negroes there were different.

"How do you mean?" he asked.

"They aren't intelligent. They can't take care of themselves," Lusson said. "We have to give them everything. Clothes, food, houses. If the Yankees won and set the Negroes free they'd all die. It would be cruel."

"But the Yankees won't win." Dawson rolled onto his bunk.

Lusson set his boots side by side. "What people don't know is that we take care of them. We always have." He looked at Dawson. "People don't understand that. It's our duty as Christians."

Dawson nodded, confused.

The ship was beginning to heel, tilting ponderously against the wind. The bunks began to slant, and Dawson braced his back against the rail. The ship creaked loudly, making deep intimate sounds, as wood strained against wood.

A week before landing, Captain Pegram made Dawson a midshipman's mate: he was now a junior officer in the Confederate navy. When they landed in Beaufort everyone was given home leave; Pegram took Dawson to stay with his family in Sussex County, Virginia. There he met Nathaniel Raines, of Oakland Plantation, Stoney Creek. Raines took an immediate liking to the young Englishman, who'd come to fight for the South. They became fast friends, and Raines wrote, "My dollars and cents I will divide with you; half my bread and meat is yours." Thereafter Dawson treated Oakland as his American home, and there he was treated as a son.

———

THE NETWORK OF friendship and kinship was spread across the South like a great shawl, patterned by education and upbringing, stamped by manners, fringed with wealth. It was loosely woven but extensive, covering the entire region—from Virginia and Georgia to Texas and Kentucky—from a certain class, a certain tribe. Membership depended on family, background, education, values—those imprecise definers of the American class system. Money was not essential: you could be a member without money, and money alone was not enough, but most members had some money, or they had had some at some time. Most members were born into the tribe, but you could join through marriage or education or circumstance. You could not force your way in. You needed an introduction. It was a powerful system that conferred on its members trust, respect, and preferential consideration.

By the time Dawson arrived in America he had joined this tribe. The Confederate officers would become his brothers in combat and his friends for life. Their mothers and sisters would welcome him into their houses and families. It was these men who taught him the South.

———

THE CONFEDERATE NAVY was disintegrating. The *Nashville* was decommissioned. Captain Pegram took Dawson and some other junior officers down to New Orleans, but before they arrived their ship was sunk. Dawson's next ship, near Richmond, was a lighter, without sails or engine. All the action was now on land, and Dawson resigned from the navy to join the army. Captain Pegram's nephew Willie was a friend, and Dawson offered himself to his artillery unit, Purcell's Battery, as a volunteer. Willie told him to wait for a unit he could join as an officer, but Dawson refused to wait. In early June he became a private in Purcell's Battery. Mr. Raines gave him a horse and he taught himself to ride.

His first battle was at Mechanicsville.

June 26, 1862. Outside Mechanicsville, Hanover County, Virginia

IN THE EARLY AFTERNOON they received orders to move out. They'd been waiting since daylight, horses saddled, gear packed. When the order came they swung up into their saddles. They were heading to Mechanicsville, across the Chickahominy. It had been raining hard, and the river was swollen. Below the bridge the water was wide and green, swirling, moving fast.

Dawson's horse was a slab-sided brown gelding who didn't like the look of the water. When he stepped onto the bridge it sounded hollow, and he didn't like that, either. He stopped dead, but Dawson clapped his legs hard against the horse. He had never made a horse walk over a bridge. He urged the horse out onto the echoing planks.

They'd been camping outside Richmond, along the Mechanicsville Turnpike. The Battery was part of General Hill's Division. As they moved out, Willie rode in front, with Dawson and the other officers just behind him. Behind them marched enlisted men, carrying bayonets and battle flags. In the rear were the cannons and caissons, pulled by big teams of horses. The marching footsteps, the metal grinding of the artillery wheels, and the hoof-beats made a sound like rolling thunder. Dawson was in the thick of things.

In Mechanicsville an overturned farm cart lay on its side. There were bags of grain still in the back, but the horses were gone. The traces lay in a tangle on the street. The town was silent. At the corner was a picket fence covered with climbing roses. Beneath the roses lay a dog, a black-and-white collie, nose covered with flies.

At the crossroads they headed east. The road led toward a cut between two high banks. The trees crowded along the road, the summer foliage lush. Nothing moved, but everyone knew the woods held snipers. Everyone went silent as they approached, and the horses danced. Ahead of the column walked the skirmishers, muskets ready.

The crack of the rifle was what Dawson was expecting, but it entered him like a shock. His horse flinched, and a puff of smoke drifted among the trees. Answering shots came from the skirmishers: sharp cracks, then puffs of smoke. The skirmishers jogged toward the woods and vanished into the trees.

The rest kept on. They rode through the cut, expecting more shots, but no one was hit. Beyond the trees the landscape opened up again. They were heading toward the sound of artillery, though they couldn't yet see it. Shots began to crash onto the road ahead and the fields alongside. The Yankees were firing blind.

They came up over a low rise; beyond it, broad hayfields ran down to a marshland tall with cattails and a wide creek. Across it were high banks and rising ground. A wooden mill stood on the far edge, its wheel still. On the high ground was the Yankee battery, a long semicircle of cannons aimed at them. As soon as they appeared a shell whistled among them and crashed onto the ground. A horse reared, panicky; another gave a high frightened whinny.

They set up the cannons facing the creek. The horses pulled them through the tall grass. Mules were better at pulling but useless in battle: under fire they went mad, kicking and plunging until they could get away. Horses were more trusting. There were four battery guns, twelve-pound Napoleon cannons, each between two spoked wheels. Each gun had a two-wheeled limber, a carrying caisson, and ammunition.

The horses were unhitched and led away. The guns made a deep crushing noise, and blue smoke rose from each shot. Dawson rode across the road to an empty corncrib. He tied the gelding to it and went back to the cannons on foot. What he wanted was a task, a way into this world of thunder and lightning.

Each gun had a team of ten numbered men, one for each task: cleaning, loading, aiming, ordering, igniting, everything. The numbers began setting up. Across the creek the tiny Yankees moved back and forth. The sound of artillery was steady and infernal. The shots were now hitting their marks. Dawson stood behind the row of cannons: he knew the drill; while they'd camped out, waiting, he'd watched them training. The cannons gave off flashes, and the shocking brightness of the flames, the roiling, weltering smoke, and the thunderous sounds made the scene like hell. A solid shot whined toward them, and two men by the cannon jerked wildly, limbs flailing. There were cries everywhere and screams from the horses. The two men were on the ground; one swept his leg wildly back and forth. Dawson ran forward to the twitching man but someone dragged him off. The other man was inert. Dawson crouched beside him and someone else ran up.

"I'll take him." The soldier grabbed his shoulders. Dark blood came from the corner of the man's mouth. The soldier started to drag him away, but Dawson shouted to give him the bag. The soldier pulled the ammunition bag off the wounded man's shoulder. He was the number five man, who ran to the limber to get ammunition from the caisson, then delivered it to the number two, who stood at the piece.

Dawson put the strap over his shoulder and ran for the limber. Around him the shots kept coming, the smoke and the monstrous noise. Dawson ran, not because they could load any faster, but because urgency was all around him.

Time didn't seem to pass. It was always only this minute, smoke drifting, explosions, the whistling shells, the screams of horses and men. Cheers, when someone scored a hit. The Yanks kept firing. Dawson ran back and forth. The number four man was hit, then the number one. They shared the tasks. The number three cleaned and sponged, dipping the long pole with the sponge into the bucket. He was sobbing silently, tears flooding down his face. Willie Pegram appeared, his gold-rimmed glasses glinting in the smoke, and took over the number one. At the end of the afternoon they were down to three. The billowing acrid smoke, the sounds of the guns. Men kept falling down. Sometimes they screamed, sometimes they were silent. It was always this minute.

Toward evening Dawson found himself on the ground. He lay on his back, looking up at the sky, confused.

Someone said, "There's that Britisher gone down."

He'd been hit, then. He couldn't move, though he could see and hear. When the feeling came back he stood up; he didn't think he was hurt. His leg felt cold, and he looked down: below the knee it was black and glistening. Blood ran thickly down his calf. He took out his handkerchief, his hands slow. He bound the handkerchief tightly just below the knee. His fingers were slippery with blood, and he had trouble making a knot. Beside him the cannon discharged with a roar, rolling violently backward. The wheel just missed his foot.

Dawson couldn't run but he could stand. He took over the number four. The battle went on like an infernal dream.

It was nine o'clock, fully dark, when the cannon fire ended and they left the field. The cart horses were hooked up again and pulled the cannons back through the tall grass. Dawson limped to the corncrib; his horse was gone. He joined a slow column of tramping soldiers, but his leg was stiffer and stiffer, and he couldn't keep up.

An ambulance wagon came through, and someone pushed him forward. He climbed into the back and lay down beside two other men. Neither spoke, though he could hear one breathing loudly. They lay in the jolting wagon. Dawson watched the stars in the darkening sky. He thought of his family at Isleworth, his father's boots. He drifted; the sky seemed to envelop him. Once he heard Tessie speak, very distinctly. *Austin*, she whispered. *I can't hear the bells*. He felt the air chilling around him.

The driver turned and asked if they were all right. Dawson said that he was. The breathing man did not answer, the other man gave a groan. Dawson could feel the man's distress coming off him like a wave of heat. The driver said they'd stop for some morphine.

When the wagon stopped, Dawson sat up, his leg throbbing. They were at a tent, open on all sides to the night. It was a field hospital. A lantern hung from the ceiling and a surgeon stood over a man stretched out on a rough table. The surgeon's sleeves were rolled up, and his arms were covered with blood; blood was everywhere, sumptuous, reeking, the smell filling the air. Under the table was a pile of something. It took a moment for Dawson to understand what it was: arms and legs, hands. A perfect foot, severed just above the ankle, pale against the darkness.

By the time they reached Richmond the man beside him had stopped breathing.

7.

April 26, 1862. Baton Rouge

IN THE AFTERNOON the wagons and drays started arriving. Everyone
heard the heavy grinding of wheels, the steady clopping of hooves. The wagons were stacked high with cotton bales that swayed with the motion, or
packed with oak barrels, shoulder to shoulder. The horses had patches of
dark sweat on their shoulders and haunches. They moved slowly, all heading
for the river. As the wagons converged, the drivers nodded soberly. They were
from plantations, up and down the river, out in the countryside. They knew
each other, but they didn't speak.

At the water's edge, the wagons drew up along the levee. Get on, the
drivers called, urging their teams closer. The mules flattened their ears, ready
to kick. The horses stretched their necks and nosed forward.

The levee was lined with wagons, all piled high with the cotton crop:
every barn and shed and warehouse had been emptied. The oak barrels held
whisky, rum, molasses. The drivers began heaving the bales onto the ground,
rolling the barrels to the water's edge. They grunted at the weight.

When the bales were piled next to the edge the men picked up axes, swinging them high overhead and bringing them down on the bales. The big swings, and the satisfying plunge of the axe into the bale, started them calling. Chop that cotton! Chop it, now! The cotton spilled out like dirty stuffing. The barrels stood behind the bales, and men walked along the line of them, raising their axes, smashing open the tops. Each stroke made a thundering crunch, splinters flew into the air. Horses threw up their heads, alarmed; mules kicked restively and a dog began to bark. As each barrel was stoven in, it was hoisted and tilted over the chopped-open bales, drenching the cotton with liquor or sugar. The planters walked behind the wagons, calling out, gleeful and angry. The mood was turning darkly festive. A federal order had been issued, promising to hang anyone who burned a single bale of cotton. All of Baton Rouge was complicit.

A planter in a wide-brimmed hat held up a burning torch; someone cheered. He dipped the flame into an opened bale, pressing against the whisky-drenched cotton until it caught. A Negro walked behind him and, as each bale flared up, he swung it, off the dock, into the water. The flaming bales began drifting out into the current, a regatta of floating pyres.

"There it goes!" someone shouted. "They want our cotton, they got it!"

"Let them pick it out of the river!"

"All that good whisky. Hope they choke!"

"Have at it, Yankees!"

Sarah and Lilly watched from the street overlooking the water. Charlie Lanoue was in charge of the burning. He stood beside a flatboat moored against the levee. Whisky-soaked bales of cotton were carried onto the flatboat, until the deck was covered. Charlie and two other planters boarded, carrying torches. The flatboat was tied to a steam launch which, when the men were aboard, towed it out into the river. There the launch stopped, the engine holding it steady. The flatboat swung with the current until it hung motionless below the launch, the towline taut. Tied to it was a skiff.

The sun was lowering over the far banks, and shafts of light slanted against the dark surface of the river. Charlie and the others began to move across the deck, pressing their torches against the rum-soaked bales until the flames rose, flickering and growing. Black smoke roiled upward, muscular, thrusting. The deck became a glowing yellow grid, and the flames leaped together. The fire became a mountain, red and roaring: the men ran for the skiff and climbed in. Charlie stumbled as he climbed into it, but righted himself and sat down. They began to pull for shore. When they were clear, the launch let go the towline.

Freed, the burning boat slowly swiveled into the center of the current and began to slide downstream. As it gathered speed, its own wind fanned the flames, and it became a bright floating inferno, crackling and roaring. The heat rolled outward, scorching the faces of the watchers.

Along the shore, people cheered. The drivers hooted and whistled and beat sticks against the wagon sides. All over town dogs began to bark. The flaming boat moved with the dark water, down the river, around the bend. The first headland was low, and after the boat rounded it, for a while the flames were visible on the far side, while the boat was hidden, as though a wildfire were moving across the land without consuming it.

Sarah and Lilly stood watching.

"Aren't you proud, Lilly?" Sarah asked.

"I don't want my husband shot," Lilly said.

"We're all in this," Sarah said. "They'd have to shoot every one of us."

"I don't want them to start with Charlie." Lilly held her hand up to shade her eyes against the sunset.

"They can start with me," said Sarah. "I'll shoot back."

"You have a gun?" Lilly turned to look at her.

"A little revolver," Sarah said. "George got it for me. I carry it in my little bag under my skirt."

"When will you use it?"

"I don't know. Emergencies. If a Yankee insults me I'm ready."

In New Orleans, when the Union soldiers took over the city, women drew their skirts back and wrinkled their noses when a Yankee passed them on the sidewalk. General Butler, whom everyone hated, announced that if the New Orleans ladies refused to act like ladies and insulted his soldiers he would allow his soldiers to insult them back. Everyone knew he meant assault. They called him Beast Butler.

"Would you really shoot one?" Lilly asked.

"I don't want them here. They say we can't fly the Bonnie Blue flag, but I've made one out of silk and I'm going to pin it to my dress and wear it in the street." All the seceding states were flying the Bonnie Blue, one brave star on a blue field.

"What if they take you to jail? What will happen to Mother?"

"She'll have Miriam."

"What if they shoot you as a traitor?"

"I'll have died for my country, and I'll be proud."

"You'll be an idiot," said Lilly.

Men were loading the empty barrels onto the wagons. Drivers were pulling on the reins and calling out. The horses tossed their heads, they didn't like backing up.

———

DURING THE WEEK of the anniversary of Hal's death she thought of him, remembering those awful days.

That Friday the men had all gone to a meeting about conscription, and afterward they'd gone to a friend's house and sat on the galerie. Hal asked someone to sing a song. The song was slightly off-color, "Annie Laurie." At the end old Mr. Sparks said he was going home, and Hal asked if they'd offended him. No, he said, I'm only tired. But after he left young Sparks accused Hal of offending his father. Hal denied it, and then Sparks called him a liar.

That was the word, Sarah wrote in her diary, that no honorable man could endure. No Morgan, certainly.

Hal jumped to his feet, denying the charge. Sparks stood up, too. Hal took his walking stick (his father's) and brought it down on Sparks's shoulder. But the cane was a sword stick, and at the impact, the sheath came loose, clattering onto the floor. Sparks shouted foul play, calling Hal a coward for attacking an unarmed man.

Hal threw the sword down on the floor and held out his empty hands, to show he had no weapon. Sparks pulled a knife from his belt and started toward Hal. Two friends jumped at him and held his arms.

After that, there was nothing for it but a duel.

8.

1862. Baton Rouge

SARAH MORGAN'S DIARY

May 9, 1862

This is a dreadful war to make even the hearts of women so bitter! I hardly know myself these last few weeks. I, who have such a horror of bloodshed, consider even killing in self defense murder, who cannot wish them the slightest evil, whose only prayer is to have them sent back in peace to their own country, *I* talk of killing them! for what else do I wear a pistol and carving knife? I am afraid I *will* try them on the first one who says an insolent word to me. Yes, and repent for ever after in sack cloth and ashes! O if I was only a man! Then I could don the breeches, and slay them with a will! If some few Southern women were in the ranks, they could set the men an example they would not blush to follow. Pshaw! there are *no* women here! We are *all* men!

May 30, 1862

Wednesday . . . we rose very early, and had breakfast sooner than usual, it would seem for the express design of becoming famished before dinner. I picked up some of my letters and papers, and set them where I could find them whenever we were ready to go to [summer cabin at] Greenwell . . . I was packing up my traveling desk with all Harry's little articles that were left me, and other things, and saying (to myself) that my affairs were in such confusion, that if obliged to run unexpectedly I would not know what to save, when I heard Lilly's voice down stairs crying as she ran in—she had been out shopping—"Mr Castle has killed a Federal officer on a ship, and they are going to shell—" Bang! went a cannon at the word, and that was all our warning.

Mother had just come in, and was lying down, but sprang to her feet and added her screams to the general confusion. Miriam . . . ran up to quiet her, Lilly gathered her children crying hysterically all the time, and ran to the front door with them as they were; Lucy [a servant] saved the baby, naked as she took her from her bath, only throwing a quilt over her. I bethought me of my "running" bag which I had used on a former case, and in a moment my few precious articles were secured under my hoops, and with a sunbonnet on, stood ready for any thing.

The firing still continued; they must have fired half a dozen times before we could coax mother off. What awful screams! I had hoped never to hear them again, after Harry died. Charlie had gone to Greenwell before daybreak, to prepare the house, so we four women, with all these children and servants, were left to save ourselves. I did not forget my poor little [canary] Jimmy . . . I caught up his cage, and ran down, just at this moment mother recovered enough to insist on saving father's papers—which was impossible, as she had not an idea of where the important ones were—I heard Miriam plead, argue, insist, command her to run, Lilly shriek . . . the children screaming within, women running by without, crying and moaning, but I could not join in. I was going I knew not where; it was impossible to take my bird, for even if I could carry him, he would starve. So I took him out of his cage, kissed his little yellow head, and tossed him up. He gave one feeble little chirp as if uncertain where to go, and then for the first and last time I cried . . . O how it hurt me to lose my little bird, one Jimmy had given me, too!

But the next minute we were all off, in safety. A square from home, I discovered that boy shoes [described elsewhere in the diary as "my new boots, too large, and made of alligator-skin"] were not the most comfortable things to run in, so ran back, in spite of cannonading, entreaties, etc, to get another pair. I got home, found an old pair . . . by no means respectable which I seized . . . and . . . thought it would be so nice to save at least Miriam's, and my toothbrushes, so slipped them in my corsets. These in, of course we must have a comb—that was added—then how could we stand the sun without starch to cool our faces? This included the powder bag, then I must save that beautiful lace collar, and my hair was tumbling down, so in went the tucking comb and hair pins with the rest, until, if there had been any one to speculate, they would have wondered a long while at the singular appearance of a girl who is considered as very slight, usually. By this time, Miriam, alarmed for me, returned to find me . . . and we started off together. We had hardly gone a square, when we decided to return a second time, and get at least a few articles for the children and ourselves, who had nothing except what we happened to have on when the shelling commenced. She picked up any little thing and threw them to me, while I filled a pillow-case jerked from the bed, and placed my powder and brushes in it . . . Before we could leave, mother, alarmed for both, came to find us, with Tiche. All this time they had been shelling, but there was quite a lull when she got there, and she commenced picking up father's papers, vowing all the time she would not leave.

Every argument we could use, was of no avail, and we were desperate as to what course to pursue, when the shelling recommenced in a few minutes. Then mother recommenced her screams and was ready to fly any where, and holding her box of papers, with a faint idea of saving something, she picked up two dirty underskirts and an old cloak, and by dint of Miriam's vehement appeals, aided by a great deal of pulling, we got her down to the back door . . .

As we stood in the door, four or five shells sailed over our heads at the same time, seeming to make a perfect corkscrew of the air—for it sounded as though it went in circles. Miriam cried never mind the door! Mother screamed anew, and I staid behind to lock the door, with this new music in my ears. We reached the back gate . . . when another shell passed us, and Miriam jumped behind the fence for protection. We had only gone half a square when Dr Castleton [appeared and?] begged of us to take another street, as they were firing up that one. We took his advice, but found our new street worse than the old, for the shells seemed to whistle their strange songs with redoubled vigor. The height of my ambition was now attained. I had heard Jimmy laugh about the singular sensation produced by the rifled balls spinning around one's head, and hear [sic] I heard the same peculiar sound, ran the same risk, and was equal to the rest of the boys, for was I not in the midst of flying shells, in the middle of a bombardment? I think I was rather proud of it.

We were alone on the road; all had run away before . . . When mother was perfectly exhausted . . . and unable to proceed . . . we met a gentleman in a buggy who kindly took charge of her . . . As soon as she was safe we felt as though a load had been removed from our shoulders; and after exhorting her not to be uneasy . . . and reminding her we had a pistol and dagger—I had secured a "for true" one the day before, fortunately—she drove off, and we trudged on alone, the only people in sight, on foot . . .

We were two miles away when we sat down . . . to rest, and have a laugh. Here were two women married, and able to take care of themselves, flying for their lives and leaving two lorn girls alone on the road, to protect each other! . . . While we were yet resting, we saw a cart coming, and giving up all idea of our walking to Greenwell, called the people to stop. To our great delight, it proved to be a cart loaded with Mrs Brunots affairs, driven by two of her negroes, who kindly took us up with them, on the top of their baggage, and we drove off . . . Miriam was in a hollow between a flour barrel and a mattress, and I at the end, astride, I am afraid, of a tremendous bundle . . . These servants were good enough to lend us their umbrella, with out which I am afraid we would have suffered severely, for the day was intensely warm.

Three miles from town we began to overtake the fugitives. Hundreds of women and children were walking along, some bare headed, and in all costumes. Little girls of twelve and fourteen were wandering on alone. I called to one I knew, and asked where her mother was; she didn't know; she would walk on until she found out. It seems her mother lost a nursing baby too, which was not found until ten that night. White and black were all mixed together, and were as confidential as though related. All called to us and asked where we were going, and many we knew, laughed at us for riding on a cart; but as they had walked only five miles, I imagined they would like even these poor accommodations, if they were in their reach.

The negroes deserve the greatest praise for their conduct. Hundreds were walking with babies, or bundles; ask them what they had saved, it was invariably "My mistress's clothes, or silver, or baby." Ask what they had for themselves, it was "Bless your heart honey, I was glad to get away with mistress things; I didn't think 'bout mine."

It was a heartrending scene. Women searching for their babies along the road . . . others sitting in the dust crying and wringing their hands, for by this time, we had not an idea but what Baton Rouge was either in ashes, or being plundered, and we had saved nothing. I had one dress, Miriam two, but Tiche had them, and we had lost her, before we left home.

Presently we came on a Guerilla camp. Men and horses were resting on each side of the road, some sick, some moving about carrying water to the women and children . . . They would ask us the news, and one, drunk with excitement or whisky informed us that it was our own fault if we had saved nothing, the people must have been —— fools not to know trouble would come before long, and that it was the fault of the men who were aware of it, that the women were thus forced to fly. In vain we pleaded that there was no warning, no means of forseeing this; he cried "*You* are ruined; so am I, and my brothers too! And by —— there is nothing left but to die now, and I'll die!" "Good!" I said. "But die fighting for us!" He waved his hand black with powder and shouted "That I will!" after us, and that was the only swearing guerilla that we met; the others seemed to have too much respect for us to talk aloud.

Lucy had met us before this . . . Lilly had sent her back to get some baby clothes, but a shell exploding within a few feet of her, she took alarm, and ran up another road for three miles . . .

About five miles from home, we overtook mother [now walking]. The gentleman had been obliged to go for his wife, so Mary gave her her seat . . . and walked with Lucy . . . All the talk by the road side was of burning homes, houses knocked to pieces by balls, famine, murder, desolation; so I comforted myself singing "Better days are coming" and "I hope to die shouting the Lord will provide;" while Lucy . . . answered with a chorus of "I'm a runnin', a runnin' up to Glor-y."

It was three o'clock when we reached Mr Davids, and found Lilly . . . A hasty meal, which tasted like a feast after our fatigue, gave us fresh strength, and Lilly and Miriam got in an old cart with the children to drive out [to the cabin], leaving me with mother and Dellie to follow next day. About sunset, Charlie came flying down the road, on his way to town. I decided to go, and after an obstinate debate with mother, in which I am afraid I showed more determination than amiability, I wrung a reluctant consent from her, and promising not to enter if it was being fired or plundered, drove off in triumph . . . I knew Charlie could take care of me, and if he was killed I could take care of myself; so I went.

It was long after nine when we got there, and my first act was to look around the deserted house. What a scene of confusion! Armoirs spread open, with clothes tumbled in every direction, inside, and out, ribbons, laces on floors, chairs overturned, my desk wide open covered with letters, trinkets, etc; bureau drawers half out, the bed filled with odds and ends of everything. I no longer recognized my little room. On the bolster was a little box, at the sight of which I burst out laughing. Five minutes before the alarm, Miriam had been selecting those articles she meant to take to Greenwell, and holding up her box, said "If we were forced to run for our lives with out a moment's warning, I'd risk my life to save this, rather than leave it!" Yet here lay the box, and she was safe at Greenwell! It took me two hours to pack father's papers, then I packed Miriam's trunk, then some of mother's, and mine, listening all the while for the report of a cannon; for men were constantly tramping past the house, and only on condition our guerrillas did not disturb them, had they promised not to recommence the shelling. Charlie went out to hear the news, and I packed alone.

It seems the only thing that saved the town, was two gentlemen who rowed out to the ships, and informed the illustrious commander that there were no men there to be hurt, and he was only killing women and children. The answer was "he was sorry he had hurt them; he thought of course the town had been evacuated before the men were fools enough to fire on them, and had only shelled the principal streets to intimidate the people!" Those streets, were the very ones crowded with flying women and children, which they must have seen with their own eyes . . .

So ended the momentous shelling of Baton Rouge, during which the valiant Faragut killed one whole woman, wounded three, struck some twenty houses several times a piece, and indirectly caused the death of two little children who were drowned in their flight, one poor little baby who was born in the woods . . . There were many similar cases. Hurrah for the illustrious Farragut, the "Woman Killer!!!"

It was three o'clock before I left off packing, and took refuge in a tub of cold water . . . Tiche was thoughtful enough to provide it; . . . we found her safe at home, having lost all trace of us, preparing to start on foot to Greenwell in the morning. What a luxury the water was! and when I changed my underclothes, I felt like a new being. To be sure I pulled off the skin of my heel entirely, where it had been blistered by the walk, dust, sun, etc, but that was a trifle . . . For three hours I dreamed of rifled shells and battles, and at half past six, I was up and at work again. Mother came soon after, and after hard work, we got safely off at three, saving nothing but our clothes and silver. All else is gone. It cost me a pang to leave my guitar, and Miriam's piano, but . . . there was no help for it . . .

It was dark night when we reached here. A bright fire was blazing in front, but the house looked so desolate, that I wanted to cry. Miriam cried when I told her her piano was left behind. Supper was a new sensation, after having been without any thing except a *glass* of clabber . . . and a piece of bread since half past six. I laid down on the hard floor . . . thankful that I was so fortunate as to be able to lie down at all. In my dozing state, I heard the wagon come, and Miriam ordering a mattress to be put in the room for me . . .

She and Lucy made a bed and rolled me in it with no more questions.

July 20, 1862
If I was a man—! O wouldn't I be in Richmond with the boys! . . .

Why was I not a man? what is the use of all these worthless women, in war times? If they attack, I shall don the breeches, and join the assailants, and fight . . . How do breeches and coats feel, I wonder? I am actually afraid of them. I kept a suit of Jimmy's hanging in the armoir for six weeks waiting for the Yankees to come, thinking fright would give me courage to try it, (what a seeming paradox!) but I never succeeded. Lilly one day insisted on my trying it, and I advanced so far as to lay it on the bed, and then carried my bird out—I was ashamed to let even my canary see me—but when I took a second look, my courage deserted me, and there ended my first and last attempt at disguise. I have heard so many girls boast of having worn men's clothes; I wonder where they get the courage.

9.

1864. Brother Philip Hicky's house, 178 Camp Street,
New Orleans

SARAH MORGAN'S DIARY

February 1864

Friday the fifth, as I was running through Miriam's room, I saw Brother pass the door, and heard him ask Miriam for mother. The voice, the bowed head, the look of utter despair on his face, struck through me like a knife. "Gibbes! Gibbes!" was my sole thought; but Miriam and I stood motionless looking at each other without a word. "Gibbes is dead!" said mother as he stood before her. He did not speak; and then we went in.

We did not ask how, or when. That he was dead was enough for us. But after a while he told us uncle James had written that he had died at two o'clock on Thursday the twenty first. Still we did not know how he had died. Several letters that had been brought remained unopened on the floor. One, Brother opened . . . It was from Col. Steedman to Miriam and me, written a few hours after his death, and contained the sad story of our dear brother's last hours. He had been in Col. Steedman's ward of the hospital for more than a week, with headache and sore throat; but it was thought nothing; he seemed to improve, and expected to be discharged in a few days. On the twenty first he complained that his throat pained him again. After prescribing for him, and talking cheerfully with him for some time, Col. Steedman left him surrounded by his friends, to attend to his other patients. He had hardly reached his room when someone ran to him saying Capt. Morgan was dying. He hurried to his bedside, and found him dead. Capt. Steedman [the colonel's brother], sick in the next bed, and those around him said he had been talking pleasantly with them, when he sat up to reach his cup of water on the table. As soon as he drank it he seemed to suffocate; and after tossing his arms wildly in the air, and making several fearful efforts to breathe, he died.

O Gibbes! Gibbes! When you took me in your arms and cried so bitterly over that sad parting, it was indeed your last farewell! My brothers! my brothers! Dear Lord how can we live without our boys? . . .

On Thursday the eleventh, as we sat talking to mother, striving to make her forget the weary days we had cried through with that fearful sound of dead! dead! ringing ever in our ears, some one asked for Miriam. She went down, and presently I heard her thanking some body for a letter. "You could not have brought me anything more acceptable! It is from my sister, though she can hardly have heard from us yet!" I ran back, and sitting at mother's feet, told her Miriam was coming with a letter from Lydia [Gibbes's wife]. Mother cried at the mention of her name. O my little sister! you know how dear you are to us!

"Mother! Mother!" a horrible voice cried, and before I could think who it was, Miriam rushed in holding an open letter in her hand, and perfectly wild. "George is dead!" she shrieked and fell heavily to the ground. O my God! I could have prayed thee to take mother too, when I looked at her! I thought—I almost hoped she was dead, and that pang spared! But I was wild myself. I could have screamed!— laughed! "It is false! do you hear me mother? God would not take both! George is not dead!" I cried trying in vain to rouse her from her horrible state or bring one ray of reason to her eye. I spoke to a body alive only to pain; not a sound of my voice seemed to reach her; only fearful moans showed she was yet alive. Miriam lay raving on the ground. Poor Miriam! her heart's idol torn away. God help my darling! I did not understand that George *could* die until I looked at her. In vain I strove to raise her from the ground, or check her wild shrieks for death. "George! only George!" she would cry; until at last with the horror of seeing both die before me, I mastered strength enough to go for the servant and bid her run quickly for Brother.

How long I stood there alone, I never knew. I remember Ada coming in hurriedly and asking what it was. I told her George was dead. It was a relief to see her cry. I could not; but I felt the pain afresh, as though it were her brother she was crying over, not mine. And the sight of her tears brought mine too. We could only cry over mother and Miriam; we could not rouse them; we did not know what to do . . .

Miriam had been taken to her room more dead than alive—mother lay speechless in hers. The shock of this second blow had obliterated, with them, all recollection of the first. It was a mercy I envied them; for I remembered both until loss of consciousness would have seemed a blessing. I shall never forget mother's shriek of horror when towards evening she recalled it . . .

How will the world seem to us now? What will life be without the boys?

10.

1865. Richmond, Virginia

WHEN THE WAR ENDED he was in Richmond. He'd been wounded again, shot in the shoulder and taken from the field to someone's house. He was lying in a darkened room when he heard people shouting in the streets. The light burned in fiery lines through the closed shutters. He heard sporadic gunshots, the grinding of wagon wheels. He listened, trying to tell who was winning. Dogs barked. A woman called, "Where are you?" He raised his head, but couldn't see through the shutters.

He thought the city had fallen, but it was the Confederacy. The South.

———·—·———

DAWSON HAD TO his name a three-cent postage stamp and a five-dollar bill, sent by a friend in Baltimore. His Confederate money was worthless. He changed the bill into coins, so it would seem like more. The first luxuries he bought were cigars and oranges.

He looked for any kind of job: driving a dray, bookkeeping, agent for an express company. He and a friend started a newspaper, but what they wrote offended the federal officers, who closed it down. When Mr. Raines offered him the job of managing his plantation in Sussex County, Dawson accepted. He knew little about running a plantation, but he was sure he could learn, and this place had been his second home during the war. Captain Pegram had introduced him to old Mr. Raines, who was the son of an Englishman. He'd opened his house and his heart to Dawson, treating him like a son, providing him with horses, money, and a home. Dawson accepted the job. He was in Richmond saying goodbye when someone handed him a telegram. It was an offer to work at the *Daily Richmond Examiner.*

Henry Rives Pollard was the editor then. He was lazy, vain, and dissolute. Also belligerent. He was inclined to threaten people with shootings, and used Dawson as his second. Offended by an article in another paper, Pollard told Dawson to get his pistol and find the editor so Pollard could whip him. Dawson found the man at the capitol, in the Rotunda. Pollard waited outside and jumped him when the man came out. Both drew pistols and fired, though no one was hit. There were other incidents: he threatened to horsewhip someone from *The New York Times.*

Later, after Dawson left, Pollard published an article about the elopement of a Miss Grant. Her brother, James Grant, took exception. To defend his sister's honor he waited in a window that Pollard passed on his way to work. When Pollard walked by Grant opened fire with a double-barreled shotgun. Pollard was dead by the time he hit the sidewalk. Grant was acquitted. Everyone agreed that he had provocation.

While he was working at the *Examiner* Dawson met Bartholomew Riordan. He was the opposite of Pollard, a slim, quiet, modest man, astute, intelligent, and enterprising. He hadn't fought in the war (he was slightly lame) but had been a journalist. For a while he'd worked for the *Charleston Mercury.* He thought that city needed a first-rate newspaper, and that he and Dawson should provide it. He went first.

In the fall of 1866 Dawson became assistant editor at the *Charleston Mercury.* This belonged to the Rhetts, father and son from an old Charleston family. Old R. B. Rhett, and Colonel R. B. Rhett, Jr., were Fire-Eaters: secessionists and ferocious supporters of the Confederacy. The South was full of people like the Rhetts: still angry at the North, contemptuous of the Union, committed to the "Lost Cause." Why wouldn't they be? They'd lost everything, their way of life, their economy, their power and presence, the knowledge that they were at the center of the world.

Dawson, only twenty-six years old and a foreigner, went in one day to tell his boss, old Mr. Rhett, that the *Mercury* should tell its readers to swallow the Fourteenth Amendment. They should swallow the fact that Negroes were citizens, and could vote. Dawson told Rhett it would save misery later. Also, he said, it would be the making of the paper. Rhett was so angry—pink creeping up his neck from his collar—he could hardly speak. He nearly fired Dawson on the spot.

Swallow this? They'd been at the center of the world. The huge engine of the Southern economy had supplied the entire world with something essential: cheap cotton. It had superseded the Silk Road and it had flooded the European markets. American cotton was king everywhere.

The North, ignorant and hypocritical, had destroyed this empire. Hadn't the North been involved in the slave trade, and benefited from it? Yes, it had. The North had no moral authority; it had no business provoking this war.

And yet it had. The North had invaded their territory and burned their houses and run off their stock. The North had killed hundreds of thousands of their good boys, who would never come back. The North had destroyed their plantations and their economy and their families: everything of value. The North had humiliated them in the eyes of the world, and for that the South would never forgive it.

The North became even more the enemy as the South watched their own slow slide downward. The South saw themselves turning to shadows, as if now their lives had become their own negatives in the photographs. Their great beautiful edifice had turned dark and empty, their eyes had gone white, their details blurred. They were no longer at the center of the world.

The South seethed. The war was over, and Northerners were leaving their lands, but they could take out their rage on the Negroes.

That fall Riordan and Dawson bought controlling interest in the failing *Charleston News*. In the first issue they announced: "The new proprietors of the paper will bend all their energies honestly, fearlessly and consistently with but the single aim—to maintain the honor and promote the welfare of the Southern people."

PART II

11.

The Late Affray in Yorkville.

The ladies of the Presbyterian Church got up a Christmas tree and party . . . for the benefit of the Sunday school. During its progress some things were thrown back and forward from the window and the street, which . . . led to a quarrel and a street fight, which ended in the death of one young man and severely [sic] stabbing of another . . . It seems that a piece of wood, thrown from the window, struck both [Thos.] Smith and [Wm.] Snyder, which irritated them—also that stones . . . thrown into the window . . . irritated the young men in the hall . . . Harsh words were used. After the . . . party, Smith and Snyder, with several others, waited for Mr. D. Jones . . . and demanded that he should retract what he said, which he would not do. They then attacked him . . . [Jones] drew his knife . . . The scuffle continued for only a few moments, when both Smith and Snyder exclaimed that they were cut, and ran to Dr. Jackson's room, where Smith died . . . his throat being cut in a most frightful manner.

None of the parties were intoxicated . . . [Everyone] sympathizes with the families of the three young men, they being . . . steady and orderly boys.

—*CHARLESTON MERCURY*, JANUARY 2, 1868

12.

A "SOUTHERN DIFFICULTY."

**Terrible Tragedy Yesterday in Columbia, S.C.—A Free
Fight, Fisticuffs and Then Deadly Shooting—The
Wrong Man Killed, of Course—The Principals Unhurt.**

Judge S. W. Melton, one of the most prominent native republicans in the State, who was nominated for the Attorney Generalship . . . has recently been designated in a published card as a liar, poltroon and coward by C. W. Montgomery, Senator from Newberry county, and now President of the Senate pro tem.

Melton . . . took no notice of these foul aspersions further than to indicate that he would settle all such difficulties after the election . . . [I]t was known Melton, true to his chivalric antecedents, would not fail to resent an insult even at the risk of his life. The dénouement proved that the latter was the case . . .

Melton had accused Montgomery . . . of issuing fraudulent pay certificates . . .

Thus matters rested until this evening, when Montgomery and a gentleman named George Tupper were in the dining saloon of the Pollock House awaiting dinner . . . Judge Melton, who had been upstairs, came down, and, looking into the dining room, saw his foe Montgomery.

Melton was accompanied by John D. Caldwell . . . and Major Morgan, son-in-law of George A. Trenholm, late Secretary of the Confederate Treasury . . . Judge Melton rushed upon Montgomery, who was seated at the dining table, and . . . began a most vigorous pummelling of his physiognomy. In a moment all the parties present jumped to their feet, and soon the room was a confused mass of scuffling men. Caldwell and Morgan sprung forward, and endeavored to separate the combatants.

The excitement at this juncture was very great, the two principal parties being still clinched, when two pistol shots were heard, and Caldwell, pressing his hands to his sides, fell dead upon the floor. Scarcely had this happened when Morgan received a shot in the shoulder and exclaimed, "I'm shot."

—*NEW YORK HERALD*, SEPTEMBER 22, 1872

September 1872. Hampton's Plantation, outside Columbia, South Carolina

THE PLANTATION LAY four miles outside Columbia, along the Congaree River.

It had taken some time for his troops to find, but General Sherman had given them particular orders to burn it: he held a grudge against the Hampton family. They owned several plantations here, and Sherman's troops found them all and left them all like this, rubble and blackened brick. Family furniture and silver and portraits; books and beds, toys. Nightgowns, boots, shawls. Lockets and watches, letters, diaries: all the physical connections to life, gone. Sometimes the owners came later to pick through the charred wood and dirty ashes, searching for anything that connected them to the world they'd lost. A blackened saucer, a broken mirror.

A hundred and fifty years later the families would still be resentful. They would never forgive Sherman, never forgive the North. This one had been the grandest of the Hampton plantations. Presidents and diplomats had visited, as well as Sarah's grandfather, George Morgan. He'd written home that he'd seen a hundred men out plowing. It was six thousand acres of good bottomland.

Ten years after the war, the Negroes still lived in their settlements. They paid no rent but would not leave, and it was impossible to deny that they had a certain moral right to the place. They also refused to work for the new owner. The Negroes would not forgive, either. They'd been judged by the color of their skin, and now they'd judge the owners by the color of theirs.

After the war, Northerners came down and told the Negroes the land was rightfully theirs. They told them it was their work that had made the land valuable. They told them that if the plantation owners didn't give them what they wanted, the Negroes should burn down their houses. They told them a small child could light a match. Quite a lot of fires started mysteriously during the night. Negroes were owed, the Northerners told them, and this was true. But how much, and who was to pay them?

After the big house at Hampton's had been burned down during the war, the sisters had built a smaller one. They tried to keep the place going; it had been in the family for over a hundred years. But finally they couldn't pay the taxes, and had to sell. The plantations were worth almost nothing now. Even if the Negroes would agree to work they wanted to be paid, and that was a problem. It turned out that cotton wasn't actually a paying crop unless the labor was free.

PASSENGERS FOR HAMPTON'S got off at The Pump. This was just a whistle-stop, a clearing in the woods. The train slowed, gave a brief breathy blast, and paused. It was still inching forward as Dawson swung down. When he hit the ground the conductor leaned out and called something and the train started up again.

Across the clearing was a buggy drawn by a thin bay horse. The driver was an elderly black man in a white shirt, the sleeves rolled up. He lifted his whip in salute as Dawson approached.

"Captain Dawson," he said. "I'm Levi."

"Afternoon, Levi." Dawson swung his bag into the back and climbed up beside him. Dawson braced his feet against the buckboard, Levi turned the mare, who was mouthing at her bit, and they started off.

"Tell me, Levi," he said, "how is Major Morgan?"

"Poorly," he said. "Doing poorly."

The telegram had said: J. M. MORGAN DYING COME AT ONCE.

———

DAWSON AND MORGAN had met during the war, outside New Orleans. Captain Pegram had been sent down to command a ship, and he brought Dawson with him, and some of the other young officers from the *Nashville*. They traveled down by train, but just before they reached New Orleans they were ordered off the train in Opelousas. There they learned the battle was over and the city had fallen. They were ordered back to Richmond, and waited for a northbound train. These came up from New Orleans, full of soldiers retreating from the city. When Dawson and the others finally found a car with room for them, Little Morgan was in it. He was huddled in the corner, with a raging case of the yellow fever. He'd been so sick he'd been sent ashore from his ship, the *McRae*. He'd been in bed at Philip Hicky's house on Camp Street when the *McRae* went down.

The trip to Richmond took three weeks, and by the time they arrived Morgan and Dawson were friends. During the rest of the war they'd stayed in touch, and last spring they'd met again, on a ship coming back from England. Dawson had been visiting his family in London; Morgan had been coming back from Egypt.

Right after the war Jem had gotten married to Helen Trenholm. Sarah came up from New Orleans for the wedding; that was her first visit to Charleston. Helen was the daughter of George Trenholm, Secretary of the Treasury under the Confederacy. Trenholm's shipping company had run the blockade all during the war, so unlike everyone else he was richer after it than he'd been before. Trenholm was famously generous. He had saved Jem's life by sending him a nurse for the yellow fever before they even met. That was how they met—Jem's roommate died of the fever, and Trenholm knew the boy's father. He helped out with the funeral, then sent a nurse to look after Jem. Then he invited him to recuperate at his big house, Ashley Hall. Jem promptly fell in love with Helen. That was during the war.

Helen was the beautiful daughter. She was the one on the Confederate ten-dollar bill, dressed as a Greek goddess. A year after they were married Helen gave birth to baby Emily, and ten days later Helen died of the yellow fever. Jem was a father and a widower at the age of twenty. The Trenholms took the baby, and Jem went to Egypt to ride in the Khedive's cavalry. He was there for six years. He left out of loneliness: he admired the horses, but the Egyptians wouldn't introduce him to their women, and he didn't speak the language. Jem went back to Charleston.

Plantations were being auctioned off then for nonpayment of taxes. No one could make them pay, and they sold for next to nothing. George Trenholm had bought several. Jem wanted to buy one from him, Hampton's. Trenholm told him it was a bad idea, that no one could make these places pay now. Jem had never run a plantation, but he was pretty sure he could make it work. He persuaded Trenholm to give him Hampton's in exchange for some railroad bonds.

———•———

THE ROAD LED through woods lit by long shafts of slanting light. The green deerflies were small and vicious. The mare switched her tail and tossed her head, and Dawson slapped his cheek, leaving a smear of dark blood. He'd come as soon as he'd gotten the telegram, but it was an eight-hour trip. He didn't know if he'd arrive too late. He didn't how he'd be able to help. He didn't know who was in the household; he didn't even know who had sent the telegram.

They came out into low rolling fields, ragged and untended. A driveway came in from the left, flanked by tall square brick pillars. Levi pointed his whip.

"Hampton's," he said.

The drive ran for nearly a mile in a straight line. On either side were huge old live oaks, meeting overhead in an airy green filigree. At the end stood a row of twelve charred pillars, sooty blackened brick. Only four were whole, the rest were stumps. They would once have been fluted white columns, supporting a pediment. Coming up the driveway, through the green arch of the live oaks, the house would have looked like a Greek temple.

He thought they should be pulled down, all these ruins. They did nothing but remind people what they'd lost.

The drive curved left toward a smaller house, plain white clapboard, with a two-story porch supported by square pillars. Levi pulled up in front.

"We here," he said.

On the porch stood several rocking chairs. An old red hound lay sprawled on the floor. At Dawson's approach she gave a brief yodeling bark and struggled to stand. Her old pads slipped on the smooth surface, as she scrabbled for purchase. After several tries she gave up, legs sliding out from under her as she collapsed onto the floor. She raised her nose and gave the hootling bark again.

As Dawson walked up the steps the door opened and a young woman came out. The afternoon light slanted across the verandah, and as she stepped into it her face turned suddenly radiant. She raised her hand to shade her eyes. Her skin was very white. She walked quickly toward him and the thought came to him, *This is the woman I'm meant to marry.* Though he was already married.

"The fever's broken." She smiled at him, intimate and joyful, as though she knew him. "He's going to live."

"Thank God," Dawson said. He took off his hat, and held it down at his side.

"You're Captain Dawson," she said. "I'm Sarah Morgan, Jem's sister."

"Miss Morgan." He bowed.

The sun lit up her honey-colored hair, her face. She seemed to give off light.

"Come in," she said. "He's waiting for you."

He stepped inside behind her. When she shut the door they were alone in the long hall. She smiled and turned to lead him. The house was dim and silent, and the air motionless. The slanting sun made bright lozenges on the dark floor. Radiant motes hung in the beams. She walked ahead. Their footsteps were loud against the bare boards. She held herself very straight, and her skirts made a light shushing sound. Her tawny hair was piled thickly on the back of her head, and loose strands curled at the nape.

The bedroom was on the ground floor, beyond the staircase. The shades were lowered, the room dim. A bed stood against the far wall. An older woman sat beside it.

"Here's Captain Dawson, mother," Sarah said.

"Mrs. Morgan," Dawson said, bowing.

Jem lay against the pillow, his right arm in a sling. His face was pale, and greenish bruises spread like clouds along one cheek and jaw. His eyelids were heavy and swollen. He grinned.

"Frank Dawson," Jem said. "All the way from Charleston."

"I'd have come farther," said Dawson. "How are you?"

"Capital," Jem said. His voice was a croak.

"He nearly died, Captain." Mrs. Morgan held grievance wrapped around her like a shawl.

Sarah dipped a cloth into a basin and smoothed it over Jem's forehead. He closed his eyes.

"Worth the bullet, the attention."

"I can see that," Dawson said.

Sarah put her wrist against Jem's forehead. "Cool." She looked at Dawson, triumphant. He nodded, as though they were partners.

They took turns telling Jem's story. Jem had gone to lunch in Columbia with his friend John Caldwell. They'd gone to the upstairs room in Pollocks Restaurant. A friend came over to speak to Caldwell. When he left Caldwell explained that he was Judge Melton, and in the midst of a public feud with Senator C. W. Montgomery, who happened to be downstairs. Caldwell wanted to make sure there was no trouble.

Caldwell and Jem went down after Melton, who saw Montgomery, sitting with his friends. Melton went straight for him. They grappled, falling over onto the floor. Caldwell and Morgan followed at a run. George Tupper, a friend of Montgomery, stood up as they approached. He pulled out his pistol and fired into Caldwell's chest. Caldwell fell backward, and Morgan caught him and laid him down on the carpet. He was dead.

"I went after Tupper," Jem said, recovering energy. "I was going to throw him out the window. I got my arms around him and tried to wrestle him over to it, but while I was getting there he got his gun hand up underneath my arm. He reached around and shot me in the shoulder."

"And then what?" Dawson asked.

"Then the police arrested Jem," Sally said.

"You?" Dawson asked.

"For trying to throw that man out the window," Sally said. "Mr. Tupper."

"But Tupper's the one who shot Jem," Dawson said. "Who killed Caldwell."

"They put Mr. Tupper in prison for a few weeks," Sarah said. "He pleaded self-defense and they let him out."

"That poor Mr. Caldwell, his whole life ahead of him," Sally said fiercely. "He was just trying to help."

"Tupper was just trying to help, too," Jem said.

Sally ignored him. "Luckily, Mr. Trenholm came up from Charleston. He got Jem out of jail and found him a doctor."

"The doctors were worse than getting shot," Jem said. "They started digging for the bullet. They spent days in there, prospecting. Finally I told them they were killing me, and they had to quit. Then the fever started. I thought that was the end of it. I thought I was dying, and asked for a bottle of champagne. They thought I was dying, and they brought it. That's what saved me. I drank it and the fever stopped."

As he talked, his eyes were beginning to droop. He was running out of energy. Talking was an effort.

"That's enough." Sarah drew up the sheet. "You need some rest. We're going to leave you alone."

As they left, Jem called after them, his voice rusty. "The funny thing is," he said, "I don't like champagne. I never have."

On the porch Sarah brought out a tea tray. Dawson watched her white hands moving among the cups. Her fingers were small and blunt, like a child's.

"How long have you and your mother been here?"

"Since June," she said. "We'd been living in New Orleans with my brother since the war."

"And how do you like South Carolina?" He expected her to praise it; she did not.

"We're learning to like it."

"Jem must be grateful to have you here," Dawson said.

"I always wanted to keep house for my brothers," Sarah said. Her gaze was level, not flirtatious. He didn't quite understand her, there was something unyielding about her. He liked it.

"We're fortunate to be here, Captain Dawson," said Sally.

"Where were you during the war, Mrs. Morgan?" he asked.

"Hither and yon, Captain," Sally said. "Hither and yon." Her faded blue eyes were large and confiding. He could see she'd been a beauty; she still gave off a whiff of coquetry. "Toward the end we were fortunate to move in with Sarah's brother, Philip Hicky Morgan, in New Orleans." She emphasized the name, as though he were famous. "So we were safe. But our house in Baton Rouge was pillaged. The Yankees destroyed everything. And we lost three of our boys." Her voice carried blame. "And my husband."

"Not all to the war, Mother," Sarah said. She had heard this before.

"During it. Two of my sons were lost on the battlefield, Captain," she said. "Gibbes and George." There was something avid and fierce about her. "My husband died of illness shortly after it began, and my eldest son, Hal, just before."

Her faded eyes were fixed on him, as though he knew who was to blame.

"I'm sorry," said Dawson. "Those are terrible losses."

"Thank you," said Mrs. Morgan.

He could see this was not enough.

"But now we're here at Hampton's," Sarah said.

"Jem can't get anyone to work for him," Sally said. "He lets them stay here, but they won't work for him. They poisoned his poor dog and stole his chickens."

Dawson shook his head.

"One of them stole his milk cow. He butchered her and nailed her poor hide on the cabin wall. When Jem took it down the man had him arrested for trespassing. And the judge gave Jem a fine. It was his cabin." Sally stirred her tea, then set the spoon in the saucer. "They're all Negroes now, you know. Judges, mayors, everyone."

He saw that, for her, this life, everything about it, this strange new house and unfriendly people, was provisional. She had been robbed of her real life. She was waiting to return to it, her sons and her husband, Baton Rouge, her friends, her furniture, her place in the world. Her lost family.

She still was living somehow in her real life, the one with her sons and family, in their house. The chandelier in the dining room, its prisms catching the early light. Tiche pushing through the swinging door with the breakfast tray. The soft linen sheets with her monogram, which she'd mended over and over. Her husband coming out of his study holding a book, his finger holding his place.

"I never saw my sons' bodies," she said.

"Mother," said Sarah.

Grief had taken hold, settling in gray drifts across this wide Southern landscape. The deaths lay like a pall over them all. No one could fit themselves around those empty spaces.

The hound, for no reason, began to thump her tail. She looked at Sarah, ears pricked.

"Good girl," Sarah said, crooning. She turned to Dawson. "Last summer Duchess saved our lives. One night the lamp caught fire, down in the front hall. Duchess woke everyone up. Mother and I were upstairs, and we'd have been trapped. The whole house would have gone but for Duchess." She smiled at the dog, who dropped her ears and thumped harder. "And you, Captain Dawson? Will you go home to England or stay here?"

"This is home now," he said. "I became a citizen right after the war."

"So you're one of us," Sarah said.

He nodded. He felt he was.

"What made you become a citizen?" She cradled her saucer in her palm. Her face was in shadow, but when she moved it flickered into the sunlight.

"A Belshazzar Thoroughbred." It was a famous bloodline, though maybe she didn't know horses.

"A horse?" Sarah was laughing.

"I bought him during the war. He was a big handsome gelding, seventeen hands, pure black except for a white snip on his nose. I was going to name him Caesar, but my servant Aleck got there first. He called him Pete, and I never went against Aleck. I trusted him with everything: clothes, meals, my pocketbook. My horses.

"But one morning when I got up Aleck was gone, and so were two of my horses. A friend and I rode after them, but Pete was faster than our horses, and finally we had to turn back.

"That summer, after the war ended, I saw Aleck on the street in Petersburg. I asked him why he'd stolen my horses. He just laughed. He said he hadn't meant to thieve them, he'd only meant to visit a girl in Winchester.

When he got there some Yankees stopped him and took the horses. He didn't say why he'd needed two horses to visit the girl."

"So the Yankees had your horse?" Sally said.

"They did. In the fall I saw him, being ridden by a federal officer. I told him that was my horse, he disputed it, and I went to the police. It was common enough, Yankees stole our horses and afterward we claimed them. But the police said I couldn't file a claim unless I was a citizen. So right there I asked for a Bible, swore my allegiance, and got my horse back."

Mrs. Morgan looked scandalized. "You became a citizen for a horse?"

Sarah laughed. "That's not very flattering, Captain Dawson."

"I've never regretted it," Dawson said.

Mrs. Morgan set her cup down in the center of the saucer. "Are you married, Captain Dawson?"

Dawson hesitated. "I am."

"A Southern girl, I hope," said Mrs. Morgan.

"A Charleston girl," Dawson said. "Virginia Fourgeaud. We've been married for five years."

"My felicitations," said Mrs. Morgan, bowing.

"Thank you." Dawson paused before he altered things. "But my wife has consumption. She became ill soon after we married. Four years ago."

Sarah looked at him, stricken. "I'm so sorry."

"Captain," said Sally, "I hope people have been kind. The South owes you a great deal."

"Very," said Dawson, bowing, "but the South owes me nothing. I'm here because I want to be."

"And what is it you do, Captain Dawson?" asked Sally. "I'm afraid I've forgotten."

"I'm fortunate enough to be the editor of the *Charleston News*," Dawson said, trying not to sound proud.

"The editor!" said Sally. "You're an important man."

Dawson laughed, pleased. "Not to everyone."

"How interesting." Sarah leaned back in her chair. "Tell me, Captain, how do you go about being editor?"

He knew Southern women, how they asked men questions in order to make the talk glide along. It was not because they were interested. He'd learned that. It was a parlor game.

"I don't do much." Dawson smiled at her. "The reporters bring in stories and we juggle them around and make them fit onto the page, and then we print the whole thing up and send it onto the street."

Sarah's blue gaze was level. "You're condescending to me, Captain."

"I beg your pardon," he said.

"Do you print national news?" she asked. "Or only local? How do you find the news? Do you write about books? Do you take positions on politics?"

Chastened, Dawson leaned forward. "I'll be glad to tell you." He set down the cup and told her what he and Riordan did, and how the paper worked. She listened, serious, attentive.

"And do you have a mission?" Sarah asked. "At the paper. A message? Or are you just entertaining your readers?"

He looked at her, delighted. No one ever asked this, though he and Riordan discussed it endlessly. "We do," he said. "To maintain the honor and promote the welfare of the Southern people." He hoped he didn't sound pompous or pretentious. He was afraid he did.

"You sound like my father," she said.

Dawson hoped it was a compliment.

———•———

EIGHT HOURS WAS not, actually, so long a trip. Dawson got on the train in the morning and was there by evening.

All fall, while Jem recuperated, Dawson visited. When he grew stronger, Jem came out and sat in the parlor. The talk was still about the war, even now. It was so large and present, it had gone on so long, there were so many stories to tell. They told each other what had happened to them, to their friends, to their houses. Yankees had pillaged the house in Baton Rouge. Gibbes had been there during the war, and had seen it. Smashed mirrors, plundered drawers, letters strewn on the floor. The portrait of Sally by Thomas Sully, all ivory skin and flashing eyes, slashed to canvas rags. Miriam's best blue dress hoisted on a sword-point and carried out into the street, pumped disgustingly up and down. The soldier slashed at it with his knife and yelled,

"That damned secesh woman." A neighbor had watched it all. They were in New Orleans by then.

"We haven't been back," Sarah said.

"I don't want to remember it like that," Sally said. "I have it in my mind the way it always was."

"The wisest way," Dawson said, nodding.

There were funny stories: Dawson told them about the time he and another soldier had been surprised by Yankee soldiers. It was at night, in a back street. The two were unarmed, but it had been rainy that evening, and they both carried umbrellas. When they saw the Yankees at the end of the street they raised the furled umbrellas like rifles and aimed them at the Yankees, who fled.

So many stories, near misses, awful coincidences, miraculous saves. Once Dawson had leaned over to fix his boot and a sniper's bullet had thumped into the tree trunk behind him, just at eye level. When he was at Oakland, recovering from a wound, Union scouts arrived and the Raineses hid him in the cellar, under a horse blanket. He lay still, listening to the boots overhead.

Sarah and Sally told him about the time the Yankees shelled Baton Rouge and they all walked to Greenwell.

"We were terrified," Sarah told Dawson. "We'd been packing to leave, but when the shelling started, everything flew out of our heads."

Sally laughed. "I took an old cloak and some books."

"I took two toothbrushes and some hairpins," said Sarah. "Some powder against the sun, but no clothes."

"The hairpins were essential," Jem said. He turned to Dawson. "Do you know about Sarah's hair?"

"Should I?" said Dawson.

Jem rose from his chair. "Stand up, Zay."

"Jem," Sarah said, shaking her head.

"Stand up!" He was laughing.

"I'm not to be ordered about," Sarah said, but she was laughing, too. Jem beckoned.

"Come here," Jem said. "And you, Dawson. Now, Zay. Take it down."

It was late afternoon. The sun painted parallelograms on the wall. Sarah was still laughing, the color rising in her bright face.

"Take it down," Jem said again.

Sarah stood up and raised her hands to the back of her head, to the heavy mass of hair. She began drawing out the pins, and the mass began to fall, heavy and loose, rolling and sliding down until it hung like a long, soft golden shawl, down to her ankles.

Tilting her head, she parted her hair with her hands, exposing the white nape of her neck. Dawson felt a jolt at the sight. Jem handed one hank to Dawson, and took the other himself. He lifted it like a tawny rope, stepping backward. Dawson did the same, and they both retreated, step by step, until their backs were against the walls. Sarah stood in the middle, her face rosy, the long ropes of hair spanning the room.

Dawson felt the heft of it in his hand. It was soft and living; he could smell it. The intimacy of the touch swept through him. Sarah laughed and blushed, but held her head high. She looked like a tribal queen. He couldn't speak, something had risen in his throat.

IN EARLY DECEMBER Virginia died. Her health had been failing steadily, then in the last few weeks, precipitously. He and his parents-in-law had been taking turns sitting up with her. Dawson and Virginia had always lived with her parents, at first from economy, then, when they all realized that Virginia was ill, from grief. That night Dawson was asleep when his father-in-law knocked on his door. "It's time," Eugene said. He carried a candle, and the rising light and sharp shadows made him look like Satan. Dawson got up and followed him, pulling on his robe. In Virginia's room Celena was kneeling by the bed, holding her daughter's hand. Virginia was motionless, her eyelids half-closed, her skin icy white. Dawson felt a deep flood of sadness, coupled with the hard fist of relief. He had been mourning Virginia for years.

He had a photograph of her mounted on porcelain, and gave a copy to Sarah. Each time he saw the picture he felt a double strand of feeling, a stab of pain and a sense of relief. The Fourgeauds wanted him to stay on with them, and it would have been cruel to leave. They had no other children, and he was a link to their daughter. But the house was silent and terrible. The blinds were drawn, the rooms seething with grief. He dreaded going home.

13.

For the last week we have averaged a murder per diem in the city and suburbs.

—*THE NEWS AND COURIER*, JUNE 21, 1873

———

IN JANUARY Sarah and Dawson began *Middlemarch*, taking turns reading it aloud. In the winter the fire was always lit in the parlor. Dawson sat in the chair; Sarah lay on the sofa. When he finished his chapter he handed the book to Sarah. "What do you think?"

She shook her head. "I think Dodo is an appalling prig," she said. "Casaubon is old enough to be her father. And he's so dull! She mustn't marry him."

"What if she loves him?"

"She doesn't," said Sarah, sitting up. "She'd never be happy. She'd only be doing it because she thinks she should. Which is exactly why I'll never marry."

"You wouldn't marry because you thought you should," said Dawson. "You'd only marry because you wanted to."

"I'll never marry because I don't want to," Sarah said. "Women are expected to marry, and I won't do it just because I'm expected to."

Dawson shook his head. "You make no more sense than Dodo."

"I'm just telling the truth." Sarah put her hand out for the book. "Let's find out what she does next, this Dodo."

Dawson handed it to her. "Such fierce opinions," he said. "What would you think of writing for the paper?"

Sarah raised her eyebrows. "I wouldn't dream of it," she said loftily. But he could see she was pleased.

"Why not?"

"I have nothing worth saying, and I'd never use my name in public."

"You do, and you could use another one," Dawson said. "Use a man's. George Eliot."

Sarah laughed, but Dawson was serious, though he said no more then.

The next morning, when he was leaving, he stood at the front door with her to say goodbye.

"Miss Sarah," he said, "I have a request. When I'm back in Charleston, may I write to you?"

There was a pause.

"We have so much to say." Was he pleading? He was afraid she'd refuse.

After a moment Sarah said, "You may write me, Captain. But with a three-letter rule: three letters from you to each one of mine."

It was the first time he'd seen her frankly flirtatious. He laughed. "I'll be delighted. I'll number mine, to keep track. You'll be shocked at how fast your debt will mount."

January 15, 1873. Charleston

FRANCIS WARRINGTON DAWSON TO SARAH MORGAN

My dear Miss Sarah:

I wrote you a long letter last night, but I was so miserable that I thought I had better sleep on it. This is the result—for better or for worse, in the words of a service which a lady never reads. I found my business in a very satisfactory condition, with mountains of dry work to be done. "Home," as it is called, is inexpressibly dreary. Enough of me!

I have sent you some New Orleans papers and to-day I have sent . . . the second volume of Middlemarch, the French Revolution, & Valerie Aylmer. What can I say of Middlemarch, except that I shrink now from reading more than we read together. The Carlyle you will, of course, read leisurely. With Lamartine's [Histoire des] Girondins & [Dickens's] the Tale of the Two Cities, it will give you a vivid understanding of the causes and excuses of the crimes committed in Liberty's name. (My hand trembles fearfully. Why is it that even writing to you affects me so?) . . . Those days at Hampton's were amongst the happiest of my life & so shall remain. The pines are as plainly seen as when I last looked upon them, & there is a wealth of meaning in their gray lights & dreamy shadows. Of this be certain: You have sealed me with your seal, and, God willing, you shall never be ashamed of me. Proud of me you will not be: you may, in some new happiness, forget all about me, but you live, & will live, as freshly & tenderly to me as when you were quietly saying that winter as well as summer romances must fade away. You see, I fancy I am at Hampton's again. Would that I were! For me you have abundant work to do, if you care to do it. As you determine I shall linger in the plain or breast the mountain height. Do as you will with me, and ask anything except that I forget you. Do write to me if you may, & as kindly as you can. I am not well in mind or in body, but my head is clear . . . Give my love to your dear Mother & brother . . . And for you I pray, that Our Lady may keep you & watch over you now & always. This is the best (of what you have not) that can be given you by your poor servant.

F. W. Dawson

———•———

IN LATE JANUARY, Jem married again. His new wife was Gabriella de Saussure Burroughs, called Ella. Her sister was married to a Trenholm, so Jem hadn't really left the family. Ella joined the household at Hampton's, with Sarah and Sally. Within a week she moved all the furniture.

———•———

EARLY FEBRUARY, one afternoon, Dawson and Sarah set out across the field for a walk with Duchess. The field was dun-colored, and the dried stalks were noisy underfoot. A pheasant scuttled along the edge, firing off a series of urgent metallic clucks. As they approached he took laborious flight, wings pumping, heavy body rising at a low angled slant, then vanishing among the trees. Beyond the field was the path into the pine woods, where the gray trunks closed around them, and the soft red-needled floor muffled their steps.

He was aware of every part of her, the small neat feet, the trim square-ness of her shoulders. The way her arms swung, quick and limber; the small cloud of curls at the nape of her neck. It seemed a waste not to look at her all the time. He wanted to look at her and he wanted something more.

Beyond the woods a field sloped down to a creek; the pale grass was beaten down by winter. By the water stood a willow, the long whips drooping into the water. The sky was muted and soft, like gray silk. Far above a hawk circled slowly, dark against the sky. In the distance a woodpecker interrogated the bark of a tree. They were alone.

"You were kind to send those things for Mother," Sarah said. "The books and magazines for me." A faint wisp of steam marked her breath.

"It was my pleasure." Dawson wasn't sure about their finances. "Let me know of anything you need." He felt flattened by something, something large that was approaching him.

"It's so cold here." Sarah pulled her shawl more tightly around herself. "It was never so cold in Baton Rouge."

"You miss it," Dawson said, "Baton Rouge." He wanted her to be happy here.

"I miss the way it used to be, all of us together. But that's gone. I don't want to go back now."

"So when you've sold the house you'll stay?"

"I don't think Ella wants us at Hampton's."

"Why don't you think so?" The things she was saying seemed impossible.

"Just that she's moved every single stick of furniture in the house from where we'd had it," Sarah said. "She dragged the little rocking chair across the parlor and set it by the window. She cocked her head and said, 'Doesn't it look darling?' Mother and I didn't dare look at each other."

"She can't be so obvious," Dawson said.

"And yet she is."

"But are you happy in South Carolina?" He wanted her to stay. He wanted her to know what he was going to say.

"We're not settled," she said. "Jem's having a hard time, and Ella wants us gone. I don't want to go back to Brother."

"Where would you most like to be?" Dawson asked. He wanted her to say Charleston. He'd find them rooms, servants, friends, everything. He wanted to take care of her. He wanted her nearby, on a tree-lined street, within reach. He wanted her.

"Provence," Sarah said.

"Provence?" He was lost.

"In a stone house with a wrought-iron balcony and blue shutters," Sarah said. "Everyone speaking French. I've always wanted to live in France."

"Provence." He nodded.

Well, then. He could sell his shares in the paper to Riordan. He spoke French, he could work as a journalist. He could move to Provence. But he could not organize his thoughts, with all this thudding, the blood pounding in his head. He took a breath.

"Sarah." His chest had tightened. He saw that she knew what he was about to say. She looked stricken.

"I want to ask you," he began, but the words he'd prepared were gone. "I want to tell you." He had to get the words out.

Sarah raised her hand to stop him. "Captain."

"Marry me," Dawson said. "Please." There was more, but he couldn't now remember it. Something inside him was expanding; fear and excitement. "You are at the center of my heart."

The sloping field, the pale grass, and the leaning tree were tilting beneath him. He could feel the turning of the planet. Her eyes were brilliant blue.

"Please don't ask me this," she said.

He waited, searching her face. The words were final, though her voice was not. "But you'll think it over. You'll let me ask you again."

"I've always planned to take care of my brothers."

"Your brothers are married," he said.

"I must take care of my mother."

"Your mother would be part of our life," Dawson said.

She looked at him, but said nothing.

"I'll persuade you." He wouldn't let her say no.

She opened her arms like a bird spreading its wings, the shawl's fringe fluttering like feathers. She drew it more tightly around her shoulders. "I wouldn't be a good wife."

"What do you mean?"

"When I was nineteen," she said, "I was in a serious carriage accident. I was thrown out. For three months I couldn't walk." She looked at him directly. "My spine was damaged. I may become an invalid."

"I'll take care of you," Dawson said steadily.

"You've already had an invalid wife. I wouldn't give you another."

He smiled gently. "That's for me to decide."

She turned away. "So I can't have children."

"I'd rather have you."

She looked up, frowning against the winter sunlight.

"Is that all?" he asked.

She said nothing. The breeze caught the fringe on the shawl, the wisps of hair around her forehead.

"Give me six months," he said. "I'll ask you again."

Duchess galloped suddenly across the field toward them. Wagging, grinning, she made big ragged sideways leaps around them. They greeted her with delight, as though she were a lost child.

"Duchess! Duchess!" Sarah leaned over the dog, clapping her hands. Inside her wrist was a delta of blue veins. He remembered the weight of her hair in his hand.

———•———

FRANCIS WARRINGTON DAWSON TO SARAH MORGAN

August 5, 1873

How was it that we came to attach so much more importance to this day than to any another? It could have been understood if my lips were to have been sealed until the coming of this particular day; but those lips refuse to be sealed, & can no more refrain from telling their love for you & to you than they can cease to breathe the fragrant breath of life. The one will end with the other. Yet we did agree that this should be an eventful day "big with the fate," not of Cato and of Rome but of a very ordinary man & a very lovely woman . . . However much either of us may try to ignore it, the certainty is that sooner or later you must decide whether you can bear with me for always, and when, if you desert me, I must learn whether I can live without you. And, whenever the time comes, you will have means of judging that you could not have had six months ago. I think I may say that I have proved that my affection for you is not a mere fancy of a day, or a month, but the deep undying and ever-increasing love of a life-time. I have proved to you that I understand you, & that the greatest intimacy leads to no jarring between us. I have proved to you that even confirmed ill-health, which you dread, will only increase and intensify my tender care of you. I have proved to you that your people are my people, & that they can love me as warmly as I love them. These are things which very few men can say to any woman whom they ask in marriage, but I can say them to you, because you know this truth. I do not press you for any decision. There is time enough for that. I only wish, on this day of all days, to remind you of what time has done, and to repeat to you, solemnly, my vows of constant and unselfish love. And it makes me glad to know that, whether it be requited or not, you never doubt now the truth of my love for you. My one aim in life is to win your hand; that gained, I have gained all that I wish for, more to me, indeed, than riches or public fame, or the honors that most men crave.

Yours always

F. W. Dawson

———•———

THEY WERE MARRIED in January.

They were living in Charleston by then. Dawson had found them rooms at Gadsden House, which was tall and distinguished, Georgian brick. They were married in the high-ceilinged front parlor by Bishop Lynch. Sarah had agreed reluctantly to a Catholic service: she would never forgive the Church for her mother's forced novitiate, but Dawson told her he would not feel married by a Protestant service. Sarah wore her mother's lace veil and a cream silk dress; at thirty-two she was too old for white. Jem walked her down the little aisle, between chairs carried in from all over the house. She carried a small bouquet of ivory freesias with golden throats, and the fragrance moved with her as she walked. Sally sat in the front row next to Celena Fourgeaud; they both wept. Ella sat beside them, stiff-backed.

Dawson stood by the bishop, in front of the fireplace. It was cold; they had lit a fire, and he could feel the warmth behind him. He watched Sarah coming toward him slowly. He could see from the veil that she was trembling. She seemed too bright to look at, like the sun. Her eyes were down at first, then she raised them and looked directly at him. It was like looking into the sun, and he felt something inside his chest swell and thicken. He could not speak.

14.

A shocking murder occurred in Opelika, Ala., on the 23d ultimo, the victim being Mr. Thomas Phillips, an elderly and respectable citizen, and the perpetrator a young man, named John Hooper, a nephew of the author of "Simon Soggs." Phillips had by accident become an eye-witness, with others, of some scandalous conduct on the part of Hooper. As the matter became the subject of public gossip, Hooper charged Phillips with giving currency to the reports, and, upon his assurance that he had not done so, demanded that he should explicitly deny all cognizance of the subject matter of the scandal. Phillips refused to utter this falsehood, whereupon Hooper deliberately drew a pistol and shot him dead. Hooper then surrendered himself, and, strange to say, was admitted to bail.

—*THE NEWS AND COURIER, JUNE 3, 1873*

15.

The year 1875 opened brightly for South Carolina . . . A good understanding between whites and blacks seemed to have been established, and . . . it seemed certain that, in South Carolina, a peaceful solution of the problems of emancipation and enfranchisement would be found, in a continuous cooperation of the better citizens of all classes and shades of opinion, in the work of governmental reform.

—*THE NEWS AND COURIER*, JANUARY 1, 1876

July 4, 1876. Hamburg, South Carolina

HAMBURG WAS A small town on the Savannah River, just across from Augusta, Georgia. Three bridges (two train, one wagon) connected the two towns, but Hamburg was in South Carolina, in the old Edgefield District. It lay on low swampy land, and when the river rose the water flooded into the streets.

The town had been founded thirty years earlier as a market center, selling slaves, whisky, and cotton. The cotton came on wagons from the countryside and left on trains heading down the river. The market was lively, but the town kept flooding, and when the railroad bridges went in, trade moved across the river to higher ground. The town dwindled, and white people moved away. By this time Hamburg held only about five hundred people, mostly Negroes, though also some Jews. The mayor, magistrate, marshal, and police chief were all Negroes.

Communities like these sprang up after the war. Freedmen didn't want to stay on plantations, and they moved to towns and cities. Now they could go to school, own land, and vote. In 1872 freedmen held 105 of the 156 seats in the state legislature. Negroes were a majority here, because South Carolinians had been some of the largest slaveholders in the country. Before the war the Negroes were slaves; now they were voters. The change was unsettling to the whites.

———•———

HAMBURG CELEBRATED THE Fourth with a reading of the Declaration of Independence and then a parade. The whole town turned out, standing along the edge of the dusty street. Mothers in long skirts and bright kerchiefs held babies in their arms, little children by their hands. Young women, with polished dark faces and white teeth, leaned against each other. Small boys dodged among the grown-ups. Men in dark jackets and straw hats stood watching.

Sam Cook, the intendant, read the Declaration. At the end of each line, people called out "Amen" or "Yes, Lord." After the intendant finished, the crowd cheered, and everyone looked up Market Street. Company A of the Ninth Regiment of the National Guard, all Negro, in uniform and in formation, carrying rifles, were marching toward them, heads high, arms swinging. They were singing. A drummer and a fifer on a six-hole cane fife rattled out the song.

> Mine eyes have seen the glory of the coming of the Lord:
> He is trampling out the vintage where the grapes of wrath are stored;
> He hath loosed the fateful lightning of His terrible swift sword:
> His truth is marching on.

The crowd took it up. They were celebrating two kinds of independence: one from the English king, one from the white master. Not everyone knew the verses, but they all knew the chorus: *Glory, glory, hallelujah!*

Captain Dock Adams, chin high, walked beside his men. He was solid, with a barrel chest and short arms. He looked straight ahead. The crowd began to clap. A woman hoisted up her toddler, his back against her shoulder, his feet on her forearm, so he could see. Company A had been founded six years earlier by the governor. It was a state militia: after the war, when the white people resisted the new laws, the state governments established armed militias to enforce them. Company A was one of these. Its first commander was Prince Rivers, who was now town magistrate. Six months ago, when Dock Adams took over the company, he expanded it to eighty-four members, and started weekly drills on Market Street.

Market Street ran parallel to the river, from the Augusta bridge to the Edgefield road. It was more like a plaza than a street—over a hundred feet wide, so the big cotton wagons could maneuver. On one side were warehouses; on the other side tall grass stretched all the way to the river. It was flat and smooth, with a carriage track down its center, just wheel ruts through the grass.

Company A marched in four columns, twenty men in each. The center columns took the carriage ruts; the outer ones marched through the grass, trampling it.

A horse and buggy had been standing at the far end of Market Street, near the bridge to Augusta. The two white men sitting in it watched as the Declaration was read. The militia marched toward the crowd, their rifle barrels catching the sun. The crowd lined the edge of Market Street. Older ladies fanned themselves. The children were playing, not paying attention; the mothers were talking and laughing.

When the troops approached the podium, the horse and buggy began to move, heading down Market Street toward the marchers. The horse was a chestnut, smooth and glossy. He jogged slowly, tossing his head. The driver had touched him with the whip, but held the reins tight, making him nervous. The roof of the buggy shadowed the men inside, so it wasn't until it got close that Dock Adams could see their faces. It was Henry Getzen and Thomas Butler, from Edgefield.

They leaned forward, staring at him. The horse threw up his head, and flecks of white saliva flew from his mouth. Adams marched his men along the ruts toward the horse. One of the white men shouted, making a sweeping gesture with his arm. But Adams was the officer in charge of a military unit, and these were civilians. He marched his men straight toward the carriage.

The horse jerked his head up and down and the driver flicked him on the rump. The horse flattened his ears: he was being driven into a herd of humans.

Along the street everyone grew quiet, watching. People drew back, and the young girls stopped laughing. The woman lowered her two-year-old from her shoulder, sitting him on her hip and wrapping her arm around his ribs.

Adams, his chin high, marched on, his arm swinging, the rifle on his shoulder. Twenty feet from the buggy he shouted, "Company, halt!"

At the sound the horse flung his head up and the driver, Henry Getzen, angrily shouted, "Whoa!"

The men stood in columns. The fife and drum were silent, the singing had stopped. Adams stood at parade rest, his arm stiff at his side.

The roadway was wide there. The buggy had big wheels, and the land was flat and open. For the white men to give way meant only turning the horse's head and making a detour of ten feet over the grass. For Adams it was asking eighty-four men on government business to change their course.

Henry Getzen was twenty-five, and married to Frances, Thomas Butler's sister. Thomas was twenty-two, son of an Edgefield farmer. Thomas's father, Robert Butler, owned a plantation in Edgefield, but he was best known for his pack of scent hounds. Before the war, tracking runaway slaves was big business, and his dogs were famous among both whites and blacks.

All these men knew one another. They had lived in this small community their whole lives.

"Mr. Getzen," Adams said, "why you doin' me this way?"

"What way?" Getzen asked loudly. His hands were set wide, his legs braced against the buckboard.

"Aiming to drive through my company," said Adams.

"I'm driving on the road," Getzen said. "Where I always drive." The horse threw his head up, and Getzen yanked on the reins. "You're bothering my horse."

"There's room enough outside this for you to drive, Mr. Getzen," Adams said.

"These are my ruts." A certain tone had come into Getzen's voice. "It's where I always travel." His eyes were fixed on Adams. Getzen was stocky, with a broad red face and a thick mustache that drooped at the corners.

Along the edge of the street, people moved away from the parade, closer to the buildings. Mothers looked around for small children.

"That's as may be," Adams said, "but if you had a company out here I'da not treated you in this way. I'da shown you some respect, and gone around."

"Well," Getzen said, "this is the rut I always travel, and I don't intend to get out of it for no damn niggers. Now get out of my way." He was angry; he hadn't expected Adams to talk about respect.

The mothers, watching, tightened their holds on the children's hands. The men frowned, shifting their weight.

"Get out of the way," Thomas Butler said.

Around there, white people didn't celebrate Independence Day. In Columbia, the state capital, the stores were closed, but only the Negroes celebrated. Southern whites felt resentful at the notion of independence. In Edgefield maybe they felt particularly resentful.

———•———

THE SIGHT OF black men marching with guns was disconcerting to these white men. All over the South were quasi-military rifle clubs and gun clubs for white men. They had no official purpose, but the unofficial one was clear. As long as there had been slaves, masters had needed weapons, to remind slaves of their situation.

Violence is integral to slavery. No one can be coaxed or persuaded into enslavement: physical coercion is necessary. Violence is essential, and so are its infernal aids: whips, collars, bits, shackles, nooses, chains. The threat of death and death itself. The constant reminder, swift and savage, of who owns the body. That was a lesson learned by both sides, black and white.

Violence was embedded in their lives; slaves must always be aware of the harm that could come to their bodies. They had to witness violence visited upon other bodies. They had to feel it on their own. This had been a part of Southern culture for a very long time.

Because of slavery, and this need, the South has always been more violent than the North. In the year 1878, Massachusetts, New Hampshire, and Vermont each reported one murder. South Carolina reported 128.

So after emancipation white people didn't like the idea of Negroes carrying guns. They felt that was power—and implied violence—in the wrong hands. Power had always been in the hands of white people.

They didn't like the idea of Negroes voting, either. More power in the wrong hands. Negroes wielding any kind of power went against their grain. What slavery had done was make every white man a lord. White men were born with power, which meant they felt they deserved it. Whatever you have feels like yours. The idea of emancipation was directly at odds with this: but how could a government nullify innate power? White people felt they were born with rights over black people.

That was what many white people believed in South Carolina. The idea of emancipation rankled. It felt like tyranny, and enforcement felt like oppression. Some people still didn't really believe they'd lost the war. They thought they were in a dip, a pause. Their motto was "The South shall rise again."

Many white Southerners felt personally oppressed by emancipation, and they opposed what happened at Appomattox. Had anyone asked them personally to surrender? Many of them wouldn't have. Many still didn't accept what had happened.

Before the war, in South Carolina, a group called the Fire-Eaters supported secession and defended slavery. After the war they were outraged by the new laws. They believed that the races were separate and unequal before God. Hadn't Negroes always been subordinate to them? They felt, on the deepest level, wronged. They felt the natural order had been challenged.

They believed this was an affair of honor, and that they were honor bound to uphold a sacred principle. This was the principle of white supremacy. They believed that the war was unfair, and that somehow they were victims (though they themselves started and ended the war). They believed that the South had taken on the holy aspect of a martyr. They believed that the South would rise again.

Also, they were accustomed to using violence to get their way; they didn't actually believe in the rule of law.

———————

HAMBURG WAS IN Aiken County, part of the Edgefield District.

The District lay in western South Carolina, alongside the meandering Savannah River, which separated the state from Georgia. It contained Edgefield County and four others: Aiken, Saluda, Greenwood, and McCormick. White colonials began settling there in the middle of the eighteenth century, part of a wave of immigrants from the Border countries of England and Scotland. These people came to America to find a better life; the one at home was unlivable.

They were called Scotch-Irish (some were from Ireland), and they arrived in big family groups. They were fair-skinned, blue-eyed, and long-limbed; also proud, tetchy, and violent. Especially violent: this was part of their culture, a long tradition of savage fighting. The border wars between England and Scotland were bloody and brutal, involving families, children, livestock. Houses and villages were burned, stock driven off, belongings stolen. Enemies were ambushed and tortured and killed. One family flayed its enemies, tacking the grisly skins on the outside walls of their houses.

This guerrilla warfare went on for seven hundred years. Governments were weak and temporary; there was no rule of law. Border people were self-reliant, vigilant, and ruthless. Some clans lived by stealing, plundering, and killing. Kinship was the only trustworthy bond, and families—clans—became small states. Blood feuds burned deep into the community, lasting for generations. Pride, fortitude, and a savage hatred of government intrusion were part of the culture they brought to America.

Arriving in Philadelphia, these immigrants were noted for arrogance and violence. They seemed unlikely to settle peaceably into the community founded by Quakers, and were encouraged to move on into the mountains. They settled throughout Appalachia, along the spine of the Southeast, spilling into the lowlands. One destination, Edgefield, was famous for violence from its very beginnings.

The District offered good land, with lots of game, loamy soil, and plenty of water. Cherokee lived there before white people arrived, and when the settlers declared it theirs, the Cherokee differed. A long, bloody conflict began, of a kind familiar to the settlers. By the time the Cherokee were driven off, the District was devastated. Livestock had been stolen and houses burned. Families were gone; there was no community. It was called "Bloody Edgefield." The veterans of the Cherokee wars were outlaws who had robbed and pillaged, raiding plantations, abducting women, and torturing landowners. The rule of law did not exist. In response to this, the Regulators were formed, perhaps the first American vigilantes. Volunteer landowners took the law into their own hands, riding through the countryside and dispensing rough justice: shooting, whipping, beating, and hanging anyone they declared guilty.

The Revolution burnished Edgefield's savage reputation. In 1781, thirty Revolutionaries were brutally executed at Cloud Creek. Among them were a father and son, both named James Butler, members of a Scotch-Irish family who'd arrived in the early 1760s.

"What! Old Edgefield again! Another murder . . . it must be pandemonium itself, a very district of devils," wrote an eighteenth-century visitor. In 1850, the homicide rate in Edgefield was twice that of the state average. After the Civil War, Congress called it the most violent region in the state.

The trigger for violence was honor. In the Borders, honor was the only inviolate possession. The idea was brought to the New World: honor was fragile, jealously guarded, and easily threatened. Anyone could insult you, and challenge your place in the world. Any real or imagined slight could result in apocalyptic violence: hand-to-hand combat, duels, ambush, murder. Men shot each other during card games, on bar stools, in parlors, on the street, through the window, over anything. A sideways glance, a misreported comment, a drunken gesture.

The upper classes had their own violent tradition, the code duello. Dueling had strict rules about procedure and weapons, but both traditions held honor to be essential, and both traditions used lethal violence to defend it.

Both traditions fit into the great tradition of violence that permeated the South because of slavery.

Edgefield had a double helix, twinned tendencies toward violence: one from seven hundred years of savage border fighting, and one from two hundred years of that peculiar institution, slavery.

———·———

SO EVEN THOUGH Hamburg was a Negro town, it wasn't safe for Negroes. The white men from Edgefield were just over the hill. They drove through all the time, making trouble.

———·———

BUTLER AND GETZEN leaned forward. The horse, hearing rising voices, tossed his head. The people watching moved into the shadow of the empty warehouses. Children were grabbed by mothers. The young girls stiffened. The town went silent.

"By God, nigger," Getzen said, "you let us through." He picked up his revolver, which was lying on the seat.

Adams turned to his men. "Open order," he called. The men stepped to each side and the ranks opened, making a wide swath between the columns. Getzen drove the nervous horse through them. Butler held his revolver pointing upward as they went through the ranks.

"The first nigger touches our horse is dead," he said.

The uniformed men stood still, staring straight ahead as the chestnut horse jogged between them.

16.

PLAN OF CAMPAIGN

1st Determine if necessary to kill every White Radical in this county—2 Every mulatto Radical leader

3rd Every negro leader—make no individual threats but let this be known as a fixed settled thing—

4th We must send speakers to all of their political meetings, who must denounce the rascality of these leaders face to face. The moral effects of this denunciation will be of great effect—

5th Thorough military organization in order to intimidate the negro

6th Every white man must be at the polls by five o clock in the morning of the day of election, and must go prepared to remain there until the votes are counted

7th Make no threats—"Suave in modo fortite in re"

8th There is no use in arguments for the negro

—CIVIL WAR EX-GENERAL MARTIN WITHERSPOON GARY, EDGEFIELD, S.C., SUMMARIZING A LETTER FROM S. W. FERGUSON, GREENVILLE, MISSISSIPPI, JANUARY 7, 1876. FERGUSON LAID OUT A STRATEGY FOR THE ISSUE OF BLACK VOTING.

M. W. GARY HAD BEEN at Appomattox, but he hadn't surrendered. Instead he drove his spurs into his horse's sides and galloped off the field to protest what was happening. That made him a hero to some.

Ten years later, Gary was still angry. He was a lawyer then, with a farm outside Edgefield. He was tall and bald, with a long nose and a permanent scowl, which gave him his nickname, the Bald Eagle. He didn't like the way Reconstruction was going. He didn't like the tax raises, he didn't like paying Negroes to work. He didn't like Negroes voting. He didn't like the white people—Radicals—who thought all this was legitimate.

He wasn't alone. He'd gotten up a group of more than a hundred local landowners, all angry. They didn't like Reconstruction and they didn't like the governor, Daniel Chamberlain, an outsider from Massachusetts who supported the laws on Negro voting. Most of the Southern Democrats were white, and most of the Republicans were black. The black population was larger than the white, which gave them political power. Gary's friends didn't like this. They didn't like Negroes holding office, and they especially didn't like Negroes carrying guns. That seemed against the natural order of things.

They complained about literacy. During slavery it had been illegal for slaves to learn to read and write, and now, ten years afterward, the black population was still not as well educated as the white one. Which meant there were illiterate people holding office. Gary and his group complained about this. They put a notice in the paper announcing that they were going to restore white supremacy. They were drawing up a list of Negroes to whom they wouldn't rent farmland. White people owned almost all the land, so if they refused to rent any to a local black neighbor, he was out of luck. The white men listed the names of the Negroes who didn't understand their proper position. Who were insolent, and wanted to be paid for their work, and wanted to vote. Gary had a plan to deal with all this, modeled on one from Mississippi.

Jim Cook was the Hamburg marshal then. He was colored, but he stood up to white men. He held both colored and white accountable to the law. Just outside town was a little spring, clear water that ran down into a hollowed-out rock. A sign forbade people from drinking straight from it, as a matter of hygiene. They were requested to drink from the dipper instead. A white man from Edgefield came by one afternoon and set his whole face right down in the water and sucked it straight up. Afterward he threw the sign down and trampled on it. Jim Cook fined him. That was something, a Negro telling a white man how to drink water. That was an insult to white men.

The boys from Edgefield liked to gallop through the dirt streets of Hamburg, raising dust and shooting off their pistols. Hollering and swearing, threatening people. It was just for fun, just a little excitement, but Jim Cook fined them for disturbing the peace. The boys resented this. The day before the parade, Tommy Butler had driven his wagon at a fast clip through town, stirring up dust into the faces of people sitting on the porches. It was a question of courtesy. Some of the people on the porches had complained, and he hadn't liked that.

The day after the parade, Tommy Butler's father, Robert J. Butler, the one with that pack of good scent-hounds, came in and filed a formal complaint against Dock Adams. It wasn't the first time. Two years earlier he'd filed a complaint against the marshal, William Nelson. This was over a dispute over the use of Market Street, for which his son Tommy claimed to have special rights. His father paid a monthly fee to the town for special use, sending his heavy wagons to Augusta. Tommy felt this gave him a kind of ownership over the roadway. That's why he had told Dock Adams he was driving in his own ruts. Two years ago R. J. Butler had claimed that William Nelson and a colored cotton buyer called Samuel Spencer had threatened to kill Tommy. Nelson and Spencer were ordered to put up two hundred dollars as bond money and promise to keep the peace for a year. That bond money was a serious burden.

Prince Rivers was the trial justice, which was what they called the magistrate. He was a tall, handsome man, with jet-black skin and an imposing presence. He'd been a slave, but had taught himself to read and write. His slave job had been coachman, and during the war he'd stolen his master's coach horse, took it out of the traces, and escaped. He rode a hundred miles, through Confederate lines, from Edgefield to Port Royal, to reach the Union troops. He volunteered to serve in the Union army, became a sergeant, and performed outstandingly. He was commended for his service. After the war he was elected to the state legislature.

Butler and Getzen accused Dock Adams and his company of blocking a public road. After they made their claims Rivers summoned Adams, Butler, and Getzen to appear the next day. Getzen said that the black soldiers carried loaded rifles, and had been insolent and threatening. Adams denied this. Rivers ordered a hearing three days later, at four o'clock on the eighth of July, a Saturday.

At noon that day there was a meeting of the Sweetwater Sabre Club. It had about fifty members, all white men. They met in the Sweetwater Baptist Church, and they called themselves a rifle club. They had uniforms and weapons, mostly Springfield rifles.

They were a rifle club, but also a citizens' militia. There were a lot of these in the South. Before emancipation there had been good reasons for white men to go out in groups with guns. There were good reasons for night patrols, good reasons to hunt down slaves who had no business being out then. Sometimes they hunted them just for fun, to hear them whoop and holler. Beg for mercy.

Before the war white men had good reasons for emergency communication systems, for armed readiness, vigilance. White people needed all this: they were living on top of a volcano. They could feel it underneath them, the shift, the roiling. They knew it was there. They had always used violence preemptively, to prevent the possibility of violence coming from someone else. Guns and violence had always been part of their lives, but before the war those things were reserved for white people. Now the balance was changed. The federal government had set up Negro national guards. Negroes were carrying guns, and that was dangerous. The white men didn't like it.

Young Ben Tillman and his brother George were members of the Sabre Club. They were from Edgefield; everyone in the club was. The Tillmans were a plantation family with a violent heritage. Their father, who'd died when they were young, had killed a man. George, the older brother, had shot a man during a card game. He hid out for a while in Mexico, then came home and served two years in jail. He carried on his law practice from behind bars, and later he was elected to the state senate. Another Tillman had been killed in a duel and a third during a domestic dispute. Ben was the youngest brother. He'd inherited some family land and had bought more. He now owned over twelve hundred acres. He'd lost an eye to cancer, and he wore a black patch over the bad one. It gave him a sinister, raffish look, which he enjoyed.

The Sabre Club admired the Bald Eagle's plan and they wanted to teach the Negroes a lesson. They wanted to redeem the state from Negro and carpetbag rule. They called their plan "Redemption"; they were all church-goers. They believed that this was a noble cause, that they were saving white society from defilement. They believed that white supremacy was part of the natural order.

The head of the Sabre Club was another Butler from Edgefield, Colonel A. P. Butler. That Saturday in July the members met in the Sweetwater Church at Summer Hill, about three miles above Hamburg. They were all told to attend the Butler trial, officially to provide protection for the two Edgefield boys, in case there was trouble. Actually their mission was to start a fight, if the Negroes offered any kind of opportunity. If no opportunity was offered, the Sabre Club boys were told to make one. They were not to wear uniforms, and not to carry guns, only pistols. Many of them took rifles any-way. They didn't want this to look like an organized military campaign, though it was. They were told to spread the word throughout the countryside.

By then everyone had heard what had happened on the Fourth, about the insolent Negroes who'd refused to yield to white men. That story had gone all around the District.

—•—

ON THE DAY of the trial, Harry Mays, colored, walked home from work. He was a porter at a store in Augusta, and on Saturdays the store closed early. When he reached the South Carolina side he saw groups of white men in the streets, talking loudly. They were everywhere, on every block. A bunch of them stood around the liquor store on Center Street. They were all carrying guns, pistols mostly, but a few had rifles. The door to the liquor store was open, and the men went in and out. As Mays made his way through the streets, more white men with guns kept coming in from the Edgefield road.

When Mays reached his own street he saw A. P. Butler on the corner.

A.P. had a farm in Edgefield, and Mays worked for him sometimes. After they'd said hello Mays asked Butler what was going on.

Butler told him that they were going to take away the Negroes' guns. He said it straight-out.

Mays said that those guns belonged to the U.S. government, and maybe the U.S. government would have something to say about that.

Butler said the U.S. government had nothing to do with it. He told Mays there was no Constitution now. He said, "It has been one hundred years since the Declaration of Independence, and the Constitution is played out now, and every man can do just as he pleases. There is nothing to be done about it."

He told Mays about their plan, how the white men were going to take away their guns and keep the niggers from voting. He told Mays that all the white men were set on it, and there was nothing to be done about it.

Mays went on home. He didn't like the look of things, and planned to stay inside.

At about three o'clock Butler's buggy came up the main street to the courthouse, carrying R. J. Butler and his lawyer, General Matthew Calbraith Butler. The general was also from Edgefield, though if he was related to R.J. it was too complicated to figure out.

It was a hot afternoon, and the door to the magistrate's office stood open. Constable William Nelson sat with his feet up on the doorframe, catching any breeze that came through. Nelson was nearly forty, a stocky man with a round face and hooded eyes. His manner was calm, and he had a settled way of speaking. The buggy pulled up outside with Butler in it. Tommy Butler and Henry Getzen were riding alongside on horseback. Getzen had a rifle, a sixteen-shooter, slung across the shoulders of his horse.

The general saw Nelson sitting in the doorway and called out to him.

"Where's Rivers?" It sounded like an order.

General M. C. Butler had narrow blue eyes, a thin mouth, and a long, narrow beaked nose. His reddish-blond hair was meager on top, but thick around his mouth and along the sides of his face. His skin was smooth and tight over the bones of his skull. He was fierce and handsome.

"Rivers is over at his house, I reckon," Nelson said. "He'll be here directly."

"Well, go get him, boy," said Butler, impatient. "Tell him to come here to me."

It was a little after three. The hearing wasn't to start until four.

"No, sir," said Nelson carefully. "I'm not Mr. Rivers's office boy. I'm a constable, and I'm here tending to my business."

The general stared at Nelson. "Do you know who you're talking to?"

"Yes, sir," Nelson said. "I believe I'm talking to General Butler."

"Well, God damn you, bring me some paper out here. I'll write something to send him."

"In here's the office, and in here's the paper, sir," said Nelson, "and here's the chairs for all the attorneys to sit down in."

It was intolerable that this man wouldn't show him more respect. "God damn you, bring it to me, sir," said Butler.

But Nelson wouldn't be sworn at. "No, sir, I won't," he said. "Come in, sir, and sit at the table."

The general got down from the buggy, the springs creaking as his weight left it. He walked up the steps. He limped a bit: one of his legs was wooden; he'd lost his own in the war. Henry Getzen got off his horse and followed. He was holding a pistol, which he pointed casually in Nelson's direction. Tommy Butler was still on his horse, out in the street. He held a pistol, too, pointing it in a general way at Nelson. Not ready to fire, but aimed in a way that drew attention.

The general came inside. He was tall and narrow-shouldered, with small hands and feet. His face was bright red. "Give me a chair."

Nelson gestured. "There's a chair, sir." A table and two chairs stood against the back of the room.

"God damn you," said Butler. "Give me the chair you're sitting in."

There was a pause.

"All right," said Nelson, standing up. "If this one suits you better." He stepped away. "Take it." He didn't touch the chair.

The general didn't move.

"You goddamned leather-headed son of a bitch," he said in a low voice, "sitting there fanning yourself in a chair, goddamn you."

Nelson said, "I'm fanning myself sitting in my own office, tending to my own business, sir." Nelson had had to put up a two-hundred-dollar bond for the man sitting on his horse in the street, holding the pistol aimed loosely at him.

"You goddamned son of a bitch," said M.C. "You want to have a hole put through before you can move."

Robert Butler climbed down from the buggy and came in. He was holding a big navy pistol. It was aimed generally toward Nelson.

Nelson didn't like all the pistols aimed at him, and he wanted to calm things down. He said, "Mr. Butler, now you know what kind of a man I am. You know me. I have always tried to behave when you came in my office."

"I know you, Nelson," said Butler, "but this goddamned drilling has got to stop. Now go and get Rivers."

"No, sir," said Nelson. "I have no right to go and get Rivers. I'm not going."

"Well, goddamn you," said Butler. His skin was thin and translucent, and the red had colored it all up. His taut cheeks and beaky nose, his neck were all brilliant scarlet. "You will be a dead man, and then you'll wish you'd gone."

Nelson shook his head slowly.

"I'm but one man," he said. "If you're going to kill me, then just kill me. That's all you can do."

"Well, goddamn you, we're going to take our time about that. You goddamned son of a bitch."

Nelson held Butler's gaze but said nothing.

"Goddamn you," said Butler, "sitting down there with your feet cocked up."

———— ·—— ————

DOCK ADAMS, master carpenter, and commander of the militia that refused to move, came home from work at around two thirty. As he walked home he saw the white men gathered along the sidewalks. They were all carrying guns. More kept coming in on the road from Edgefield, carrying guns and talking loudly.

At first Adams didn't pay too much attention to them, but they kept flooding in. At home he went upstairs. From the second-floor window he watched the men in the streets. He could hear them talking. They were going to kill the niggers. He heard his own name. *Dock Adams, he's the head of them.* They said they were going to kill him. They were going to kill every god-damned nigger in Hamburg.

He watched them milling about, going in and out of the liquor stores: Nunberger's, Coger's, Davis's. He watched young Bill Morgan jump over someone's fence into the backyard, and cut himself a switch from a cherry tree. He walked about cutting at people's shoulders and saying what he was going to do to the niggers. Most of the men were either drunk or acting drunk. Dock thought they were drunk.

Dock left by the back way and went to Prince Rivers's house. He told Rivers he wouldn't show up at the courthouse: there were now several hundred white men crowding through the streets, carrying guns and saying they were going to kill him. He told Rivers he didn't like the look of it. Rivers told Dock he was being too cautious. M. C. Butler just wanted to meet with him and the other militia officers. Adams said he'd agree to meet with Butler, but not at the courthouse.

Rivers headed over to the courthouse to talk to Butler.

The long, hot afternoon was beginning to slide toward evening. The liquor stores were all open, and more and more white men went in and out of them. Loud talk and jostling. Dogs got up from where they lay along the edges of the streets, moving off into alleys, out of the way.

The men kept flooding in. Some were on horseback, and milled about, walking their horses in circles, on long reins, leaning down to take a bottle out of someone's hand, swigging from it.

When Rivers came back he told Adams that Butler was willing to meet him at S. B. Spencer's house. But a big mob of white men with guns was already gathered there, and Adams refused. He told Prince that he'd be willing to meet Butler halfway between, if he'd keep back his men.

Butler refused. He said that all the guns must be given up to him. And that he wouldn't guarantee any protection to Adams and his men. Adams said he refused to meet: he and his men would be at the mercy of Butler and his men. He said he couldn't surrender the arms to a civilian, only to an official of the government that issued them. Rivers suggested that he take the weapons and send them directly to Governor Chamberlain.

Butler had had enough. No, he said, and got back into his buggy. He headed across the bridge to Augusta. He was gone for about half an hour. The white men were getting louder, shouting about killing all the niggers in town. Butler came back followed by a crowd of armed men. Sam Cook, the intendant, went up to him where the road turns onto Market Street. Sam Cook told Butler that things were looking squally, and he was worried they'd get worse. He asked Butler if he could get the women and children out of town before anything started. Butler told Cook he could have fifteen minutes. The intendant asked Butler if there was any way to settle things peacefully, and Butler said the Negroes would have to surrender their arms.

Adams refused. First of all, he told Cook, if they turned over their guns they'd all be killed by the white men. And these were government weapons. He couldn't hand them over to a civilian. He'd surrender them only to a government officer who had a right to them. He wrote this down in a note to Butler.

Butler sent back word that Adams had fifteen minutes to hand them over. Butler was incensed to be taken for a civilian. He was a general; everyone knew that.

Adams sent word that he couldn't surrender the arms.

The weapons and ammunition were kept in the Sibley Building, a solid brick two-story structure on the corner of Market and Center. It was next to Dock Adams's house, with a connecting door. Sometimes the men drilled there. Adams got word out, ordering his men to muster there at once. Thirty-eight men gathered in the drill room on the second floor. Adams watched out the window as Butler lined his men up outside, on the far side of the street and behind the abutment of the railroad bridge. The streets were now completely filled with white men carrying guns, hundreds of them.

Adams had little ammunition; they'd never had much. He told his men to use it sparingly. It would be risky to shoot from the windows, where they'd be targets. They'd only be able to aim at an angle.

The men took up their guns and concealed themselves beside the windows. Outside they could hear the white men talking, and then Adams heard a signal gun go off. The white men began firing. Most of the bullets hit the brick walls, though some came shattering through the glass. Every so often one of the men jumped in front of a window and took a shot. Adams was looking out when he heard a crack, and then saw someone over by the train abutment suddenly jerk his head up, then fall. It was Mackie Merriwether, and now they'd killed a white man. The Edgefield boys started yelling at the top of their lungs, and shooting into the Sibley. The bullets thumped into the walls. Most of the Negroes were lying flat on the floor.

Outside, Butler shouted to Walker McFeeny to go across the river and bring two kegs of powder from Augusta: they were going to blow up the building. Dock stood by the window, watching from the side. What they actually did was to bring a cannon across the bridge. They set it up in front of the building and began to fire.

Behind the Sibley Building the ground sloped away. They were on the second floor, and needed a ladder to get out the back window. Adams went next door for his carpenters' tools while the others ripped up the floorboards. He put together a ladder, which they lowered out the back window. Adams sent most of the men down it, but he and a few others stayed upstairs. Every once in a while they shot out the window to make the white men think everyone was still inside. By then it was nearly dark, and the moon was starting to rise. It was round and full and cast a dark radiance over the town.

The men hurried down the ladder to crouch in the darkness. Adams came down after them and moved them to the outskirts of town, into a corn field. He ordered them to wait there, and then he went back up the ladder. He went into his own house and up onto the roof, where he could watch and listen. He heard the white men talking and shouting.

His militia didn't stay where they'd been ordered to stay. They started moving through the streets, trying to get away.

Harry Mays lived at the other end of the block from the Sibley Building. While this was happening he was at home, watching from upstairs. He saw M. C. Butler giving orders. He thought between nine hundred and a thousand white men were there in the streets.

Months later he told Congress what happened.

They fired with small-arms until about eleven o'clock. Then I heard a cannon fire, and when I heard that I said, "Jesus! God! we are all done killed!" I . . . peeped out of the window. The moon was shining as bright as day, and I heard Harrison Butler say, "Here they come," and they fired at the niggers and the niggers fired at them. I saw both fires . . . The niggers had done come out and was going across the street . . . Every time they would see a nigger they would shoot at him, and would holler, "Here he comes." They got a fellow in Davis Lepfield's yard . . . and they fotch him out. There was white men all around. Good God! I don't know how many. There was about twenty-five men around him, and I think half of them shot him. He fell . . .

There was another man, Jim Cook, and I heard them say, "I've got the son of a bitch." I heard him holler. I know his voice. He said, "O Lord!" They said, "You call on the Lord, you damned son of a bitch." And it seemed to me that fifteen or twenty of them shot him then. By that time they got done shooting niggers in the street . . . Then the next man they got was me myself. I was living in the house next to Rivers . . . I heard them in Rivers's house. From the smashing up of things and going-on I felt pretty bad myself. I thought the next turn would be mine. And sure enough . . . When I heard them strike the middle door with the butts of their guns I unlocked my door and walked out on the porch, and there was about ten or twelve at the foot of the steps. They hollered, "Come down, you damned big son of a bitch." I said, "I hav'n't done nothing." They said, "None of you hain't done nothing." Then they took me around into this ring . . .

They had a whole parcel of men there, and you couldn't see outside after you got inside. You couldn't see among the white folks at all. Then they had us in the ring. After they got me there the next man they got was Attaway . . . They set him right down close by the side of me. He said, "Mays . . . do you think they will kill any of us?" I said, "Yes, I do think so . . ." He said, "Do you think they will kill me." I said, "I do . . . All you have got to do now is to pray to God to save your soul. Just give up your wife and children and everything else, for they are going to kill you." And then he hung his head and commenced crying . . .

There had been lies told on him, and they said he was going to kill white folks; the niggers had made up lies on him, and the white folks had been making such awful threats against him . . .

They were all going to get on one side of us and then were going to fire right into us [but then someone stopped it, and some of them went off and talked.] They carried us about twenty yards . . . and they stopped us in a ring and all circled about us and said, "Stop here;" and we all sat down in the dirt and sand. [There were] between twenty-five and thirty [of us] . . .

The first man they killed was Attaway . . . They called Attaway. Attaway says, "Gentlemen, I am not prepared for death." Some of the white men said . . . "I don't care; we are going to kill you;" and they took him off over the hill, and I heard the guns fire. When they come back they called for Dave Phillips. Dave got up just like a soldier. He looked like he didn't care no more for it than he would about eating, and he walked right along. I heard the guns fire, and they came back, but Dave didn't come. Then they came back and called Pompey Curry. He was sitting right by me. Me and him was cousins. I says, "Pompey, you run," just so, and Pompey got up and darted out, and got away from them . . . They shot him right here, [pointing,] but the ball only scalped his leg, and he got away. The next one they killed was Hamp Stevens. He was sick. He says, "O, gentlemen, I haven't done nothing." They says, "Come out here." He was a big mulatto fellow—a young man. They took him out, and I heard the guns fire, and they came back, but Hamp didn't come. The next time they called Alfred Minyard. He was a small fellow, and was sick. He was grown, but he was only a little fellow. One of the white men said, "O, let that boy alone; he is sick;" but they said, "O, God damn him; we'll fix him too." I heard the guns fire, and they came back, but Alfred didn't come. That was the last one they killed. He didn't die then, not till the next day, at nine o'clock. I saw him after he was killed, and I saw where they had cut off a big piece of meat from off his rump.

—U.S. CONGRESS, DECEMBER 5, 1876, REPORT OF THE OFFICIAL U.S. INVESTIGATION, *TESTIMONY AS TO THE DENIAL OF THE ELECTIVE FRANCHISE IN SOUTH CAROLINA AT THE ELECTIONS OF 1875 AND 1876*

17.

We find little, if any, excuse for the conflict itself, and absolutely none for the cowardly killing of the seven negro prisoners who were shot down like rabbits long after they had surrendered . . .

The killing of seven of the prisoners was barbarous in the extreme. We have no words strong enough to express our condemnation of such a crime.

The Hamburg militiamen . . . had given no special offence, and certainly had committed no such overt act as would justify the onslaught of the men from Edgefield. Their offence lay, we fear, in being negroes and in bearing arms . . .

In our judgment, the whole affair, from beginning to end, was shamefully wrong, and we owe it to the State to say so. We shall be told, no doubt, that it does not become a Democratic newspaper in South Carolina to give "aid and comfort" to the Radicals by denouncing, as criminal, any act of a body of white South Carolinians. Our answer to that is, that there is only one right and one wrong, for Democrat and Republican. What is wrong we must condemn. We will not consent to cover up a wrong, because it is committed by our political associates or personal friends.

—*THE NEWS AND COURIER*, JULY 10 AND 11, 1876

WHEN RIORDAN WAS TIRED, his left leg dragged slightly. In the mornings this was nearly unnoticeable, but later in the day it began to show. That afternoon he paused in the doorway of Dawson's office to lift his hip, so he could swing his leg over the sill.

Dawson's office was large and light, with two windows overlooking Broad Street. On one wall was a large map of Charleston, bookshelves beneath it. Between the windows hung a wall clock with a glass case for the pendulum below. Dawson was leaning over a manuscript on his desk, a pencil in his hand. He looked up as Riordan came in.

"What do you think?" Dawson asked.

"Our readers will be outraged." Riordan sat down across from him.

"They should be. It's outrageous behavior."

"By your response," said Riordan. "How far do we want to go in alienating them?"

"No one can stomach this," Dawson said. "Shooting down prisoners like animals. I saw nothing like this in the war. Decent men will agree with me."

"That won't help if we lose all our subscribers," said Riordan. "They'll kick like mules at this."

Their subscribers were fickle, canceling in a huff, firing off outraged letters, renewing without explanation. Circulation rose and fell in a continuing wave. But generally his readers agreed with Dawson, and if they left he trusted them to return. Where else would they get their news? *The News and Courier* was the best paper in the state, maybe in the South. The paper was booming.

"They'll kick but they'll come 'round," he said. "This is a matter of honor. They'll understand that."

Riordan shook his head. "Their code of honor doesn't apply here."

"We can't have two different moral codes," Dawson said.

Riordan raised his eyebrows.

The cancellations flooded in; two days later Riordan was back.

"Forty-seven today." Riordan came in and sat down.

"Is that all?" Dawson asked.

He was already focused on something else, the gubernatorial election. He wanted to reelect Chamberlain. "What are our chances, do you think?"

"He is an outsider," Riordan said.

"From that foreign land, Massachusetts," said Dawson. "But he's so much better than the others. He's cleaning up the state. Everyone can see that, can't they?"

Riordan shrugged. "Self-interest plays a large part in politics."

"But it's in the interest of the whole state to elect him," Dawson said. "Everyone."

Riordan shook his head and said nothing.

"I'm going all out for him," Dawson said.

The office boy came in. Bouton was eighteen, lanky and awkward, with watery blue eyes and an anxious manner. He did a million things: clipped articles, pasted them up, carried messages, ran up and down stairs, did as he was told. He wasn't allowed to write anything yet, though he wanted to.

He'd brought up the mail, and handed a stack to Dawson.

"More love notes from our readers," said Dawson. He picked up his letter opener, a narrow ivory knife. It was a gift from Sarah. He slit the first envelope. He read the letter and tossed it on his desk. He read two more, then looked up at Riordan.

"They do feel rather strongly."

"I'm keeping count." Riordan rose to leave. "I was a cotton broker before I became a journalist. I can always go back to it."

"Riordan," Dawson said. "If all we're doing is courting subscribers, what are we doing?" He waited. "Principle was the whole point."

"Yes," said Riordan. "There's a difference between holding firm to principle and rubbing the public's nose in something offensive."

The cancellations flooded in. Dawson didn't care. Every morning he opened the mail with the ivory knife.

"Twenty-three," said Riordan, coming in.

"And General Butler has denied having anything to do with the executions. He said he'd left when the mob was too unruly to obey commands. He said he left in disgust."

"What will you reply?"

"It's probably true. I hope it is. I hope a distinguished general wasn't in charge of that contemptible operation. And they'd been drinking all afternoon."

"Armed and drunk," said Riordan. "A recipe for success."

"These gun clubs are a force for chaos," said Dawson.

The Bald Eagle wrote an angry letter to a rival paper, calling Dawson cowardly for refusing to fight a duel. Dawson, who enjoyed dustups, wrote back at once. He strode into Riordan's office and put his answer on the desk. Riordan read it while Dawson waited, his hands in his pockets.

Riordan looked up. "'Slanderer and braggart!' That's a bit strong."

Dawson shook his head. "He called me cowardly."

"He'll never give way, you know," Riordan said. "He wouldn't surrender at Appomattox. He thinks the war can still be won. Do we want him our enemy for life?"

"Does he want me his enemy for life?"

"These people are looking for enemies," Riordan said. "It gives them focus."

"They'll do better choosing someone else."

Riordan handed back the page. "We'll stand firm. I hope the Bald Eagle settles his feathers."

"That's up to him," Dawson said.

That afternoon he received a hand-delivered message: the Bald Eagle challenged him to a duel.

Dawson took it in to Riordan. "From General Gary," he said. "Delivered by General Butler, colleague and second."

Riordan was going over an account book. He jotted down a number in the margin, then put his hand out for the note.

"Two generals," Riordan said. "Impressive." He scanned the letter. "It's a good thing you won't duel. You'd have been dead years ago."

"A barbaric institution," he said. "I want to have it banned."

Downstairs they heard a commotion, voices rising, shouts, then laughter: it was the reporters. They were like dogs, thought Dawson, barking in a frenzy, wagging their tails, running in circles.

"Do you ever think of getting a dog?" Dawson asked.

Riordan shook his head. "Not now."

"I suppose not," said Dawson. Riordan's wife had left him (scandalously, for another man), and Riordan had custody of his two children. He had put them in a local boarding school, and now he lived with his bachelor brother. You couldn't have a dog without a wife, a household. Dawson thought of tiny Ethel, her wild blue eyes and outstretched arms, staggering clumsily toward his legs. She wasn't old enough.

"I had a dog when I was a boy," said Riordan. "A little setter with brown spots. We called him Ajax."

"I'd like a terrier," Dawson said. "Or a Newfoundland."

Riordan laughed. "Quite a difference."

"Maybe both," Dawson said. "I enjoy extremes."

Downstairs they were laughing again, and then the front door opened and shut, the bell on it sounding. Someone had left, and the noise died. "How many cancellations do we have now?"

"A hundred and twenty," said Riordan. "Cotton brokering calls. I can always go back."

"But you won't," Dawson said. "Have some pity. That would be the end of me."

Riordan smiled and shook his head.

"It was good, you know," he said. "Your piece."

———

YOUNG BARNWELL RHETT insulted Dawson in his paper, the *Journal*. Dawson didn't mind. He remembered telling old Barnwell Rhett, at the *Mercury,* to swallow the Fourteenth Amendment. Rhett's furious red face, his eyes like tiny chips of blue stone. But Dawson had been right.

Dawson showed the letter to Riordan.

"Another challenge?" asked Riordan.

"Only an insult," said Dawson. "Or maybe three. 'Liar, ingrate, and coward.' Is that one or three? I'm curious about ingrate, but since we're not on speaking terms I can't ask. But no challenge. By the code it's up to me to challenge him. Which I won't."

"But you'll reply."

Dawson nodded.

———

THEY WAITED IN Dawson's office, Riordan, Jem Morgan, and Carlyle McKinley. McKinley was tall, lanky, serious, with a long Irish face. He'd been with the paper nearly from the start. Dawson trusted him.

It was just before noon. Dawson stood by the window, looking toward Rhett's office at the *Journal*. It was a block away, on East Bay.

"Can you see him?" Jem asked. He came over to stand beside Dawson. He was shorter by several inches, still Little Morgan. His mustache was extravagant, and curled up at the ends. Jem was between jobs, as he often was, but always ready for excitement.

Dawson shook his head. "The sidewalks are full. We have an audience."

"What time is it?" Riordan asked.

Jem took out his watch. "Eight minutes of."

"What did your note say?" McKinley asked.

Dawson turned from the window. He tugged down his waistcoat and shot his cuffs.

"'Captain Dawson requests the honor of meeting you on Broad Street, twelve noon, August eleventh.'"

"Have you a pistol?" McKinley asked.

Dawson shook his head. "I don't carry one."

"Have you?" McKinley asked Jem.

Jem raised his eyebrows and said nothing.

"We're not setting out to fight," said Dawson.

"You're not," said Riordan. "But he might be. This is South Carolina."

"By the code he can't shoot first," said Dawson. "He has to wait for me to respond."

"You've responded in print," said Riordan.

"I didn't challenge him. By the code he can't shoot first. Either I shoot or no one does," said Dawson.

"The code has been broken before," Riordan said.

"I rely on his honor," Dawson said. "Isn't that the point?"

"What about the honor of his seconds?" Riordan said.

"Who are his seconds?" asked McKinley.

"McHugh and Williams," Dawson said. "Write it all down, McKinley. In case anything happens."

McKinley took out his notebook. There was noise out on the street. Everyone knew about this.

Dawson took out his watch and flipped it open. "Time."

They went down the wide creaking staircase. Dawson went first, buttoning his jacket. Jem clattered behind like a tugboat, small but important. As he went down he pressed his elbow against his side pocket, where the pistol was. The others followed.

Dawson and Jem stepped outside and turned toward East Bay. At first there was excited talking, but then the crowd quieted. No one spoke. A man leaned out of an upstairs window. Two policemen stood along the curb. Everyone watched Dawson. Jem walked jauntily beside him. Dawson moved with long, deliberate strides.

At the far end of the block, three men approached on the other side of the street. Rhett and his seconds held themselves erect, looking straight ahead.

The street was silent. A buggy passed, the driver and passenger watching. Rhett and his men held their arms slightly away from their bodies, hands floating in the air. Jem held his arms away from his sides, but Dawson's arms swung freely. He gazed straight ahead. One of Rhett's men turned his head, staring at Dawson. It was one long block from the office to East Bay. A seagull flew overhead, crying.

In the middle of the block the men passed without pausing. Their seconds watched with sidelong gazes but didn't turn their heads. The footsteps were loud. The crowd watched in silence. Someone whistled, and another gull wheeled above. Dawson and Jem walked on, and when they reached East Bay they turned, away from the crowds. McKinley was a few steps behind.

After another block they stopped, now alone.

"I think it's over," Dawson said.

"I was hoping for a little more excitement," Jem said. "I got up early for this."

McKinley took out his notebook and began writing.

"There's nothing to write," Jem said. "Nothing happened."

For Dawson the light had turned oddly spangled. He put his hands in his pockets and bent over from the waist. When he straightened the world crowded around. The tall brick house beside him was immense, its white trim brilliant. The ironwork fence was hung with garlands of wisteria. How precisely pointed the leaves were, how green! The windowpanes gleamed darkly. The sun was directly overhead; he was walking on his shadow. It was miraculous. He thought of Sarah's blue gaze: she, too, was miraculous. It was miraculous that she was his wife. He was alive in the world.

On each side, each man thought he'd won.

———·———

SARAH SAT UPSTAIRS in her bedroom. She'd drawn the filmy inner curtains, but the sunlight filtered through. She sat with her back to the window, a parasol leaning on the sill to keep the slightest ray from her skin. She was trying to read; she couldn't concentrate. She was always afraid for him. Whenever he was late the thought of his death entered her mind. Now she sat with a magazine, starting the same paragraph over and over. The handle of the parasol kept sliding off the back of the chair. Each time it slipped, it startled her.

When she heard the front door she was afraid it would be someone with a message. She wondered what she would say to Ethel. But when she went down she saw it was Dawson.

"All done," he said. He put his arms around her.

"I was frightened," she said.

"But you needn't have been."

———·———

IN AUGUST the Democratic Convention met, and Dawson learned that his readers would not take his advice. They would not support Daniel Chamberlain. The convention elected Wade Hampton as their candidate for governor. Hampton was the grandson of a Revolutionary hero, and a Civil War hero himself. His family had been one of the largest slave owners in the South, and he still owned vast properties.

Riordan came in to his office. Dawson stood at the window, looking down into the street. His hands were in his pockets, rattling the things there: a cigar cutter, change purse, a small knife.

"I've heard," Riordan said.

Dawson nodded without turning.

"It's a blow," Riordan said.

Dawson turned around. "We're the voice of the people. We support the process and the office. If they've chosen Hampton, we'll support him."

Riordan nodded.

"I don't agree with them, but if that's the way the current is moving we must stay in it," Dawson said. "We can't be left on the bank."

Riordan took out his watch. "Only thirty-six days, nineteen hours, and twenty-two minutes."

"That it took for me to see I was wrong?" Dawson said. "But I might have been right. I might have swung them round. If it hadn't been for Hamburg."

The trial of the Hamburg defendants took place in September. Eighty-seven white men—all the members of the Sweetwater Sabre Club, plus others from the District—were charged with murder and conspiracy to murder. They were ordered to appear at the courthouse in Aiken. Later Ben Tillman would write that that they merely agreed to appear, not that they obeyed an order. As he remembered that day, the Sabre Club was in charge, not the court. The defendants wore the Bloody Shirt.

The Bloody Shirt was like the Confederate flag, it roused something deep and primal. It was a reminder that blood had been shed, that the South had been victimized by the North. The Bloody Shirt reminded people that the South suffered. It was at once violent and sentimental.

The myth of the Bloody Shirt began in 1856, when Senator Charles Sumner gave an antislavery speech, criticizing Senator Andrew Butler, who was from Edgefield. A few days later, Butler's cousin Preston Brooks, also from Edgefield, accosted Sumner in the Senate chamber. Brooks and his friend Laurence Keitt approached Sumner as he sat at his desk. Sumner had become famous because of his speech, and he was signing copies of it for the public. Brooks told Sumner he'd insulted his cousin. He raised his gold-headed cane in the air and brought down the heavy end on Sumner's head. Sumner struggled to rise, but Brooks pounded savagely on his skull. He beat Sumner so hard he finally broke the cane. Sumner managed to stand but Brooks kept on beating him as he staggered away, and Sumner finally collapsed, bloody and unconscious, on the floor. Laurence Keitt brandished a pistol, warning off interference. Someone finally urged Brooks to stop before he killed Sumner. Sumner nearly died from his injuries, and suffered for the rest of his life from chronic pain and trauma.

Some responses to the incident were gleeful, urging Brooks to do it again and finish the job. There were reports that Sumner traveled about with the blood-stained shirt, asking for pity. It was said he'd gone to Boston and to England, flaunting the shirt. This behavior was considered evidence that Sumner was not a gentleman, that the North did not understand the South's gallant code. Some Southerners despised Sumner for showing the Bloody Shirt as if he'd been a victim, as if he claimed to deserve attention, apology, sympathy, compensation.

But there was no bloody shirt. The whole story was a fabrication. Sumner never showed any shirt to anyone. Yet the story spread like wildfire, and the phrase passed into the language of the South. The Bloody Shirt was a rallying cry, a reference to the sniveling victim and a threat of violence. Sumner's critics took to wearing the Bloody Shirt themselves. It became part of the Mississippi Plan to terrorize Negroes, and it spread throughout the South.

In late August, Red Shirts rode in a torchlight parade through Charleston. Everyone knew what the shirts meant; everyone understood that the blood was not the blood of the wearer.

Before the Sabre Club trial, Ben Tillman had shirts made for all eighty-seven men accused of murder. He bought Venetian red pigment himself, though some of the boys used pokeberry juice, to stain their shirts. Tillman had a gigantic effigy made, a flagstaff with a head. The figure wore an enormous bloody shirt. The head was made of two Negro masks, topped with a kinky black wig. At the bottom was a motto, from Milton's *Paradise Lost*: "Awake, arise, or be forever fallen." This was Satan's appeal to the fallen angels, in which he tells them that though "defeat hath lost us Heaven," still, "all is not lost." Tillman had allied himself with Satan.

The white men rode into Aiken, the gigantic crucified Negro swaying above their bloody shirts. White people stood on the sidewalks and cheered. Negroes stayed indoors.

The men filed in to the courthouse, pistols in their belts. The judge set bail: they all got the same amount. They all provided affidavits for one another, proving that none of them was anywhere near Hamburg on the night in question. They all got off.

Dawson wrote high praise of Wade Hampton, the Democrats' dream candidate.

"All I ask," Dawson said to Riordan, "is that you don't quit and go back to cotton brokering."

Riordan smiled but didn't answer.

On election day the Sabre Club turned out armed and in force. They threatened and harassed the Negro voters. They closed down some Negro polling places altogether. Their efforts were completely successful: Edgefield reported more votes for Wade Hampton than there were residents in the town.

But both the gubernatorial and presidential results were disputed. South Carolina, and several other Southern states, submitted two different sets of voting results, and both Chamberlain and Hampton declared victory. Uncertainty reigned. To maintain the peace federal troops entered Columbia, but so did armed Red Shirts. They claimed to be protecting Democrats, but they were so numerous and unruly that their presence itself was a threat. Chamberlain and his government were virtually under siege.

Dawson and others went to Washington to negotiate a solution. The result was the Compromise of 1877: South Carolina gave its electoral votes to Rutherford B. Hayes, the Republican presidential candidate, and its state votes to Wade Hampton, the Democratic gubernatorial candidate. In return South Carolina received federal assistance for Dawson's favorite projects: railroads, commercial development, infrastructure. Most importantly, the delegation had demanded that federal troops depart from Southern soil. That promise was kept. Federal troops withdrew, leaving Negro voters without protection.

Dawson was confident that they didn't need protection. Once federal troops left South Carolina the Red Shirts would settle down. Negroes were now in high office. He reminded his readers that Negroes were succeeding.

—◦—

Wm. N. Stevens, a full-blooded negro, is said to be one of the most eloquent speakers in the Virginia Senate. He is a graduate of two colleges, and was born a slave.

—*THE NEWS AND COURIER*, FEBRUARY 23, 1878

18.

THE GOGGINS MURDER.

—•—

**The Widow and Brothers of the Deceased Charged with
the Crime—Not a Tear Shed by any of the Family—
A Bloodstained Neighborhood.**

A special reporter of the Ninety-Six Herald throws some light on the recent
mysterious murder in Edgefield County. He says:

The jury of inquest into the murder of Pickens Goggins, near Good Hope
Church, in Edgefield County, on the 6th instant, closed its labors on Monday last after a protracted investigation . . . The verdict of the jury charges
John Goggins, Henry Goggins, and Mrs. Emma Goggins, widow of the deceased, with having committed the murder. Pickens Goggins, the murdered
man, and Miss Emma May entered into the state of connubial felicity only
a few weeks ago . . . Mrs. Emma Goggins, widow of the deceased, is a bloom-
ing brunette of about fifteen summers, beneath the long lashes of whose
dark eyes could be detected the smouldering fires of intense passion. Over
her straight dark hair, without a curl or ripple, was jauntily perched a

pearl-colored felt hat, with lavender trimmings and an ostrich feather. A purple worsted dress, with maroon trimmings, and a gaudy neck ribbon fastened on her bosom with a showy tinsel pin, completed her outfit . . .

She appeared before the court when called, and gave her testimony in an easy and nonchalant manner. She stated that when the murder occurred she was in the kitchen with a negro girl getting supper; heard the shot fired in the room in which she had left Mr. Goggins; called "Pick," (the deceased,) but he did not answer; then called for Mr. Clyburn, who lives perhaps one hundred and fifty yards distant, and told him when he came that she thought "Pick" was shot; did not go into the room where he lay until Mr. Clyburn came. Mr. Clyburn came at the call, and found Goggins dead, with a pistol shot in the head.

The witness exhibited no feeling whatever, and made her statement without a quaver of voice or the suspicion of a tear. Indeed, there was not a tear shed by any of the family, or any one else, during the day, so far as your reporter's observations extended . . .

On the way to the scene of the murder we passed what had been the residence of Mr. Louis E. Holloway, who was murdered last year . . . Just beyond this are the remains of the shanty of Cash Harris, who was hung last summer for the murder of Holloway. We were also told that Goggins was murdered in the same room where his father was killed about three years ago.

—THE NEWS AND COURIER, FEBRUARY 23, 1878

PART III

19.

Sir: I see that you have had the extreme bravery to accuse the Editor of the Columbia Register of publishing "lies," "falsehoods," "untruths" &c. There might appear to be something manly in this if we could forget that you have done so behind the protection of that darling pet of yours and of all other cowards & slanderers, which is known as the "Anti Duelling Act." When we remember this we are at no loss to recognize it as a piece of "chivalry" worthy only of the bully who took refuge behind the Church from Col Rhett at one time and from Gen Gary at another—whose religion never bridles his tongue or pen but serves only as a protection from those he has wantonly insulted. And then to call yourself Captain too. What kind of a Captain are you or were you? Do you remember what Dame Quickly in Shakespeare said to Ancient Pistol when *he* was styled Captain in her presence? "If Captains were of my opinion they would cudgel thee for taking their name upon thee." Are you not ashamed of yourself, knowing that you are an object of so much contempt? The people of this state like bravery. They like for a man *to be* a man and to be responsible for what insults he may give. If a man is too religious to fight he should certainly be too religious to insult any one. It is folly to suppose that duelling is at an end in South Carolina. It never was, for fifty years back at least, of frequent occurrence here, but it has been and still is regarded by the "gentlemen" who seem to be such a terror to you, as the only way of putting the strong and the weak on terms of equality when they *must* fight, and it will be resorted to again notwithstanding the Anti Duelling humbug, whenever occasion shall occur, and no jury of twelve South Carolinians will be found so lost to all sense of *right* and *justice* as to find a man guilty of any crime in defending his honor and manhood or the good name of his family, no matter what may be said by a fellow, as the Macon Telegraph says, "whose hands are befouled with the swag wrung from a prostrate people by political pariahs," and one who is so plainly seeking to hide his cowardice under a guise of religion and philanthropy. Take my advice, and make up your mind to be a man, if possible, in future and, as you *are* a man of talent you may yet be regarded with some little respect, perhaps more than I think possible.

A Citizen

20.

TREATED AS BRUTES.

Pastor Heard's Description of the "Jim Crow Car" on the Georgia Railroad.

The Rev. W. H. Heard, pastor of Mount Zion A.M.E. Church, in this city, had made complaint to the Inter-State commerce commission that he and several members of his congregation having purchased first-class tickets over the Georgia Railroad, from Atlanta to Charleston, were forbidden entry to the first-class coaches and compelled to ride in a dirty and uncomfortable car, one-half of which was a smoking car.

—*THE NEWS AND COURIER*, JUNE 29, 1887

"I was on my way from Cincinnati to Charleston," said Mr. Heard yesterday, "and had a first-class through ticket which I purchased in Cincinnati. I travelled in the first-class coaches and enjoyed all the conveniences and comforts that my ticket entitled me to until I reached Atlanta. There we changed cars. As our party was about to enter the first-class coach on the train that was to go to Augusta a brakeman in uniform said to us: 'Don't go in there. This is the car for your people.' Dr. Gaines said to me, 'Let's go in there. We can't afford to raise a fuss. The brakeman is simply carrying out his orders' . . . The car was the half of a dingy old car much inferior to the second-class coaches on the railroads in South Carolina. It was divided from the rest of the car by a thin partition that did not reach to the top of the car, and over which came clouds of tobacco smoke and very offensive smells . . . Crowds of railroad hands, in dirty clothing, with their buckets and picks, came into this alleged first-class car, and, by their loud talking and boisterous conduct, made themselves disagreeable to refined people with sensitive nerves. Several passengers came into the car, bringing chickens and bags of meal . . . There was no carpet on the floor and there was no ice in the water tank. It is well that we were told that we were in a first-class car, for the liveliest imagination would never have entertained such an idea.

"When the conductor came around to collect tickets, I said to him, 'This is not the way to treat men with first-class tickets.' He replied: 'You will have to ride here or get off the car.'"

—*THE NEWS AND COURIER*, JUNE 30, 1887

"The Jim Crow Car."

As we have said before, it is not unlawful to separate the white from the colored people. But it is not right or just that a colored passenger to whom the railroad company has sold a first-class ticket shall be crowded into a dirty car along with "chickens, railroad hands and dogs," while the white passenger, who has purchased a first-class ticket has infinitely better accommodations for the same money. If chickens, railroad hands and dogs can be hauled in the first-class car for colored passengers, dogs, railroad hands and chickens should not be kept out of the first-class car for white passengers. In this case it is the amount of money that the railroad company receives for its tickets, and not the color of the ticket-buyer, that must decide the question of accommodations.

—*THE NEWS AND COURIER*, JUNE 30, 1887

"Change Cars."

The answer of the Georgia Railroad Company to the complaint of the colored man, W. H. Heard, that he had been refused the first class accommodation for which he had paid, and had been compelled to ride in the "Jim-Crow car," does not in any wise help the case of the company.

The remarkable assertion is made, in the first instance, that the company is not aware that any of its cars have been spoken of as Jim-Crow cars. As this name is familiar to every one who has ever travelled on the company's road, it is very singular, to say the least, that the company has never heard it. Perhaps, however, it is as ignorant as it claims to be, and this would account for its other remarkable assertion that the differences between the cars provided for the colored people and the cars provided for the white people, "relate to matters aesthetical only, and consist in higher ornamentation and matters of that sort, rather than in those which affect the substantial conditions of safety, comfort and convenience" . . .

There is a very practical way of putting all the assertions of . . . this railway to the test, and that is by issuing an order that, for one week, the white passengers shall occupy the cars now assigned to the colored people, and the colored people shall occupy the cars now reserved for the whites . . .

The colored people want to ride in the first-class cars, and the railroad company declares that there is no reason why the white people should not be delighted to ride in the Jim-Crow cars. We challenge the company then to put its counsel's assertion to the proof . . . and we risk nothing in saying that the new arrangement, with all its beauties, would not stand for twenty-four hours. It would have the effect, however, of exposing the deceptive character of the statements which were made to the Inter-State Commerce Commission, and would probably lead to justice being shown to first-class colored people who pay first-class fare.

—*THE NEWS AND COURIER*, AUGUST 1, 1887

21.

To the people of the South the race problem is the most stupendous problem of the century. It meets us at every turn. It obtrudes itself upon us in our political and industrial life. It touches every element of present progress and stands up like a great black wall against the future. All expedients for its solution which are not grounded in the spirit of absolute justice between man and man, or race and race, will fall to the ground.

—*THE NEWS AND COURIER*, JANUARY 2, 1889

January 15, 1889. Charleston

A COLD WIND had come up from the harbor, squalling through the streets, catching hats, snapping the furled corners of umbrellas. Dawson stood on the sidewalk outside *The News and Courier* talking to the mayor. He was wearing his new black wool overcoat from London. The wind gave a sudden swirl, lifting Dawson's hat, and he raised his hand to it. The sensation— his hat, the wind, the new warm coat—made him feel ebullient. He'd just sat through a long meeting on tax codes and now he was liberated.

Mayor Bryan was a cautious man, with a small face and short neck. He talked slowly, and was cautious about city funds, storm drainage, building renovations, everything. It made Dawson want to whistle.

"I've gone into these new raises very carefully," Bryan said. "From one point of view it makes perfect sense."

"The city certainly needs the income," said Dawson. He shifted his walking stick on the pavement, setting the metal tip an inch farther to the left, as though this might hurry the conversation along.

"I don't want to put too great a burden on the taxpayers," said Bryan. "I spoke to the comptroller just now."

"And he thinks?" asked Dawson, though he was quite sure he knew what the comptroller thought.

Over Bryan's shoulder he saw two well-dressed men approaching. One of them he knew: Reverend Dart, of the Morris Street Colored Baptist Church. He and Dawson had worked together after the earthquake. The other man was white, a stranger. They were heading straight for Dawson.

"That it isn't nearly enough," said Bryan.

"Always the issue," said Dawson. "Finding the balance between needs and resources. You have a difficult job, Mayor."

His tone contained a note of finality. Smiling, he looked at Bryan and also past him, at the two men in black overcoats. They stopped just beyond Bryan, hovering politely. Reverend Dart was tall and thin and dignified, with hunched shoulders, a lined face and round glasses. The white man had a long flat face and a high forehead, his hair rising in wrinkled waves. He had narrow eyes and a dark challenging stare.

Bryan, seeing Dawson's gaze slide past him, turned.

"Good morning, Mayor," Dart said, bowing. "Captain Dawson. If you have a moment."

"Morning, Dart," Bryan said. "I'll be off, then."

"Good morning, Reverend," Dawson said.

"Captain," said Dart. "I'd like to introduce a distinguished visitor from Virginia."

Dawson had pulled off his glove. He took the man's hand as Dart was finishing the introduction. He was gripping the other man's fingers when Dart said, "Professor John Langston, Captain Dawson."

Dawson knew who Langston was. He was not white. Dawson was shaking the hand of a colored man. At the realization he gripped harder. He held the grasp for an extra second, meeting the man's eyes with particular intensity, as though carrying out a dare.

"Professor Langston," said Dawson, his voice hearty. "Welcome."

"The professor has a favor to ask," Dart said.

"Glad to do whatever I can," Dawson said. "Come inside, out of this wind."

Inside, the front room was full of reporters. Red-headed O'Hare sat with his back to them, his finger jammed in his ear. He was jiggling it like an idiot. Moroso was standing up, gathering his papers. A boy jogged down the stairs with a wire basket of trash. The door to the printing room was open, and full of clacking noise.

Proud of his domain, pleased by its energy, irritated by O'Hare's jiggling finger, Dawson led the men upstairs. He tried to remember what he knew about Langston: Was he the president of a Negro college? The head of a Negro law school? He'd run for Congress in Virginia, but things had gone wrong. Election fraud, voter suppression, intimidation, the usual mess. They were shameless in Virginia.

Dawson ushered them into his office. They took off their coats and sat down. Dawson rubbed his hands briskly.

"Professor, welcome to Charleston," he said. "I think you gave a speech last night, at Reverend Dart's church. How was it?" They'd put a notice in the paper.

"I was pleased," Langston said, though he didn't seem so. His eyes were hooded, his gaze guarded.

"Very good." Dawson nodded and looked at Dart.

Dart said carefully, "There was some confusion about the location."

"Oh?" Dawson asked.

"The notice said the Morris Church, not the Morris Street Church. They are different establishments. Some people went to the other church."

Dawson nodded, waiting. Then he understood.

"Did we get it wrong in the paper? Was it our fault?"

Dart said nothing.

"My dear Reverend, I'm so sorry," Dawson said. "What a blunder. I hope your audience came to the right place in the end."

Dart looked relieved. "It's quite all right, Captain."

"No, I do apologize. We do our best, but we make mistakes." Dawson turned to Langston. "Perhaps you'll tell me what your talk was about, Professor."

"Progress." Even sitting down Langston was perfectly erect, his shoulders militantly square. "For the Negro race."

"A salutary topic," Dawson said. "And what's the key, in your opinion?"

"Education," Langston said. "If the blacks are to take their place in society, they must have education."

"Undeniably," said Dawson. "And you're head of the law school at Howard, is that right? Is that your alma mater?"

"Oberlin," Langston said. "But it had no law school for Negroes when I graduated. I had to apprentice with a lawyer. Which is precisely the problem we face."

Langston's eyes were fixed on him as though he held Dawson responsible. What was confusing was that Langston spoke like a white man. An educated, Northern white man. With his pale skin and light eyes and his precise speech, he seemed white. It was mesmerizing: Langston seemed to change from race to race before Dawson's eyes. It wasn't only his skin and accent but his confident manner, his ramrod posture. His impatience. His lack of deference: he acted like a white man. But he was here with Reverend Dart, who spoke in the local accent, whose head was humbly lowered, his shoulders hunched, who waited for Dawson to speak before he did.

"Absolutely," said Dawson, nodding.

He was remembering more about Langston: His mother had been a freed slave, his father a white plantation owner. They'd both died when he was a child; the boy had been taken in by a white Quaker family in Ohio, friends of his father. So he'd been raised white. He'd always spoken like this, this was his real voice. It gave Dawson a strange feeling. He'd never heard a black American man who sounded white. He remembered the Negro at the Sorbonne.

"We're losing ground," Langston said sternly. "It's almost worse now than it was before the war. Negroes are held back from education, from good jobs. From voting."

"It's a terrible problem," said Dawson. He agreed with this, but there was something accusatory about Langston's manner. It was disagreeable. "What do you recommend?"

"Legislation," Langston said. "Negroes must have more political power. I ran for Congress last fall in Virginia."

"And what happened?" asked Dawson.

"I won, but the results were challenged," said Langston. "There was ballot fraud, interference, harassment. Lynchings. The whites try to prevent black voters from voting."

"The lynching is utterly barbaric," Dawson said shortly.

But it was awkward, talking about this to a black man. It was different from talking to Riordan or McKinley. With Langston he had a different relationship to the issue; he felt challenged in some way. He changed the subject.

"What do you think of the return to Liberia?" Dawson asked. Black leaders had endorsed the idea, and hundreds of people had bought tickets on ships to the homeland.

"Utterly ridiculous," Langston said crisply. "Blacks have lived here for centuries. This is their native land. They should no more be sent back to Africa than you should be sent back to England."

Crispness was unexpected.

Now Dawson remembered something else: Langston's father had been English. This gave him a strange doubling feeling. He tried to imagine himself as a Negro, looking at his white father. It was disorienting, Langston's light eyes, his uncompromising gaze, his accusatory voice. His accent: he seemed like Dawson, only hidden behind something else. Dawson wondered where in England Langston's father was from. He didn't ask; the question seemed somehow risky.

"American blacks have a white heritage as well," Langston added. "Why should they be sent to Africa when half their families are white?"

But this was distasteful. Racial mixing was not discussed. Whatever had happened during slavery was shadowy and unsavory; whatever happened now was illegal. All miscegenation carried some ethical stain. Langston raised it so baldly; he was so upright, so composed, so unashamed.

Reverend Dart sat silent, his hat in his lap.

Dawson changed the subject again. "Tell me what we can do for you, Professor."

"I'd like to look at some of your back issues," Langston said. "To document what happened in my campaign."

"We'll be glad to help you." Dawson banged the bell on his desk for the office boy. While they waited he asked Langston what dates he wanted. Langston gave the dates, and told him more about the attacks in Virginia. At the end of every sentence he fixed his black eyes on Dawson, his spine perfectly erect. It felt somehow like an accusation.

Dawson listened, increasingly uncomfortable. He knew white men were bitter over their losses; he knew they wanted to recover the world they'd known. He understood their anger, but he couldn't countenance their rage, this violence. He felt these brutal stories like blows deep in his heart. Hearing them, knowing what they meant, was like looking at Langston, seeing him shift from race to race. This was like hearing the South shift from honorable to savage. It felt like an accusation. Dawson banged again on the bell.

For the rest of the day he felt uneasy, as though something hurried behind him, rapid, incessant.

22.

A BITTER FIGHT IN LOUISIANA.

It Ends with the Defeat of McEnery and a Victory for the Reform Element—The Struggle Marked by Bloodshed—Five Men Killed and a Dozen or More Wounded.

NEW ORLEANS, January 6.—The campaign which ended last night, by the election of fifty-six Nicholls and forty-eight McEnery delegates in this city, virtually determines the Government of the State of Louisiana and of the City of New Orleans for four years to come . . . The contest between the rival factions of the party has been the most savage and bitter ever known . . .

As the campaign grew warmer the pistol was appealed to. It was opened by a political murder of a very aggravated kind. Then Judge Trimble and Editor Ramsey met and killed each other over the question of McEnery's reception in Farmerville. The next day the chief of police of Opelousas and a merchant of that town killed each other over their choice for Governor, and on New Year's Day the "Reform" leader, the Hon Pat Mealey, was killed in an affray resulting from the two factions cheering their respective candidates. The wounded in these political disturbances have numbered over a dozen, some of whom may yet die.

—*THE NEWS AND COURIER*, JANUARY 9, 1888

February 1, 1889. Charleston

MARIE-HÉLÈNE BURDAYRON, the Swiss girl, sat at the kitchen table, the cook's baby on her lap. He was nine months old, heavy and loose-limbed, liquid eyes, soft red mouth, fair greasy hair. His mother, Celia Riels, was a stout young German with a red face and gray eyes. She stood at the other end of the table, her arms bare. She was leaning over the pale carcass of a whiting, boning it. Hélène was holding the baby until the doctor arrived. The baby was feverish and fretful. She jiggled him on her knees, but he wouldn't quiet. He fussed, making little coughing cries.

Jane Jackson, the parlormaid, came in from the yard, a man behind her.

"Here's Dr. McDow," she said.

Dr. Thomas McDow was in his midthirties, slight, hollow-chested, slope-shouldered. He had a long, pale undertaker's face, dark hair, a thick drooping mustache, and a weak mouth. His eyes were black and bold.

"Doctor," said Celia. She was still holding the knife, her hands slimy with fish.

He didn't answer. He pulled out a chair and sat down in front of Hélène. Instead of leaning forward to look at the baby he leaned back, fingering his mustache, and looked at Hélène. He asked about the child.

Hélène said it was not hers.

"The baby iss mine," said Celia Riels, wiping her hands on her apron. "He iss crying through the night," she said anxiously. Eighteen days after the baby was born her husband had died in a fall. He'd been a carpenter, and he had been fixing a roof. Now she was alone, and frightened all the time.

"How old is he?" The doctor was still staring at Hélène.

"He has nine months," said Hélène. She pretended her English was better than it was. She heard the English words, they flowed through her mind, but she couldn't make them flow through her mouth. The Dawson family spoke only French at home.

"Put him on the table." The doctor opened his bag. He watched as Hélène spread out a cloth with one hand, holding the baby with the other.

Hélène tried to lay the child down on his back, but he struggled to sit up. "Ah, non," she said under her breath. "Reposes-toi. Tais-toi." She felt the doctor watching her. The baby twisted, fussing. Finally the doctor asked Hélène to pick him up for the examination. She sat on the table and held the child facing out, his back against her chest. The doctor stood in front of her and put his palm against the child's forehead, then pressed his fingers under his jaw. He stood very close to Hélène. His legs were near her thighs. Her legs were tightly closed.

McDow frowned. He slid his hand inside the baby's nightshirt, against his hot skin. He tapped on the chest, listening. He looked into the baby's throat; Hélène could hear him breathing. His hands, moving on the baby, were very close to Hélène's body. Once his knuckles brushed against her breast. Her nipple, actually. His touch was quick and intent. It was thrilling. She looked up to find his eyes directly on hers.

Celia had dried her hands and came over to Hélène. "Give me him," she said, and Hélène handed her the baby.

The doctor asked more: Does he cough? Is he eating? He told Celia to turn the child around, so he could examine him from the back. While she was doing this he looked again at Hélène. His black eyes drilled into hers, direct and intimate, as though he knew her very well. It gave Hélène a fine thrill, like a needle. She felt it in her body. It felt like power.

She lifted her chin and turned away.

As Celia held up the baby, Hélène nodded goodbye to everyone. As she left the room she felt his eyes on her.

MARIE-HÉLÈNE BURDAYRON WAS twenty-two years old, and from Geneva. The Dawsons called her Hélène, which was more distinguished than the common Marie. She had met Madame Dawson at the agency in Lausanne, when she and the children were in Europe. It had been Frank's idea. "If you find a nice young woman, bring her back with you," he had written Sarah, "so we can all speak French with her at home." Sarah had offered her a position. The situation was good: the pay was generous, the children well behaved, the parents correct.

Hélène liked living in this tall white house, driving in the Dawson carriage. She admired the handsome captain, who was an important person in this city. (Hélène thought he was the most important person. She had never met the mayor.) The household was distinguished, and Hélène liked being part of it. She enjoyed her position, which was superior to the servants. Jane and Celia and the young parlormaid and Isaac and his family all lived out in the kitchen building, the *dependence*, in the backyard.

But Hélène lived in the house with the family. She ate breakfast with the children, and dinner with the whole family. She was like an adopted daughter. The captain and Madame petted and teased her as though she were their own child.

She'd agreed to stay for two more years. When she went home, with her references and her savings, she'd be a person of distinction. She'd find a good position, a good husband.

She hurried across the wintry yard, hugging herself against the cold. The yard was big and open, with trees along the back edge. The trees were bare now, the lawn gray. Her breath rose in little plumes, like a dragon's. She thought about the doctor's gaze. She'd enjoyed it. She knew how she looked to the world: beautiful. She had a beautiful young body, strong legs and soft hands, white skin and dark eyes. When she fixed her hair in the morning she admired her face, her broad forehead, straight nose, dimples. Her eyes were dark and heavy-lidded. *Des beaux yeux.* A man in Lausanne told her that once, in a café. *Que tu as des beaux yeux, ma petite.* It was not what he'd said about her eyes, but the fact that he'd called her *ma petite* that made a liquid shiver run through her. As though he owned her. She liked it. He didn't own her, but she liked the shiver.

In the morning, watching her fine eyes in the mirror, she arranged her lace cap over her hair, pulling some soft wisps out from under the ruffle. Her white lace ruff lay neatly over her black collar. She knew she dressed neatly and moved prettily; she knew her small feet in trim boots, her narrow waist, neat hands. She felt herself pleasing as she walked through the Dawsons' high-ceilinged rooms. She was an ornament to the household.

Hélène went through the front hall and up the stairs. She used the front stairs, the ones the family used, the spiral stairs. Not the steep, straight, narrow servants' stairs in back.

The children were at school. They'd gotten off late this morning, because Ethel had taken so long to dress. They'd had to take the cars, instead of walking the ten blocks downtown. Ethel had to go in to her parents to ask for the fare. Hélène disapproved. Ethel was spoiled. Warrington was her favorite.

Hélène would tidy their rooms, and then she'd sew, sitting in the window and singing. She had a pretty voice, everyone told her that. (Madame called her "ma rossignol," *my nightingale*. Madame loved her.) Sometimes Hélène imagined that someone on the street would hear her. A man would look up and want to know who she is, the beautiful young woman in the window. Like a fairy tale.

She could be a character in a fairy tale. She'd come here from across the sea. She was living in a sort of tower, awaiting her future. A stranger might want to take her away with him.

Running up the stairs, her steps quick and light, she could feel something around her, the next thing, like mist in a canyon. Her future was so close she could nearly touch it. Soon it would begin.

She was ready: she was young. That was her secret.

Madame was elegant and correct, she dressed beautifully and spoke perfect French. Hélène respected her for all that. But Madame was old, though she didn't realize it. She didn't know that age was lapping at her feet.

Madame was old and Hélène was young, which gave Hélène a kind of power. Age had no connection with Hélène. Hélène's hair was not so long as Madame's (she'd never seen anyone with such long hair), but Hélène's was thicker. It would always be thicker, because she would always be younger. She was entitled to this. She couldn't imagine being anything but young. Her body, moving quickly through these rooms, was like that of a princess. She was a princess of youth, la princesse de la jeunesse.

Hélène's bedroom was on the third floor, beyond Warrington's room. A painted iron bed, a little chair, a bureau. The window looked out on the back garden, but it wasn't here that she sat. She took her sewing box and a jacket of Warrington's and went to sit in his room. This window looked out to the side of the house. It overlooked the backs of the houses on Rutledge Avenue, at right angles to this one. Hélène raised the window a sliver and felt the sudden slice of cold air against her knees. She sat down and began to sing. She was a nightingale.

In the kitchen the doctor finished examining the child. Beef tea, he said to Celia Riels, every two hours. Hot compresses on the chest.

Celia nodded anxiously, holding the child against her. He fussed, mouth crumpling with unhappiness.

He'll be fine, the doctor said. Celia nodded, jiggling the baby. "Thank you, Doctor," she said.

The doctor started packing his things. His face turned away, he asked her about the French woman. What is her name, and how old is she? Where is she from? Is she married? Where does she sleep, out here, or in the house?

Celia told him the family called her Hélène, but her real name was Marie. She slept in the house.

Jane came in and stood listening. She set her hands on the back of a chair and lifted her foot, scratching one ankle with the other. She had fair skin, and got rashes easily. In the winter her hands and feet were always cold, her fingers chapped.

The doctor repeated the name. "Marie," he said. He closed his bag. "If I ever want another wife, I'll think about her!"

He said this jovially, smiling at them as though he expected them to laugh.

After he left, Celia held the baby against her chest. Shush, she said. She was thinking about the night, how he would sleep through. She'd start making the beef tea right now. He was still whimpering, little explosive snorts like a kettle.

Jane set down her foot, still holding on to the chair as though she were steering it. "I'm thinking he was drunk, the doctor," she said. She was Irish, and had had some experience with this. Her father, in particular.

Celia said he was not. She didn't want to have had her child examined by a drunkard.

"Will you have a look at his eyes," said Jane. "Those heavy lids. And all that talk about Marie, what is he thinking? He's a married man. He'd never have said all that sober." Jane nodded to herself. Having said it, she now believed it.

"He was not," said Celia, indignant. She turned from Jane, joggling the child. Shush, shush, she said.

Jane held her elbows, scratching them through the fabric of her uniform. In the winter she itched all the time. She felt slighted by the doctor, who had not looked at her. And she wasn't fond of Hélène, who put on airs.

The next afternoon Hélène took the children to dancing school. They went in the big phaeton, with Isaac driving, wearing his frock coat. Ethel and Warrington, dressed up for class, sat on either side of Hélène, arguing in French. Hélène sat very straight and pretended that the carriage was hers.

Ethel leaned across her to slap at Warrington and Hélène grabbed her wrist. "Taisez-vous! Soyez sages!" *Be quiet*, she said fiercely. *Be good.* "Vous vous battez comme des loups." *You fight like wolves.*

"Yes," Warrington said triumphantly to Ethel. "Sois sage, loup!" *Be good, wolf!* He bared his teeth at her.

Ethel gave him a venomous look and turned to stare at the houses. They'd just turned onto Rutledge, heading downtown. A man stood outside one of the houses. It was long and narrow, set sideways. Along its side stretched a garden, from the street to the fence behind, beyond which was the Dawsons'. The man stood in the front of the garden, near the street. As the carriage passed, Hélène saw it was the doctor.

He bowed, his eyes fixed on her. She bowed with great formality, like the queen. She was young and beautiful, and a member of the Dawson household.

———

AFTER THAT Hélène saw him often, standing in the front of the garden, or out on the street. Sometimes he was in the back of his garden, looking over the fence into the Dawsons' backyard. When he saw Hélène he bowed, holding her eyes with his.

In the kitchen, they'd told her he'd asked about her. They'd told her what he'd said about becoming his wife. Hélène had lifted her chin, shaking her head. He's a married man, she'd said primly. Jane and Celia were watching, she could feel their stares. Inside she smiled.

In the kitchen they knew all about the McDows. They knew all about everything. Servants' gossip flows through backyards and kitchens, then into their families, through the bedrooms, the dining rooms, then into the parlors.

The McDows had only moved to Rutledge Avenue a few months ago. At first it was just the doctor, his wife, Katie, and their daughter, Gladys. Then Katie's father moved in. C. D. Ahrens was a widower, a stout fair-skinned German, affable and prosperous. He'd started the big wholesale grocery store down on King Street, and for a long time he and his family had lived over the shop. But first Katie moved out to marry Thomas, and then later his wife died. That was when C.D. bought Katie and Thomas the big hand-some three-story house on Rutledge. He moved in with them for a while, but then he moved downtown to the Waverly Hotel. Katie was like her father, fair and heavy, with thin flyaway hair and turned-in feet. Unlike him she was anxious, her little blue eyes always darting around. Another woman seemed to live with them, too, or anyway she spent much of her time there. Her name was Julia Smith, and she was an old friend of Katie's.

In the kitchen they knew all about Julia Smith, who lived a block and a half down Bull Street, in the carriage house behind Mrs. Calder's hotel. Julia was the young widow of William Smith, who was one of the Benjamin Smiths, who'd built the elegant Bee's Row houses. Those Smiths were re-lated to the wife of Senator Augustine Smythe—and neither the Smiths nor the Smythes had been happy when William married Julia. Her father had been a pharmacist, and in trade. She had not grown up with senators' daughters, but with shopkeepers' daughters, like Katie Ahrens. After William died (a shooting accident, out duck hunting) Julia was relegated to the out-skirts of the Smiths' tribe. The Dawsons knew about her, but they didn't know her. They didn't see her. They didn't know anyone who saw her.

In the Dawson kitchen they knew all this. In the kitchen they were deeply snobbish, and could calibrate the social levels with exact precision. They were proud of the Dawsons' position, which was elevated, and they knew exactly where other families stood in relation to it. The Dawsons didn't know the McDows, either.

In the kitchen they knew that McDow was from up-country, and somehow disreputable, with some stain hovering around him. He'd had legal trouble in Tennessee, or Mississippi. He'd shot someone. At least one person, maybe more. His patients weren't from the upper circles either: they were Negroes and poor whites. Servants. There had been talk about another scandal, dead bodies and insurance companies, fake death certificates. It had been last year. Corpses had been dug up from a potter's field and then people claimed them as relatives, saying they'd just died. Insurance claims were filed, and doctors had signed death certificates. McDow hadn't been charged, but his name was mentioned. In the Dawson kitchen they felt superior to the McDow kitchen. The McDows had only two servants, both black: a cook, Emma Drayton, and a coachman, Moses Johnson.

Now Hélène saw the doctor every time she left the house. In the morning, when she walked the children to school, he always seemed to be standing where he could see them pass. He bowed, and she returned the bow without speaking. On the way home he was there again. He bowed again, his black eyes on her. He took off his hat with an elaborate gesture.

———

HÉLÈNE WAS SENT OUT to Sullivan's Island for the day. The Dawsons had rented a little summer house there, as did everyone they knew. Sarah had asked her to meet with the caretaker, to start getting the house ready.

Hélène came back on the last ferry. It was dark by the time she took the car up Rutledge Avenue. She got down at Bull Street. The air was cool and damp, and the streetlamp cast a glowing circle on the ground. The houses were dim, the streets empty. Night had drawn itself smoothly across the city.

Hélène's footsteps sounded loud in the silence. As she crossed the street she saw a man standing on the sidewalk, near the corner. He was watching her. When she reached the sidewalk he stepped toward her.

"Good evening," said the doctor.

She bowed, but kept walking, very erect.

"Good evening, mademoiselle." He mispronounced the word. He stepped forward, blocking her way, and doffing his hat with a clumsy flourish.

"Good evening, Dr. McDow." She stopped.

"You're out very late," he said.

"I have come from Sullivan's Island," she said with some pride. She pronounced the difficult name carefully. "Madame Dawson asks me to make some commissions there."

"Very nice," McDow said. "And how is the baby?" He added, "The cook's baby."

"He keeps very well," Hélène said. "Thank you." She could see his eyes in the dimness.

"Very good," McDow said. "And how do you like it here in Charleston, mademoiselle?"

"I like it here very much."

"How long have you been here?" he asked. "Our fair city." He said this as though it were a joke; she didn't know why.

"I come two year ago," she said. "I will stay two more year."

"Two more years," he said. "A long time before you see France again."

She was not from France, but didn't correct him. People here thought France was more glamorous than Switzerland. "I have made an arrangement with the Dawsons. I will stay two more year."

"You don't want to go back before that?" He was smiling still, looking into her eyes, intimate, intent. "You could leave the Dawsons."

"The Dawsons are good to me," she said primly. "Captain Dawson is like my father. I could not leave without permission," she added practically. "They would not give me a reference, and I would not find another position."

"What if you came to France as my wife," said the doctor.

"You are already married, monsieur," Hélène said. She was excited by the word "wife."

"Not happily married." He stared, smiling, daring her to respond.

She wondered if he'd been drinking. There was something loose and unpredictable about him.

"You are married now." She could feel he was attracted to her. Her body had become electric. She glowed, invisibly.

"I should have married you." His smile spread across his face. He leaned slightly toward her.

"Non," Hélène said. But she had seen his wife, coarse and heavy, with small eyes like a boar's. "I must go home. It's late. I can't stay in the street."

She felt herself powerful and beautiful. She felt his gaze on her. She felt his urgency. The city was hushed around them. She gave him a queenly smile and said good night. She walked away, trailing fire, a wake of glowing sparks.

She heard him following her. She opened the wrought-iron gate into the carriage drive, and as she passed through she felt him behind her. When the gate closed they were both now on Dawson property. She turned to him.

"You may not come in, monsieur le docteur."

"When can I meet you again? I want to see you."

"Non, non," she said. "It's not possible."

Though she felt that it was possible. Her own body was aware of his.

"It's not possible," she said again, and turned away. He stepped closer, moving between her and the house.

"Tell me when I can see you again." His voice was low. "Marie," he said.

She raised her eyes, hearing her name in his mouth.

"I want to see you again." His eyes bored into hers.

She felt the house at her back, the lighted windows where Madame or the captain might be seated. Anyone might look out and see her.

"You must go." She put her hand on his chest to push him away. He seized her hand and pressed it against himself.

"Only if you tell me when I can see you again. I'll meet you here tomorrow. Tell me what time."

He repeated her name in a whisper. His fingers caressed her hand lightly, lightly. Whisky. The sense of his body was dark and powerful. His eyes shone in the darkness. Her own body was electric.

"When?" he said.

"Tomorrow," she said. "I will meet you here tomorrow morning. At ten o'clock. When I return from school."

"Ten o'clock," he said.

He let go her hand and moved off. She turned and walked toward the house. Up on the third floor the light was on in the captain's room. He stayed up very late, working. She admired this. She walked up the front steps, feeling his eyes on her.

In the morning, when she came back from school, McDow was waiting at the gate. He carried a small bouquet.

"Good morning." His gaze was now focused. When he smiled his gums showed, pale and glossy. He held out the bunch of flowers.

She thanked him. "They are beautiful."

"For a beautiful lady," he said. He was quieter now, but his gaze was still locked on hers. Her whole body brightened under it. She remembered him examining the baby in her arms. His hand pressing on her breast.

She looked down at the wintry pink flowers. They were bruised, already limp. She felt queenly.

"We'll take a little walk down the street," he said. He wanted to touch her.

———•———

THOMAS'S OFFICE WAS on the ground floor of his house. One door led to Rutledge Avenue, the other, facing it across the room, led to the inside staircase. There was no waiting room, only a tiny vestibule. Two windows looked into the side garden. In between them stood a settee, on which he examined his patients. In the middle of the room was a round table. In the corner was a tall slant-front secretary. The upper part was full of medical books. Below was a cupboard where he kept a bottle.

That day he went down to his office and wrote a letter to his brother, Arthur. Arthur was younger, and still living in Rock Creek, where they'd grown up. He was a security guard for an express company, something like that. Thomas told him to come to Charleston. He said he had a proposition, and gave him the name of a rooming house.

That night, as they were getting ready to go to bed, Thomas told Katie he was going to sleep in his dressing room. He felt restless, he said, and he didn't want to keep her awake.

"You won't keep me awake." Katie reached up to take down her hair. The sleeves of her dressing gown slid back, showing the heavy flesh of her upper arms. Her skin was pink and mottled. She turned to look at him.

"No, I'd wake you up," he said. "I'm not going to sleep here."

He kept a bottle in his dressing room, too. Sometimes he sat in the dark, looking out the window and drinking.

Sometimes Julia spent the night at their house, up on the third floor in the guest room. When everything was quiet Thomas went up to her. He'd told Julia he wanted to leave Katie. He'd told her that with his arms wrapped around her naked body.

That night Julia wasn't there, but Thomas wasn't thinking about her. He was thinking about Hélène. He went into his dressing room, which was small, with a window that looked over the garden. He looked out it at an angle, toward the Dawsons' house. He thought he knew which was her bedroom. He saw someone moving behind the filmy curtains, until the heavy ones were drawn for the night. Then he could only see a narrow slit at the top, where light leaked into the darkness. He stared at that until it went out, and then he stared into the darkness. He'd set the bottle on the floor between his feet.

23.

Murdered by a Mob.

In November last John Lee Goode, a young white lad, the son of a well-known farmer in York County, was murdered under circumstances of peculiar brutality . . . The finding of the coroner's jury was that Goode was killed because he had accidentally detected his murderers in the perpetration of a robbery. The negroes who committed the crime, it was also proved, were bound together by a solemn oath to rob and plunder, and "to murder all persons who might detect them in their lawlessness." They were formed into a lodge . . . It was ascertained by the preliminary investigation of the case that other murders had been freely discussed and planned. Before the coroner had concluded his work twenty-six negroes were arrested and lodged in jail at Yorkville for complicity . . .

At the time of these occurrences *The News and Courier* protested against lynching or violence of any kind, upon the ground that the crime could be fully and promptly established in a Court of justice, and that outraged society should condemn the wrong and punish sternly the wrong-doers, through those channels by which alone society can effectively speak and act. It was believed and hoped that all the proceedings would be in conformity with law . . .

Yesterday morning, however, without awaiting the action of the law, the jail at Yorkville was forcibly entered by sixty men, who seized the prisoners, and having taken them outside the corporate limits of the town, strung them up by their necks and left the corpses of the five miserable wretches dangling in the air.

The murder of young Goode was bad enough, but the lynching of his murderers was worse. It is a shame to the State that such a tragedy could take place anywhere within her borders. It is an offence against the law and an outrage against the peace and good order of society. No apologies or excuses can be urged for the perpetration of this later and greater crime. It is the darkest of the deeds of blood which stand out in great red clots upon the pages of our recent history. It is a sign, moreover, which shows how rapidly we are drifting into a condition of lawlessness, and, unless something be done to check our progress, the time will soon come when each man's hand "will be against every man, and every man's hand against him." We owe it to ourselves and our children, to the majesty of outraged law and to every private and public interest, that no stone shall be left unturned to discover and punish the perpetrators of the monstrous crime which was committed at Yorkville yesterday. All the machinery of the Court should be set in motion, and all the power of the State should be exhausted in the effort to hunt down those who have sacrificed the lives of five helpless and defenceless prisoners to an insane desire for vengeance.

It will not do to dismiss the matter with the verdict of the coroner's jury that the deceased came to their deaths at the hands of persons unknown to the jury. There were sixty men in the squad of lynchers who broke down the door of the cell . . . They were seen by the sheriff of the county. They were not disguised. They went about their horrible work without any attempt to conceal their identity. It is not possible that they could have escaped observation, and it is due to the law they have violated that they shall be indicted for murder and punished. They may call themselves lynchers, but they are, in fact and in deed, wholesale murderers, and as such they should be treated.

—*THE NEWS AND COURIER*, APRIL 6, 1887

February 3, 1889. Charleston

RUDOLPH SIEGLING'S OFFICE overlooked Broad Street. It was just down the street from both *The News and Courier* and the Bank of Charleston. Siegling was president of both boards, and could step around easily from office to office.

When Dawson had written him to say he'd call, he'd hesitated over the greeting. Siegling was a friend and colleague—he'd been on the newspaper board for years, and the president since 1882. Usually Dawson wrote "My dear Siegling." But just now this seemed too intimate, too casual. He'd written "Dear General."

Siegling stood as Dawson came in. He had heavy dark side-whiskers and a short upper lip. He was thickset, with a broad chest and very powerful arms.

"Dawson, come in," he said. "Sorry about the smell. They're trying to get rid of the ants. They're invading us, apparently." He waved his hand. "So we're using some vile substance to make them leave. I may go before they do."

Dawson sat down. He felt an odd impulse to draw the chair close to the desk, like a supplicant. He pushed the chair slightly away, leaning back.

Siegling slid him the humidor, flipping it open onto the banked cigars, dark and fragrant. They each took one. Dawson took out his gold cutter and snipped the end. Siegling held the flame to his cigar and Dawson drew a long breath as the tip turned brilliant. Armed with these fiery tokens of manhood and friendship, they leaned back in their chairs.

"I saw you at the opera house last week," said Siegling. "What did you think of Signor Campanini?"

Music was a language they both spoke. Siegling's whole family was musical; his father had made instruments and been a music publisher, and his sister Marie was a composer. Siegling knew every piece of music Dawson had ever heard. Charleston had an opera house but no company, and it depended on traveling troupes.

"I enjoyed it," Dawson said. "Particularly the Faust."

"We rarely get Faust," said Siegling. "Americans like Puccini better than Gounod."

"I wish we'd get a full opera. I've heard those arias so often I no longer remember what they're from. And they make no sense: *Casta diva*, followed by the Toreador's Song, then something from *La sonnambula*. I've lost all sense of story."

"The story of *La sonnambula*," said Siegling, "is so absurd you're better off not remembering it."

"Like most operas," said Dawson. "Ridiculous stories set to glorious music."

"I saw a great *Così* last year in New York," Siegling said. "At the new opera house. D'you think we'll ever have our own company?"

For a moment Dawson didn't answer.

It would be a great thing. For a moment he let himself imagine an opening night, the tenor drawing breath, turning toward the woman in red satin, her back to him, the sound of his voice rising into the filmy air, the hushed house. But it was unobtainable. To reach it meant creating a bonfire, rallying, gathering names, writing letters, meeting with wealthy men, powerful women, persuading, urging, declaring. He would be the flame, his energy the fuel. He'd done all this before, raised funds for the cathedral, rallied support after the earthquake, organized the festival week. He'd raised money, stoked enthusiasm, made a bonfire. Now it seemed beyond him.

"It would be difficult," Dawson said. He tapped the cigar, dropping a weightless gray disk into the ashtray. "Filling the house every night, all season. I'm not sure we'd get the support." He waited for Siegling to protest, urging Dawson to start the drumbeat, certain he could do it.

"You're right," said Siegling. "So we'll have to be content with the arias. Trips to New York." He drew a long breath, making the tip glow. "And how are things at the paper?"

Dawson nodded. "Quite well." The English use of the word.

"What about the *World*?"

Dawson shook his head. "We're going to wear them out. We have the stamina. They have nothing." One of the *World*'s backers, Huger, sat on the board of the bank. Dawson couldn't be as candid as he'd have liked.

"And how is it working?"

"The main problem is persuading the public that real news is more valuable than scandal. But I have faith in the public."

Siegling snorted. "Why?"

"That's how we succeeded in the first place," Dawson said. "The ideal of excellence. It's always worked."

"But not now." Siegling tapped his cigar.

"That remains to be seen," Dawson said. "We've had to cut back on reporters, so we've had less to offer. We need more reporters. It's a vicious circle."

Siegling nodded. "Exactly so."

A law firm was quieter than a newspaper; the building around them was soundless. Siegling drew another long breath. When he exhaled the blue stream dissolved into the air.

Dawson cleared his throat, which had gone oddly tight. "I'll need another loan. To pay for running expenses. We can't cut any more on content, we'll lose subscribers."

Siegling looked at his cigar and tapped it again.

"We can't let the paper fail," Dawson said.

"We had this conversation last fall," Siegling said.

"*The News and Courier* is an institution," Dawson said.

Siegling looked at him.

"It's known all over the country. People look to it."

"But do they subscribe to it?"

"We can't let this happen." This was like trying to run through deep water; the weight was more than he could manage. "We can't let a great paper be destroyed. They're not better, you know. It's trash." Heat rose through his neck.

"Dawson," Siegling said. "I've said yes once. I want to help. But I'm not going to go on sending supplies to a sinking ship."

"It's not sinking." The word enraged him. "It's not sinking." He stood up. "The *World* will fail. It will sink. There's nothing at its center. It has no mission, no substance. It can't succeed."

Siegling shook his head. "*The News and Courier* has been losing money and subscribers for the last year. I can't support those losses indefinitely. I have a responsibility to the shareholders here at the bank."

"You're president of the board of the newspaper," Dawson said. "You have a responsibility to the shareholders there."

"I'm sorry," Siegling said.

Dawson stared at him. "You refuse." He could feel something gathering in him, heat rising through his body, his belly, his chest and shoulders. His neck grew larger.

"I'm sorry," Siegling repeated.

Dawson saw he was not sorry; the word was simply a way to end the conversation. He could feel Siegling withdrawing, hoisting sail, setting off, out of reach, smug and unassailable, with his financial heft, his banal musical aperçus.

"Siegling." Dawson leaned forward, over the desk. "You can't do this."

"I can't lend you the money," Siegling said.

Dawson knew this was not true; Siegling was drawing a line between them. But he was prepared for this. He'd been stalled before; they'd tried to stop him from buying the *Courier*. He'd found a way. There was always a way.

"I'll apply for a personal loan," said Dawson. "I'll put up my *News and Courier* shares as collateral."

Siegling spread his palms open, the cigar held between thumb and forefinger. "We'll be glad to oblige."

When Dawson left the bank he felt energetic and powerful. He had the money. He knew he was right. It wouldn't take long, he just had to hold out.

24.

Is it probable that the white people of the South, for any reason or motive, under any circumstances that are likely to arise, will ever regard the negroes among whom they live with much less aversion,—or with more favor, if that term be preferred,—than they now entertain towards them?

The answer must be an emphatic, unqualified negative . . . The prejudice of race has always been exhibited, and is still exhibited, by every white man, woman and child in the South. It is rooted in the minds of fifteen millions of people. Argument does not touch it . . .

There is not a white person in the old Slave States—not one—who advocates a change in any respect in the social relations of the two races; not one entertains the thought of change.

—CARLYLE McKINLEY, *AN APPEAL TO PHARAOH: THE NEGRO PROBLEM, AND ITS RADICAL SOLUTION*, 1889

February 5, 1889. Charleston

BROAD STREET WAS empty. The night was dark, and the wind was spitting rain. From the sound against the pane it might have been sleet. The windows in Dawson's office were blurred with moisture. The gas chandelier hissed steadily and the wall clock, hanging between the windows, repeated its modest hurrying tick. The building was quiet; it was past nine, the day shift gone.

Dawson sat at his desk with a manuscript before him. He edited with big sweeping marks, crossing out, underlining, making query marks, scribbling notes. His pencils wore down quickly, he bore down hard. He carried extras in his pocket, and a small penknife for sharpening.

When McKinley appeared in the door Dawson looked up.

"McKinley, good. I can't read any more of this." He leaned back in his chair. It was dark red leather and starting to crack. Dawson was hard on objects.

McKinley came in and sat down, folding his long body into the chair. His clothes were always slightly rumpled, and he seemed never to have quite grown into himself. Though he was forty-two, married, and the father of two, he was always trying to find room for his arms and legs.

Carlyle McKinley was from Georgia. After college, and the war, he'd gone on to seminary in Columbia. He'd planned to become a minister, but he had a certain unbending quality, and some thistly part of the Presbyterian doctrine stuck in his craw. He could not swallow it, and so he coughed it out. He left the ministry to teach in Columbia, and started sending pieces to *The News and Courier*. He'd left teaching nearly fifteen years ago and had become a trusted colleague. Since Riordan had left, Dawson depended on McKinley even more. Particularly on ethical questions, moral ones. McKinley was a man of absolute principle. Dawson trusted him in all ways.

But the sight of him here, late at night, was unexpected. Dawson hoped McKinley wasn't going to ask for a raise or announce he was leaving for the *World*. He couldn't afford to give him a raise, and he couldn't afford to lose him. The thought of the *World* was sickening. He felt the silver blade twist inside him.

"What brings you here?" he asked, and McKinley shrugged and shook his head.

"Tell me everything. What's going on in Columbia?" Dawson leaned back in his chair. "What's Tillman up to?"

"Making trouble," McKinley said. "Riling up the backcountry against the Low Country. Which has too much power."

It was true that the Low Country had disproportionately large representation in the state legislature. This caused resentment, but it wasn't new. Dawson waited, but McKinley said nothing more. He seemed oddly quiet.

"Why's he doing this?"

"He's planning to run for governor."

"Again? Didn't we make it clear? We don't want him."

"He's giving speeches about Hamburg," said McKinley.

"Hamburg?" Dawson frowned. "Ten years ago."

"He's boasting that he was a ringleader," said McKinley. "Claiming credit."

"He wants credit for Hamburg?" Dawson asked. "There was a congressional investigation. It made us look like savages. Why would he want credit for that?" He took the penknife from his pocket and snapped it open.

"It did just what he wanted," said McKinley. "The Negroes were terrorized and the white men went free. Hampton was elected. All according to the Bald Eagle's plan. It was a victory for him."

"It was a disgrace for us," said Dawson. "We should put it behind us." He drew the scrap basket over between his knees and took up the pencil and the knife. He leaned over and began whittling at his pencil. Each stroke lifted a pale curling chip. There was a silence.

"But we haven't," said McKinley. "Put it behind us."

Dawson looked up. "Meaning?"

"Things are getting worse," said McKinley. "For the Negroes."

"In what way?"

"All ways," said McKinley. "They're no better off now than they were at emancipation."

"I hardly think that's true," said Dawson. He looked down again. He turned the pencil, scraping at the point.

McKinley raised his eyebrows and said nothing. Behind him on the wall hung the office clock, the pendulum hurrying back and forth in the case.

"All this takes time," said Dawson. "During Reconstruction men were elected to office who couldn't read or write. We can't have illiterate officials." He looked up. "We can't. Education takes time."

"It's twenty-five years since emancipation," said McKinley. "They're no better off now. Worse, in some ways. They're still dirt-poor, and still uneducated. They've gotten nowhere. We don't let them. We keep them impoverished. We allow them only the worst jobs," he said, "the ones we don't want. The Negro can't move forward unless we allow it. We don't allow it because we don't want it."

"Hold hard," Dawson said, raising his hand. "We have quite a solid black middle class in Charleston. Master carpenters, mechanics. Ministers. Doctors. Distinguished members of the bar." Dawson held the pencil up to look at it. He set it down, folded the knife, and slid it into his pocket.

"Mostly craftsmen," said McKinley. "If they're professionals they only work for each other. White men wouldn't use a Negro lawyer. Would you send your wife to a Negro doctor?"

"People tend toward their own kind," Dawson said. "That's a fact."

"The fact is that we keep them subordinate in every way."

Dawson shook his head. "You make this sound like a concerted effort," he said. "I've always supported their progress. I've done so from the beginning, and old Barnwell Rhett nearly fired me for it. I tried to get Negroes on the aldermanic ticket, in 1868. I arranged the first meeting between Negro candidates and Democrats. I hired the hall and I carried the chairs down the street. At the paper we've always supported them."

"Whatever we do," said McKinley, "is not enough."

There was silence in the room.

"What's your point?" Dawson asked.

"We should never have brought them here," said McKinley.

"True. But we did," said Dawson. "They're here."

"And we've freed them. And now what? We don't take care of them and they can't take care of themselves. They're destitute. They're in rags. They're starving."

"We do take care of them," said Dawson. "We have an obligation. I pay our coachman a good salary. I also let him live rent-free in our backyard, with his wife and his many children. They raise chickens on our property.

They feed them on scraps from our kitchen. Then they sell us the eggs. They raise vegetables on our land. They make jam from our fruit trees. They sell it all to us. They take advantage of us; we both know it. But that's the system."

"It's based on inequality. White people own everything. The Negroes need a way out of poverty," said McKinley. "They're dying, you know. Their mortality rates are twice ours."

"Poverty," said Dawson, frowning. "Poor hygiene. Lack of education."

"But that's their lot: poverty and poor hygiene and no education. How can they make progress?"

"What progress do you have in mind? Social equality?" asked Dawson.

"Not even Lincoln suggested that," McKinley said. "God made them members of a lesser race. But they're human beings. We can't treat them this way. Their misery is our fault."

The room was silent. The sleet rustled coldly against the windowpane.

Dawson sighed. He tapped the pencil once on his desk. "It's the problem of the age. Our duty to solve it."

"Giving them the vote made things worse," said McKinley. "The Red Shirts have started the war all over again. Now we have rule of violence instead of rule of law."

"Do you have a solution?"

"Liberia," said McKinley.

"Send them all back to Africa?"

McKinley nodded.

"They don't all want to go, you know," Dawson said.

"Hundreds have signed up," McKinley said. "It's the only fair thing. Lincoln thought so."

"But we can't decide for them," said Dawson. "Langston thinks it's absurd. He's the president of a law school. He doesn't want to be bundled off to Liberia." Dawson shifted in his chair. "We owe them something, but not summary deportation."

"But we do owe them something," McKinley said. "Besides two centuries' pay."

"A legitimate claim," Dawson said. "Though hard to carry out."

"We owe them a place where their rights are honored."

The room was silent except for the clock.

"And where is that place?" McKinley asked.

There was a long pause. The clock gave its percussive hurrying tick.

"What I can't bear is the lynching," Dawson said.

———

MCKINLEY WAS WRITING a book about this; that's why he'd come.

As he finished them he sent the chapters to Dawson, who read them at night. Sometimes he read them to Sarah, while the two of them sat alone at the top of the house. They were incendiary.

"'We brought him here for purely selfish reasons, under horrible conditions, and bred him, and worked him, and bought and sold him . . . for our own profit. His back and breast are scarred with the stripes we inflicted on him,'" Dawson read. "'It's a dreadful story from beginning to its end. We cannot bear to have it told in its naked truth, and we have no love for him who tells it, even though he be one of ourselves. It must be told and retold, however. We have sinned against him, and against ourselves, and against God.'"

Sarah looked up, frowning. "Why must this be told and retold? Does he want to start the war over again?"

"Race is the problem of our age," Dawson said.

"McKinley makes it sound like some hideous torture chamber. It wasn't like that."

"What was it like?" Dawson was sitting in his armchair. "Having slaves?"

"They were servants, and part of our family," Sarah said. "We'd never have hurt them. I didn't know anyone who hurt their servants. All that about stripes and scars is Northern talk."

"I'm sure your family was kind," Dawson said, "but the institution was not. Your own servants lived in the house, but what about the ones who worked in the fields?"

"You have no idea what it was like. We belonged to each other." Sarah remembered Tiche holding her, kissing her, the night her father died, so she'd wake to the news in the arms of someone who loved her. "The time we ran from the Yankee bombardment, Tiche carried the family silver. She and I shared a quilt on the floor during the war. I used to give the maids Bible lessons. We looked after them. You and I took on Levi, after Jem sold Hampton's. We took care of him when he was ill, until he died. He wrote to me while I was in France, I still have his letters." She looked up. "In England, did you look after your servants for their entire lives?"

"We didn't own them," Dawson said. "We banned slavery in 1830."

"Just stop," Sarah said. "Are you going to publish all this? It will make trouble. Why do you keep stirring things up? And don't do it while I'm away. I don't want anything to happen while I'm gone."

"I'm not going to publish it. It's a book, not an article," Dawson said. "And nothing will happen while you're away."

"Nine days," she said. "I've never been away from the children that long in my life."

"You were away from me for two years in Europe," he said.

"That wasn't my idea."

"It was your idea to stay with the children," he said.

"But it was yours, my darling chuck-chuck, to send the children away."

"All I wanted was for them to have a good education," he said.

"All you wanted was to send them to boarding school in England," said Sarah. "Which was much, much too far away, and they were too young."

"Any boarding school would have done," he said. "Any one that taught them what I was taught."

"They don't have schools like that here," she said. "All those languages. Classical literature and the catechism. Anyway, I don't approve of boarding schools. In my family we taught the children at home."

"And in my family we sent them to boarding school. Where they learned all those languages, and art and music, and classical literature and the catechism," he said. "I was sent away to St. Mary's at eight years old, and it ruined me, as you can see."

Sarah said nothing. She tucked her scissors into their case and began swiftly winding the loose thread onto the spool.

He rose from his chair and went over to her. He sank onto his knees and took her hands.

"My darling," he said. "I'm teasing you."

"Ah, now you love me," she said, not looking at him.

"Now I do love you, chuck-chuck," he said. "And now you're back home again, with our children, who now speak French, and all is well. And you'll be gone only nine days."

"Which is quite a long time," Sarah said, still not looking at him. "Longer than I've ever spent apart from them."

"Your children will be absolutely fine. They are nearly grown up," said Dawson, "and you have an excellent and reliable staff in me. And Hélène."

He didn't read her more of McKinley's book. Each chapter was an elaboration on his four points: it had been a mistake to bring the Negro to America, a mistake to keep him there, a mistake to make him a slave, and a mistake to give him the vote. The Negro race, as inferior, could never achieve equality with the white; still Negroes could achieve more than they had. It was whites who were preventing their progress. It was whites who were entirely responsible for the Negroes' misery.

As Dawson read it he thought of that meeting he'd arranged, on Haynes Street. He'd brought pitchers of cold water, and glasses. After one of the black members of the group had poured himself a glass, the white members wouldn't even touch the pitcher.

And he kept thinking of Langston, the way he'd seemed to change from race to race before his eyes. The memory made him uncomfortable, as though there were something he'd forgotten, something he should be doing that he was not.

25.

February 7, 1889. Charleston

THE BOARDING HOUSE was on a side street. It was shabby, the white-wash peeling off the bricks, and inside it smelled of fish. The woman who came out into the hall told Thomas McDow that his brother was on the third floor, last on the left. Thomas went upstairs and walked quietly down the hall. At the door he stood still for a moment, then seized the handle, trying to wrench it open. It was locked. Arthur was five years younger than he; Thomas felt he shouldn't have to knock. He stood before the door, waiting. He knew Arthur was listening.

Finally he said, "Open."

Arthur opened the door and the brothers faced each other. They both had pale skin, dark hair, and dark eyes, but Arthur was taller. His face was broader, and pockmarked. He stepped back warily, letting Thomas inside.

The room was small, with an iron bedstead, a wooden chair, and a tall hulking wardrobe. A curtainless window gave onto the alley. Thomas sat on the chair, Arthur on the unmade bed. The springs creaked as he settled.

Thomas took a flask from his breast pocket and offered it. Arthur took a short swallow and passed it back to Thomas, who took a long one, the burn rising in his throat. He put the flask back in his pocket.

Arthur asked, "What's the important business you wrote?"

Thomas didn't want Arthur to take charge.

"How you doing?" he asked. "Job all right?"

Arthur nodded.

"Wondered if you could use some cash," Thomas said.

"Depends." Arthur kept his eyes on his brother. "On what I have to do for it."

"Not much," Thomas said. The gas lamp on the wall above him cast black shadows on his face.

Arthur said nothing. He didn't trust Thomas.

"I have a problem," Thomas said. "Need someone to help me out. The person would come into a good bit of cash."

"What's the problem?" Arthur asked, then corrected himself. "How much?"

Thomas raised his hands and patted the air as though he was tamping something. "Slow down," he said. "Slow way down."

Arthur kept his eyes on his brother.

"A family problem," Thomas said. "It would be a lot of money. In the hundreds." He added, "Maybe."

Arthur shrugged. "Can't say till I know what you're talking about."

Thomas leaned forward. "It's my father-in-law. C.D. He has a big grocery store down on King Street."

"And?" Arthur said.

"I need someone to take care of him," said Thomas. He took out the flask again, eyes fixed on Arthur. He swallowed and screwed the top back on. "Easiest thing in the world. He lives at the Waverly Hotel, other end of King. He walks home along that street every night. Someone waits in the alley, steps out onto the sidewalk, pops him off, and steps back into the alley. No risk at all."

"Then what happens?" Arthur said.

"He's a rich man," Thomas said. "His wife died last year. Katie's an only child, she'll get everything."

"Who you think would take care of him?" Arthur asked, though he knew.

"You," Thomas said.

Arthur shook his head. "I got no need to do this." He didn't want to get tangled up in his brother's messes.

"The money." Thomas tapped his forefinger in the air as though he were tapping it against Arthur's chest. "You'll get a share. A big one."

Arthur narrowed his eyes.

"You're lucky I'm giving you a chance," Thomas told him. "I could ask anyone to do this. They'd jump at it." He watched his brother. "It'll be simple. Wait in the alley, step out of the dark, raise your pistol." Thomas snapped his fingers. "Goodbye." He closed his hand, rolled it over, and opened it wide. "You're gone, vanished. No one even knows you were in town."

Arthur shook his head. "I don't want to."

"Yes, you do," Thomas said. "Yes, you do. The money."

Arthur looked at him, considering. He always carried a pistol, he had one right now in his jacket pocket.

"No one would think it was you," Thomas said. "That's why it's such a good plan. You have no connection to him. He's rich! He gives Katie jewelry. Gold bracelets. Diamond earrings. All the time."

Arthur thought about it. "Then what happens?"

"Then I take care of Katie," Thomas said. "That will be easy, too. I'll just drop something in her tea."

"They'll suspect you."

Thomas shook his head. "She's always ailing," he said. "Headaches, this and that. I know what to use. No one will know."

The lamp lit Arthur's pale forehead and bony nose, his red mouth in the black tangle of his beard. Thomas's long face was in shadow, but his eyes gleamed. Thomas wanted something: this was familiar to Arthur. He felt he should say no, but he wasn't sure why.

Outside a cat gave a high squalling sound, ready to fight.

"How would I know it was him?" Arthur asked.

"Go in to his shop," Thomas said. "He's always there. Tall and stout, going bald. Reddish hair. Ask someone."

"What if someone's with him?" he asked. "When I step out?"

"Do it the next night."

"What if he goes home a different way?"

"There is no different way," said Thomas. "His shop and the hotel are both on King Street. Only one way to go."

Arthur said nothing.

After a moment Thomas's face changed.

"You want the money or not?" He leaned back, his eyes on Arthur. "I'm giving you a chance. I don't have to. I can do it myself. I'm giving you an opportunity."

Arthur looked down at his hands. He turned them over, considering. He didn't trust his brother. He looked up.

"What will you do with the money?"

"I have a girl," said Thomas. "I'll go away with her."

"Who is she?"

"A friend of Katie's," Thomas said. "She lives with us."

"In your house?" Arthur asked.

"Most of the time," Thomas said. "She has her own room up on the top floor. Stays with us." He was bragging. He wanted Arthur to understand the arrangement. How powerful he was.

But Arthur was thinking of something else. The bedsprings creaked as Arthur breathed, considering. Outside, the cat gave his low dangerous squall. He was joined by another, their voices in dire harmony.

"I'll have a look," Arthur said. "See how the land lies. I'll let you know."

He wanted to learn more about Thomas.

———•———

THE NEXT AFTERNOON Arthur stood near the livery stable on Rutledge Avenue. An old groundnut woman was on the corner, her baskets spread out around her. He bought peanuts in a twist of paper, and carried them back to eat them as he watched his brother's house. On the short side of the house was the office door, opening onto the street. At the end of the house was a fence that ran along the sidewalk. A gate led into the garden and on to the front door, which was on the long side of the house. On that side was a two-storied piazza, with an outside staircase. Arthur watched the house as he fished the boiled peanuts out of the paper twist with his index fingers. A colored woman went into the office door and came out. Three white men went in and came out. When Thomas came out, carrying his doctor's bag, Arthur ducked his head and turned his back. When he heard his brother pass him on the other side of the street he turned and followed him at a distance, as he went on his rounds.

After dark, Arthur came back alone. Standing on the sidewalk, he put one hand on the iron fence and swung himself into the yard. He went quietly up the outside staircase to the second floor, where he raised a big window. He slipped inside, into the hall. He stood listening to the clinking of dishes, silverware, voices. Supper. If he was seen, he was here on a visit. He was family.

He went quietly up to the next floor. He peered through the doorway into a child's room, then his brother's and Katie's, dark wallpaper, heavy curtains, a double bed with a massive headboard. Next to it was a small dressing room, with a single bed and an armoire. He went up to the next floor. Only one room seemed occupied: another big bed, a bureau. A folded shawl on the dresser. A pair of women's shoes under a chair.

He went back down to Thomas and Katie's room. The only light came from the moon. Against the wall stood a dressing table with a tall mirror, a woman's brush and comb set. Arthur opened the drawers and felt the contents: odds and ends, ribbons, nothing. On top of the table was a small chest. He opened it and felt inside the compartment. He felt hard, heavy, worked shapes: jewelry. Pins and brooches, bangles. A thick coin. He scooped it all up and put it in his pockets.

He moved faster now. On the ground-floor piazza he stopped to listen. A small wind shifting branches, distant hoofbeats. A dog somewhere. He put his hand on the fence and swung himself back over it.

———————

THREE DAYS LATER Arthur rang the bell at the office. Thomas opened the door a crack. When he saw his brother he frowned.

"You shouldn't come here," Thomas said.

"No one saw." Arthur walked past his brother to the table in the middle of the room. "I have something for you." He took out the mass of jewelry and dropped it. It was a mess, the diamond earrings tangled in the gold chain, the brooch caught in the bracelets. The five-dollar coin rolled, wavering, toward the edge of the desk. Thomas smacked it flat with his hand and looked up.

"What is this?" he asked.

"Something you might want."

Thomas stared at him. "Where did you get this?" Katie had been wild when she saw she'd been robbed. He'd called the police that same morning, and they'd sent a Detective McManus over to investigate. Thomas hadn't liked him a bit.

"Found it," Arthur said.

"What are you up to?" asked Thomas.

Arthur shook his head.

"Stay out of my house," Thomas said. "I already called the police."

"You got it back," Arthur said. "You can uncall them."

There was a pause. Thomas stared at him.

"When are you going to do it?" Thomas asked.

"Working up to it," Arthur said. "Seeing how the land lies." He dusted his hands together over the little mound of jewelry. "There, you got it all. I'll be on my way."

"You need to get onto this," Thomas said. "You can't wait on it."

Arthur smiled at his brother.

The groundnut woman was still there, her baskets close around her. Arthur set off toward his boarding house. If Thomas told the police he had the jewelry, he'd have to tell them how he'd gotten it back, and he'd be implicated.

Now Arthur had some power over Thomas. Thomas thought he was so smart, but Arthur was smarter. And he had another plan.

———

TWO NIGHTS LATER Arthur went over the fence again, up the outside staircase. He slipped inside and listened. There were voices in the dining room: Thomas and Katie at supper. And another woman's voice: Thomas's girl, Julia. The two women talked to each other. Occasionally Thomas spoke, his lower voice an interruption.

On the third floor Arthur headed for the back bedroom. Moonlight came in from the window at the end of the hall. He was like a hunting dog on the scent. He could sense the prey nearby, poised, plump, helpless.

He slipped inside Julia's room. There was the bed against the wall, a chair heaped with clothes, a bureau, a lamp on the wall. A mirror over the bureau gave back a moving shadow: his own dark-fringed face and gleaming eyes. He opened his hand to touch the things on the bureau top, just feeling them lightly under his fingers. A brush, a comb, a little cut-glass jar. He crossed the room and lay down on the floor and rolled under the bed.

He slid all the way in and settled onto his back. He lay still, waiting. He scratched his jaw, then yawned. That dog was barking somewhere. On his lower gum was a canker sore, he explored it with his tongue. Around him the nighttime settled. He was going to get back at Thomas.

He thought of the time Thomas took him snake hunting. They had pistols and went out across the fields. It was early spring; Thomas said the snakes were slow at this time of year, easy to kill. Arthur hated snakes. A black band of terror folded tight around his chest at the sight of one. He didn't want to go looking for them but he didn't dare tell Thomas that. They walked around, kicking over rocks, prying up logs. His heart thundering.

When he saw one, a big black one lying along a crevice in the rock, his heart slammed against his chest. He fired at it twice, and a bullet ricocheted off the rock and his ear suddenly blazed with heat. He nearly screamed; blood dripped down the side of his head. Thomas laughed and laughed, holding his arms tight across his belly. There was no snake, it was a shadow.

After medical school Thomas taught in Tennessee, but he had to leave over a shooting. The sheriff came to their house, asking for him, but their father shook his head and said he didn't know where Thomas was.

The floorboards were hard against Arthur's pelvis, his shoulder blades, the back of his skull. He wanted to know if Thomas was telling the truth about Julia. He'd seen her. She was small and slight, energetic, with dark hair and square shoulders. Prettier than Katie.

He wondered how long they'd be, and if he might go to sleep by accident. He probed with his tongue at the canker. His pistol bit into his hip, and he moved. He hadn't realized Ahrens's market was so big. The old man was rich, Thomas was right. Thomas would be rich.

Voices, then footsteps coming upstairs. Arthur stilled. The door opened and she came in: the sudden glow of the lamp. Her feet, back and forth. The whisper of cloth. A dress was laid across a chair, and the weight of its folds pulled it sideways. It began to slide off, was caught, laid back. The shoes came off, the feet stripped of stockings. The feet were pale and bare. She came toward the bed; the feet vanished and the springs creaked. He felt her weight above him. She was waiting. She lay stretched out, restive. Arthur timed his breaths to match hers so she wouldn't hear him. He was lying just inches beneath her. They lay expectantly, one above the other.

Finally another set of footsteps, slower and heavier. The door opened and Thomas came in.

"I've been waiting," said Julia.

"Well, I'm here." Thomas's voice was thick with drink.

"You took a long time," said Julia. "Katie keep you?"

"I couldn't come until she was asleep," said Thomas.

The bed creaked as he sat. He undid something. Arthur smelled the sharp vinegar smell of his bare feet. He took something off, then there was a great rustling of covers and creaking of springs.

"I don't like this," said Julia.

"Like what?" Thomas said.

"Sneaking around," said Julia. "Waiting for Katie to go to sleep."

"Won't be for long," said Thomas. "We'll get married."

"You say that," said Julia.

"It's true," said Thomas.

"When?" asked Julia. "How are you going to marry me?"

"Going to get rid of Katie and her father, then I'll marry you. We'll be rich and we'll go away."

After a moment Julia said, "What do you mean?"

"I'm going to get rid of them both," said Thomas. "It's you I want. I never wanted to marry Katie."

"So why did you?"

The bed creaked. "Financial considerations."

Julia gave a low helpless laugh. "Stop that," she said. "Stop. What do you mean, get rid of her?"

"Get rid of her and her father. Him first, so she'll inherit. Then her, so I'll inherit."

"Gladys would inherit," said Julia. "Stop it!"

"I'm Gladys's father," said Thomas. "I'll inherit, too."

"Wait," Julia said, turning serious. "Get rid of her?"

Thomas said nothing. There was a long pause.

"That's risky," said Julia. "Very risky."

"It's not," said Thomas. "No one will suspect. I have a plan that will keep me completely clean. And what will happen to Katie, no one will ever know."

After a pause there was more shifting and rustling. The bed began creaking, a quickening rhythm of breaths and sighs, thudding springs, rising in velocity. Then Thomas grunted twice, heavily, and everything stopped. The bed creaked again as they moved apart. They said a few words, Arthur couldn't catch them. They lay silent. After a while the bed creaked again and Thomas's feet thudded onto the floor. His breathing was heavy. Alcohol spread through the air. He went out and closed the door behind him.

Arthur breathed with Julia. The slanted patch of moonlight moved slowly across the floor. Finally a light grumbling sound: Julia was snoring. He counted to a hundred, then slid slowly sideways. He crept across the room, crouching. By the door he straightened. His knee cracked, and Julia's breathing stopped. He stayed motionless. When the grumbling began again Arthur slipped through the door. He slid open the hall window, the night air flooded around him. He stepped outside and lowered the sash.

Now he'd got him. Thomas.

26.

February 15, 1889. Charleston

ARTHUR WOKE EARLY. The room smelled of mildew. From where he was in bed he could see a segment of sky: it was oyster-colored, overcast. He tested the canker sore with his tongue. It was exquisitely tender, a small star of pain, irresistible. Thomas had once held him underwater in the pond. He'd clawed at his brother's slippery white arms, yellow mud rising around him in dense clouds.

He sat up and set his feet on the cold floorboards.

He had never trusted Thomas. He knew Thomas hadn't bought that big house with what he got from his practice. His patients were poor, and his house calls were on back streets in shabby neighborhoods. He wasn't making money that way. And he was up to something: those white men who went in together to his office weren't patients. Thomas had married money. He'd gotten the house from his father-in-law. And he was up to something.

Arthur picked up his pants from the chair. Thomas's plan meant for Arthur to take the risk while Thomas got the money. No reason in the world why he should do this. He had no intention of shooting Ahrens. He was smarter than Thomas, though Thomas didn't know it. He was already ahead of Thomas with the matter of the jewelry. Now, if Thomas admitted to having it, he'd have to explain that he'd gotten it from Arthur. And if Arthur were charged with the crime, he'd say he gave the jewelry back.

Now he'd use Thomas's plan against him. He'd go himself to Ahrens and tell him he had information that he'd provide in exchange for compensation. That was the word he'd use. Ahrens should pay a lot for this: Arthur would be saving his life. He felt generous. He felt exultant and powerful.

Arthur pulled on his pants, balancing on one bare foot, then the other. Old man Ahrens should be grateful. Arthur pulled the suspender straps over his shoulders and stuffed his shirt below his waistband. He was ready to go into the world. He put on his jacket and patted the pocket heavy with the pistol. He could feel himself heating up, expanding into the landscape. He had power. He was saving the man's life.

C. D. Ahrens Groceries Ltd. was large and bustling, with three wide aisles and a counter at the back. It was a merchandising company, not just a shop. Arthur left a note for Ahrens with the men at the counter, saying he'd call at the Waverly Hotel at five. He said he wanted to give Ahrens some useful information. He signed it "Arthur McDow. Bro. of Thos. Doctor."

The note reached Ahrens in his office. He sat behind his wide desk, a big bluff good-natured man with pink skin and pale eyelashes, big dark freckles on his balding pate. He didn't like anything about the note: the clumsy handwriting, poor grammar, misspellings, the vaguely threatening tone, the family connection. He didn't want to meet this man alone. He called the police department and asked for the man who investigated Katie's robbery.

At four o'clock the detective arrived at Ahrens's rooms at Waverly House. McManus was six foot three and thin as a whip, black-haired and blue-eyed, with a thick black mustache, a broken nose, and protruding ears. He stood very straight, and had a stern, official manner. He wore a big tarnished star pinned to his lapel. He was imposing except for the ears.

Ahrens showed him the letter. He wondered aloud if Thomas could have had a connection to the robbery. McManus read it and nodded: it did seem like an inside job, he said. Nothing had been broken, nothing else was taken, and the thief knew just where to go. Now Thomas's brother had turned up.

"It was curious," McManus said. "It might have been this fellow."

"I don't want to see him in here alone," said Ahrens.

McManus looked around the room. A low round table was in the center of it; to one side was a big armchair and a lamp. Against the far wall was a tall bureau.

"I could conceal myself," McManus said formally, "behind that piece of furnishing. I'd hear whatever he has to say, with no risk to you."

At five o'clock the two men were waiting, McManus hidden behind the far side of the bureau, Ahrens in his armchair, holding the newspaper. He was scanning it, but he couldn't actually concentrate. When McDow knocked on the door Ahrens went to it and let him in.

Arthur stepped inside quietly. His eyes flicked around the room. He was on high alert.

"Mr. Ahrens," he said. He ran his tongue over his dry lip and looked around again.

"Mr. McDow." Ahrens gestured at a straight chair and then sat down in his armchair. "You're the brother of my son-in-law, I believe. What can I do for you?"

"Yes," Arthur said. He didn't like the way he was standing and Ahrens was sitting. There was something wrong with that, as though Ahrens were his superior, but he didn't know how to fix it.

"Please have a seat," Ahrens said, nodding at the straight chair. But now Arthur didn't want to sit down. He didn't want to obey orders from Ahrens.

"I'll stay up as I wish." His eyes flicked again around the room.

"What can I do for you, Mr. McDow?" Ahrens repeated. He folded his hands on his lap.

Arthur studied him, the small blue eyes and sandy lashes, the heavy lower lip.

"It's more something I can do for you," Arthur said, pleased with this presentation.

"And what is that?" Ahrens asked pleasantly.

Now he felt there was something wrong: Ahrens was too comfortable, too composed. Arthur meant his presence to be disturbing, but the old man acted as though Arthur were nothing, merely a deliveryman. Ahrens leaned back in his armchair, legs crossed as though he were at a tea party. He spoke loudly and slowly, as though he wanted someone else to hear.

Arthur looked around again, wondering if someone else was there. Under the bed, or beyond the big wardrobe. He could feel the gun in his pocket. Instead of answering he stepped forward, moving quietly. He could feel his heart beating. Now he was on the job. He felt energy gathering within him, he became hot and molten, huge.

At this—at Arthur moving across the room—Ahrens turned alert, pale eyes now attentive. Arthur walked past him, across the room to the big wardrobe. He peered around the end of it to see a man staring directly into his eyes.

Arthur leaped back and bolted for the door, McManus after him. Arthur had a head start, but McManus jumped over the low table and passed him in the air, knocking off the newspaper, reaching the door first and throwing himself across it. He turned to face McDow, back set against the closed door.

"Mr. Arthur McDow," he said loudly, his face thunderous. "Detective McManus."

"I done nothing," Arthur said, furious. He'd been double-crossed. The air in the room had become black and turbulent. "I don't know why you're here. You can't arrest me. I done nothing."

"This gentleman requested police protection," McManus said. "I'm here as an observer. You may continue your conversation." He folded his arms across his chest, his shoulders against the door.

Arthur said nothing.

McManus urged, "Go right along. Tell the gentleman what you wanted to tell him. What you said in the letter."

Arthur looked around. No window, no other door.

"You wrote Mr. Ahrens a letter, told him you had something to say," McManus reminded him. "Here he is. Tell him what you come to say."

"Why I come," Arthur said to Ahrens. "To tell you you'd better leave this city." He'd brazen it out.

"Why would I leave?" Ahrens asked. "I have my business, and my daughter."

"Your daughter, too. You both stand to meet danger."

"What sort of danger?" Ahrens asked. "What is this about?"

Arthur shook his head. "I can't say under present circumstances." He cut his eyes toward McManus. "All I can say is you should leave Charleston."

"Why can't you tell me?" Ahrens asked.

"The fact is," Arthur said sulkily, "I won't tell you with this gentleman here." He lifted his chin at McManus. "Ask him to go out and I'll tell you."

"Absolutely not," said Ahrens.

"I'm not leaving," McManus said. "In fact, Mr. Ahrens, I'd like to ask you to leave, sir. I'd like a few minutes alone with this fellow myself."

Ahrens stood, buttoning his jacket. McManus took hold of Arthur's shoulder as Ahrens walked past. When he was gone McManus locked the door.

"Arms up." He searched Arthur, finding the gun.

"Against the law, Mr. McDow," he said. "You'll get a warrant for carrying a concealed weapon. Loaded, too."

"I've done nothing," Arthur said.

McManus pulled out a crumpled piece of paper from his breast pocket. "I charge you, Arthur McDow," McManus said, "for stealing jewelry from your brother's house on the eighth instance." He read out, "One set of diamond earrings, one gold watch, one gold chain, one diamond brooch, one gold ring, one set of gold bracelets, one gold five-dollar piece."

It was the way McManus lifted his eyes and stared at him that silenced Arthur. McManus was much taller than Arthur, and the cold blue stare was somehow unanswerable. McManus stood again with his back to the door, his big star hanging off the bottom of his lapel, the law behind him. Even his big ears, glowing red and flaring, carried the threat of the law. Arthur felt all the blood drain down in a deadly rush from his heart, from his chest. He was chilled, cowed. He was in the hands of the law.

When Ahrens came back Arthur had confessed. He put the blame on his brother. "If you don't believe me," he told McManus, "come to my room at the boarding house. I'll tell Thomas to call on me. I got a bureau you can hide in. It's all his idea," Arthur said.

Ahrens sent for Katie, and when she arrived her father told her everything. She heard all of it, the robbery, about her husband's plan to put poison in her tea, but what she said was, "Thomas has my jewelry? He has it?" She rubbed her plump wrist, as though feeling for the bracelets. She stared at her father. Her pale blue eyes were watery. She couldn't seem to address the poison.

"You and Gladys must come and stay with me," her father said. "I want you out of that house."

"Yes," she said, but they could all see she didn't want to leave.

———

IN THE DAWSON KITCHEN they heard rumors about the McDows. They heard all the neighborhood rumors. The servants all knew one another. Every few blocks was a little corner store; there was one at Bull and Rutledge, where everyone stopped in, everyone talked. In the kitchen they heard the doctor's family had left him. Katie, her father, and the little girl—they'd all moved out. They heard the doctor was living alone. Then they heard the wife and child had moved back in. But the doctor was seen outside, alone in his garden, at all hours. Scandal spread from the kitchen into the parlors; the servants mentioned what they'd heard to their employers. Their employers listened with half an ear; it was kitchen gossip and they didn't approve; certainly they didn't join in. But they heard. Sarah heard the rumors from other people's parlors. She told Celia she was not to use Dr. McDow again. No one in the household was to have anything to do with him.

But Dr. McDow was popular with the coloreds, so when they talked about him in the Dawson kitchen Isaac took his side. The other servants, who liked gossip, took the Dawsons'.

"He drinks," Jane said. She grimaced and sucked at her thumb where she'd burned it on the teakettle. "His wife has left him."

Isaac had just come in from serving. He wore a white jacket when he waited on table, a black frock coat when he drove. He set down the tureen.

"He ain' drink," Isaac said. "He a good doctor."

But Jane shook her head. She'd seen him walking unsteadily, staring over the fence.

"Not only does he drink," she said, "he's got mixed up with the police."

"Not the police," Isaac said, shaking his head.

"The police," said Jane. "So I heard. An insurance fraud. A deception." She pronounced each syllable with precision. "They dig up a dead body and they say he just died in an accident. A doctor signs a death certificate and they file a claim. The insurance companies pay, and they all share the money. The doctors do it. He's one of them."

"He never," Isaac said.

"What do you mean?" Celia asked.

"It was in the paper," Jane said. "A woman called her neighbor to come in, and there was a dead body on her kitchen table. The woman said it was her husband. She told the neighbor it was very sad, that they'd been estranged and then her husband had finally come home. But as soon as he came home he slipped and fell on the stairs and died. She wept and all. But the neighbor said she'd never seen the man before. And she said the smell was very pronounced. Very of-fen-sive." Jane looked around at them. "He was lying there on the kitchen table." She tapped the table with her finger.

"On the kitchen table!" Celia was shocked.

"How could she lift him alone?" asked Jane. "It's not easy to lift a dead body onto a table. That's a heavy load. It's help she had."

Isaac shook his head. "Dat a lie," he said.

"It was in the paper, so," Jane said, not looking at him. In that household, the newspaper was sacred.

Hélène was not part of this discussion. She was in the dining room, with the Dawsons.

27.

February 27, 1889. Charleston

THE AIR WAS SOFT, earth-smelling, the morning cool and misty. The cobblestones shone with damp. Spring was imminent. Sarah was on her way to visit Celena Fourgeaud, who was dying. Isaac was driving Brownie, who shook his head. Sarah leaned back in the swaying carriage and thought of Miss Celena, the mother of Frank's first wife.

Frank had a photograph of Virginia in his desk. Sometimes when she was alone Sarah used to hold it close to her face, examining the high rounded forehead, small bow mouth, dark confiding eyes. Sarah tried to make her out, this young woman who thought she'd share Frank's life. Frank had only kind words for her. Sarah was sure she was all those things—sweet, loyal, loving—but she wondered what else Virginia was. She'd never know: death ends the conversation. Afterward, you couldn't call someone a fool, or remember his grating laugh. Death beatifies.

She wouldn't say a word against Hal. Not that he had no flaws, but they were irrelevant now. The dead were beyond criticism because they were beyond change. They had lived their lives, they were fixed forever. She imagined the dead, motionless and somber, lying in long ranks in the earth, while the living chattered.

She knew for a fact that Virginia had poor taste in music: Frank wouldn't play the sentimental songs from her sheet music, still in the piano bench. Sarah suspected that Virginia wasn't intelligent enough for her husband. She didn't like the idea of Frank trapped in a marriage without conversation.

She felt pity for Virginia, thinking she was setting out on a long path, only to find her footing give way, the earth begin to slide away beneath her. Fading strength, lessening breath, blood on her pillow. It made Sarah feel guilty at her own good fortune.

The Fourgeauds treated Frank as a son, his children as their grandchildren. Miss Celena used to play hide-and-seek, Warrington crouched behind the sofa, she with her hands over her eyes, counting. Frank had taken care of both of them, first Eugene, as he failed, and now Miss Celena.

The trees along the lower end of Rutledge Avenue were now softened by rain. Her first visit here had been with her mother, when they'd first moved to Charleston. When she and Frank became engaged, he brought them to meet Miss Celena as though she were his mother.

"We're so happy for Frank," Celena told them, in her whispery voice. Miss Celena sat in a little chair by the fireplace, and each time she sat down her cat jumped into her lap. It was a big ginger cat, and when Miss Celena stood up she had to lift him down onto the carpet, where he stood crossly, lashing his tail. She gave Sarah a brooch that had been Virginia's, a cameo with a Greek goddess in profile. She'd used to wear it, but the front half of the face had fallen off; the beautiful profile had dropped, just like that. It lay now in the back of a drawer. The thought of it made her feel guilty, as though she'd been living her life at Virginia's expense, and hadn't valued it properly.

Isaac drew up before the house. The walk was edged with hellebores, their dark glossy leaves half hiding the flowers. Miss Celena had given Sarah seedlings; they flourished along the edge of her path.

Nancy, the maid, opened the door. She was long-faced and lean, with trembling hands and fine gray hair. When Sarah asked how Miss Celena was, Nancy shook her head.

"Tolerable," she said. "Just tolerable."

In the bedroom, Miss Celena, tiny and wasted, lay propped up on pillows. The air was close, smelling of eucalyptus and something else, something darker and softer, less pleasant.

"Good morning, Miss Celena." Sarah sat down and took her hand. It was fragile and light, as though the bones had become hollow.

"Sarah." Miss Celena spoke with difficulty.

"How are you feeling?" Sarah asked.

"Moderate," Celena whispered, as always.

"I've come to say goodbye for a little while," Sarah said. "Tomorrow I'm going to Washington to see Miriam, my sister. And Jem, my brother."

"A family visit," said Miss Celena. Her breathing was audible.

Nancy brought in the tea tray.

"Coming over here today," Sarah said, "I remembered how kind you were, when I first came here. And to my mother."

"You were Frank's wife," Miss Celena said.

"Not yet," Sarah said. "You made us feel welcome. I've always been grateful."

"Frank took care of us," Miss Celena said. "We were grateful." She tried to swallow; something struggled in her throat.

"You had a big cat," Sarah said. "He kept jumping into your lap."

"Archimedes," whispered Miss Celena. "He shed so."

"I'll only be gone for a week," Sarah said. "I'll come and see you when I get back."

"I may not be here," she whispered.

"Of course you will," said Sarah, though she was doubtful.

Miss Celena's eyes were pale, the irises rimmed unevenly with white. The small seamed face was colorless. It was her soul, quick and living, that illuminated her gaze.

Here was the end of her own life with Miss Celena, Sarah thought. This tiny lined face, the pursed, lipless mouth, the hand plucking at the sheet. Here was the end, Nancy standing outside the door, long mouth turned down with anxiety. Miss Celena was worn out; life had had its way with her.

When she said goodbye Sarah kissed the back of Miss Celena's hand and placed it against her cheek. There was nothing she could do, the current that would carry her away was gathering force. She could feel the pulse, rapid and uneven. It was like holding a bird in her hand.

In the carriage Sarah wept a little, out of sorrow for Miss Celena, but also with a guilty surge of gratitude, for her own husband and children, vivid with life. Brownie, who knew he was going home, threw up his head and tried to trot. Out of respect to Mrs. Fourgeaud, who was dying, Isaac held him sternly to a walk.

In the afternoon the weather darkened. Clouds moved in low, muffling the city. The trees turned vague in the desultory rain. The trunk had been brought upstairs, and Sarah was packing. She already missed the children. She thought of Warrington's luminous eyes, his weak chest. And this was the dangerous season, winter melting treacherously into spring, damp air seeping into lungs. She moved between armoire and trunk, laying out her clothes on the bed, smoothing out the wrinkles, folding them carefully. She stepped around Bruno, Frank's giant Newfoundland. Dark-pelted, white-pawed, he was always underfoot. Turning back from the armoire she stumbled onto his paw. He yelped and yanked it back. Exasperated, she whispered, "*Bruno.*" He looked up, his moist eyes earnest, thumping his tail in apology.

Presents for Miriam: lemon soap, perfume; and for her daughter Lucille a beaded purse. A tiny white lawn nightgown for Jem's new baby. She was looking forward to being surrounded again by her family, swimming in that thick Morgan soup. All those years in Baton Rouge there were cousins up and down the river, at every party, every holiday, every wedding and funeral. Now it was just her and Miriam and Jem. She thought of Jem settling his chin into his neck when he laughed. She thought of Hal's face, though it was dim now. It seemed as though the house on Church Street were still there, and if she went there she could step inside and find everything the same: the red lantern in the hall, her father reading in his study. The polished table in the dining room, Tiche pushing through the swinging door. The mockingbird singing in the middle of the night, high in the magnolia tree.

Instead, Miriam was living alone with Lucille in Washington. She'd left her dreadful husband, Alcée, who drank, but now she was living as a divorcée, and what would Mother have said to that? Jem was on his third wife, Frances (the awful Ella had died of the typhus, poor thing)—and had a new baby, Frederica. They lived on a farm outside Washington, though Jem's last attempt at farming had gone so poorly. He couldn't seem to settle: a diplomatic post in Australia hadn't gone well, either. Still, he was the merriest of them all.

Taking down a skirt from the armoire, she thought of her father in his study, his beautiful long fingers on the carved arm of his chair. He seemed suddenly present; she felt him in the room.

She heard herself speak: "Father." The word was shocking in the quiet air. She waited for a second, as though something might happen.

But she could not leave her children for nine days. She could feel them in her arms, warm, impatient, their angular limbs, their whorled, mysterious ears.

The front door opened and she heard them start up the stairs, footsteps pounding. Warrington was always first; he burst into the room, still in his coat. Ethel came behind, holding something. Warrington was already talking, complaining about school. He came across the room, jumping to avoid Bruno.

"I knew the answer, and he didn't call on me," he said. "I had my hand up and he wouldn't call."

He looked up. His skin was translucent. Beneath his eyes were smudges of purplish-green.

"I'm sorry." Sarah smoothed his head. His hair was lank and pale, fine as silk thread. "I'm sure he didn't see you." She stooped and put her arms around him; he curved backward, flexible, indifferent.

"I'm sure he did," Warrington said. He climbed onto her bed and sat, his feet dangling over the side.

"You always say that, afterward, that you knew the answer and he didn't call on you," said Ethel. "What was the answer that you knew so well?" She came over to stand by the bed, looming over him.

She was tall and lanky, a dense cloud of crinkly blond hair massed on her back. Her skin was so pale it was greenish, like Warrington's.

Were they ill, her children? Should they not be pink and white, not this strange, wan greenish hue, like lilies? Their narrow chests, this changeable weather.

"Not your affair," Warrington said. He had sat on the stack of scarves, crushing them.

"Don't argue," Sarah said. She said to Ethel, "Was today your music class? Did you remember your piece?"

"I did," Ethel said. "Except for one passage. I had to repeat it. Don't tell Papa."

"No," said Sarah. She smoothed Ethel's hair away from her high bony forehead. She had a greyhound's long nose. "Will you play it for me?"

"What if I forget it again?" Her eyes were anxious.

Sarah shook her head. "No one will mind."

"You said I must learn it properly," Ethel said.

"Yes, but forgetting is part of learning it properly. There are lots of times before it's learned when you'll forget it."

On the eve of departure she was infinitely indulgent. Her children were beloved. She could feel their hearts beating in her chest.

"I knew my whole piece," Warrington said.

He was still in his coat. And muddy shoes. If he kicked his feet, if he moved them one inch he would leave muddy smears on her white bedspread. Hélène was meant to be in charge of this.

"Where is Hélène?" she asked.

"Disparu," said Warrington. He picked at the edge of one of the shawls, bouncing the fringe on his fingers. *Disappeared.*

———

IN THE EVENING she drove with Frank down to the office. It was raining harder, fine needles rattling against the phaeton roof. Isaac sat hunched beneath the huge black umbrella. Frank stepped down and turned, squinting against the rain as he kissed his hand to her. Driving back through the chill twilight, bundled up in her shawl, Sarah thought of her trip and felt a flush of anticipation. She thought of Jem tucking his chin down. She thought of Frank's squinting smile, the fling of the kiss. Impulsively she leaned forward and asked Isaac to take her to Marie Chazal's.

Frank wouldn't approve, but Marie was brilliant at fortunes, the things that weren't rational, but were real, part of her life.

At the front door she stepped inside and called, "Marie, it's me." Her heart was pounding as she drew off her gloves. She felt as though she were on a secret mission.

They went into the parlor and sat down. Marie put a folding screen across her lap. She shuffled the deck, then began to lay out the cards, one by one.

———•———

LATER SHE WAITED upstairs for Frank, listening. She knew the rhythm of his footsteps, how they sounded coming down the sidewalk from the corner. They'd stop at the gate, and she'd hear the click of the lock, the creak of the hinges. She'd hear him mounting the front steps. She was reading, but really she was listening. After dark he was more present, closer to the surface of her mind. It had stopped raining by then, and the night was still. She went to the window and drew open the curtains. She raised the metal shaft, twisting and sliding it, then pushed open the tall French windows. She swung them out onto the night and stood, listening.

Outside, the city was quiet. The air was chill and damp. A small breeze sifted against her skin. A dog barked in the distance, alone. The city seemed hushed, waiting. She listened, listened, listened: the air seemed to tingle. She could feel the great animal of the city around her, hushed and dark, but full of hidden life. Like the ocean, full of subtle inscrutable movement. She drew in a long sweet breath, like cold water.

Something rustled suddenly above, a rapid fluttering: a bird had come inside. Or a bat. She turned around, hearing anxious wings. She saw nothing. The door to Frank's study was open, and the one to the hall. She closed the door to the hall and went into his study: the bird was there, balancing nervously on a lampshade. It was a gray phoebe; they nested every year under the eaves. She was watching Sarah, her black eyes brilliant, her long tail twitching. Sarah went back to her bedroom and opened the French windows farther, a great black gape onto the night, and then went back to the study. The bird watched her, the tail jerking.

Sarah moved toward the bird. "Outside," she said quietly. The bird lofted up toward the ceiling, hovering clumsily in the air. Sarah passed underneath her, then raised her arms slowly, walking back, gently herding her. "Outside," she said again softly. Panicked, the bird fluttered along the top of a gilt picture frame, then flew back out into Sarah's room. Sarah followed and shut the door to the study. The bird, vibrating with anxiety, trembled in the air up near the ceiling.

"Outside." Sarah whispered it. She raised her arms again, the movement wide and slow, as though she herself were about to fly. The bird, her eyes bright with fear, dropped down into midair and hovered, desperate. Sarah stepped closer, and suddenly the bird understood the black rectangle. She lofted into the darkness and was gone.

As she drew the windows closed Sarah heard his steps on the sidewalk. She went to the dressing table and leaned over to look in the mirror. She drew in her breath. She smoothed her hair, then settled the lace at her collar. No matter how late Frank was, Sarah was always soignée.

They had supper alone. The house was silent, servants gone, children in bed. The candles made a light-filled space, holding the shadows in the corners. In the center of the table was a silver bowl heaped with crystal grapes. The soft light reflected on the grapes.

She asked if he liked the sauce on the chicken. "If I have to tell Celia you don't she will quit."

"It's very good," he said.

"She threatens it constantly," Sarah said. "Quitting. And Jane asks to borrow money."

"You must be firm," Dawson said. "But generous. If they need money who else can they ask?"

"Yes," said Sarah. "Only I'm never quite sure if they really need it."

"It's so disagreeable to ask," Dawson said, "I assume no one would do it unless things were dire." He tore off a piece of bread. "Tell me what you did this evening."

"Something foolish," Sarah confessed. "You won't approve."

"Try me," he said.

"I went to Marie's."

Frank frowned. "Why? And it was raining."

"I was wrapped up," she said. "I had a sudden urge."

"What did she say?" asked Frank, irritated. All this was nonsense. It was the fashion now, to have tea parties and a fortune-teller. Sarah had given one a month ago; the children were there.

"She was brilliant," Sarah said. "You'll be amazed."

He waited.

"First she said I'd just said goodbye to someone who was about to die. Someone who loved me, but had no connection to me."

"And who was that?" Frank asked.

"Miss Celena," Sarah said. "I saw her this morning."

Frank inclined his head and said nothing.

"Then she talked about you, my darling," Sarah said, as though she were giving him a present. "She said that in two weeks' time you'll have your heart's desire."

"My heart's desire," said Frank. "I can't think what that is."

"Two weeks," Sarah repeated. "March the twelfth."

"Peace and quiet, that's what I'd like." Frank started eating his salad. "An end to all this furor at the paper."

"That's a very modest request," said Sarah.

Frank said nothing. It was actually a large request; things were getting worse. Every day he kept thinking the tide would turn in his favor, and every day it did not. He might need another loan from Siegling, which he dreaded requesting. Two more of his staff had left. He might have to go back to New York for a loan. He now had to worry about meeting his payroll. He felt the silver blade.

"All your friends will gather," Sarah went on. "You'll receive great honors. I picture you on the balcony at City Hall, receiving a medal."

He didn't want to remember that balcony. "Doesn't sound like peace and quiet to me."

She changed the subject. "Also, there's some terrible danger threatening Jemmie."

Frank said nothing. Jem had always been reckless.

"But I can't believe it's true," she added.

"Why not? You believe everything else she says."

"Why are you such a skeptic? Marie sees things she couldn't possibly know. She told me about a terrible scandal, everything but the woman's name, which I already knew."

"Who was it?" Dawson asked, diverted.

"I can't possibly repeat it," she said. "It's the most appalling gossip."

"Sarah!" he said. "Now you must."

"In two weeks," she said, "I'll tell you everything."

He shook his head.

"Another thing," she said. "This is very strange. In two weeks someone will bring me a bundle of clothes, during the night, in the rain. It's something that shouldn't come to me. It looks like soiled clothes, but they're fresh. They've been dragged in the dirt, and they're stained. Marie asked me what on earth I thought it meant. I said it must be a baby, left at our gate, like the one at Mrs. Wyttle's."

"I hope you know what to do if a baby were left here," Dawson said.

"I'd look after it until we found out where to take it," Sarah said.

"You certainly would not," Dawson said. "I had no idea you were so ignorant on such matters."

"I'm sure I'm ignorant on many matters."

"You'd call the police," said Dawson. "Don't touch the baby. Call the police, and let them handle it."

"But there are times when you'd take matters into your own hands. You wouldn't wait for the police."

"If it's a matter for the police," said Dawson, "no one else should interfere. Please pay attention to me."

"Well, it wasn't a baby," said Sarah. "Just a bundle of clothes."

"It wasn't anything," Dawson said. "It was words made up by Marie. The cards don't say anything about a scandal, you know that. Or a bundle of clothes. The cards are just cards. A ten of clubs is not a bundle of dirty clothes."

"Marie is gifted," Sarah said. "It's a kind of art."

"It's not an art," said Frank. "You like Marie because she's Creole. She speaks French."

"Hardly," said Sarah, now haughty. "There are lots of Creoles here I don't speak to. And this is a gift. Marie said the same thing at my tea. The cards said the same thing. The children heard it."

"I don't like that nonsense told in front of the children," Dawson said. "It's against the Church, among other things. I don't want them listening to soothsayers and fortune-tellers. We'll have the gypsies in next."

Sarah said nothing. She began cutting her meat into small pieces. Without looking up she said, "Do you remember writing to me at Hampton's, telling me you felt me in the room with you?" She looked up. "It was just past nine at night, and you asked if I'd been thinking of you at that moment."

That moment: he'd been in his room at the Fourgeauds', reading. He'd been startled. He looked up from his book, the sense of her flooding through him like a wash of warm air. He was staring at a print on the wall, an image of classical ruins, a temple, while feeling her presence, vivid, unmistakable. She was there with him. He could smell her hair.

"All right," he said. "I remember." He took a swallow of water. "But I wasn't making a prophecy from a pack of cards."

She raised her eyebrows and looked down at her plate.

"What is this about Jem? What danger?" he said. "Probably financial, which is not news."

Actually, Marie hadn't said anything about Jem. She'd said that the person Sarah loved best in the world was in danger. Who could that be? Sarah decided that Frank would say it was Jem. Then Marie had used Frank's name.

"She also said that you were in danger, from a small dark man. A stranger. A professional man, maybe a doctor." Sarah looked at Frank. "I told her that was nonsense. You're too well-known to be attacked. You have enemies, but you know who they are."

"It is nonsense," said Dawson.

"But maybe you should be careful," she said.

"What should I do? Careful about what?"

"This man," Sarah said. "Protect yourself from him."

"What man? The man Marie Chazal made up from reading a pack of cards? Should I watch out for the jack of clubs?" He stared at her, vexed. "There is no man. I won't carry a gun, if that's what you mean."

"No, no, I know," Sarah said. She thought of Marie's face, turning up to her, over the cards. "Maybe for a day or so."

"It's a matter of principle," Dawson said. "I will not carry a gun. And there is no man."

They ate in silence. The candles flickered, the shadows wavered in the corners. Overhead, the light faded upward, rising toward the dim ceiling.

Marie had said she saw Sarah in the twilight, surrounded by a crowd of men. She said sorrow would come to Sarah. Sarah thought of sorrow like a dark mist, moving toward her. She thought of the servants, how they bothered her. How she never knew whether or not to believe them.

If Dawson could get another loan he'd hire another reporter. He wanted more news, more energy. When he allowed himself to admit it he felt some terrible sapping taking place. He was afraid that the essence of the paper was draining away. He didn't know how it began, how to stop it. In the morning, stepping into the downstairs office, he'd always felt charged with energy and purpose at the sight of the reporters at their desks, busy and intent. They'd looked up and nodded, smiling, calling out greetings, in the thick of their work. Now they looked up silently, cool, restrained. He was afraid they were planning their exits; he didn't know how to greet them now. He couldn't remember how he'd greeted them before. Did he nod? Did he speak? Now, curt, uncomfortable, he nodded, frowning, walking through them on his way upstairs. He wished Riordan were still there. He remembered when the paper was a churning center of energy, people walking back and forth, calling out, laughing. He remembered when he thought they were like dogs, wagging and barking. All that excitement had drained away. He was thinking of paying a wire service for a weekend package of columns and jokes. He'd never done this, he'd always wanted his own writers' voices to make the paper, but he couldn't afford to pay his writers to produce all this anymore.

Thinking now of walking into the office the next morning he felt as though he were drowning, as though something were rising up his body, pressing cold against his waist, his chest, rising to his shoulders, lapping at his neck. He remembered the balcony at City Hall, the faces of the crowd lit up by torches. He picked up the silver salt cellar, the little silver basket set on curved legs, and shifted it to the left, as though he could correct what was happening inside him by this gesture.

He looked up at Sarah.

"My heart's desire," he said, "would be to spend more time with you and the children."

Her face in the candlelight opened like a flower.

"We'd all like that," she said. Marie's comments became trinkets, to be laid out and exclaimed over, then put away. Sarah put them away, all but the heart's desire.

"Perhaps we should move to Provence," Frank said.

"Marie did say I'll move to a foreign land," Sarah said. "She says I'll die there."

Why had Marie reappeared in the conversation? Dawson frowned. "That will be after I die."

"But don't die," Sarah said. She put her finger on her own lips, to keep him from using the word.

"I have no plans to," said Frank. "I can't afford it." He gave a short laugh. "I can't get life insurance."

"And why is that?" Sarah asked.

He didn't want to tell her about the ulcer. "I'm changing companies." He was looking for one that would give him at least partial insurance.

At the station the next morning he settled her in her compartment, then waited on the platform. When the train started off he walked alongside it, and as it pulled away he kissed his hand to her. She kissed hers to him, suddenly bereft. When the train pulled away she sat down again. The seat was red plush, and she didn't rest her head against it for fear of lice. The train moved through the back streets, past untidy backyards with clotheslines and henhouses. An old man stood chopping kindling. He was bent over, even as he raised the hatchet. She missed her children. Her heart was being torn from her chest. It was wrong to leave them for so long. She felt she should atone somehow.

Jem and Miriam were the only people now who called her "Zay," though growing up it had been her name.

28.

February 29, 1889. Charleston

WHEN THE DOORBELL RANG Hélène was upstairs making Ethel's bed. She was leaning over, smoothing the sheet, when she heard the sound and knew at once who it was. She left the bed and hurried down to reach the door before Jane.

He was standing on the porch. It was a shock to see him here. He stared at her. She couldn't look away.

"Good morning, Marie." He spoke slowly. "May I come in?"

Hélène didn't move.

"The captain's gone to the office, I saw him," he said. "And she's away. I've come to see you."

He kept his eyes on hers and made a little gesture with his shoulder, as though he were pushing at her body. His skin was very pale. A small lock of dark hair fell across his forehead. His mustache was dark and springy. "Take me inside, Marie." His voice was intimate. She stepped back to let him in.

In the front hall he stood still, looking slowly around, as if he had just bought the property. His gaze was avid. He looked at the red hanging lamp above his head, the framed paintings on the wall, the patterned carpet beneath his feet. The curving staircase, leading to somewhere he did not know.

"Please," Hélène said, and led him into the little study off the dining room. Two tall bookcases faced each other; on the third wall hung a painting, a shawl draped stylishly over one corner. Carved wooden chairs flanked a mahogany table, on which was a bronze sculpture of a struggling man, naked. Beside it was a telephone, with its curling cord and complicated receiver.

McDow looked at everything, the statue, the hanging shawl. All the books.

"Books," he said scornfully. "Captain Brains. Is that who he is?"

Hélène smiled, baffled.

"Thinks he's very smart," McDow said. He nodded several times with satisfaction. "Very smart."

"Yes," Hélène agreed, nodding. "He is very smart."

But he frowned at that.

"I brought you something." McDow took an envelope from his breast pocket and handed it to her. He moved close as she opened it. Inside was a thin sheet of paper covered with lines of handwriting: poetry.

"You see?" He murmured as though this made something clear. "I told you. I want you to marry me."

"Very beautiful." She nodded and looked up.

"You see?" He held her eyes with his. She could hear his breathing. He wasn't yet touching her but she felt his nearness. She felt her body waiting for the touch.

He moved closer. "We'll fly away, mademoiselle. Would you like that?" He pronounced it "mamedeselle." He was staring into her eyes, into her mind.

"I don't know how to fly." She didn't move away. Very slowly he reached around and touched her back, the angel wing of her shoulder, with just the tips of his fingers. At the touch she shuddered violently.

"Oh," he said, nodding. "You have wings, Marie. You have wings. I'll show you how to use them."

She smiled, as if this were a game she understood.

"No," she said, "I don't know how to use them."

He waited, and she stepped away from him.

"But I have something for you," she said. She'd put it in the corner of the bookcase. It had a handsome red cover, with elegant lettering: *The Lure of the Lantern*. She wasn't sure what a lantern was, but she'd heard them talking about the book at dinner. Madame said they shouldn't allow it in the house, a married man and a single woman. The captain said all books should be allowed in the house. Hélène had gone to find it on the shelf to look at it. She couldn't read English very well.

McDow took it in both hands and turned it over. "Very nice." He looked up. "A present for me, Marie?"

She nodded.

He leaned toward her and she could smell his thick male scent. Alcohol, always that, and something dark. He moved his mouth close to hers, staring at her. She waited.

Suddenly the telephone gave off a noise. It was like an alarm, shrill and high; McDow jumped like a nervous horse. He made a small flat sound as he jerked away, crouching slightly, as if ready to fend something off.

Hélène covered her mouth; a little snort escaped her.

"What is that?" McDow asked, angry.

"Telephone," she said. She was laughing.

"I know that!" he said, lying. "But why did it ring?"

Hélène raised her shoulders mysteriously. "Someone wish to call the captain."

"Is he watching me?" McDow asked. He was hissing. "The captain."

Hélène laughed out loud. "You cannot see through it. Only hear. It's for talk and hearing."

McDow straightened. He smoothed his mustache with both index fingers.

The telephone shrilled again, bright and metallic. This time he didn't move. They both watched it as the sound died into silence.

"Are you sure he's not here?" He looked at the doorway.

"He is not here. Maybe it is the office calling to find him. He left some time before." She shrugged.

He nodded. He raised his hand and fingered his mustache, smoothing the short hairs down.

"You see what I brought you," he said.

"Yes, thank you," Hélène said, nodding.

She smiled at him.

"I want to marry you," he said. He was unsettled and angry. His eyes kept darting around the room. He put his hand on her shoulder and squeezed it hard, twice, staring at her.

29.

March 5, 1889. Charleston

DAWSON WAS ALONE at breakfast, Sarah still in Washington, the children gone to school. The morning mail was stacked beside his plate: a letter from Sarah, several letters for her, one from his brother, Joey. A few others.

He read Sarah's first. She was enjoying herself. They'd gone to tea with an old friend from Baton Rouge. They'd all started speaking French, and didn't realize it until the others there looked at them oddly. They'd gone out to Jem's farm to see his new baby: tiny, with big wild eyes like a lemur. "I miss you terribly," she wrote. She couldn't wait to come home.

He thought of her at her dressing table, braiding her hair for the night. Her fingers flicking in and out. He felt a physical urge to make her happy. Right now the world seemed to be sliding out from under his feet.

Joey's letter would be long, full of church politics and a request for money for one of his projects. One of the worst things about the situation was that Dawson couldn't offer to help people. He had always done it; this inability sickened him.

He turned over the large official-looking envelope. The return address was Nicholas Musser, *St. Louis Globe*. The *Globe* was famous, populist, a bit rabble-rousing, but principled. "My dear Captain Dawson," the letter began. Musser (who was the owner and publisher) announced that he had long known Dawson's work. He admired Dawson's independence and forthrightness, his courage, his vision, his writing style.

"Would you consider coming to St. Louis to work for us?" He reminded Dawson that they fought for progress, would not tolerate injustice or corruption, challenged demagogues. He hoped Dawson would consider his offer; he looked forward to an early reply.

Dawson read the letter again.

"I would be honored to call you my colleague," Musser ended. Dawson wondered on what terms he'd be called colleague. Musser was a Hungarian immigrant who had started with nothing, and made his way into the newspaper business. He was much admired for his success, though people were divided over his principles. Musser was famously tough and smart, but some said he was a muckraker, not a visionary. He owned three newspapers now, a national presence. His headlines screamed. Did Dawson want to call him colleague? He could walk away from all this: Courtenay, Tillman, Huger, the rest.

He thought of St. Louis, deep in the interior. He'd never been there. He imagined wide prairies, dull plains. Clouds of dust. He thought of sailing here in the bay, with Warrington. Tacking back and forth across the bright water.

Would it be cowardly to walk away? Or was it time? Editor in chief of the *St. Louis Globe*. At least it was a choice, another possibility. He felt his chest loosen.

The last letter carried no return address. The paper was flimsy, the handwriting looping and uneven, with pretentious curlicues.

Dear Captain Dawson,

I would like to inform you that your children's governess is spending time in assignations with a married man. She has been seen many times on the street and in other houses with this man. It is an insult to your family's honor that she should act this way. You should stop this happening at once. I am referring to your governess Marie Burdon.

Signed, A Friend

Dawson read it again, then set it down, apart from the others. He actually didn't want it touching them, certainly not Sarah's. Who had written it? The man's wife? A self-righteous sister? A busybody neighbor? He wondered if it was true.

He rang for more coffee. Jane came in holding the coffeepot with both hands. Her boots creaked with each step. Her long apron was pinned to her dress, her white cap covered her thick red hair. She leaned over to fill his cup, her mouth tight in concentration. She'd know something about this, though Dawson wouldn't ask her. He wouldn't gossip with servants.

He asked if she knew where Hélène was. Her boiled blue eyes flicked up at him.

She's not yet back from taking the children, she said. Was there anything more? He shook his head and she left, creaking.

Miss Isabel Ashby Smith's school started at nine. It was fifteen minutes away on foot. By ten o'clock, when Dawson left for the office, Hélène had not yet returned.

30.

March 6, Ash Wednesday, 1889. Charleston

IT WAS DARK when Dawson got up, the windows still black. He shaved by the light of the gas lamp, leaning close to the mirror. With one hand he held his cheek taut, with the other he drew the razor against the snowy mounds of cream. He could hear his own breathing. The house was silent.

This was a day of reflection and penitence. Here at the top of the house, in the darkness, he was aware of the presence of God inside himself, like a soft humming mist, not quite visible but real, immanent. Or some presence, something he couldn't quite grasp or understand, whatever it was that his prayers and thoughts referred to. Part of the strength was the mystery. This early silent rising separated him from the world, reminded him of his solitary self and God.

The world outside was slowly turning toward the light; he heard the first soft twitterings as the birds entered the day. Birds, with their hollow bones and downy chests, the rapid tapping of their tiny hearts. Their unfathomable lives; the miracle of flight. Lofting through the oceans of the air, breasting the warm currents. In the scale of things, he was a small tapping heart.

He went downstairs, moving quietly through the dark house. When he stepped onto the front porch the sky was beginning to turn light. It was a pale ash, not quite day, but somewhere beyond darkness. The air was cool and bracing against his naked cheek. He walked down the front steps, past the blurred shadows of the garden. The street was empty and silent. Dawson walked through the misty air, beneath the dark masses of the trees. At the corner he turned down Rutledge. His heels sounded against the damp brick, the brass tip of his walking stick clicked with every other stride.

He would try Siegling again. He would try the bank in New York again. Maybe Riordan would know of a different one. With a loan he'd hire more reporters.

Contemplation and penance, humility. This was what his Church asked of him. He felt the familiar tension between the world and the Church, what he was asked and what he could offer. For a moment he felt something yield, some soft barrier inside himself give way, as sometimes happened: his grasp on the world, his own presence giving way to something larger, and in that moment he felt himself dissolve. He felt the soft dark presence of the Holy Spirit, like an intimate request to the soul. For a beat he felt its nearness, then almost at once it was gone. What he wanted was to lay himself bare, open himself to the examination of his heart, but already it was over. He was walking down a public street, his stick ringing against the bricks, the stitch in his gut tightening slightly at each step. He'd nicked the edge of his chin, shaving in the dim light; he wondered if he was bleeding.

Before him stretched the low horizon, the tree-fringed streets. When he'd first arrived the city had reminded him of London: the soft old brick, fluted white pillars, neoclassical arches and pediments. An eighteenth-century city, though softer and quieter than London. He thought of St. Louis, frowning, Teutonic, full of ponderous stone buildings. He could walk away from this, Courtenay, Tillman. Bayard Swinton, the cashier who'd leaked news to the *World* before he quit and joined it.

He wondered what sort of offer Musser would make. He wouldn't take a beginner's salary, didn't like the idea of working for someone else. But Nicholas Musser was distinguished and principled. It would be a great thing to walk away into partnership with Nicholas Musser. The offer made him feel powerful.

Humility and penance. Meditation. He struggled to envelop himself again in the soft gray mist, but day was spreading itself through the streets. Walking toward him was an oyster-woman, a wide basket balanced on her head. "Yashta," she called, the syllables drawn out, "yashta." Her long faded skirt brushed against her bare feet, her lean brown toes. She looked at him. One eye was milky, gone.

Hélène had walked along here with the children, on their way to school, coming home alone. Where had she been seen?

By the time he reached Queen Street morning was coming on, and the air had turned bright and ordinary. The pro-cathedral stood behind the ruins. The old cathedral had burned down in the war, a huge square tower flanked by tall Gothic spires. For thirty years the congregation had used the pro-cathedral, and then Bishop Northrop had asked Dawson if he'd help rebuild. Dawson, who loved being asked for help, had told the bishop to start the construction: he'd promised to rouse support through the paper. The reconstruction had begun, and a haphazard skyline of scaffolding had gone up. Dawson had published an appeal and the money started coming in.

On the steps stood a group of men. Dawson nodded but didn't speak. He didn't like to talk before the service, holding himself intact from earthly contact, so the Holy Spirit could enter him. But by now that was unlikely. The mystery that had seemed so close as he'd walked down the silent street had dissolved.

There was J. T. Curley, who owned a big hardware shop downtown. He used to advertise regularly in the paper, but he'd stopped. Dawson didn't want to know if he'd moved to the *World*. He nodded to Curley as he passed. He thought of Siegling, his cold gray eyes.

Humility. Contemplation and penance.

Dawson pushed through the door. There must be other possibilities, banks, businessmen. New York investors; he'd find them. This had happened when he and Riordan bought the *Courier*. He'd manage. Inside he was met by a hushed ecclesiastical silence, the faint dry tingle of incense. The room was bare except for the old altar, an ornate Gothic spire saved from the fire. Dawson made his way up to his pew, near the front. Sometimes he brought the children here. Warrington was indifferent, but Ethel liked the ritual, the chants, the beads, the robes. Opulence and ceremony. Before they'd married, Sarah had promised the bishop she'd raise the children in the Church, but she hadn't. Dawson had hoped that school in Europe would make the children into Catholics, but it had not. Now Sarah usually took the children to the Episcopal service at St. Michael's; sometimes they came with him as well. He thought of the youngest, little Philip Hicky, who'd only lived six months: he might have been a Catholic. The lost child, the dark mist of his presence.

The room hushed. Bishop Northrop, in his deep purple robe, came swaying slowly up the aisle. The censer swung its steady rhythm, spreading pungent clouds. At the altar the bishop turned and made the sign of the cross. He began the chant; the congregation answered in sibilant half whispers. The swinging globe, the rich robes, the obedient response were all comforting. The Church was larger than he, powerful, ancient, unknowable. It stretched like an airy cathedral through time and space, soaring, lofty, full of shadows and mystery, demanding the interior leap into the space of faith.

Dawson kneeled. He held on to the smooth mahogany pew and set his forehead against his hands. The bishop's voice rose and fell like plainsong. He thought of the early church on Torcello, the figures high on the wall, Christ Pantocrator. Dawson sat up, then kneeled again. It would be cowardly to leave. Chanting, murmuring, crossing himself in unison with the bishop, the congregation, he felt confidence rising. He moved into the aisle for the Eucharist. The man in front of him, J. T. Townsend, face like a big platter, was on the city council. That nonsense over waterfront ordinances, and Townsend had taken sides against Dawson. He would put it from his mind. He would not judge; Townsend was a man like himself. Townsend struggled, like everyone else. Humility and penance.

The line of congregants moved slowly, approaching the rail. When Dawson reached the bishop, he met Dawson's eyes, formal and impersonal. In daily life the bishop was a friend, but now, here, he was distant and remote, changed by his office. He was tall, pale, with bleached skin, a long bony nose. He raised his hand with its darkened thumb and Dawson bowed his head. The bishop touched his forehead. "Memento, homo, quia pulvis es, et in pulverem reverteris," the bishop murmured. *Remember that you are dust, and to dust you shall return.* Dawson closed his eyes as he received the mark, trying to dissolve himself into the spirit.

All day he wore the sign of approaching death.

———·—·———

BEFORE DINNER he asked Hélène to come into the library. He stood with his back to the bay window, and when she came in he asked her to close the paneled doors. She drew them shut and turned back to face him. The closing of the doors made her serious. Her face was sober, and she folded her hands at her waist.

Dawson spoke in French. "I wanted you to come in because I've received some information that I need to ask you about."

"Oui, monsieur." Hélène seemed mystified.

"I've heard that you've been seeing a man," Dawson said.

"A man?" Hélène widened her eyes as though she hardly knew the word.

"A married man." He was irritated by the widened eyes, the repetition.

On either side of the doorway hung portraits of the children: Warrington, mournful in a long green coat; Ethel, fey, in a swooping straw hat, a pink ribbon around her waist.

"Monsieur." Hélène shook her head.

The letter might be untrue, of course.

"Here you are in my charge," Dawson said. "I take the place of your father. I am responsible for your safety and your honor."

She watched him, her hands clasped.

"If you have formed an alliance with an honorable man, Madame Dawson and I will be happy to have you married from this house."

Hélène ducked her chin.

"But if you're seeing someone unsuitable," Dawson continued, "someone already married, you must stop. It will destroy your reputation and cast a shadow upon this household. I cannot permit it."

Still she said nothing.

He raised his voice slightly. "Do you understand?"

"Oui, monsieur," she said. "I understand."

"You must reply," Dawson said.

Hélène shook her head. "I don't know what you could have heard. I would never put your family under any dishonor. I respect them too much."

He didn't want to bully her. He couldn't remember where, exactly, she'd come from. The agency had been in Lausanne, but she'd have had references from another family. European or English? Sarah would know, but he didn't want to tell her yet. The letter might be untrue, he didn't want to raise suspicion.

"You have never met with a married man?" he asked.

Hélène shook her head. "You may trust me, monsieur," she said. "I would never give you reason to do otherwise."

"Thank you, Hélène," he said. "You understand that you must tell me the truth. If you are not telling the truth, I will learn of it."

"Je vous dis la verité," she said. *I am telling you the truth.*

She went upstairs, feeling exalted. She had stood up to the charge, she had not given way. She was like Joan of Arc, though she couldn't remember exactly what Joan had done. Stood up to kings, defended her honor, was that it? Refused to yield. Hélène felt a kinship with Joan. Though she would not go so far as to be burned at the stake.

McDow would be furious.

She called the children for dinner. "Hurry up," she said. "Your father waits for you." She used "your father" like a title, like "the king." They hurried down; he didn't like to be kept waiting.

At the table he asked them about the day.

"Ethel-pet," he said, "tell me about school."

Ethel gave him a considering look. Her eyes were like Sarah's. "We have a new girl called Eleanor. She has kidskin boots cut low on the sides." She made a curve in the air to show the shape.

"And who is this elegant Eleanor?" asked Dawson. "Where does she come from, this Eleanor-of-the-low-boots?"

"Her name is Eleanor Legendre and I don't know where she comes from. She has long thick curly black hair. She's beautiful," Ethel said slowly. "I love her."

"She must come from somewhere," Dawson said.

"But I don't know where," said Ethel. "She has long hair, down to here." She set her hand against her forearm.

"Ah!" said Dawson. "She comes from the Country of Long Hair. Your mother probably knows her parents. You may even be related."

"I'm going to have hair as long as Mamma's." Ethel tipped her head back, so her hair hung down farther. "Down to my ankles."

"You might," Dawson said.

"I will," Ethel told him.

"You can't choose, pet. You might have hair that long, but it's rare," Dawson said. "No one else in her family does."

"Not Aunt Miriam? Aunt Lilly?" Ethel asked. "No one?"

Dawson shook his head, proud.

"Well, I will." Ethel pointed her chin straight up and put her hand behind her back to feel how far down her hair hung. "I'll never cut it."

"It might be as long as your mama's," Dawson said. "But it might not. People's hair make their own decisions. I couldn't grow a mustache when I was in the war, though I wanted to." He touched his mustache.

"You couldn't?" asked Warrington, shocked.

"Everyone had one but me," Dawson said. "I felt very left out. I felt it made me look young."

"But you were young," said Ethel. "Weren't you?"

"I didn't think so," Dawson said. "I thought I was very grown-up."

"Did anyone else think so?" Warrington asked.

"No one," said Dawson. "But finally the mustache came, and then they knew."

"I'm going to be an explorer," said Warrington.

"Aha," said Dawson. "Not a pirate?"

Warrington shook his head. "An explorer. Isaac is coming with me to help with the horses."

Isaac, white-coated, leaned over Warrington with a dish. He held one hand behind his back. When Warrington said his name, Isaac nodded. His eyes nearly vanished when he smiled. His skin was a smooth light brown.

"Is that right, Isaac?" Dawson asked. "Are you leaving me to go off with Warrington? Are you taking Brownie?"

"That's right, Captain."

"And Bruno," Warrington said.

"Bruno!" Dawson said. "My dog?"

Delighted, Warrington nodded. "You'll just have to manage, Papa."

Dawson laughed: this was what Sarah told them.

Ethel announced, "I got a bad grade in arithmetic." She hoped this was a good time to say it, while her father was laughing.

"I'm sorry, pet."

"Will Mamma be cross?"

"I hope not."

For some reason they'd all been speaking English. Hélène looked from one to the other. Dawson thought of her in the library, her hands clasped. He wondered if she was telling the truth.

"Alors," he said, "on a fini."

Ethel pushed back her chair, but Warrington carefully folded his napkin and slid it into the silver ring marked with his initials. He liked ceremony.

———·———

HÉLÈNE CARRIED THE salad bowl out to the kitchen. She was in charge of the complex ritual of salad, tearing the leaves of lettuce, making the vinaigrette. And the instruments, the oiled wooden bowl, the silver-handled ebony fork and spoon.

Celia looked up when she came in, irritated at once. "Don't set that here," she said. "Take it to the scullery." She was slicing potatoes, the juicy white flesh bright against her red fingers.

Hélène went into the scullery without answering. She washed the bowl, then brought it back to the kitchen.

"How did the captain like that beef?" asked Celia.

Hélène shook her head. "He did not say about the beef." She would give Celia nothing.

Celia tightened her mouth.

Jane called from the scullery. "He ate every morsel and licked his plate."

Hélène said, "Before dinner, le Capitaine Dawson asked to speak to me in private. In the parlor."

Celia narrowed her eyes. "What about?"

"He had heard some talk," Hélène said.

"What talk?" Celia asked.

"He want to know if I am seeing a married man."

Jane came in with a stack of wet plates. She set them down at the other end of the table.

"What did you tell him?" She sat down on a stool and began to dry the plates.

"I tell him he was wrong," Hélène said, as though this was obvious.

"You told him he was wrong?" Jane repeated. "He was righter than the rain. We see you over there every night. With that doctor. Do you think we have no eyes in our heads?"

"The captain is wrong to ask me," Hélène said. "What I do is my own affair. I do nothing wrong."

"We don't know that," said Celia.

"I am saying it," said Hélène.

"And how would you know what's right and what's wrong?" Jane said. "You're French."

Hélène made a sound of contempt. "You are jealous," she said. "The doctor is my friend. I have done nothing wrong."

"Suppose the captain knew how often you see the doctor?" asked Celia. "Suppose he knew you brought him into this house yesterday? Would he say that was right or wrong?"

"It is none of his affair," said Hélène. "We did nothing wrong. We talk only."

"None of his affair?" Jane's face had gone pink, the freckles nearly invisible in the rush of color that rose from throat to hairline. "It's his house. I think he'll think it's his business, you bringing that doctor inside."

"It is also my house," said Hélène grandly.

"It most certainly is not your house," said Jane. "It most certainly is not."

"It is where I live," Hélène said.

"It's the captain's house," said Jane. "You brought in a man who was plotting to murder his wife!"

"This is not true," Hélène said, contemptuous. "This is talk. You know nothing." She stood with her arms at her sides, her hands in fists.

Celia set down her knife. "Then why did his wife leave him?"

"They are not happy," said Hélène, prim. "He is not happy with his wife. He has never loved her."

"His wife left because his brother was going to murder the father and then he was going to murder his wife," said Jane. "Everyone in Charleston knows."

"Then everyone is wrong," said Hélène. "No one knows what happened. She has come back. It is all talk."

Jane folded her arms. "If you don't stop seeing that man," she said, "we'll tell Mrs. Dawson you brought him into the house. Now you've lied to the captain. It's a disgrace you are to the family."

Hélène made the noise of contempt. "Madame Dawson will not believe you."

"We'll all tell her." Celia set her hands on her hips. "We'll tell her together. Isaac, too. We've all seen you."

"You will not," Hélène said. "You will not say one word. I will tell Madame to fire you. Every one."

Isaac stood in the doorway, his face troubled. He lived here, with his family. All his children. He said nothing. He trusted none of these women.

"Madame Dawson loves me," Hélène said. "She will believe me. I am like her daughter." She narrowed her eyes. "If you say one word, I'll tell her to fire all of you." She looked at Isaac. "You, Isaac."

Celia stood by the table, her face pink. She stared at Hélène with dislike and said something under her breath.

"What do you say?" Hélène demanded, fierce.

Celia didn't answer. She bent again over the potatoes.

Jane stared at Hélène. Hélène turned on her heel and went out into the backyard.

It was cold, and the air made her face tingle. She felt excited, as though she were rising up in the world. The captain had no business asking her about her private life. She was an adult, in charge of her affairs. The doctor was in love with her. He was going to leave his wife. She was at the center of everything.

She had done nothing. She was honest and loyal. She thought of the Maid of Orleans, who rode a white horse and led an army.

That night, after the children were in bed, Dawson still at the office, Hélène wrapped herself in one of Madame's shawls and went outside. He was waiting in his garden. She saw him standing in the shadows as she opened the gate. She slipped through and came up to him, smiling in the darkness.

"You're late," he said.

He didn't touch her. Usually he stepped close as soon as she arrived, putting his arm around her.

"It's the children," said Hélène. She could see that he was angry. "What is it?"

"'What is it?'" McDow repeated, mockingly. "You know what it is."

Hélène shook her head. "I don't know."

"I saw you in there." McDow said.

Hélène thought of her conversation in the kitchen. Was he angry that she'd called him just a friend?

"In there?" She nodded at the kitchen building.

"With the captain," McDow said.

He was close to her. She felt the heat coming from him; he was furious.

"The captain?"

"Don't repeat what I say. What were you doing with him, in that room? I saw you."

"What room?"

"That room." He motioned with his head. "Right there."

When he slid his fingers down the curve of her hip she felt a long charge run up and down her body. Now she felt his heat, but it was a different sort: rage. Her body became alert, attentive.

"You should not look through other people's windows," Hélène said.

"I'll look wherever I like," McDow said. "I saw you close the door and stand in there alone with him."

"He is my employer," Hélène said. "I have no choice. I must talk to him if he wishes."

"He has no right to say anything to you," said McDow. "I don't want you going into a room with him. I want you to come away with me. I'm going to divorce my wife and marry you."

"But when will you divorce your wife?" Hélène asked.

"She's moved out," McDow said. "The first step."

"But why did she?" Hélène said.

"I told her I didn't love her. I told her I loved you."

"This is not what I hear," said Hélène.

"I don't care what you hear," McDow said. He paused. "What did you hear?"

"I hear she is back." She didn't quite have the nerve to mention the murder plot.

"She moved out because I told her I would divorce her. I never loved her. Look at her! She's fat. She's a German pig. She has hair in her ears. I married her for her money." He paused. "She came back because she wants me to change my mind, but I won't. I'm going to divorce her in North Carolina, I told you."

"But she is not the woman in your house," said Hélène. "Perhaps it's that other woman you must divorce."

McDow laughed, pleased. "Julia's an old friend. Don't worry about her."

He put his arm around her shoulder and pulled her close. He put the back of his hand against her neck and stroked her with his knuckles. "She's furious, you know. I'll toss her away. That's what you'd like, isn't it?"

Hélène shrugged. "I don't have a feeling about her."

"Yes, you do have a feeling," McDow said. He squeezed her shoulder hard. "And she has a feeling about you. She's crazy jealous of you. Green-eyed."

"Jealous of me! I don't know why," said Hélène. This thrilled her. She had no idea why Julia would have green eyes. "I don't know her."

"She knows you. She knows I want to marry you."

"First," said Hélène, "you must divorce your wife." She unwrapped his hand from her shoulder.

McDow grabbed her again. "First you must stop going into a room alone with Dawson. What does he say to you?"

"Madame Dawson is away," Hélène said. "I am in charge. He was giving me directions for the children."

"What kind of directions?" McDow was angry again. "Why did he shut the door? Does he touch you?"

Hélène moved restively. "Of course not. He is a man of honor. A gentleman."

McDow stared at her in the darkness. He was pressed hard against her. She felt him ready to hurt her.

"If the captain touches you I will kill him," he said, and then repeated it. The sentence made him feel powerful. "I will kill him." Alcohol was on his breath.

"I must go. They will miss me." She didn't want to come into the house smelling of drink.

"Captain Dawson will miss you."

"The children," she said.

"I think he is in love with you," said McDow.

"You are wrong," said Hélène.

"You are lying," said McDow.

"I am not," said Hélène. She thought of Joan.

He pulled her close again, and whispered against her hair. "Are you lying to me?" He closed his fingers on her wrist like a handcuff.

"I must go," Hélène said, and pulled away.

"I'm coming tomorrow morning," McDow said, "when you get back from school. I want to come inside."

"Good night." She wrapped her shawl around her shoulders. He was drunk. She moved away. He reached for her arm, but she pulled free, and he staggered a little.

The moonlight drifted down through the branches, making pale patches on the ground; his face was deep in shadow. The doctor's breathing was slow and thick.

"Good night," she said, wanting something. But he said nothing, and she went back out through the gate.

She slipped into the house. Upstairs she went through Warrington's room (he was curled into a ball, asleep) to her own. She turned on the lamp and the room sprang into light: her bed with the embroidered coverlet, the little chair. She took off Madame's shawl. Her heart was still pounding. She looked in the mirror: her fine eyes were flashing. The doctor had no business speaking to her like this. She folded the shawl. She did not meet him to be insulted. She was not a liar. She had nothing to hide. Both the captain and the doctor accused her of lying.

She sat down on her green chair. The doctor had given her many bouquets of flowers, and a book. The book was in English, so she couldn't read it, but it was prettily bound in dark green, with gold-stamped covers. And he'd given her a gold watch, which she kept in a small wooden box. She took it out to look at it. On the back was an inscription: *Ma cher Marie, from your Thomas.*

It should have been "chère." The mistake made her feel superior. She traced the words with her finger: real gold. She held it to her ear to hear the tiny, impossibly rapid ticking. It was Swiss, from her country. Fast, reliable, perfect.

She was a good woman, honorable, but her life had split in two. This part was none of the captain's business: she had her own life now. A doctor, a man of importance, was in love with her. He was ready to change everything for her. He was ready to leave his wife. She was powerful, she exerted an irresistible spell over him. The captain had nothing to do with this. She thought again of Joan of Arc, who was becoming an old friend.

———•———

WHEN SHE CAME HOME from school the next morning he was there on the sidewalk.

"Take me inside," he said.

"It's not good today," she said.

"Take me inside." His face was red. He glared at her, furious. She led him up the steps.

Inside she went into the little study off the dining room.

"Tell me what he said to you."

"Who?" she said, though she knew.

McDow gestured with his head. "Him," he said. "The captain. Le capitaine."

"I've told you," she said.

"Tell me again." McDow stood with his legs spread, his head thrust forward.

"He say I cannot see you again," Hélène said.

"But you are seeing me again," McDow said, grinning. His teeth were bright with saliva. There was a small gap between the two front ones. "Why is that?"

"I do what I like," Hélène said, tossing her head like Joan.

He walked up and down, looking at the books. He put out his hand and ran his fingers along the spines.

"Captain Brains," he said. "Captain Braggart. He's no more a captain than I am." He turned to look at her. "He has no business telling you what to do. I'll see what he says to me."

"You must not speak to him," Hélène said.

"I'll decide that," McDow said, raising his voice. "If he thinks he can tell me what to do I'll fix him. I'll take care of his business."

"Business?" she asked. "At the newspaper?"

"I'll take care of him." McDow glared at her.

She frowned. There were so many English words she didn't know. "'Take care of him?'" she repeated. *Il le gardera?*

He nodded.

31.

March 8–11, 1889. Charleston

SHE RECOGNIZED HIS footsteps on the platform before she saw him. She watched from the window, and when he appeared she gave a little wave. When he reached her car he stepped inside, and then he was with her, his lovely smell, starch and wool and delicious skin.

"You're here," he said.

She took his arm and they walked toward the station. Beside them the train panted heavily.

"The children are mad with excitement," Dawson said. "They've made you a surprise. You'll have to act astonished."

"I will be," she said. "I don't know what it is."

"You'll see."

"I missed you all." Now it seemed impossible that she could have left them, even for a day.

He put his gloved hand over hers, and she felt a flush of affection, and admiration for his elegant gloves, his polished boots, his lustrous new overcoat. Gratitude for his meeting her, taking charge of her luggage. For the way he put his hand over hers.

The day was cool and overcast, so the top was up on the phaeton, making a dim little private space. Dawson drove. Sarah talked in snatches, telling him things she'd forgotten, or were too digressive or complicated to put in the letters. Dawson listened. A fresh breeze moved against their faces. Clouds moved swiftly overhead, like big dim landscapes shifting across the sky.

"Now tell me about the children," Sarah said. "Tell me everything that happened while I was gone."

"Ethel has a new friend," he said. "Who has special boots. Warrington plans to be an explorer."

"An explorer! He wouldn't survive for a moment. With his chest." She made a clicking sound. "I should never have gone away. What else? Has Hélène been helpful?"

Hélène had been helpful, he said. "Can you do something about Jane's boots? They creak like a sailing ship."

"Jane's boots?"

"They're so noisy," he said. "They drown us out at the table. Buy her some new ones."

"If I bought Jane new boots the others would have tantrums," Sarah said. "Celia would quit."

"But do something about the boots, for my sanity."

Near the corner of King and Calhoun Streets Chief Golden was walking with another officer. Dawson reined in the horse.

"Chief Golden," Dawson said, "I wonder if you'd be able to stop by my office later this afternoon."

"Is it urgent?" Golden asked. "Would tomorrow afternoon be all right instead?"

"Exceedingly so," Dawson said. "Thank you, Chief."

He lifted the reins. As they drove off he apologized to Sarah for the interruption, but didn't explain.

At Citadel Green there were children running in ragged circles. They were chasing a lean spaniel, who dodged and spun, his tongue hanging out. In one corner stood a cluster of palmettos, dark corrugated trunks and shaggy heads. As Dawson drove past, he nodded to them as though they were friends.

"Why do you like palmettos so much?" Sarah asked.

"I'd never seen any before I came here," he said. "They were so exotic. It always tickled me, to think this was my new country. They reminded me how far I'd come."

"We should have one," said Sarah. "I'll give you one for your birthday. It'll make you a real Charlestonian."

"Aren't I already?" he asked. "Twenty years." He thought of Courtenay's note.

"That's not so long, here. There are people who think of us as newcomers."

"Everyone in America is a newcomer."

"True. But some families have been here for several hundred years."

"Ah, now you're condescending," he said. "Because my family made the unforgivable error of not coming here two hundred years ago, when yours arrived."

"All I mean," she said, "is that people in Charleston go back a considerable while."

"Going back to the war is sufficient," said Dawson. "I think we've established our credentials here." He tapped Brownie, who swung into a slow jog. "But all right. Let's send for the tree man. Let's order a palmetto. While we're at it, let's replace the trees we lost in the earthquake."

Sarah looked at him. "Is this the moment?" she asked. "Can we afford to spend money on new trees?"

But he couldn't afford to believe that the way he'd always lived was over.

"Exactly the moment," he said.

——•——

SARAH'S TRUNK STOOD OPEN. The air bloomed faintly from the sachets tucked along the sides, sweet and sharp, clove and citrus.

Dawson settled into her striped slipper chair, which was too small for him.

"You're going to break it, you know," Sarah said.

"I've sat in it for years."

"It's stayed the same size," she said. "You've grown."

"Only more prosperous," he said comfortably. "Now, tell me all. Tell me about Jem's new wife."

"Frances," she said. "She's very nice. She has big eyes and big cheeks. I like her. She's sweet to Jem."

"And what about him? Is he going to try farming again?"

She didn't want to talk about Jem's plans. "What's the children's surprise?"

"You'll see," Dawson said.

"Is it a flower?" She turned to him, smiling.

One afternoon he'd come home to find the children hovering on the verandah, Bruno beside them open-mouthed, wagging. As he started up the steps they started calling out. "Papa, look around! Look around!"

"What am I looking for?"

"Just look!" shouted Warrington. At the top of the steps was a century plant, an aloe, meant to bloom every hundred years. But apparently it had chosen that moment. Its spiky leaves were dotted with red berries.

Dawson clapped his brow, beneath his hat. Warrington hopped on one foot. Bruno opened his mouth, shifting from foot to foot in his excitement.

"Good heavens," Dawson said.

"The century plant has flowered!" shouted Warrington. "Amazing!"

"A miracle!" said Ethel, then clapped her hand over her mouth, remembering: "miracle" was only to be used about the Church.

They had taken the buds from a red pepper bush and set them along the fleshy spiny leaves of the plant.

Dawson laughed, and the children came to stand on either side of him. He put his hands on their small warm heads. He felt their fine scratchy hair, the heft of their skulls, their heat.

"Remarkable!" he said. "I never thought I'd live long enough."

Now he laughs, remembering.

"No," he says. "Not a flower."

Sarah smoothed the wrinkles from a dress and carried it to the armoire. As she opened the door the shadowy interior appeared. Was it a man, crouching inside? Black jacket and striped trousers, a hat balanced at the top. Her breath caught for a moment.

"That's the surprise," Dawson said. "It's meant to be me. They thought you'd be surprised to find me in your closet."

"But you're sitting here," she said. "How could I think you'd be in there at the same time?"

"I cannot explain the reasoning processes of your children."

"My children," said Sarah. She took down the hat; the man disintegrated.

"Tell me more. How is Miriam?" Dawson asked. She was a favorite of his.

"She wants to become a stenographer." She said the word "stenographer" like "murderer."

"Good for her!"

She turned. "How can you say that? It's so unseemly."

"People from good families do all sorts of unseemly things," he said. "Miriam married a man who drinks."

"Which I begged her not to do," said Sarah tartly, as though that proved her point.

"But now she's shed him," he said. "She'll have a good life on her own. This will make her independent."

"So you think she should do it."

"I think it's perfectly sensible," he said. "I have a stenographer. It's the way of the future."

"Spending her day in an office full of men. Taking money for her work."

"You took money for your writing," said Dawson. "So does George Eliot."

"I needed the money," Sarah said. "And no one knew it was me."

"So does Miriam need it. And a great many people knew it was you," Dawson said. "You were quite popular, Mr. Fowler."

Sarah said nothing. She'd been secretly flattered that her thoughts should have reached other people's minds.

"Women should earn money if they need to," Dawson said. "Why not?"

"Miriam wants to send Lucille to the conservatory in Ohio, to study voice." Sarah looked at him. "I'm afraid you'll be asked to pay."

"I'm very fond of Miriam," he said.

It pleased him to pay for education, as his aunt Dawson had done. He'd sent money home for Tessie's tuition. After the war it had been his turn, and he'd helped out the Raines family for years. He'd sent Nathaniel's granddaughter, Susan, to college. He wondered what the Oberlin tuition was.

O'Hare's long face came suddenly into his mind, with an expression so challenging it was as though he'd spoken out loud: he's leaving for the *World*. Dawson felt the silver knife twist.

"What is it?" Sarah paused, holding a stack of shawls.

"Siegling turned me down for a loan," he said.

"Is he mad?" she asked. "It's his paper, too. How can he consider letting it fail?"

It was the first time she'd used that word. She thought it possible, then.

"What would you think of moving to St. Louis?"

She set the shawls in the armoire and turned to look at him. "St. Louis."

He handed her the letter. "It's an honor to be asked. I don't know what he'd offer."

She read it. "So you could walk away from all this. If it's a good offer you could pay off everything and walk away."

"Would I like being an employee?" he said. "After owning my own paper for twenty years?"

"You could ask for an interest." Sarah sat down on the bed. "Make it part of the negotiations."

"Yes," said Dawson. He steepled his hands and set them against his lips. "I thought I'd made my life here."

"We all thought that," she said. "We can all make them somewhere else. I thought I'd made my life in Baton Rouge."

"You wouldn't want to leave this house," he said.

"Frank," she said. "Wherever you want. Really."

Dawson rubbed his face. "It would mean I'd failed here."

"It would not," Sarah said. "Any more than it meant you'd failed in London before you came here. Or failed in Richmond before you came to Charleston. It would just be part of your career."

"I think O'Hare will quit," he said. "That will make three."

"Ingrates!" Sarah said. "Especially O'Hare. He owes everything to you. Walk out on all of them. Siegling, Swinton, O'Hare, all of them. Where would they be without you?"

"St. Louis is more German than French," he said.

Now Sarah looked doubtful.

"German language, beer companies. Big dark stone buildings."

"You didn't tell me that," she said.

They stayed upstairs all afternoon. Later, when the office called to ask when he was coming in, Dawson said, "In the morning." He didn't want to see O'Hare. He got back into bed and drew the covers over them both.

MOST SATURDAY MORNINGS Dawson went to the office, but that day he told the children he'd stay at home to fix the telephore, a contraption he'd set up the week before. It was a cross between a telephone and a funicular. He'd strung a rope from the front porch of their house to the back porch of the house on the corner of Bull and Rutledge, where little Marie Lafitte lived. Dawson had attached a basket to the rope, and all week the children had hauled it back and forth, sending notes and calling out to each other what was in them. Now the children wanted a bigger basket.

"You shall have it," Dawson said. "I've got a new rope."

"I'll tell Marie," Ethel said, sliding off her chair. "May I be excused." She was already gone.

"Put on your bonnet," Sarah said.

"There's no sun!" Ethel said.

"There's always sun," Sarah said, "and you only have one complexion. You mustn't get freckles. I don't want you looking like a servant."

Warrington set his napkin in the ring. "May-I-be-excused," he said, all in one word.

"You may," Dawson said, and they vanished.

"Put on coats," Sarah called.

The second-floor balcony looked out onto Bull Street. Dawson knelt by the railing and began drawing in the old rope, hand over hand, to find the splice. Bruno stood beside him, wagging his heavy tail. Hélène was in the doorway, watching.

The air was cool, but spring was making itself known in Charleston. The air was freshening, the lawn starting to turn bright. The tight-fisted buds were starting to open their fingers.

The Lafittes' house stood on the corner, facing Rutledge. It stood side by side with the doctor's, both houses backing onto the Dawsons' front drive.

The children were already out on the Lafittes' porch. They leaned over the railing, calling.

"What?" Dawson put a hand behind his ear.

"We want it strong enough to carry a basket!" called Ethel.

"A mascot?" he called back.

"What did you say, Papa?" called Warrington.

"Eh?" called Dawson.

"*Food in a basket.*" Ethel set her hands at her mouth like a megaphone.

"Send Bruno?" asked Dawson. "As a mascot?"

The children fell about. Warrington shouted, "Bruno!" Hearing his name the dog pushed close, stepping on Frank's legs. Dawson asked Sarah to coil the new rope, which lay in a thick brown snarl by the door. Sarah tried to lift it, but it was heavy and she was afraid she'd hurt her back. She turned to Hélène, who was crouching, for some reason, in the doorway. When Sarah asked for help, Hélène moved grudgingly forward. Still crouching, she began to coil the rope.

A fence ran along the Dawsons' driveway, marking the property line. Beyond it were the back gardens of the houses on Rutledge. In the back of the McDows' yard, near the fence, stood a man holding a watering can. He was still, his eyes raised, fixed on the Dawsons.

Hélène crouched, trying to coil the rope without being seen. She didn't want McDow's eyes on her. She could see from his posture he was in a state. He was staring up at them. He held the watering can like an axe. Fear quickened her heartbeat. She tugged at the heavy coils.

She looked up, hoping McDow hadn't heard. But he called her Marie. She stayed crouched.

"Please pass the knife," Dawson said in French. He was kneeling at the railing. His old bowie knife lay on a table by the door. Hélène handed it to him, the long blade gleaming.

"Pas comme ça!" said Dawson. *Not like that!* "You must always pass a knife by the blade. You must hold it by the blade, you give the other person the handle. C'est le code ancien de la chevalerie," he told her. *The ancient code of chivalry.* "It's a matter of courtesy. You must offer the other person the chance to attack you."

"But I will not attack you, Captain," she said.

"I hope not," Dawson said cheerfully. He began to splice the new rope onto the old, tying and braiding the strands.

"I want to ride in the basket," Warrington called.

"He's too big, Papa," called Ethel. "Tell him he can't."

"I'm going to ride in it first," Dawson called to them. "I'll be the test."

Hélène pulled at the heavy coils, her head down. He was watching them. She could feel his eyes, voracious.

THAT AFTERNOON, in his office, Dawson heard Chief Golden's ponderous step on the stairs. He stood up to receive him.

"Chief Golden."

"Captain Dawson." Golden was slightly out of breath. He was double-chinned, with blue jowls and a red mouth. He took out his handkerchief and ran it meticulously across his upper lip. He sat down facing the desk.

Dawson handed him the letter. "This came last week."

Golden read it slowly. "D'you know who wrote it?"

"No idea," said Dawson.

"It is always an interested party," said Golden. "Maybe the man's wife."

"We don't know who the man is."

"What would you like me to do?" asked Golden.

"Have the young woman followed," Dawson said. "See if she's meeting anyone."

Golden nodded. "We can do that."

"She leaves our house every morning at about nine fifteen, to take the children to school," Dawson said.

"I'll have someone there on Monday," Golden said. He leaned forward, setting his hands on his knees to push himself up.

"Ask your man to be discreet," said Dawson. "If the letter's false, I don't want her shamed."

32.

March 11, 1889. Charleston

AFTER SUPPER Dawson sat at his desk, writing. Sarah was in the red chair, mending a torn paisley shawl. The lamp cast a glow on the shawl, on its rich ochres and scarlet. She'd torn it, catching it on a door handle.

"What are you writing about?" Sarah held the shawl up to the light to see the tear.

"Pickens."

Of course he was. The whole state was talking about Pickens County.

Last year, right after Christmas, a thirteen-year-old girl called Lula Sherman had been at home one afternoon with her eight-year-old sister. Their parents were sharecroppers, and they were both out just then, her father at work, her mother helping a sick neighbor. A local man called Manse Waldrop, who worked on a neighbor's farm, was seen out walking near the Shermans' house. People noticed him because he had a shotgun but no dog. That was a strange thing, because you couldn't hunt without a dog. Waldrop came to the Sherman house and knocked on the door, and the girls let him inside. They were wearing their new Christmas dresses. It was a small place, only a two-room cabin, so the younger sister saw everything. When Lula put up her arms against Waldrop he used the stock of the gun, battering her arms and face. Then he pushed her down on the floor beside the flour barrel and lay on top of her. She had stopped making any sound by then. When he stood up she lay still. She was bleeding. She'd been torn inside. To stop the bloody seeping, Waldrop stuffed a wad of cotton up inside her before he left. When her parents came home Lula was too ashamed to tell them what had happened, though she was bruised and in pain. The back of her head was pale with flour dust. She said nothing that night. The dirty cotton stuffed inside her was breeding infection, and her bloodstream was turning septic. The next day she was clogged with poison, her veins thick with it. Failing, Lula told her parents what had happened. She died that afternoon.

At the inquest the doctor declared criminal assault. Manse Waldrop was brought into the courtroom and Lula's sister pointed at him. That's the man, she said. Waldrop was arrested. By the time everything was over it was late. Some people urged the sheriff to wait until the next day, but he was determined to get Waldrop in jail. He and a deputy set out with Waldrop, his hands tied behind him, in a mule-drawn buggy. The sheriff and Waldrop sat on the seat; the deputy said he'd walk. It was midnight when they started. They hadn't gone a mile before a man stepped out of the darkness and took the mule by the bridle. You can't make a mule go if someone's holding the bridle; they were stopped dead. There were six men with guns. They told the sheriff they were taking Manse Waldrop. They made him climb down from the wagon. In the morning he was found hanging from a tree.

Lynching was common enough. It was rough justice, handed down from the old vigilante system, when the people took the law into their own hands. It had something to do with the Border countries, the dangerous frontier between England and Scotland, something to do with the code of honor. People were lynched for murder, for arson, for any serious offense, but especially for what the press called "the usual crime": the rape of a white woman by a black man. That was considered an abomination, and punishment for it was considered outside the law, a necessary act. Which meant that no one was ever prosecuted for lynching. In the courts, lynching seemed not to exist. It drifted through the legal system like mist.

Until the Pickens case. The thing about Lula Sherman was that she was black, and her attacker was white. Five of Waldrop's six attackers were black. This had never happened, black men lynching a white man. For the first time, lynchers were being prosecuted by the law, and four of them had been sentenced to death. One of the lynchers was Cato Sherman, Lula's father.

This had caused a ruckus. A petition for clemency had roared around the state, gathering three thousand signatures. The first trial had been declared a mistrial. At the second trial a new verdict was reached: two colored men were still condemned to death, but Cato Sherman, two other colored men, and the white man would all go free. The press was divided on the issue. The *Greenville News* called it outrageous to punish black men for a crime that was committed with impunity by white men.

"What will you say?" Sarah was making small stitches, coaxing the fabric across the tear. The lamp cast highlights on her hair, on the ruffle on her shoulder, her pale hands.

"That I disagree with the *Greenville News*." Dawson enjoyed disagreeing with other editors; he liked to set the record straight.

"Why?" asked Sarah. "Certainly they're right."

"This is a chance to raise the issue of lynching," Dawson said. "All lynchers flout the law. No one should be above it."

"And so?"

"Someone has to take the consequences," he said. "If there are white lynchers, there will be black ones. Whites set the example by lynching in the first place, and now blacks are following it. If the black men are punished, it will establish a precedent. And that will deter the whites."

"So you think they should all be hanged, as a matter of principle?" asked Sarah. "Frank, this man is her father. His daughter has died."

"The father's been acquitted," he said. "He won't be hanged. But these men have committed a serious crime. There must be consequences." He looked at her. "You understand that. The rule of law."

She said nothing.

"Lynching is barbaric," he said. "People can't take the law into their own hands."

Sarah frowned, looking down at the shawl, slipping the silver needle in and out.

"Well, Waldrop should have been punished," she said. "He killed that girl."

"Punished by law," Dawson said, "not by lynching."

Sarah didn't answer. She thought he should be punished not only for murder but for the other crime, the one she wouldn't name. The idea of it was horrifying. The mixing of the races was an abomination.

She thought of her black maid, Mary, who'd left service when she became too pregnant to work. After the baby was born, Mary came back to show her baby to the household. Ethel came running upstairs to find Sarah. *Come down to the kitchen,* she said. *Mary's brought the baby!*

Mary was sitting at the table with the servants, a basket set before her. As Sarah came in Mary stood up to greet her, embarrassed, deferential. She was smiling, but she kept her eyes cast down. The baby was in the basket. It was a sweltering day, the air thick and humid, but the basket was covered in a heavy veil. *Take off the veil,* Sarah told her. *It's too hot for that.*

Mary didn't answer. She was a pretty young woman, long-limbed and graceful. She didn't look at Sarah. After a moment she lifted the veil.

Sarah leaned in to see the baby's tiny face, soft and rosy. Rosy pink: the baby was white. Sarah felt the shock of it in her body; it was like the sight of a crime. The baby raised her tiny pale fists and beat them in the air. Mary's eyes were lowered; Sarah couldn't speak.

Sarah went on setting tiny stitches into the shawl. Dawson went on writing, his pen making a quiet rustling sound. He wrote fast, crossing out phrases, writing over them, his pen hurrying across the page. When Sarah had drawn the torn fabric back together she finished off the stitching, then took out her sewing scissors and snipped the thread. The scissors were vermeil, and in the shape of a stork. Her mother had given them to her. She held up the shawl against the light: the hole was gone. She folded the shawl into a square.

She went over to Dawson, at his desk.

"I'm going to bed," she said. She stood beside his chair.

"You don't agree with me," he said.

"I don't," she said. "It's horrible."

"Lynching is a horrible crime. I want to have it banned."

"It's still horrible to advocate hanging those men," she said.

"It's not that I want them hanged," he said.

"I know," she said. "It's principle. Tell me something. Are we moving to St. Louis?"

Dawson leaned back in his chair. "It seems harder and harder to think of leaving here."

"During the war we had to leave everything," Sarah said. "Over and over. We had to walk out of the house, not knowing if we'd ever come back. The day of the bombardment I let my canary out of its cage." She remembered him fluttering up to the rafters on the galerie. "And when we finally went to Brother's, when we arrived in New Orleans we had to swear allegiance to the Union. Which was a foreign country."

He waited.

"You left your country to come here," she said. "If we leave here it will be all right." She put out her hand and smoothed his hair. "We'll be all right. We can always learn German."

"We're not leaving," he said, as if her touch had made him certain. "We'll stay here, fight it out. When we leave it will be for France."

"All right, then," she said.

She went into the other room and he heard her moving about. The creak of her chair as she sat to take off her shoes. The click of the armoire door opening, the tiny thud as it closed. She would be in her nightgown now, voluminous and white. Taking down her hair, braiding it for the night. Then the metal creak of the bedsprings. She called in to him.

"Good night, chuck-chuck." She nearly whispered, so the children wouldn't wake.

"Chuck-chuck," he whispered back.

Dawson's pen strode across the page. "Lynching taints every man who acquiesces in it," he wrote. "It has proved wholly ineffectual to prevent the crime for which it is its punishment."

The house was silent. The night had closed around it like a soft fist. The children were nearby; he could feel them sleeping. The dark pressed against the window, and a screech owl gave its ghostly whinny. He was alone, awake, the steward of the sleeping house. It was like night watch, looking out on the moonlit ocean as the ship slid through the heaving surge.

He thought of Ethel, the way she used to pose in the staircase niche. There were two of those niches hollowed out in the stairwell. The children used to stand in them like little statues. Ethel stood on tiptoe, arms raised, head lifted. Her raised arms were so thin, like matchsticks. She was the same age as Lula Sherman.

He felt he was fending off something.

"The world is horrified by a black man attacking a white woman," he wrote, "but not by a white man attacking a colored woman. This is ugly but it is true." He meant the white world.

The owl called again, nearer now. Who cooks, who cooks for you, she called. He must set this straight, this wrongheaded notion that the Pickens lynchers should go free.

"There is no safety for a community outside of the law, under any circumstances."

In the darkness he felt the world was turning, the light moving away from him. He felt the steady loss of subscribers, like the tide drawing out. His debts piling up. He remembered, with amazement, as though it were someone else who had done it, that he had told Sarah to order a whole grove of trees, as though they were rich, and could afford it. Now he felt the house balanced on his shoulders. Three of his best journalists had left for the *World*, and though most of the time—during the daylight hours—he believed he would fix all this, there were times, like right now, when he wasn't sure he could. There were times when it felt as though the path beneath him, which had been solid rock, was now crumbling away beneath his step, as though he were about to fall into deep space. He wrote fast to keep his footing, to hold his place in the world. His thoughts were important. He needed to set them down, to put them in order.

"There are signs of a better life," he wrote.

He'd done this before, fought his way back up from the bottom. He wrote swiftly, filling up the page. He wrote to explain the world to itself.

———·———

ON SUNDAY it was raining, a steady drumming on the roof of the carriage. The sodden horse plodded stolidly through the streets. Periodically she shook her head, as if she could toss away the whole rainstorm; silver strings of water were flung from her ears. They were going to visit Mrs. Fourgeaud's grave. She'd died while Sarah was in Washington; Frank had arranged the funeral. She was buried in St. Lawrence, the Catholic cemetery next to the Anglican Magnolia.

Celena Fourgeaud lay now between the stained marble stones of her husband and her daughter. The living Dawsons, sheltering beneath big black umbrellas, stood dutifully before the graves. Miss Celena's was only a sunken rectangle of sodden earth. There was no headstone.

Shivering, Sarah looked at the three graves, the end of a family.

"I'm glad I said goodbye before I left," she said. "Was it a good funeral?"

"The service was," said Frank, "but during the burial there was a torrential rainstorm. People could hardly drag their feet through the mud. You couldn't hear the priest."

"You could only hear the rain," Warrington said.

"I hope that doesn't happen at my funeral," Dawson said.

"I won't be there," said Sarah.

"Don't talk about your funeral." Ethel put her hands over her ears.

"I can hardly walk," said Sarah. Her boots were smeared and heavy with pale clay.

When Virginia had died Dawson bought the adjoining plot for himself; the two families would be united forever. She and Frank would lie there someday. Their last child was already there, Philip Hicky Dawson, who'd died of the heat at six months old. Sarah didn't want to think about Philip Hicky. She could feel his small hot body heavy in her arms, arching away from her, head thrown back. She didn't look directly, though she saw the small white stone from the corner of her eye. She felt a current of cold rise inside her, as though she were passing over a spring in a lake.

The children fought over who should hold the umbrella. They jostled, muddying their boots. The horse stood still, her head low, her ears laid back, her coat dark with rain.

ON MONDAY AFTERNOON Dawson read the police report by Sergeant Dunn.

At 8:56 Hélène had dropped off the children at Miss Smith's School, then walked on downtown and met another young woman. They went into several stores, then separated. Hélène walked to Nunan Street and went inside a house for a few minutes. Then she walked back home. She met no one else. Apparently she attracted a great deal of attention on the street on account of her dress.

Dawson read it carefully. It was distasteful to him that she should attract attention on the street. She was a member of his household. He thought of the way she had stood in the parlor, hands folded demurely.

He wrote Golden, asking to have her followed again the next day.

33.

A MIDNIGHT MURDER.

THE DREADFUL DEATH OF
MR WILLIAM MUNZENMAIER.

Slain in the Vigor of his Young Manhood—
A Death-dealing Razor—The investigation To day.

A homicide, atrocious in its perpetration and sickening in its details, was committed within the first quarter of the first hour of this Sunday morning. William Munzenmaier, a young man well known in Charleston and who has for years been engaged in honorable employment, was killed . . . but a short distance from his own home . . .

FROM EAR TO EAR

It was a fearful gash, deep, wide and long enough to have killed the unfortunate man on the instant of its commission. From the bloody head and face and neck of the victim a distinct stream of blood had flowed towards the pavement . . .

From early in the evening there was a number of young men . . . at the northwest corner of Spring street and King street. Among them were William Munzenmaier, O. Weir, Mervin Johnson, Blodgett Baker . . . and the young men already mentioned. Some of them were playing cards and in the course of the game one of the party slapped and crushed a fellow player's hat. This crushing was done by either Weir or Johnson, whereupon Munzenmaier interfered in a friendly way, and said that one friend should not treat another in that way. Both men resented this interference, but before anything looking to a row had taken place the proprietors announced that they had to close the store. This must have been within a few minutes of midnight . . . There was a good deal of bickering going on when the party went out but nothing which would warrant so serious a result. The whole party then started down King street. Munzenmaier and Johnson and Weir and Baker were well together and as to the rest, some were ahead and some behind. They then began throwing bricks at each other, Weir's friends . . . trying to hit Munzenmaier and Munzenmaier's friends trying to hit Weir. This was kept up until the party reached the spot where Munzenmaier was killed. "Just here there was an indiscriminate melee. I saw Weir with a knife—it might have been a razor . . . He had it out, and just then Baker picked up a brick and Munzenmaier hit him in the jaw, and then this fellow Baker went off. I heard somebody say: 'Did you draw a knife on me?' Another man said, 'Yes, I did.' Then Weir said, '———' and then he jugged him."

"Who jugged him?"

"Weir cut Munzenmaier's throat, sir, with a knife or a razor, but I saw him do it. I was standing right beside Billy, (Munzenmaier,) and he turned towards me as he fell and the blood spurted out of his throat. Weir then ran off and I halloeed to the boys 'He killed him,' and we all took after him. He didn't run far. We all reached him together. He fell down and we all fell on him in a heap. I think he had the razor in his hand when we fell on him."

—*THE NEWS AND COURIER*, MARCH 10, 1889

34.

IT'S JUST PAST nine o'clock in the morning. Hélène stands on the sidewalk on Broad Street. It's chilly, the shadows are still long and cool. She shivers, lifts one foot, and presses it against her ankle, for warmth.

She's just left the children at Miss Smith's, standing in the arched doorway, letting go their hands, loosing them into the stream of children surging inside. Ethel's face was still set in aggrievement over losing her books. She'd found them, of course, and now holds them tightly against her chest, but her eyebrows are raised plaintively as though she'd somehow been the victim. Because of this they'd had to take the streetcar, and she'd had to ask her parents for the fare.

Hélène has no patience with Ethel, who should have put the books out the night before, as Warrington does. Hélène prefers Warrington and so does Madame Dawson. Ethel should not believe, just because she's the elder, that she is better than her brother. She is not.

—·—

HÉLÈNE'S WAITING FOR the red streetcar, which McDow will board farther uptown. He'd reminded her of this last night, asking her if she knew the instructions, as though she were a child.

"Now, which car do you take?" he asked. They were in his garden, at the back, just inside his gate.

"The red," she said, "the red car."

He put his arm around her waist and gave her a hard squeeze.

"Keep that watch wound up." He nuzzled against her face. His nose was unpleasantly wet, and she drew back. "Is it wound up tight?"

"Yes," Hélène said.

"Tight," he said, pulling her close.

"Yes." She let him hold her close at the waist but leaned back from his face.

He looked around in the darkness, as though someone was watching.

"Make sure you're on it." He tugged her waist close again.

Now she sees the red tramcar approaching, the big horses nodding patiently with each step, the car rolling smoothly along the metal tracks. Hélène raises her hand to hail it and steps off the curb into the street. She's aware of her body against the fresh morning air. Her dress is black jersey, a tight bodice with a white ruffle at the neck. Over this is a silky black cloak. Men pass by, in carriages, along the sidewalk. She feels their gazes. A man in a bowler hat is standing behind her, waiting for the car. She's aware of him. He's been looking at her, but she doesn't look at him. She looks only at the approaching car. Her new boots lace tightly over her instep, clasping her ankles.

She takes a seat in the middle of the car. It's empty except for two other people: an old man at the very front by the conductor, and a young woman halfway down, her face turned to the window. The man in the bowler moves to the back. Hélène sits very straight, like a princess. She knows that men look at her. She crosses her feet neatly, feeling them enhanced by the new boots. She settles the full dark sweep of her skirts. The car starts off. At the next stop the old man gets off. Hélène watches for McDow. He wants to take her somewhere.

Once he'd insisted on going out to the Dawsons' kitchen building, where the servants live. He wanted to see the rooms upstairs. Hélène took him to the cook's bedroom, but as soon as they stepped inside McDow put his arm around her and tried to kiss her. She turned her face aside and slid out of his embrace. All the servants knew she was up there. She could feel them downstairs, listening. She stepped away from him.

"Here it is. You see?" She waved her hand over the narrow bed, the chest of drawers. McDow looked at the bed.

"My own is much nicer," Hélène said. "In the family house."

"I'd like to see that," McDow said, coming close to her. Stepping toward her he stubbed his boot into her new shoe and she stepped back.

"Ah, no," she said, shaking her head. "You may not come there. The Dawsons' rooms are next to mine. And the children."

"I wouldn't make a sound," McDow said. He wanted her body in his hands, he wanted to press his fingers against her cushiony flesh and feel it spring back, but she stepped away and moved to the doorway.

"We must go down," she said.

He stared at her, angry, but she shook her head. He had to walk past her as she stood in the doorway.

Now Hélène sees McDow out the window. He's on the sidewalk, waiting. When he gets on the car he doesn't look at her but moves toward the back. He nods to the man in the bowler hat. They talk, polite, desultory. McDow turns once, glancing at Hélène, but makes no sign. The car rumbles along, clicking and shifting on its metal tracks. McDow strokes his mustache, then leans back in his seat. He rubs his hands on his thighs. He doesn't look at Hélène.

They're going north. The buildings become smaller and farther apart, shabbier. They've long since passed Bull Street. The other woman has gotten off; only Hélène and McDow and the bowler man are left. McDow stares moodily at the street outside. She knows something is wrong.

Hélène stands to pull the checkrein, strung through loops along the wall. The bell rings, the car comes to a halt. She doesn't know the street, doesn't know the neighborhood. Hélène steps down without looking at McDow. From the corner of her eye she sees him getting out on the other side. He starts walking along the street, away from her. She follows, on her side.

He's walking fast and wildly. She hurries to keep up. He turns at the corner and she follows. She doesn't know this neighborhood, which is colored. McDow stops and she comes up to him in front of a big white church. It looms over them, tall blank pointed windows and high walls.

McDow is scowling. "We've been seen," he says accusingly, as she comes up.

"We are not seen," Hélène says, looking around. "There is no one."

"Don't speak to me," McDow says.

"You are speaking to me," Hélène points out.

They're in a remote part of town. There's no point here in her beautiful soft black jersey, the new boots. There are no well-dressed businessmen walking past to see her. She feels wasted.

"That man on the car is a detective. His name is Dunn." McDow is hissing. "I know him. He's seen us." His eyes are wild.

He turns and walks away again. She hurries after him.

"Where are we going?" she asks.

He stops. "I've told you not to speak to me," he hisses, then turns away again. They go on for another block, nearly running. The new boots are beginning to hurt, the right one especially. It chafes at the toe.

A buggy is approaching, driven by a middle-aged white man. McDow turns suddenly off the sidewalk and grabs Hélène's hand. He pulls her through a little gate and into a messy yard with an unpainted fence. The house is small and shabby, with a tin roof. A magnolia tree towers over it. A dirt path leads through the weedy grass to the house.

"Why do we go in here?" Hélène pulls her hand away.

"We can't stay on the street." McDow looks furtively back at the buggy.

"We are not on the street," Hélène says. "What do we do here?"

Two colored children are playing at the edge of the porch. They stop to watch. An elderly woman steps out, holding a shawl around her shoulders. She's lean and bony, long-jawed and fierce-eyed.

McDow walks up the dirt path. The woman watches him, unsmiling. "Morning, maum," he says.

She nods, her eyes narrowed. Her skin is like soft coal.

"I wonder if you could let us come inside." McDow's voice is low, persuasive. "Just step inside for a few minutes."

The woman narrows her eyes more. "Why you want to step inside?"

"There's a man after us," McDow says, keeping his voice low.

The woman looks past him to the street. The horse and buggy are nearing.

"No, sir," she says.

"Just for a little time," McDow repeats, and takes a step toward her. She shakes her head. Another older woman comes out from the doorway. She's unsmiling. McDow turns to look toward the street. The driver glances in at them as the buggy goes by. McDow turns again to the woman.

McDow keeps his voice low, but the woman's voice rises.

"No, sir, you can't come in here," she says. "That's all." She juts out her long chin.

McDow turns away and pushes past Hélène, grabbing her hand again. The woman stands on the porch, watching them leave. The children stare, motionless. McDow pulls her out onto the sidewalk.

On the street Hélène pulls her hand away.

"The scandal has begun," McDow says.

"I don't know what you mean," Hélène says.

"It seems that everyone I know in Charleston happens to have seen us this morning," he says. "That man in the buggy is a doctor called Melville. He knows my father. He saw us. And so did the detective on the car. It's just my luck."

He's furious. He looks up and down the street. On the next block sits a groundnut woman, her baskets spread around her on the sidewalk. Standing before her is the man with the black bowler hat, face turned away.

"He's here!" McDow says, whispering. He makes a fist and shakes it, close to his chest. "That's Dunn, the detective. And I know who sent him: Dawson. I know what's going on. Dawson has done all this. I'd like to beat him to a pulp. If I were younger I'd beat them all to a pulp."

He makes a strange gesture with his mouth, opening his lips to bare his teeth. His lower teeth are irregular, like an animal's. The cords in his thin neck stand out.

The baring of the teeth bothers her. Wildness comes from him like a smell.

"I'll beat them all bloody." His words are slurred. "I'll do them all in.

I'll do him in, Dawson." He's half smiling, excited. Something lights him up inside.

Hélène turns and starts walking back toward Rutledge. He's frightening her.

He comes after her. "Where are you going?"

"Home," she says. She keeps walking.

At Rutledge she waits for the car. When it comes they both get on, but sit separately. She tucks her feet beneath her and smooths her skirts down over her legs so they cover her new boots. Her toe throbs. She hears him talking to himself. At first he whispers, and she strains to hear, then his voice gets louder and louder.

"Just my luck," he says, looking up and down the car. "Everyone I know in Charleston is out on the street today. Just my luck." He rubs his hands on his thighs. "I know who it is, it's Dawson." He shakes his head in a loose, strange way. "I'll do him in," he says, dropping his voice to an whisper. "I won't stand for it." He looks up at the front of the car, his head held oddly low. "I have the right to go where I want with my friends. I won't stand for this." He shakes his head. "I'll do him in." This makes him feel better and he nods. He looks straight at Hélène. "You know what that means?"

She turns away and looks out the window. Do him in. She thinks she does know.

It's quarter to ten in the morning.

———

FRANK AND SARAH are late coming down to breakfast.

The children have left for school, Hélène's not yet back. In the dining room the sunlight sifts in through the leaves outside. The crystal grapes— clear, soft amber, pale amethyst—catch the light. Jane comes in with the breakfast tray. Her boots creak, and when she turns her back to set down the tray Dawson looks at Sarah and raises his eyebrows. Sarah ignores him.

"The nurseryman is coming with the trees today," Sarah reminds him.

"Well done," Dawson says. "And my palmetto."

"Which will make you a real Charlestonian."

"If I'm not one by now, I'll never be," Dawson says.

"Which reminds me of the portrait of you," says Sarah. "Is that artist here yet? Landon? That's what I want for my birthday."

"I forgot to tell you," he says. "If you still want it, the sitting will have to be today. Landon will only be in Charleston a few days."

"I do want it," she says. "I want to hang it there." She points at the wall over the sideboard. "Where my father's was in our dining room."

"And what about a portrait of you?"

She shakes her head, smiling. "I'd rather die."

"You set up a drastic choice," he says. "I'm not so adamant. But if you want this you must make me do it. Come and pick me up at three. You must carry me off, no matter what I say. I'll tell you I can't, I'm too busy, but you must tell me I promised."

"I'll be fierce," she says. "Adamant."

Outside, the gravel crunches under the phaeton wheels. Isaac is driving down the driveway to wait for them on the street. It's after ten, and Sarah leaves to get her hat and cloak. Hélène is just coming in the front door, and follows her upstairs to her room.

Sarah takes her cloak from the armoire. "You're late again," Sarah says in French.

Hélène raises her eyebrows. "Madame?"

"The children are due at school before nine. The trip takes less than twenty minutes. You should be home by quarter past nine. Twenty past at the latest." She looks at her watch. "It's after ten."

"Does Madame think I am late?" Hélène asks, meek.

"I think you are sometimes," says Sarah. "I think you must stop."

"I only go to the school and back," Hélène says. "But you won't need to say this to me again, Madame." Her eyes are full of something.

Sarah turns to her. "What's the matter?"

"Nothing, Madame," Hélène says. "Do you think there is something wrong?"

"Obviously there is," Sarah says, but she has no time now to talk. She stands before the mirror and settles her hat over the mass of her hair. She brings the veil down over her face; it makes a shadowy scrim against her skin. She pulls it taut and draws the long ends behind her neck.

"Let me help you." Standing behind her, Hélène takes the long ends and ties them at the nape of Sarah's neck. Hélène watches Sarah in the mirror. Sarah watches herself. Hélène makes a loose bow, then tucks the ends neatly into the collar of Sarah's cloak.

"Voilà," Hélène says, looking at her in the mirror. "Madame est très chic."

"Perfect. Thank you." Sarah smiles at her. Hélène is young, and far from home. Perhaps she's being too hard on her.

Sarah starts down to Frank. Usually Hélène walks Sarah out to the carriage, but now Hélène stops at the top of the stairs. Frank waits at the foot.

"Do you want me to come?" Hélène calls, not moving.

Sarah, now feeling guilty, calls, "No, no, you needn't."

Frank reaches out to take her hand. She'd fallen once, they'd fallen together, from the top of the stairs. The two of them thudding horribly down, and he'd been so frightened for her spine. Now she reaches the bottom and smiles at him.

"Is Hélène coming?" he asks, looking upstairs.

"I told her she needn't."

"Then I'd like your help. I want to take some books to the office." They each carry a stack to the carriage. They're in the phaeton today; Sarah has errands to run.

As they set off Dawson says, "I haven't seen Hélène in days. I feel as if she's hiding. Is something wrong?"

"Maybe she's embarrassed," says Sarah. "I told her she takes too long coming home from school."

"What did she say?" Dawson turns to look at her.

"That she only goes there and back," says Sarah. "She promised not to be late again."

That day, Tuesday, the light is cool and promising, the air fresh. They turn down Rutledge: Charleston has launched itself into the business of the day. The street vendors are wheeling carts along the pavement, calling their wares. On Broad Street there is traffic: buggies, phaetons, mule-drawn farm wagons. Around them is the steady clop of hooves, the grinding of wheels, the clack of footsteps. People stride along the sidewalk. A white dog sits down to scratch urgently at his ear. The melon man gives his strange cry, "Barcalingo! Barcalingo!"

The sign stretches all the way across the front of the building: "News and Courier." The building is tall, three stories, and solid. It has big windows and a classical doorway, tall fluted columns, a stone pediment. Sarah feels proud when she sees it. It's so dignified, so substantial. It reassures her.

McKissick comes out onto the sidewalk. He's a reporter, a small busy man, with wide mouth and pointed ears, like a leprechaun. He's been with Frank for years. He greets Sarah cheerily, and she asks him for news about the competitors, the *Sun* and the *World*.

"I'm glad you asked, Mrs. Dawson," McKissick says. "I hear the *Sun* is closing."

"Closing!" Sarah says triumphantly.

"It's what I hear," McKissick says, pleased. He rises slightly on his toes, then settles.

"Why don't you give *me* news like that, McKissick?" Dawson climbs down to the sidewalk. He's wearing his new overcoat from London, fitted, elegant. His black bowler hat, dogskin gloves. He carries his light Malacca walking stick.

He holds up his stack of books so Sarah can set hers on top of it. As she leans down toward him, her books tip, and several slide down to the sidewalk.

"Mrs. Dawson," Dawson says. "That's the first sign of age I've seen in you. Are you losing your grip?"

"Apparently," she says.

He leans over to pick up the fallen books and his own pile tips, cascading to the sidewalk.

"Captain Dawson," she says, "that's the first sign of age I've seen in you."

He straightens, laughing, books stacked against his chest. He sets his chin on the top one, holding them in place. *He's getting jowls*, she thinks, fascinated. *That really is a sign of age.* She feels surprised and tender. They will grow old together; it has already begun. The thought makes her happy.

"Remember to pick me up at three," he says, "no matter what I tell you."

"I'll be here," she says.

"And remember the boots." He doesn't say "Jane's" because he doesn't want Isaac to hear.

She nods.

His hands on the books, he kisses the air discreetly, and turns to go. The big street windows give onto the downstairs office, and Sarah watches him stop inside to talk to a reporter, the books stacked against his chest. Even from behind his stance is familiar, the shape of his head, the line of his shoulders.

Sarah tells Isaac to move on, and he slaps the reins against Brownie's back. He says his word—she can never quite make it out. Gerrup? Get up? Chirrup?

The errands will take all morning. Isaac draws up outside the stores and the shopkeepers come out to the carriage; they all know her. At the dry goods store she asks for a jar of leather cream for Jane's boots.

At the pharmacist's, the owner comes out. Mr. Gaskell is a small man with thinning hair, very black. Sarah told Frank she thinks he dyes it; Frank said the poor man should be allowed to dye his hair if he wants. Mr. Gaskell wears a long white jacket. When he reaches the carriage he bows. He is cheerful and friendly.

"Good morning, Mrs. Dawson," he says, rubbing his hands. She gives him her list: powder for sun protection, oil of peppermint, salve, tooth powder. He goes inside while Sarah waits in the carriage. A boy comes out with her order, packages tied with string, and a carton of Pear's soap.

"Did I order that?"

"No, ma'am," he says, "but we just got some in, and I know the captain likes to keep it in stock."

"Thank you," Sarah says. It's comforting to feel known, to feel that someone keeps track of her family's needs.

Her last errand is on the outskirts of town, at the stonemason's. Slabs of stone are stacked haphazardly outside the big barnlike building. Sarah's here to order the gravestone for Miss Celena. She's been here before.

The interior is bare and dim, high ceilinged, with small windows up in the roof peak. Stepping inside Sarah feels the air gather around her. She came here before, with Frank, after the funeral. She and Frank stood together at the counter to choose the stone, and the words to put on it, but all she could think of was that small wooden casket, its tiny brass handles.

The men had stood close to the edge of the grave, holding the ropes as they let it down. The little casket—so light it had nearly slid off the ropes—descended unevenly, then disappeared. She hadn't stepped closer. She hadn't wanted to see it at the bottom, resting on the pale soil.

She puts that from her.

Mr. Roberts is lean and balding, with a sober manner. He stands behind the long counter. When Sarah comes in he has a chair brought for her. He knows every family in Charleston who owns a cemetery plot. He knows the stones that already stand in theirs; he knows where it is. He knows there are two Fourgeauds and one Dawson. So far. He takes the long view: everyone will be his customer in the end. He leans over the counter while they discuss the stone, the shape, the lettering.

A bird has gotten inside the building. It flutters up among the shadowy struts, a sudden swift flapping, then silent settling. As Sarah talks she has the confused feeling that the anxious bird, flying back and forth, is what they are trying to put at rest. She talks to Mr. Roberts about the marble, thinking about the small stone for Philip Hicky. She thinks of Miss Celena, struggling to breathe. She's glad to do this, put them to rest.

———

ON THE TRIP BACK McDow had watched Hélène from the corner of his eye. She kept her face turned away from him.

Everything had gone wrong for him. He'd wanted to go to the quiet part of town where they could walk about unobserved. He wanted the feel of her in his arms, the grip of his fingers.

He knows the colored people up there. He has patients there, people who were in that insurance business with him. They owe him favors. He's sure he could have gotten someone to let him use a room. He wanted to get Hélène down on a bed, he wanted to put his hands on her. He could feel her pillowy breasts, that soft white skin. Her skin was French. The thought of her French skin, naked against his hands, roused his blood.

Everything had gone wrong.

The detective, then that doctor. The world presses against him. Dunn, with his red mustache and big square teeth, was certainly following them. Standing there by that groundnut woman as though he'd come all the way to Cannon Street by chance.

Hélène has gone around the corner to her house. McDow opens the door to his office. He wants to hit something. He feels the world pressed up against his chest jagged and hostile. All this is because of Dawson. He remembers standing in Dawson's house when the telephone rang. How he jumped, and how she laughed at him. The memory fills him with heat. He feels scalded by shame for being startled, rage at being laughed at.

In the vestibule hangs the tin box on the wall. He checks it for messages: Mrs. Fair wants a house call. She lives nearby on Ashley Avenue.

In his office McDow opens the lower cabinet of the secretary in the corner. He takes out the bottle and sets it to his mouth. He tilts his head back and swallows once, then again. He feels the fire slide down into his chest, a relief. He puts the bottle back in the cabinet. He stands up, then leans down and opens the cabinet again. He takes out the bottle. Another swallow, then another.

Out on the sidewalk he looks toward the Dawson house. Sometimes she sits in the upstairs window, singing. Not today, though he thinks he sees a dim silhouette, back from the window. He feels her presence, a dark, glowing pulse, but she's cut off from him. This makes him angry. It's Dawson that's done this to him.

He rings the bell at Mrs. Fair's house. Her maid, elderly and rheumy-eyed, opens the door. Without speaking she takes him down the hall to the bedroom. The air is close, sweetish. Mrs. Fair lies in bed, propped up against the pillows. She's in her fifties, a dark-skinned mulatto woman, lively and opinionated. Her husband's a gambler, well-known in Charleston. Rosey Fair, he's called.

"Mrs. Fair," McDow says, "Good morning." As he comes into the room he finds himself listing slightly to one side. This takes him by surprise and he takes an extra step to stay upright. The world seems slightly uneven.

"Doctor," says Mrs. Fair. "I am so glad to see you. I've been feeling poorly." She smooths the sheet over her belly. She's a handsome woman, with a broad face and a drift of small dark freckles across her nose. Her hair is reddish, crinkled, pulled back untidily.

"I'm sorry to hear that," McDow says. "Maybe it's this in-between weather. Gets to everyone."

McDow comes over and sets his bag down, staggering slightly. He sits on the bed, to steady himself.

"I surely hope that's all it is, Doctor," says Mrs. Fair. "You know I don't have time to be sick."

She's wearing some kind of bed jacket, silk and lace, over her nightgown. Her heavy breasts are flattened against her chest but he sees the shadows of her nipples.

"What seems to be the trouble?" he asks. That's the right thing to say. His brain is clouded by something.

"It's my throat," Mrs. Fair says plaintively. She lifts her chin to show her fleshy mottled neck. Deep lines circle it as though a thread has been tightened at intervals. "I can't exactly say what's wrong, but I can hardly swallow. And my chest is tight."

"Any pain?" asks McDow. "Is it tender?" He puts his hands on her throat and palpates it, looking discreetly at the ceiling. He slides his fingers up and down its length. It's warm and pulsing.

Mrs. Fair swallows; he feels the muscular spasm beneath his fingers.

"Not exactly pain," she says, and puts her hand just below the base of her neck. "A kind of closeness. Breathlessness."

"A tightness?" asks McDow. He's not sure what he's asking. The nipples are standing out beneath the soft layers of fabric. They're more erect now. He's certain of this.

"A tightness, exactly," says Mrs. Fair. "It seems like I can hardly swallow. Or breathe, either. My chest feels full."

McDow looks down at her. Her fraying hair fans out around her face. Her full, loose body seems to press itself against his consciousness. The blowsy unbound breasts, the hump of the belly, the dark secret below. He knows what's there, warm and private. He senses it waiting for him. A kind of wildness is growing in him.

"Let me listen to your heart," he says.

He leans down toward the floor, nearly overbalancing, and takes the stethoscope from his bag. As he leans down he can smell her, a strong musky odor, with a suffocating undertone of flowery cologne. He puts the earpieces into his ears and takes the metal disc. He moves his hand down, slipping it under the covers, inside the V of her jacket, then the neck of her nightgown. He sets the metal disc on her bare skin, just below her left breast. He gazes solemnly at the ceiling. He feels the heft of her bosom, large and unconfined, spilling over his hand. He feels it against his fingers. He moves them slightly, rubbing them against her flesh, pretending to feel for the heartbeat. He knows the real heartbeat is between her legs. Still looking up at the ceiling, he slides his fingers up over the big drooping swell of the breast. He sets them on either side of the nipple, which is swollen and huge. He tweaks it.

But this is wrong.

The bed erupts, rocking and plunging, and the air explodes with noise. The woman is yelling and throwing herself around, plunging over to one side. She's yanking open the drawer in the nightstand. He's pulled his hand away as though it were burned, but she keeps on yelling his name, yelling for Maudy, as she pulls something from the drawer.

"Get out of here! Out! Out!" she yells.

It's a pistol, he can see that. He's already moving, leaning down to grab his bag. She levels the barrel at him.

"You get out of my house, you weaselly trash!" she yells. He hears someone else call out, then footsteps, but he's already moving, on his way out. He runs for the door, but he's watching her, holding her in his gaze as though that will keep her from shooting him, and when he reaches the door he finds he's miscalculated. As he turns he slams his head hard into the jamb. He draws back and keeps going, head stinging, eye tingling, his bag banging against his leg and Mrs. Fair still shouting. Maudy's in the hall, frowning, her rheumy eyes angry, but she doesn't know what to say to a white man. She stands back as he runs past.

"Doctor!" she calls after him, but he's out the door.

Out on the street he stands still. He feels as though he's been attacked by hornets. He feels the sting all over his body, the shame of being threatened by a woman with a pistol. He blinks rapidly, again and again. His whole body stings.

He heads off downtown. The hardware store on Broad Street sells guns. He won't stand for this. His own brother has a Smith & Wesson, even cowardly Arthur, who has run off home again. The vile Mrs. Fair, waving her flabby arm, the barrel glinting. Even she has a gun.

His head is thick with rage and whisky. Dawson is behind all this. It's Dawson.

35.

March 12, 1889. Charleston

SARAH REACHES HOME just before noon. The wagon from the nursery is waiting on the street, packed closely with their trees. The roots are balled in burlap, and they stand close together, like a miniature forest. The palmetto rises above the others like a tower, its leaves erupting in a green spray.

Sarah runs upstairs to take off her cloak; it's turning hot. She calls for Hélène, who sits in Warrington's window sewing.

Sarah calls to her in French. "No singing? What's happened to my nightingale?"

Hélène looks doleful. "If Madame had my problems she would not sing either."

"What problems?" Sarah asks, not wanting to hear.

Hélène shakes her head again, as though she doesn't want to talk about them. Then she does. "It's impossible to tell you what I've had to put up with while you were away, from the kitchen." She's afraid the others will tell Sarah about McDow.

Sarah knows she means the servants by "the kitchen."

"I haven't heard a word from anyone," she says. "No one has complained," Sarah says briskly. "You have no problems there. So, sing, please!"

She hurries downstairs.

The nurseryman is a big burly man with a mustache that doesn't conceal his cleft palate. Sarah can hardly understand him, but he doesn't seem to mind. He talks cheerfully and unintelligibly as they walk about. She shows him where everything will go, the scarlet oak and magnolia along the back fence, serviceberry beside the oak. She wants the palmetto by the front gate, where everyone will see it.

The man's assistant is young and lean, with very dark skin and very high cheekbones. The two hoist each tree into the wheelbarrow, and then the boy trundles it through the garden. Sarah walks with him, showing them where to dig. She herself is a gardener, and knows every plant on the place. There's a dilapidated shed against the back fence that she won't let anyone touch because a huge staghorn fern has clambered on top of it and is living there so happily. In Baton Rouge she had a narrow strip off the front porch, where every morning she ruined her nails and her complexion pruning and weeding. Digging in the damp earth: she loves the smell of it. These new trees are treasures. She pictures them when they're mature, massive: the magnolia, towering, glossy leaves and satin petals, the scarlet oak aflame. The pair of fringe trees, *Chionanthus*, will have a conversation with each other, and erupt in the spring in cream-colored sprays. A tall serviceberry, with its upright calligraphic branches. She feels enlarged by the arrival of these beauties. It's as though a company of dancers has come to take up residence.

The day has cleared and brightened, and now the pale sun is beating down. The boy takes a shovel from the back of the wagon and begins to dig the holes, starting with the palmetto. Sarah goes with him, to make sure they are in the right places, then she stands on the galerie, watching. Her forehead is damp, and she takes out her handkerchief. She presses it against her temples, first one side, then the other. The two men slide the palmetto in together. It tilts at first, and then they straighten it. It stands like a green sentinel by the gate. She can't wait for Frank to see it.

———

DAWSON IS AT his desk, scanning a new bill from the paper supplier, when McKinley comes in. He's holding a copy of the paper.

"Hello," Dawson says. "Come in. Sit down." He puts down his pen and leans back in his chair. He holds his wrist, flexing his fingers. "Do you find this? My hand gets tired now in the mornings. It used not to happen until late afternoon."

McKinley shakes his head. "If you were a reporter," he says, "you'd only have to write once a day."

"Maybe I should go back to reporting," Dawson says. "Let someone else run the paper."

But McKinley is not there to chat. He sits down, sober.

"I've read your piece on Pickens," he says. His manner is not collegial.

"Oh, yes," says Dawson. He frowns.

"I don't understand what you're trying to do," says McKinley.

"I'd have thought it was clear," Dawson says.

"Blacks will be up in arms," McKinley says.

"Oh?" says Dawson, and waits. He doesn't like this accusatory tone.

"How can you talk about them this way?" McKinley asks. He looks at the paper in his hand and reads from it. "The difference between the 'instincts, character and conduct of the two races.' Their moral purity, or lack of it. You make it sound as though they're all criminals."

"The races are different. Their crime rate is much higher than ours," says Dawson. "That's a perfectly well-known fact."

"It's a perfectly well-known fact that we keep them in poverty. They steal food to eat."

"I'm not blaming them," said Dawson. He's becoming vexed himself. "That's not the point. I'm citing facts."

"They'll be outraged," says McKinley.

"Because I say that the public is more horrified over a white woman being raped by a black man," asks Dawson, "than it is over a black girl being raped by a white man?" He pauses. "You know it's true. Public outrage is greater over one than the other."

"You make it sound as though it's justified." McKinley is definitely accusatory.

"I'm making a point, using language our readers will understand," says Dawson. "I'm saying that in the past people have found this crime—a black man raping a white woman—so horrifying that they see it as justifying an even greater crime: lynching. Because of this, no one ever prosecuted the lynchers. But in the Pickens case the public felt more horror over the lynching than they did over the rape. Suddenly lynching is seen as a crime. Which I applaud."

"Because it's a white man being lynched by black men," says McKinley.

"Race plays a part, it always does. It obscures the law. But what I'm trying to do, McKinley," Dawson says, his voice turning emphatic, "is stop lynching altogether. *I want it brought to an end.*"

He stares at McKinley, as though the reporter is challenging him.

"The ministers will turn against you," McKinley says.

"Against me?" asks Dawson. He's spent the last fifteen years supporting them. "They know perfectly well I'm on their side. I've always been."

McKinley says nothing.

"White people lynch black people because of the horror they feel at rape. But *lynching* is the horror. It poisons the body politic. The Pickens lynchers should be prosecuted. If we punish black people for lynching, then we can punish white people for it. And then we can get the whole barbaric system banned. Which is my intention. Sweet mother."

Dawson runs his hand through his hair. This is like trying to run through waist-high water. Why must he struggle with every step? Here's McKinley, his trusted ally, come in to pick a fight. Dawson's fingers hurt and so does his wrist. He has no way to pay the paper bill. The delivery drivers will be next, and then there is payroll to meet.

"God made the races different," Dawson says. "I'm simply stating facts. Do you deny it?"

McKinley stands up, buttoning his jacket. "What you've written is offensive."

Dawson's chest fills with fury. He strokes his mustache, holding McKinley's stare. He would like to lean across the desk and shout at him. He will not be told by his employees what he can say in print. He'd like to fire him, but he won't. "Out," he says. He gestures brusquely at the door. "Come back when you're civil."

McKinley turns to leave, holding the folded paper in front of him like a declaration. His neck is dark and suffused with blood.

Dawson sits down. His ears are ringing, fury rages through him. McKinley is unconscionable, coming in to challenge him. Dawson can't focus on the page. He thinks he should fire McKinley; he half rises to go to the stairs and shout this message down to the newsroom. He sits down again. He can't afford to fire anyone. He rereads the article. He can't focus, can't take in what anyone else says.

He picks up the paper and finds his own piece. He goes over to the window to reread it. The clock ticks evenly beside him, that calm hurrying beat. He can't concentrate. The races are different, but the sentence about purity is confusing.

He sees Langston's face, shifting before him black to white. The idea of Langston reading this makes him uncomfortable—but Langston is not who he means.

He sits down again, still furious. McKinley has no right to challenge him. He doesn't want to think about the editorial. He feels the silver blade within him, and shifts away from it. He'll write again tomorrow. He's done this before, written in the heat of the moment, then had second thoughts. The point is to bring lynching to a halt. That's his intention.

There are signs of a better life. He'd meant that. For both races. He takes a slow breath, shallow, so he won't feel the blade.

He exhales. He's glad he didn't shout down the staircase at McKinley.

———•———

JUST AFTER ONE THIRTY, Chief Golden arrives.

Dawson hears the distinctive footsteps on the stairs and is standing when Golden comes in.

"Golden," Dawson says. "Thank you for coming."

"You may not want to thank me, Captain," Golden says. He hands Dawson the report and sits down.

Dawson reads it, his frown growing deeper and deeper.

"Dr. Thomas McDow?" he asks, looking up. "Who is he?"

"Your neighbor," Golden says. "An unsavory piece of meat."

"What sort of unsavory?" asks Dawson.

"Insurance fraud, for one," says Golden. "He and some other doctors have worked up a very nice practice. They dig up a body and someone declares the person has just died. They claim the life insurance and everyone takes a share."

"We ran a piece about that," Dawson says. "I didn't know it was my neighbor."

"We're still investigating," Golden says. "McDow's definitely involved."

"Anything else?" Dawson asks.

"He seems to have shot a man in Tennessee," says Golden. "That's why he came here in the first place. The Medical Association turned him down over ethics."

"Anything more?"

"He seems to have tried to hire his brother to kill his father-in-law."

Dawson leans back in his chair. "Really. Kill his father-in-law."

"The plan was for his wife to inherit. She's C. D. Ahrens's daughter, the grocer. Then McDow would put something lethal in her tea," says Golden. "Then he'd run off with another woman. Or that's what the brother claims. We caught him, we have his sworn testimony."

"What happened with the brother?"

"He double-crossed Thomas. Instead of killing Ahrens, he tried to extort money from him. Ahrens told us and we nabbed him. He confessed, but there's no crime," says Golden. "Thomas lives right behind you, on Rutledge."

"So I hear. I've never met him, though." He looks over the report: the meeting, the tram ride, the walk. Hélène slowly shaking her head. *Non.* "Your man is sure of all this."

Golden nods. "He knows McDow. He saw the girl. There were only the three of them in the car."

"McDow is a hound." Dawson feels heat rising into his chest again.

Golden looks cautious: Dawson has a temper. "He hasn't committed a crime. All he's done is ride on a streetcar and walk about with her. That's not an offense."

"This young woman is under my protection," says Dawson. "He's planning to murder his wife and carry her off."

"No," says Golden, "he was planning to carry off someone else."

"Someone else?" Somehow this is worse. Now Dawson is offended on Hélène's behalf.

"A young woman called Julia Smith," says Golden. "Some connection of Senator Smythe."

Carson, the office boy, appears in the doorway, looking anxious. "Telephone, Captain," he says. "Mrs. Dawson."

"Tell her I'm in a meeting," he snaps, and Carson vanishes. "I want you to put a stop to this," he says to Golden.

"He's done nothing yet," says Golden. "It's not a crime to meet someone in the street."

"You refuse to make a move?"

"We can't stop it," Golden says.

Dawson glares. "Must I take care of it?"

"Captain, don't approach him yourself," Golden says. "McDow is dangerous. He's killed one man anyway."

"Which is why I can't have him meeting with my servant," Dawson says. "She looks after my children."

"I'm sorry, Captain," says Golden. "We're following up on the insurance fraud. Nothing else we can do right now."

"Very well. I'm grateful for the report." Dawson puts it in his breast pocket and stands up. "Thank you for coming by."

Golden stands. "We'll be in touch as soon as we learn anything."

Dawson nods. He's remembering the man standing beyond their fence, while he was fixing the telephone. He was staring up at them. He has been watching Dawson's children play on the lawn. He heard them calling back and forth to the Lafittes'. He has watched Sarah as she walked about in the garden. He can see into their windows. Dawson is sickened by this. His family has been contaminated. Each time he thinks of the man peering over the fence, his chest expands with rage.

———·———

IT'S NEARLY THREE O'CLOCK when Jane comes out to tell Sarah that the captain is on the telephone.

When she answers he says, "Good. You haven't left yet."

"I'm sorry I'm late," she says. "I've been working with the tree man."

"No, I'm calling to say don't come down to pick me up," he says. "I'll take the car. There's something I have to do on the way home."

This is a relief; she's hot and dusty, and if she changes she'll be late to pick him up. "I can't wait for you to see the trees," she says. "The palmetto is fifteen feet tall, and bigger round than you."

"I'm looking forward to it," he says, in his public voice. He must have someone in the office with him. "I'll be there very soon."

Sarah hangs up. They have both forgotten about the portrait. Hélène is in the doorway, her face watchful.

"Quelque chose a passé?" *Has something happened?*

"Rien," says Sarah. *Nothing has happened.* "The captain is coming home by car, which gives me time to dress."

"It's not bad news, then," Hélène says.

"No," Sarah says, irritated by the question. "Why do you ask? Go and get the children ready for dinner."

Dawson waits on the sidewalk outside his office. At twenty past three the car pulls up in front of his building, and just as it arrives a friend comes over to speak to Dawson. He raises a finger to the driver, who knows him and holds the car. The friend hands him a letter, which Dawson puts inside his coat. He waves to the driver and climbs on board, making his way up the aisle, nodding to acquaintances. He knows many of these men, businessmen, coming home for dinner. Dawson sits down next to his lawyer, Julien Mitchell. The men trade the news of the day as the car trundles up Rutledge Avenue.

36.

3:00, March 12, 1889. Rutledge Avenue, Charleston

MCDOW CLOSES THE street door behind him, then the inner door. He takes off his hat. His office is dim and shadowy. The windows onto Rutledge are opaque glass, and the ones onto the garden are overshadowed by the wide piazza overhead. The room seems subterranean.

McDow turns on the gas chandelier, which casts a crepuscular glow onto the round table below it, the bottle-green settee between the side windows where he examines his patients, the tall secretary in the corner.

He stands at the table. The dreadful morning comes flooding back: on the car, when he recognized Dunn, the fruitless attempt to lose him; the maddening appearance of Melville, his father's friend; the colored woman on her porch, shaking her head. The trip home, Marie's face turned to the window. The dreadful Mrs. Fair. His head still throbs from his slamming impact against the door jamb, his ears ring with her raucous cries. The whole episode—her gravelly voice, his panicky retreat—fills him with rage. He is furious that he ran from her. His fingertips feel burned where they brushed against her heavy pendulous breast, like a loosened sack of meal. The memory scalds with shame and rage.

He takes the pistol from his pocket.

He'd told the clerk at the hardware store he was familiar with it. "Very familiar," he'd said, though it wasn't true. He hasn't owned a gun since Tennessee. He knows this is a Smith & Wesson—that's what everyone has—but he's already forgotten the caliber. Is it .36 or .38?

It's heavy in his hand. The barrel is a dull pewter, the handle matte black. He takes the bullets from his pocket and makes a heap on the table. They're small, smooth-nosed cylinders. He breaks open the pistol. The clerk warned him not to carry it loaded, but why have it if it's not ready when you need it? The bullets slide smoothly into the chambers. Each turn of the cylinder makes a metallic sound. Everything locks into place. He fills all five chambers, then straightens, powerful.

Because he won't stand for this. He's had enough. He knows who's behind it all. He puts the pistol on the table and it makes two small, important sounds as first the muzzle, then the handle, meet the wooden surface.

Beside the front door is the secretary. The slant front is folded down, the writing leaf is untidy with papers. Below this is a drawer, below that the cupboard with the bottle. He opens the door of this and the bottle gleams in the dim light. The sight of it excites him. He picks it up; it makes a faint liquid sound, and this too excites him. He opens it and fits his mouth over the glass lip in a smooth embrace. He lifts the bottle and tilts his head back. He closes his eyes and swallows. The fire slides inside him. He takes three long, fortifying swallows. He deserves this. The fire fills his chest. He wipes his mouth on his sleeve. He sets the bottle back on the shelf. He pats his chest twice. He feels powerful.

The pistol is still lying on the table; he puts it in the drawer of the secretary.

He leaves by the interior door and goes up the inside staircase. Katie is in the back sitting room, standing by the window. She turns as he comes in.

"You're late," she says.

Thomas shrugs and shakes his head. This is no way for a wife to greet her husband. "I had a call." It's what he always says.

"We have to go right in," Katie says. "They're waiting."

She walks past him without speaking. She's irritated; she's always complaining about this. It irritates him that she's irritated.

In the dining room they sit down. Moses Johnson, the butler and coachman, serves them. They eat in silence until Katie says, "Where were you this morning?"

He frowns. She never asks this. "I had some calls," he said. "A patient over on Ashley."

"But you took the cars," Katie says. "I saw you get off."

"I met a colleague earlier," Thomas says. He thinks of Melville, up on Nunan Street. He cuts the meat roughly, sawing with his knife. He stuffs a messy bite into his mouth.

Katie is watching him as she eats. When she swallows, her chin jerks. "What colleague?" she asks.

She has never asked this before, and he flicks his eyes up at her.

"Never you mind," he says forbiddingly. "It's not your affair who my colleagues are."

She looks down. It's chicken, undercooked.

She changes tack. "Are you going to the dinner?"

"What dinner?" he asks, though he knows.

"The one my father asked you to. The Merchants' Dinner."

"I can't," he says.

"You said you would," Katie said. Her voice takes on edge. "You told him you would."

"Well, now I can't," he says. "I'm not a merchant," he adds, lordly.

Katie puts down her fork. "You told my father you would go with him."

Thomas nods, holding his knife and fork. He gulps and swallows. He detests this conversation. He detests the way his wife holds her head down low between her shoulders, as though she had no neck.

"And now I'm telling you I won't." Those three golden swallows have let the fire loose. He wishes the bottle were up here. "I'm not going. I'm not a merchant."

"You can't humiliate my father like that." Katie's voice has risen again, her blue eyes gleam. Is she crying?

"Stop it!" he says, slamming his hand down on the table.

She stares at him in silence, subdued by the slam.

"I won't have you making accusations!" He is feeling more and more powerful. "Close your mouth," he adds.

She watches him. She swallows, takes a drink of water. She puts the goblet down and sets her fork and knife together on the plate. Her small blue eyes redden. She starts to speak and then stops. Her voice catches in her chest. "What am I supposed to tell my father?" Now she gives a long liquid sob and begins to weep. "You have to apologize to him."

All this is distasteful. "All right, I'll go," he says angrily. He won't.

"The way you act," she says, "it's insulting to my father."

He shrugs again and says nothing.

"You may not insult him," she says. Her voice shakes.

"I haven't," he says. "And there's no reason for me to go."

Old Ahrens paid for this house, and for other things as well. This means Thomas can't really speak candidly to Katie, as a man should be able to speak to his wife, though he can hint at his feelings. Most of the merchants are German: he doesn't want to attend these roistering Teutonic celebrations.

"I'm not a merchant," he says. "I'm not German."

"You're his son-in-law," Katie says. "You promised. You may not behave like this. I won't have it."

"Oh, you won't," he says mockingly. "Well then, don't have it. Do without it."

"Don't talk to me like that." Her voice has now risen, shrill and angry, with a note of panic.

"I'll talk to you as I wish," McDow says, standing up. He slaps his napkin down. "Don't tell me how to talk to you." There's something else he wants to say, but it eludes him. He puts his fists on the table and leans toward her. "I'm not a German," he hisses.

She's frozen, staring at him.

"I'm not a German and I'm not a merchant," he repeats. He straightens. Power floods through him. Yes, this is what he meant to say. He turns to walk out of the room.

Moses pushes in through the swinging door from the kitchen, carrying the blue-and-white platter of chicken.

"No," Katie says, to both of them. "I don't want that." Moses freezes. She half stands, looking at McDow, then sits down again, looking at Moses. "We're done, Moses," she says angrily. "Can't you see?"

Moses nods. He backs out again through the swinging door, the platter tilting in his hands.

Katie's in a rage. Her face has gone pink in blotches, and the tops of her cheeks are dull red, as though the skin has been sandpapered. Her small eyes have gone smaller. He feels her swelling and bursting with hostility.

She must know, of course, where he goes, up to the bedroom on the fourth floor, when Julia spends the night here. Katie must lie in bed awake waiting for him to come back down, though she pretends to be asleep. He knows she knows all this; she disgusts him.

He feels reckless and lordly. He'd like to sweep his marriage off the table with one hard fling. He's going to France with Marie, and then he won't have to put up with either Katie or Julia. He can't think of the words just now, with which to sweep it off, but he'd like to do it. He has Marie now. Julia knows, too, where he goes, at the back of the garden, at night, watching for Marie. He thinks Julia comes down the street and stands on the sidewalk, watching their black silhouettes. She's accused him of meeting Marie. She screamed at him, and once she threw a tortoiseshell comb at him, which hit the wall and broke. All this excites him: women's tempers, the color rising up their necks, hair spilling down over their throats, eyes brilliant with rage and tears.

Now he feels Katie's anger roiling toward him. The fire has spread throughout his chest. He feels excited, ready for battle.

Downstairs, the gong sounds; someone's at his office door.

———

DAWSON PULLS THE checkrein to stop the car just before Bull Street. He walks up the sidewalk toward the corner. Ethel is upstairs in Warrington's room; she sees him from the window. She's been waiting for him.

"There's Papa." She shakes her hands, flapping them from the wrists, anxious.

No, says Hélène, it can't be.

"It is," says Ethel, but Hélène tells her no, she's mistaken.

Of course Ethel recognizes her father, his solid silhouette, upright posture, distinctive walk. The new black coat. She's been watching for him: she wants to apologize. When she came running into their room this morning she'd been upset about losing her books. She was afraid they'd be late, ashamed to have to ask for carfare: it was all her fault. She's full of guilt now, because when she heard him call she pretended she hadn't. She hadn't answered, hadn't said goodbye. All day this bothered her. It's like a debt. She's waiting to tell him she's sorry.

Dawson walks up the street. On the far corner, at the grocery store, a man stands on a ladder, painting the window trim. Across the street, outside William McBurney's house, a livery horse and carriage stand waiting. On the near corner is a groundnut woman in a bright turban and long skirts. She sits on a stool among her baskets. As Dawson passes McDow's garden he looks in, between the houses, toward his own property. McDow's garden stretches from the street all the way to the back boundary. There a fence marks the line, but anyone standing in McDow's garden can look over it into the Dawsons' backyard. Or into the dining room windows. He can see the chandelier in the dining room. Something rises and tightens inside Dawson's chest.

The groundnut maum watches Dawson, hoping for custom, but he stops at McDow's door and steps into the vestibule.

Dawson rings the bell and hears its brief liquid trill. He stands waiting, but hears nothing more, no voice or footsteps. Seconds tick by. He doesn't like being made to wait. On the wall hangs a battered tin basket for messages. It's empty, and Dawson wonders who McDow's patients are. He thinks of the insurance fraud, digging up corpses. The stench. The body on the kitchen table. He thinks of McDow and Hélène on the street. He thinks of Golden watching as he, Dawson, read the report. It was distasteful to learn of this from Golden. All of it is distasteful. The stench. It is distasteful to deal with McDow in any way: McDow stands beyond the divide that separates men of honor from the other kind. What he has done is unthinkable. Honor and principle are the foundations of a civilized society; McDow flouts them.

McDow has broken the social contract and now he owes something to Dawson. Dawson will hold him to account. He can feel the muscle in his jaw gritting; he feels the way his teeth meet, at the back. He shifts his walking stick and rings again. Now he hears movement, and the door opens.

A short, slight man in his midthirties stands inside. He has a long face and a drooping black mustache. He's frowning slightly, as though he's just remembered something. His narrow head rises from his sloping shoulders like a weasel's.

"Yes?" McDow's tone seems peremptory. He doesn't apologize for keeping Dawson waiting.

"Dr. Thomas McDow?" Dawson asks.

Dawson stands in the doorway, straight-backed, elegant in his black derby, his lustrous fitted overcoat, his pale soft leather gloves. He holds a Malacca walking stick. His luxuriant mustache curls over his lip. He's several inches taller than McDow.

"Yes," says McDow. "Come in."

McDow despises all this: the gloves, the overcoat, the mustache, all of it. It's all beyond him—he wouldn't know how to find such an overcoat, and couldn't afford it anyway. He despises it.

He steps back. Is he swaying a bit? To cover it up he exaggerates his gestures.

Dawson thinks McDow's manner is offhand, or perhaps it's mocking? The ridiculous sweep of the arm.

They step inside. The office is low-ceilinged, the whitewashed walls stained with damp. It smells of mold and something else. In the center stands a round table. On the left-hand wall, two windows give out onto the piazza. Between them is a settee.

McDow moves back toward the settee, then turns to face his visitor. "What can I do for you?"

"I am Captain Dawson," Dawson announces.

McDow's face does not change; Dawson sees that he already knows this.

"Oh, yes," McDow says carelessly. He won't be intimidated. He feels the pistol, heavy and serious, behind him in the secretary drawer. He had come downstairs angry at Katie, and when he reached his office he'd taken out the bottle. Three long swallows, the fire glowing up in his chest. He's pleased that Dawson's here. He has a reason for seeing him, though he can't summon it up at this moment.

McDow repeats, "And what can I do for you?"

He's insolent, there's no question. Dawson thinks of the man staring over the back fence into his yard, through his windows. At his children. Sarah. Dawson's chest tightens.

"Dr. McDow," says Dawson, "I've been informed that you have been making improper advances to a member of my household. Ungentlemanly."

McDow says nothing. His silence is even more insolent.

"You are a married man," Dawson says. "This young woman is under my protection. I will not permit this."

McDow smiles. "The young woman," he says, "is of age. She is under her own protection. You have no right to say who she sees. Or does not see."

The words come rolling out: he's more powerful than he knew. The air in the room has begun to glitter as though lit by phosphorescence, some bright darkness which he can't understand, but which makes the room into a place where he can say or do anything.

Dawson's mouth tightens. "Please understand me. You have no right to tell me anything about Hélène Burdayron."

"Marie," McDow corrects him. "Her name is Marie."

"Do not tell me the name of my own servant." Dawson's voice rises. The heat in his chest is moving up to his throat.

McDow feels himself lifting off the ground. "I'll tell you whatever I like," he says. He's fumbling a bit with his words. "And she's not a servant."

"Marie-Hélène Burdayron"—Dawson pronounces the French name with insulting precision; McDow feels the words thrown in his face like frigid water—"receives a salary from me. She has been retained to look after my children. Mademoiselle Burdayron is a part of my household. She depends upon me for protection."

"Ma-moi-selle," says McDow, mockingly, but he can't think of the next thing. He sways slightly.

Dawson wonders if he's drunk.

"Let me be clear, Doctor. You are not to speak to her again," Dawson says, very precisely. "Nor to meet her on the street, or anywhere else. Nor to follow her. Is that understood?"

"No, it is not!" McDow says energetically, pleased with himself.

Dawson recognizes the other smell in the room: whisky. It's McDow's breath.

"You will do as I say," Dawson says, raising his voice. "You will stop seeing her, or I will publish an account of your disgraceful behavior in the newspaper." He's breathing hard now.

Rage boils up in McDow. "I will do nothing you say," he says. "I have been inside your house many times. Marie takes me there whenever she likes. I've sat in your library, in your own chair."

This is a lie. He has never sat in Dawson's chair, but saying so emboldens him. He feels the space in the room expanding. He's rising to meet Dawson on his own territory.

"I've sat in your chair," McDow repeats, pleased with himself. "By the statue of the wrestler. Very nice," McDow says, nodding. "I had a look." He lifts his hand and wiggles his fingers suggestively, to show that they had run over the contours of the bronze body.

Dawson does have a copy of *The Dying Gladiator* on his library table. The thought of McDow's fingers on it revolts him. All this revolts him— the idea of sneaking into someone's house at the invitation of a servant. "If you speak to her again I will ruin you," Dawson says. The man is contemptible.

"I'll speak to her when I like," McDow says. He stumbles a little over "speak"; his tongue has got soft somehow. "If you publish me I'll hold you personally responsible." That means a duel. He feels powerful, threatening Captain Dawson. "I'll speak to her when I like." He stumbles again over "speak."

Dawson gives his head a small shake. Looking down, narrowing his nostrils against the smell, he turns to leave. It's impossible to deal with a man who has no moral code, no sense of honor, no principles. McDow is beneath him.

McDow understands this: the headshake, the averted eyes, the narrowed nostrils, the contemptuous turning away. They are insults. Indignation flowers within him.

"You can't ruin me, Captain," he says. For some reason he believes this is true.

Dawson doesn't answer, he won't even look at McDow. He's done. He starts toward the door, but McDow steps in front of him.

McDow recognizes contempt, he can feel it freeze against the skin. Heat and whisky boil inside him. He won't be made invisible. He will make Dawson see him.

"Don't push past me, Captain," McDow says. He can't quite control himself, and he lurches into the captain.

Dawson's mouth twists. Up close the smell is vile, and he draws his head back.

McDow staggers closer. He will make Dawson see him. He was in Dawson's own library, walking up and down with Marie. He kissed her there, he touched her breasts. He touched those books, too, laying his finger across the spines, marking them with his touch. He ran his hand over the books and he kissed Marie. This man, Dawson, pretends it never happened. Dawson won't even acknowledge his existence. He'll make Dawson see him.

The air is tightening and flowering at once, his head is bursting and he understands that he can do anything. Dawson has turned away, heading for the door. He's put his cane in his other hand and he's going to walk out without speaking. McDow steps, lurching, in front of Dawson.

Dawson is repelled by McDow's face up close, the reddened eyes and stinking breath: Has he not understood? Dawson is done with him. His nostrils tighten, his mouth turns down in distaste.

"Let me pass, sir." Dawson uses "sir" as part of an order, as he'd speak to a dog.

But McDow doesn't move. He stands unsteadily before Dawson, chin jutting, chest out. Disgusted, Dawson sets his gloved palm against McDow's chest and gives him a tremendous thrust.

McDow staggers backward into the settee. It catches him behind the knees and he goes down, sprawling awkwardly onto the couch.

Now McDow remembers why he's pleased Dawson has come: because of what he told Marie he would do. Now he sees everything has been leading smoothly up to this moment. The humiliating fiasco of this morning, the detective in the tramcar, Melville in the buggy, that Negro woman shouting from her porch, the contemptible slack-breasted Mrs. Fair: all of it has been rising toward this, right now. Dawson is to blame for it all, and he has delivered himself to McDow.

Dawson, in his fitted overcoat and black derby, turns away, toward the door. McDow lurches to his feet and pushes past him, heading for the secretary in the corner. As he jostles past Dawson the other man recoils, but McDow keeps going. He opens the drawer and takes out the pistol. The air is closing around him and his arm rises of itself. He cocks the gun and points at the big solid torso as though someone else were inside him. Everything has slowed down, every movement is delayed.

Dawson hooks his cane over his left arm and reaches for the doorknob with his other hand. He turns to open the door and lifts his arm, exposing his right side, and McDow pulls the trigger. It seems to happen by itself. The sound explodes in the room.

Dawson is standing, but now everything changes. His shape ceases to move.

The air stills. McDow feels the shock echoing through the air like ripples on water. Everything has stopped.

Dawson turns to face him. He sets the point of his stick on the floor and leans on it. His face is changing utterly. It is like an eclipse, all the color is being leached away from it. Something is spreading through his body. He stares at McDow. In the silence something enormous is happening.

"You've killed me," he says. He sounds astonished. "I'm dying."

His expression is complicated, as though there is much more to it than this. McDow is frozen, hand still raised, holding the pistol. The room is filled by what has happened. Dawson is becoming something else, something is shifting inside him.

It takes a long time for Dawson to fall. He leans over slightly from the waist. Then he shifts to one side, as though he's about to step forward on the other foot. He gropes with the tip of the cane, but he's not stepping forward, his body is doing something else. His face is fixed, his expression interior and intent, as though he's watching something no one else can see.

Dawson feels the thing coursing through him, the great eruption inside, the cold moving up through his limbs. He feels it coming like the racing wall of shadow during an eclipse. He understands there is no stopping it.

The bullet has gone into the most intimate reaches of his body. It has grazed his kidney and gone on to sever the vena cava, the great vein that receives blood from all the vessels of the body, the vein that supplies the chambers of the heart. With each thundering beat the blood is being pumped elsewhere, away from Dawson's heart. His face is whitening, his lips turning pale.

It's the lips that frighten McDow. They are gray. He can't move. He stares at Dawson.

Dawson, confounded in some deep part of himself, puts his hand uselessly against his side, where the bullet entered, as though he can now prevent the terrible racing loss inside. He tries to press the heel of his hand against the place: above his waist, just around the curve of his side, on the edge of his back. He can feel the ribs under the skin; they are still solid, but that doesn't seem to matter. He can feel the world slipping. He staggers, catches himself, struggling to stay upright, then slowly he collapses, yielding to that which would have him fall. Gravity, and the inexorable descent toward what is coming. Now he feels it gathering around him; the world itself draws near, a great sweeping accumulation, like an ocean wave, curling over and crashing down in silence, of thoughts and feelings, his beliefs and ideas, the things that populated the world he lived in. Now he sees they are irrelevant, as he slides downward onto the floor of Thomas McDow's office.

His big body comes thudding down hard. The darkness pools inside him.

Dawson feels the world closing around him, the air turning dark. The things that he was moving toward have become distant. He was doing something here, something important. Hélène comes into his mind, but that's not it, it's something larger, the whole sky lies before him, though it's dark and overcast. He thinks of Sarah, turning to look at him in the garden; of Warrington's face. He sees the wrought-iron balcony on the house in Provence, the tall green shutters. Ethel, in the niche on the staircase, her pointed chin raised. What was it he was moving toward? He was doing something, accomplishing something large. Wasn't it large, wasn't he grappling with great issues? He could feel himself groping for the shape of it, but now the world is closing around him, the things he was racing toward are disappearing, now it's only this that he can see, what's just here, and the light is fading. The newspaper itself, the magnificent engine of his life for all these years, a sense of power and urgency like a brushfire, the sense of it, glowing and hot, incandescent with energy and ideas. He can see the staircase at the office, the crack in the bottom step, and the clacking sound of the press. The reporters barking and laughing downstairs, like excited dogs. The softened seat of his leather chair, the sound it makes as he settles into it. And Sarah, Sarah's face at his bedside when he had the fever, her pale blue eyes, the bony bridge of her nose where the skin is translucent. Her pale zealot's eyes. He's leaving everything, and he can see the room darkening; he can't see the stars, even the deep sky is gone. He can't hear the bells. Whatever he wanted is gone, and the dark rises, sliding up over his head. He's drowning. He remembers the ship, the tossing waves, and the long white script of the moon on the water and the great shadows on the surface of the sea during the long night watches.

———•———

MCDOW STARES as though this were happening without any connection to him.

His chest is on fire. He can't encompass it: the sound of the shot—was it from him?—and the strange interior look on Dawson's face, that unexpected shift of his weight, the slow collapse, the dark ink spreading onto the carpet.

After a long time he moves to Dawson's side. He feels the wrist for the pulse. The flesh is flaccid, it yields. There is no beat. Dawson's eyes are open and fixed. Dull.

McDow wonders if he should get help; he thinks confusedly of calling a doctor. Medical assistance.

It's fatal. He sees that.

He should do something. His mind is blurred and fumbling.

He does nothing. Minutes pass by. He may faint; his eyes go dark. He is alone here. The room seems to close around him, the air thickens. He can hardly breathe.

37.

4:00, March 12, 1889. Charleston

CAPTAIN DAWSON LIES on the floor, inert, enormous.

The body seems to take up the entire room. The dark overcoat is flung open onto the big chest, exposing the high white collar, the silky folded tie, the black high-buttoned jacket. The legs, in striped trousers, turn outward, feet splayed. The abdomen is huge, swollen from internal bleeding. But it's the face McDow can't look away from. Dawson's head is turned to one side, and his eyes are open and still. The mouth is parted. Narrow lines of red have made their way down from the side of the mouth, the nose, down the slack cheek, disappearing into the collar. The blood is shockingly dark, nearly black. Dawson's eyes are open, the whites gleam. They seem to move. McDow thinks they follow him, that Dawson is watching him. He's both dead and watching.

McDow can't think how he has come to be here in this room with this body of death. He feels resistance, rejection of the sight. The body seems to radiate some kind of inaudible alarm. He can't stop it.

The street windows are opaque. He pulls down the blinds on the piazza side, then goes out the back door and up the outside stairs to the second floor of the piazza. He walks up and down, glancing sideways at the street to see if anyone has heard the shot. No one's walking about, though a carriage and driver stand waiting outside McBurney's house. McDow goes back downstairs and lets himself in to the office.

The body is still there. As he stands looking at it he hears the gong. The noise is loud and terrifying. Someone is at the door.

A chill moves through him: Dawson's body lies in front of the inner door. For a moment McDow does nothing, then he picks up the pistol and steps through the vestibule to the outer door. He leans over, listening: he hears shuffling, breathing. He opens the door a few inches and peers through the crack with one eye.

A man on the other side stares at him. He can see the face: it's a policeman, a light-skinned colored man called Gordon. McDow had seen him on the street earlier, coming back from the disastrous trip with Hélène. Gordon was on the corner, wearing civilian clothes. Now McDow thinks he must have been put there to watch him.

———·———

MCDOW CROUCHES SLIGHTLY, hidden behind the door. The pistol is in his right hand. He can hear his heart thundering. He says nothing, only one eye exposed.

"Dr. McDow?" Gordon says.

"Yes," McDow answers. He hears himself breathing.

"Everything all right in there?" asks Gordon.

"Yes," McDow answers. They stare at each other through the crack. McDow's heart gallops. Gordon's amber eye is wide open. They are inches apart.

"Heard there might be some trouble," Gordon says. "Someone heard a shot."

McDow feels himself loud and silent. He refuses to speak. His heart, though.

After a minute McDow draws his face away from the door. He is still watching the policeman as he closes the door on the other man's gaze. He turns back to his office.

The body is still there. The coat is still flung open, the black jacket exposed, feet splayed. It's still here in the room with him.

He must hide it. He must hide it before Gordon comes in. He'll come back.

He can bury it. There's a closet under the interior stairs. The floor is only loose wooden planks laid over earth. He's used it before to bury medical detritus, surgical scraps.

He grasps one of the hands and tugs, trying to drag the corpse across the floor. It's like dragging a sand dune, a mastodon. Dawson will barely budge. He braces himself and tugs harder, but the glove comes off in his hand and he staggers backward. He drops the glove and seizes the bare hand. The fingers are cold and unresponsive; he recoils, then regrasps the hand. He grabs the other one as well, pulling the arms over the head. He begins pulling, bracing himself for each tug. The thing shifts heavily across the carpet. The other glove comes loose; he grabs the wrist. He braces himself with each step, moving backward. When he nears it he opens the door to the stairwell. The closet door is nailed shut, he did this himself, recently, when the hinges broke. He leaves the body by the closet door.

He puts on his hat and walks out to the barn, feeling exposed and strange. He brings back a hatchet and spade, holding them low and awkwardly. Inside, the body is still there. He has to step over it to reach the closet.

He prizes the nails free with the edge of the hatchet. He takes off the door and sets it against the wall. He leans into the closet. The lintel is low, and he bangs his head on it hard. He prizes up the floorboards, exposing the earth.

The space is about eight feet long, three wide. Easily big enough. He leans in to start digging and bangs his head again, painfully. It's too dark; he needs some light.

He steps across the body again. He doesn't look at the eyes. He goes out through the piazza door and heads for the corner store. On the sidewalk he passes his neighbor Edward Lafitte, who gives him an odd look. Lafitte stops to speak but McDow ignores him.

Lafitte says, "Doctor."

McDow stops.

"Your hat," Lafitte says, pointing. "It's dented, and there's whitewash on it."

McDow doesn't answer. He takes his hat off and rubs it on his elbow. He smiles, to show Lafitte everything is fine. He can't remember exactly how to smile; he thinks it's like this, raising the lips and pulling them back. The air is seething. The world is speeding up, everything is going faster and faster.

At the store he asks for five cents' worth of apples. He doesn't want to raise suspicion by asking for candles first. The shopkeeper picks out six apples from the barrel. McDow asks carelessly for a nickel's worth of candles.

"Don't wrap them," McDow says, and counts out the coins. His heart is thudding. His chest has become huge. He puts the candles in his pocket. He walks outside with the packet of apples. Across the street, on the corner, stands Gordon, conspicuously not looking at him.

The body is still there. It's still huge. It seems ready to burst. It's so silent! McDow is appalled by it.

He steps over it. Inside the closet he lights a candle and sets it into the soil. He takes the spade and crouches, hitting his head again. He crouches lower and begins digging. The soil is loose and friable. He shovels quickly, fearful, piling the earth on either side of the hole. He thinks of Gordon knocking on the door; he thinks he hears the gong, but it's his imagination.

When the hole is large enough he backs out, crouching. He drags in the body, tugging, then pushing.

The head stops at the far end. It won't go any farther. He shoves and lunges, but it won't move. It's mostly buried, though, and now his pulse is hammering. He crouches and slides the floorboards down again over the body. The nose is the highest point, and thrusts the board into a slant. McDow uses the shovel like a sledgehammer on the board. He tries to pound down the board, flattening what's underneath it, but there isn't room to raise the shovel high enough. The plank stays on a slant, tilted by Dawson's head, his nose. McDow backs out, panting. It's mostly hidden. It doesn't need to be entirely buried. He nails the door shut again. No one will come in here.

He goes back out into his office. The body is gone, but still seems to be present. He can still hear his heart. He remembers that the eyes are still open.

He didn't close them. He slid the boards over the face and the eyes were still open.

He takes out the bottle and has three more pulls of fire. He waits for the policeman. There is no one. He hears nothing from outside. He thinks of the body crammed into the space, the floorboards against the face. He can feel the face being crushed by the planks.

The air in here is taking up the air from outside, this room is taking over the rest of the world. What's happened here is blotting out everything else. He feels his brain at the center of a huge whirling rotation, the spiral at the start of the universe. He's right at the center of it.

He must tidy up. He sets the chair in place, neatens the papers on his desk. He puts the pistol in the drawer of the secretary. He opens the bottom cabinet and takes another swallow; another; then another. He feels better. He sits down at the table.

He can feel Dawson lying under the stairs. There is a smell. He can feel the face under the floorboards. The face beneath them. The eyes.

He should dig him up. This was wrong, utterly wrong. He sees that now. He must dig him up. He goes back to the closet and sets the hatchet blade against the nails, prizing them up. Chaos swirls through his head, like a hurricane in the room. He wrestles out the filthy planks.

He pulls the body out by the feet and drags it back into the office. The face is covered with dark abrasions from the floorboards that were set on top of it. McDow stands over it, smoothing his mustache. He is at the center of something; he has no idea what. The body is dirty and disheveled, the feet lolling apart.

He goes upstairs for a rag and basin. Emma, the cook, is in the kitchen. She looks at him but says nothing. He asks where his wife is. Gone to her father! says Emma. He comes down slowly. He's holding the basin carefully, but the water slides back and forth, spilling. He sets the basin beside Dawson and crouches down. He wets the rag, wrings it out. He lays it over Dawson's face. He digs into its contours, the bridge of the nose, the yielding eyes in their sockets, the hairline. Between strokes he dips the rag in the basin, releasing a dark murky cloud. He washes everything, brushes the sand from the silky creases of the tie, flicks it from the black wool.

He carries the basin through the hall, through the lumber room, into the little back space, full of cobwebs and broken tools. He puts the basin behind a sawhorse, on the windowsill.

The glove lies on the carpet. McDow puts it in Dawson's fist and clasps the fingers around it; they don't stay clasped, and he bends them again. Slowly they open. He tucks the glove inside them, as though Dawson had just taken it off.

Five o'clock. Time lies endless before him. All these hours stretching on into the evening, and then night, like the deserts of Arabia.

He can't stay here in the same room with death. He puts on his hat and goes out, down Bull Street, past the Dawsons' house. He doesn't turn his head as he walks past, though he sees it from the corner of his eye.

Julia lives two blocks away, behind Mrs. Calder's Hotel. He turns up the driveway, his footsteps, the oyster shells crunching beneath his feet. The sound seems deafening; he resists the urge to walk on tiptoe. He walks past the main house to the carriage house. Julia's apartment is on the second floor; he steps inside and calls up the stairs. She opens her door.

"What is it?" She stays in her room, peering through the door. She doesn't like it when he comes here.

"Come down," McDow says. "I need to see you."

She comes down to stand on the step above him. On the wall beyond her is a set of steel engravings, pictures of historical events marching up the stairwell. "What is it?"

"I've killed Captain Dawson," McDow says.

He hears himself say the words. Now they are true. Behind her is the signing of the Declaration of Independence, bewigged men in a lofty room, gesturing with quill pens. She stares at him.

"What do you mean?"

"I've killed him," he says.

She steps down the last stair.

———·———

AT THE OFFICE HE unlocks the front door and they come inside. It is very quiet. Dawson is still there, lying on the floor near the back door.

Julia's face goes white. She draws a breath and puts her hand on her chest.

She turns her head away and goes over to sit on the settee. She puts her head into her hands. He hears her rapid breathing.

She says something, he can't make out what. After a minute he understands she's asking him questions.

"What happened?" She looks at him, not at the captain.

"He said he'd publish me in the paper," McDow says. He doesn't want to say anything about Marie. "He'd ruin me."

As he says it he hears that it's not enough. He makes a large gesture across his chest, as though Dawson had driven a steamroller over him. "He caned me." He remembers Dawson's huge thudding push against his chest. Did Dawson hit him with his stick at the same moment? He can't remember; he might have. It seemed like caning. He was being attacked. He touches his head, where he'd run into Mrs. Fair's doorjamb, and then against the lintel in the closet. It's tender; he blames Dawson.

Julia frowns.

There is a silence. McDow raises both hands to his mustache and smooths it outward. He thinks of saying that Dawson refused to look at him. But he can't tell her that. He can't bear saying it out loud.

"He hit me," he says.

She nods, waiting.

"With his cane," McDow says, trying it out. "He caned me and threatened to publish me in the paper."

"There's mud in his hair."

"I buried him," McDow says.

She looks appalled.

"Under the stairs," he says, gesturing. "Then I dug him up. It wouldn't work."

She looks down again. They stay motionless. He watches her; he hears her breathing. After a while she stands and smooths her skirt.

"I was standing by the settee when he hit me," he says. "I fell back onto it and he hit me again with his cane."

McDow sees the glove; it's fallen out of Dawson's fingers. He gives it to Julia, who puts it in Dawson's fist. She clasps the fingers around it; they don't stay clasped, and she bends them again. Slowly they loosen, open.

She stands and sets her hands on her hips.

"You'll have to turn yourself in," she says.

He stares at her.

While she was working on the glove it seemed that everything was slowing down and under control. When she says this, things start to speed up and swirl again.

"To the police," she says.

"Yes," he says, irritated. "I will, I will." He is offended that she doesn't know that he knows this. Everything offends him. The air is filled with stinging particles.

"I want you to stay here to look after Katie, when she comes back," he says.

"Where is she?"

"Gone to her father's, at the hotel. I want you to wait for her."

She nods. He leaves by the front door.

He'd told her he'd turn himself in. Is that what she said? He will, he'll turn himself in to the police. He looks around for Gordon, who may still be lurking nearby.

But first he needs to tell Marie. It's past six o'clock, she should be home by now.

He goes around the corner to Bull Street. He walks back and forth on the sidewalk in front of the house. Often Marie hears him, when he does that, and comes outside. She knows his footsteps, which used to please him but now alarms him. He walks up and down, but no one appears. He stops at the wrought-iron gate and stands looking at the house, up the flight of stone stairs.

He's waiting for Marie, but it's Mrs. Dawson who comes outside. She's been listening for a footstep, though not his.

She stands on the porch, looking down at him.

She doesn't recognize him. He stares at her: a small erect woman with pale eyes, at the top of the long stone stairs.

38.

SARAH MORGAN DAWSON MEMORANDUM

At four o'clock, I grew very anxious. From that moment, the conviction that he
had been murdered haunted me. Ten minutes, at the latest, would have brought
him home. He never failed to warn me by telephone, or note, or messenger,
of the least delay, knowing my anxiety and haunting fear. I had waited over
sixteen years to see his murdered body brought home. The day had come.
Our acquaintance had begun in such a threatened tragedy. I never doubted
this would be the end. He shared my belief, great as was his faith in
humanity.

At five, I had dinner for the children hastily served. I would not eat, because I
said it would make him sad to eat alone, presently. The children were due at
dancing school at five o'clock. It was ten minutes past, as they ran from the dining
room followed by Hélène. They had caught up a cake apiece, and still wondering
why "dear father" did not come, paused before McDow's window, by which

McDow had once more dragged their father's body from its hidden grave. They were wagering which of the approaching cars would bring their father. He lay just the other side of the opaque panes of glass—murdered. The murderer must have heard their laughter as he performed his ghoul's work of arranging, with Miss Smith, the mise en scène for an "act of self defense."

And I—left to myself, I could no longer dissemble. I could neither read, nor reason with my vague fears & growing terror. I could only see him murdered—doubled up—and in a dark corner. And then I was ashamed of myself.

At six, exactly, I went on the front porch, to hear his step the sooner. I know it was six, because the gardener who never worked after the first stroke of six, was just coming around the house to take away his rake & spade. I begged him to take with him the dead vines I had pulled down as I waited. As he carried them off, I stood listening intently for the step I was never to hear, and gazing at a very beautiful sunset sky which I shall never forget. Suddenly, a great horror seized me. I felt that I was in the presence of an unclean devil.

At the gate, looking intently at me through the light iron lattice work, was a slender, very dark, dirty and dishevelled man. The face was that of a devil in anguish. In horror I gazed at this incarnation of a lost soul, repeating to myself "It's a devil! He is a devil!" His very piteous, God-forsaken look seemed defilement to me. I feared that by standing so absorbed on the front porch, I had attracted the attention of a drunken tramp; and I quickly entered the house. It was the murderer, who had come to carry off Hélène, having now unburied my husband, according to his subsequent statement. I learned after, from Isaac and the other servants, that he passed through the gate at once, and went in to the kitchen, where he asked for Hélène. Isaac said she was at dancing school. Where? He neither knew nor cared. They were all impressed by the murderer's singular manner and appearance, & decided that he was, as usual, drunk, because of the terrible expression of his eyes, whose convulsive rolling he could not control.

I had hardly entered the parlor, when [my friend] Miss Gazer was announced. I tried to hide my anxiety, unwilling to court comments which would be difficult to answer. Perhaps I was never more gay. She asked how it happened that I was not driving with Capt. Dawson—"This is your hour; I confess I did not expect to find you!"

"I have not started yet for the office," I said. And for a moment I feared I would tell her "I believe he is murdered!" and so create a painful impression of my sanity.

I saw her out, and fled to his room. I sat by his bedside, looking at the sunset, & vainly endeavoring to read "The Century" which I had held the whole time. If I could but make an excuse to call the office by telephone, without betraying my fears!

The clock, which he kept so exact, struck half past six. I flew to the telephone, and summoned the upper office to answer the question that only the lower office would reply to.

"Were the wood & coal ordered for me to-day?"

They would inquire below.

"Oh! no matter. Is Capt. Dawson there?"

"No ma'am! He has not yet returned."

I closed the telephone mechanically. "Returned!" Then he had gone out—and the haunting dread of all these years—Murder—might have overtaken him. Again I stood by his bed, staring at the sunset, dreading to move or speak for fear of the formless horror on the threshold. From four o'clock, I had been able to see him only as murdered, doubled up, and thrust in a corner. Do what I would, I could not rid myself of this haunting conviction.

The telephone again called, within a very few minutes. I dashed out, thinking it was he. It was the lower office, & Mr. La Coste. Strangely enough, it was my own question: "Did you get the wood and coal?"

"No—but—"

"Is Capt. Dawson there?"

"No! Mr. La Coste! I believe he has been waylaid & murdered!"

Sharply the telephone was cut off.

I was angry with myself for not compelling him to listen to my pain. I did not know that he was repeating to the Chief of Police my cry, or that Golden was answering "His life may depend on your silence," as he ran out.

Again I returned to his window, staring at a sky that contained no morning for me. I said to myself "If he indeed lies stark and dead—doubled up—in a corner—and

I remember that I suffered all these hours doing nothing while I might have saved him—!" I turned to the dark in fresh terror.

Twenty minutes to seven. I dashed out to the telephone, determined that someone should hear me.

Mr. Armstrong answered.

I called "Mr. Armstrong, Capt. Dawson has not returned to dinner. This has never before happened without a note, or a messenger. I am *very* anxious!"

"What are you afraid of, in his perfect health and strength?" he laughed.

"He *is* in perfect health, thank God! But you do not know what I have suffered since four o'clock! I believe he has been waylaid and *murdered*!"

As I uttered that word, a wail, not of this world, came across the telephone wire. It was a soul in anguish. I have no explanation to give; I only know the terror that froze my very blood.

The next moment I heard Mr. Armstrong's voice: "Did you remember the Granite committee at seven?"

"No! or I would not have spoken! But please go to the committee room! Tell him I am sorry to be unreasonable, but that I am so unhappy about him that I can know no rest until he sends me word that all is well with him!"

"Not only that, but I will never leave him until I place him under your eyes! You shall see for yourself that nothing has harmed him!"

"Thanks! quickly, then!" I called.

The children in running to me from their dancing, had paused on the stair, followed by all the servants who came to ask further orders about the delayed dinner, etc.

Ethel threw her arms around me as I turned from the telephone.

"Pourquoi me cacher que tu étais inquiète a propos de cher papa? Je t'aurais bien vite consolér!" [*Why didn't you tell me you were worried about Papa? I'd have consoled you right away!*]

"Rien de saurait me consoler quand je crains un malheur pour ton papa," I answered. [*Nothing can console me when I'm afraid that something has happened to your father.*] Again, I now remembered Hélène's strange question "Quelque chose est donc arrivé?" [*Has something happened?*]

"Rien. Il paraît que monsieur est retenu par des affaires qui me touchent. Il arrive. Préparez vite sa salade." [*Nothing has happened. The captain is detained by business matters. He's coming. Quickly fix his salad.*]

To the cook, I gave orders to change the dinner to a hot supper, not forgetting the dessert for which he had asked for the first time that he ever asked any dish. To Isaac, I gave the order to re-set the table, substituting the blue china for the red dinner service.

Jane, as usual, wanted to borrow [money]. I gave her $5.00 & change. Celia began a very bitter and impertinent tirade. I told her that I was very tired of her ingratitude and inefficiency; that I had borne her very patiently for God's sake, and would feel greatly relieved when she could find another place, & so relieve me of an intolerable burden. I turned to finish a letter to Miriam, when [my friend] Mrs. Sinkler was announced. I remember that she talked for quite fifteen minutes, neither sitting nor pausing. I ran back to my letter. Hardly the second page was finished when Henry Baynard was announced. I ran gladly down the steps, meeting him under the crimson hall light.

"You bring me a message from Capt. Dawson!" I cried eagerly.

"No–!"

"No message? Where is he?"

"Is he not here?"

"No! If you bring me no message, Mr. Baynard—what has happened?"

"Nothing! I thought I would like to call, that is all."

"Oh! I beg your pardon, Mr. Baynard! pray come in! The fact is I am *very* anxious about my husband—so anxious that I am not civil! Where is he?"

"At the office!"

"And sent me no message? Is anything the matter, Mr. Baynard?" For I suddenly perceived that Mr. Baynard was either insane, or deeply agitated.

"Oh! *nothing* is the matter! He is well! *Very* well!" and he burst into tears and fell at my feet kneeling.

I knew that his brother Swinton deserved death at Frank's hands, and that Frank repeatedly said that ex-mayor Courtenay would yet force him to kill him, (Courtenay) by his infamous slanders and persecution. I thought Henry Baynard had come to tell me of the death of one of these, at my husband's hands.

Strange to say, this awful thought gave me superhuman strength.

"Has he killed any one? I do not care!" I cried. I meant that nothing could separate him from my love.

"He has killed no one! He would hurt no one! He is quite, quite well! In the office, you know!"

Then I knew that Henry Baynard was a madman—at least I believed it. I must humor him, and temporize until I could hear Frank's step. He must be almost at the gate, now! But my own haunting fears, and the agony of Mr. Baynard were beyond my endurance. I felt my life ebbing. I could only articulate "Mr. Baynard I am in a very critical state. I feel I shall die before many minutes. Will you put me out of pain, and tell me what has happened to you?"

His tears were raining on my hands as he knelt before the chair where I had fallen to die, as I believed.

He only sobbed "Nothing! nothing has happened to me!"

I heard hurried steps—many of them! Frank's was among them then! He would save my life! The door burst open. Mr. Hemphill and Mr. Weber stood before me.

"Mr. Hemphill! What has happened?"

"I know nothing! I came to ask!"

"Mr. Baynard knows something! make him tell me, or I shall die!"

Mr. Baynard could only cry in anguish. Mr. Hemphill led him from the room. I stood facing Mr. Weber. We never spoke or moved. As they re-entered the back parlor, I advanced calmly.

"Is my husband dead?"

"Yes."

————

LATER THAT EVENING the bundle was brought, the bundle that she should not have seen. It was the clothes, muddied and soiled, that had been taken from his body for the autopsy.

Later still they brought his body.

39.

6:00, March 12, 1889. Charleston

MCDOW STARES AT Mrs. Morgan. He has never met her; she is from another world. Their circles would never overlap. She stands at the top of the two flights of white stairs, staring at him with blazing eyes. He sees that she knows. He can't move. He doesn't dare speak to her.

She turns and goes inside. He watches the door close. He has been inside that hall, he knows the red lamp. He knows the rooms. He feels his knowledge swell and vibrate within him.

McDow goes down to the carriage gate, slips inside, and walks up the driveway to the kitchen building. He opens the door without knocking. In the kitchen Celia leans over the big table. When she sees him her face turns closed and angry. Jane comes in from the pantry, holding a basin.

"What do you want here?" Jane asks.

"Marie," McDow says. He can hardly speak. His head is swollen inside, filled with flickering and sound.

"She's not here." Jane bangs the basin down on the table and wipes her hands on her apron.

"I need to tell her something," McDow says. He looks around. Isaac sits on a chair in the corner, his white jacket unbuttoned. He stares at McDow. "Where is she?"

"Dancing school," Isaac says.

"She took the children," Jane adds.

"But where?" McDow asks. He needs to find her. She lies at the heart of all this. He's killed the captain on her behalf. She must be told.

Dawson's body is in the middle of his brain, motionless on the floor. He thinks of the chest rising, the black coat shifting as the ribcage expands. He must tell Marie, she will know what it means. She knows it had to happen. She was there this morning when he said it would happen. She's part of this.

"Where is she?" he asks, looking from person to person. He sees that they all hate him here.

Celia makes a disgusted face and turns to the stove.

"Where is she indeed," says Jane. The basin is full of string beans, and she begins snapping the ends off.

It's Isaac who knows exactly where she is, he drove the carriage. McDow looks at him. He can feel himself tilting—is he tilting? Is his body tilting? He leans surreptitiously in the other direction.

"Don't know where they are," Isaac says with finality. He stands up, holding the edge of his jacket, and leaves the room. McDow sways slightly. The two women ignore him. He waits for a moment. He feels the evening gathering around him, rushing against his brain. He needs Marie, and she's not here. He can't tell these people what has happened. He feels that he looks strange, he feels himself made into something else, but he has no control. He sways slightly, and with a great effort he turns without stumbling and goes outside.

The light is beginning to fade, the trees becoming dark overhanging silhouettes. He walks back down the driveway, out onto the sidewalk. He needs to tell someone. Julia told him he must turn himself in. That may be what he will do. He can't be sure.

On the corner is the old groundnut woman. Her head is wrapped in a red kerchief. She stares at him balefully. He sees from her glare that she knows about him. The world knows what he has done.

He will turn himself in.

At home he tells Moses to get out the horse and buggy. Moses brings it out and McDow gets onto the seat and sets off. At the corner is Officer Gordon, in plain clothes. Gordon has been sent to watch him. He understands that this is how it will be, that he will be watched. Everyone knows. The world is contracting and expanding around him, he has no control over it.

He has done everything. The body is cleaned and laid out on the carpet; the office has been straightened, his keys are in the drawer with the pistol, his papers square on the desk. This is the next step. He repeats the phrase in his mind: He caned me. He caned me. No man of courage would allow it.

The words seem lustrous, powerful.

Though he doesn't actually want to say that he's been caned. He hesitates between rousing outrage and admitting shame. He's persuaded himself now that Dawson did hit him with his walking stick when he pushed him. Thrust him away. He can still feel that insulting shove against his breastbone. And his head still hurts from Mrs. Fair's doorway, and the low closet lintel.

It's all Dawson's fault, starting with the detective on the streetcar. Though that now seems in another century, the ride through the morning sunlight, Marie climbing on board, glancing at him, then turning her head. Knowing they would get off together. After that everything spiraled into a tornado, that old woman who wouldn't let them step inside her house for three minutes, that doctor turning up in the buggy, being hounded through the streets. Mrs. Fair's maid, her horrified face, as he ran past her. All Dawson's fault, mounting into such a whirlwind. Now everything is urging him on. It's like a waterfall, the current now too powerful to resist.

Gordon watches McDow as the buggy approaches.

"Evening, Doctor," Gordon says.

"Officer," McDow says, "I want to turn myself in. I've committed a murder."

"A murder." Officer Gordon looks anxious.

"I've killed Captain Dawson," McDow says. He feels as though he's falling off the edge of something, a precipice.

———•———

BECAUSE HE HAS turned himself in, and because Dawson is famous, McDow is given certain unofficial allowances. On the way to the station he is permitted to visit the man he wants to hire as counsel, Judge Andrew Magrath.

The news has already begun to spread, and by the time he arrives at jail, McDow has become a celebrity: he has killed the most important man in Charleston. He is put in the police chief's office instead of a cell. He sits in the chief's chair and asks Detective McManus to go out to buy him cigars. When McManus returns McDow asks for better ones. He sends out for dinner. His manner is agitated and excited. He gives an interview to a reporter from the *World*, who asks him several times to calm down.

McDow tells his story: Dawson was aggressive and hostile. He commanded McDow to stop seeing Hélène, and threatened to ruin him. When McDow defied him, Dawson struck him a terrific blow on the chest and gave him a cut on the head with his cane, denting his hat. When Dawson attacked him McDow made his way across the room to seize his pistol. Afraid for his life, he fired.

McDow says nothing about the three hours that elapse between Dawson's death and his turning himself in. He doesn't mention dragging the body to the closet under the stairs, the loose floorboards, the soft dry soil. He says nothing about Julia Smith. He says nothing about the gold watch he gave Marie Burdayron, or his proposals.

A GROWING CROWD gathers around the jail. People in the street pass the word that Frank Dawson has been shot. Dawson is dead.

MAGRATH WASN'T AT HOME when McDow stopped at his house, but he received McDow's request before Sarah had been told her husband was dead, before she knew she would need help for herself. Magrath agreed to take McDow's case. This left Sarah the choice of someone less eminent, less experienced, less brilliant. She chose the firm of Jervey and Mitchell, whose partners were both friends of Dawson. Their firm had argued against Judge Magrath at an earlier trial, when Dr. Amos Bellinger had been accused of the murder of Stephney Riley, a black livery stable owner. Thomas McDow had been one of the autopsy doctors. He had watched Magrath perform. He had seen him walking up and down before the jury, orating, giving those big sweeping gestures, letting the silence grow. Thundering, whispering. Magrath was theatrical and authoritative. McDow had watched Magrath win the case. He'd seen Bellinger go free. He'd seen Jervey and Mitchell argue on the other side. He'd seen them lose.

40.

THE TRIAL WAS in late June, when Charleston was murmuring toward summer. The trees were in full leaf, the sidewalks generously dappled with shade. The roses were over by then. Dawson's favorites, the luscious pink Paul Neyron and the biscuit-colored Gloire de Dijon, had shed their satiny petals in loose cascades onto the moist earth. The phlox stood glowing in tall pale masses against the dark green box bushes, and the lacy white heliotrope made its floppy arches, giving off its sweet wedding-cake fragrance. The evenings were still cool; ladies wore wraps. Sarah seldom went out, and when she did she wore a heavy veil, two layers of thick gauzy net over her face. She wanted to meet no one's eyes.

Newspapers all over the country covered the trial.

On the first day it rained, big slashing sheets that pounded against the windows. The sky was low, muffled in heavy storm-filled clouds. The streets pooled with water. Crowds shuffled slowly along the sidewalks, awkward with umbrellas. They crammed themselves into the courthouse. Inside, the windows were steamy, the air close.

It was the first trial of a white man with a jury more black than white.

During the selection, McDow and his counsel challenged one after another until they had found seven black jurors and five white. Most of the white men on the jury were not educated: McDow did not want to be judged by his own peers, let alone Dawson's.

McDow's lawyer, Judge Magrath, was a Fire-Eater, and the former governor. He was a distinguished trial lawyer, a big handsome man, commanding, with a long nose and thin lips. His face was clean-shaven, his thick hair was brushed back from a bold forehead. He held your gaze, he held the silence. He used his arms to gesture, he strode back and forth. He was charming, wily, and aggressive.

The prosecutor was William Jervey, an old friend of Dawson's. He'd supported Wade Hampton's election, and in 1884 he'd attended the Democratic National Convention, when Dawson was the state delegate. At the trial he brought in two attorneys to assist him, Henry Smith and Julien Mitchell, both also friends of Dawson.

That first day the courtroom was packed to panting. McDow came in wearing a dark suit, his black eyes bright, his hair trim. He walked calmly into the room, composed, nodding and smiling like royalty. After he sat down he took out a white silk handkerchief and flicked at his sleeve. No one could take their eyes from him.

Until Hélène Burdayron was brought in. The crowd whispered and rustled, telling one another who she was: "The French maid!" She was dressed demurely, in black, with white lace at her collar. She had dark circles under her eyes. The bottom of her dress had gotten wet in the rain, and her skirt was heavy and sodden.

They all craned their necks to see her.

When Hélène took the stand, she did not understand the very first thing she was asked. The clerk handed her the black courtroom Bible, tattered, tied with string. He told her to kiss it. She stared at him in incomprehension.

"Kiss the book," he said, louder.

Hélène looked around the room for help. A man standing by the judge's desk stepped forward and took the Bible. He kissed it, then handed it to her, nodding. Hélène pressed it dutifully to her lips and awaited the next command.

The prosecutor asked for a translator, since the witness manifestly did not speak English. Magrath disagreed, maintaining that she was competent in the language.

He walked up to her, his hands clasped behind his back, his hair a thick white mane.

"What is your name?" he asked her. He held her gaze, smiling at her.

"Marie Burdayron."

"You are living in Charleston now?"

"Yes."

"What is your native language?"

"French," she replied.

"You came from Geneva to Charleston?"

"With Mrs. Dawson."

"Where are your relatives and friends?"

But at that Hélène shook her head, mystified. Too many words, too fast.

Smith, sitting at the table, asked again for a translator, but Magrath waved him silent. He walked up to Hélène, sitting on the raised seat.

"Do you know Dr. McDow?" asked Magrath. He spoke slowly and thoughtfully, as though these were things he'd been mulling over, ideas he'd like to share with her.

"Yes."

"What did he say to you?"

"He asked me to run away with him in France."

"What did you say?"

"I say I won't leave Mrs. Dawson for anything in the world."

"Why did he tell you he wanted to run away?"

"He didn't give me the reason."

Hélène told him how they'd met, how he'd besieged her. How she'd told McDow to attend to his marriage, and that she would not run away with him.

Magrath smiled at her, as though he liked her.

"Did it occur to you that if it was wrong in McDow, being a married man and a father, in making these addresses to you, it was wrong in you, being a single young girl, to be listening to those addresses?"

Hélène frowned, trying to understand. She thought they were discussing a moral point.

"Yes, I thought so," she said.

"And still you continued to listen to them?"

"Yes, I did," she said, truthful.

"Was his voice musical and soft?" asked Magrath, smiling.

"Yes," said Hélène, confused.

"Then was it the music of his voice that was enchanting you away?"

"I don't think it was that, it may be that he was talking English," she said uncertainly.

"Did you ever help him to talk French?"

"Yes," she said.

"What was your mode of instructing him in French?"

"I never did teach him," she answered, floundering.

"He never asked you the pronunciation of a French word?"

"Yes, two or three words I told him with pleasure."

"You helped him along?" Magrath asked gently.

"Yes."

"You just led him along by the hand that way?"

"I don't know what you say," Hélène answered. Now she'd become uneasy. She understood that there was something she didn't understand.

Magrath asked her about McDow pulling her in to the colored woman's yard. He tried to make her admit that she knew why McDow wanted a private space.

"Didn't you know without his telling you what he wanted you to go there for?"

"I did not know nothing about it."

"Didn't you know that he wanted you to go away with him?"

"Yes, I know," she said, "but I would not."

"For what purpose?"

"I don't know, he would not tell me."

"Did you suppose that he wanted you to go and play croquet with him?" He spoke gently.

"I did not suppose so," Hélène said stoutly, but she was out of her depth. Everyone could see it.

Smith asked again for a translator; the judge denied his request.

Magrath asked about the watch McDow gave her.

She never wound it, she said, because she had another one.

"Do you mean to say that it was not necessary for you to keep the watch running to keep Dr. McDow in your mind, that you could remember him without keeping the watch running?"

"Yes, I could," she said, confused.

Magrath smiled at her. He was a handsome man, with his bright blue eyes, big swath of white hair. High cheekbones.

When Hélène left the stand she looked at McDow. He gave her a little smile, as though they were complicit in something, partners still. She smiled back, but they were not complicit, not partners in anything: the strategy of the defense would be to destroy her character.

———·———

MCDOW TOLD THE COURT a different story from the one he told in the interview, on the night of his arrest. During the trial he remembered his courtesy toward Dawson, his composure, his bold, articulate response.

He described Dawson "entering . . . with a domineering air, he proceeded in an excitable and irritable voice to say, 'Dr. McDow, I have just been informed of your ungentlemanly conduct towards one of my servants.'"

Magrath stopped McDow. "Wait a moment. What was his manner?"

"Domineering and aggressive," McDow repeated.

Magrath nodded and went on. "You repelled the idea that you had been ungentlemanly in your conduct?"

"Yes, sir," said McDow briskly. "I naturally felt indignant that the man should have entered my office in such a way."

"Describe to me the general appearance of Captain Dawson," Magrath asked. He was walking slowly back and forth before the chair. "Was he a large man or a small man?"

"Rather a large man," said McDow. "Possibly over two hundred pounds in weight and well-developed, muscularly."

"Had he the appearance of being a strong man?" asked Magrath.

"He had all the appearances of being an athlete," McDow said.

"Do you think that you compared favorably with Captain Dawson in that regard?" asked Magrath.

"Well, I think comparatively I am a mere pygmy," said McDow.

Magrath wouldn't let this go. "His physical powers were much in excess of yours, were they not?"

"Very much in excess," McDow assured him.

"Then after this first salutation what followed; what did he rejoin?"

"He said, 'I give you to understand that she is under my protection and if you speak to her again I shall publish you in the papers,' and I said, 'If you do, you infernal scoundrel, I will hold you personally responsible,'" McDow said, pleased with himself.

"Do me the favor to repeat that answer?" asked Magrath.

"He said, 'I forbid you speaking to her.' I told him that I would speak to her as long as I pleased, until he showed me he had the authority to prevent it."

"Then he said . . ." Magrath said, coaxingly.

"'I give you to understand, sir, she is under my protection and if you speak to her again I shall publish you in the papers,' and I said, 'If you do, you infernal scoundrel, I will hold you personally responsible. Get out of my office.'"

McDow was pleased by the phrase "infernal scoundrel."

There were other changes in his story. In his first interview, in jail, McDow had told the reporter that the pistol had been in a desk drawer, and he'd scrambled across the room, around the table and to the far corner, while Dawson took two steps to reach the door. Now, at the trial, he said the pistol was in his right hip pocket. That he'd pulled it out to shoot Dawson in the front, to keep him from attacking McDow again. He said he'd carried a pistol for years.

The prosecution challenged this: Why would a doctor carry a gun? No doctors carry guns; it's antithetical to their calling. And no one carries a loaded gun in his pocket when he sits down to have dinner with his family. Then he got specific: McDow certainly hadn't carried this one for years, as it was clearly brand-new. On the day of the murder McDow was followed by a detective, who saw him buy it. Moreover, when McDow was asked what sort of pistol it was, he didn't know the caliber.

McDow claimed that Dawson had struck him ferociously, on the chest, with his hand, and on the head, with his cane; that the caning had bruised his head and dented his hat. But Dawson could not have dented the hat: McDow had not been wearing it when Dawson arrived. McDow had been upstairs having dinner then. He'd put on his hat later, when he went out to get the spade. As to an assault, the doctor who examined McDow found no evidence of battery, only a small scab on the left side of his head. The dent and injury might have come from bumping against the lintel of the closet as McDow buried Dawson. Or the injury might have come from McDow running into the doorframe in Mrs. Fair's bedroom. She'd written to the judge, describing McDow's gross insult to her person, and his violent encounter with the doorframe. She offered to testify, but was not permitted to do so, nor was her letter allowed in evidence.

In closing, Magrath walked up to McDow and asked him, man to man, about Hélène. Smiling, as though they were intimates, he asked a personal question. Did McDow think he behaved in an ungentlemanly manner toward her?

"Under the circumstances I don't know that I did," McDow said, "because of the willingness on the part of this woman, the acquiescence on the part of this woman, to engage in what I had been engaged in."

It was an ingenious defense, the idea that the perpetrator would be exonerated by the pliancy of the victim.

At the summation, Magrath and his colleague, Asher Cohen, made a moral assessment.

"Gentlemen, I have only this to say, that my experience and yours is that a man seldom makes the first advance. There is always something in the eye or manner that extends an invitation. There is some instinct in the heart of man put there, I think, by God for a wise purpose which causes him never or very seldom, unless a very bad man, to make the advance, unless in some mysterious manner an invitation has been extended."

Magrath added gently, "I do say that she, more than he, is responsible for all that has occurred."

So there it was. It was the fault of the French maid.

In the black community, the tide had turned against Dawson. Despite his record of supporting black progress, despite his editorials supporting black rights and the rule of law, despite his relief efforts during the earthquake, his last editorial had been unforgivable.

After Dawson's death *The News and Courier* printed eulogies from all over the country. Scores of white people praised Dawson, people who remembered meeting him, people for whom he'd done something generous.

One woman wrote to thank him for reading her essay at her college graduation. The graduating girls were not to read their own essays in public, so a man, usually one of the family, read the essay for her. But Miss Jennie Grier's essay was written in French, which no one in her family spoke. Someone at the college knew Dawson, and asked him to stand up with Miss Grier at the ceremony. The captain, she wrote, not only read the speech in French, but, when he saw the audience had no idea of what it had just heard, he'd started to sing the Marseillaise. No one knew the words, but they all knew the music. The whole crowd sang it lustily, and afterward they cheered. Miss Grier wrote to say how much that had meant to her: she had never met him before that day. Librarians, schoolteachers, community organizers, readers, professors, lawyers, and farmers wrote in to the paper to express their grief. But the sole response from a black leader came from Reverend J. L. Dart.

I have no hesitation in saying that I believe he was deeply interested in all that concerns the educational and material advancement of the colored people . . .

Capt. Dawson defended the interests of the colored people in this State in several crises, and his liberal influence and sound and healthful views regarding the welfare of this city and State, and all its people, will be greatly missed.

The longtime black leaders were silent. Many in their community trusted Thomas McDow, who'd been their doctor.

The judge allowed no evidence regarding McDow's character. The prosecution was not permitted to ask about his visits to brothels, nor the shooting in Tennessee, nor of the insurance fraud, which was still under investigation. Nor could the prosecution mention the sworn testimony by McDow's brother, declaring that McDow had tried to have his father-in-law murdered so he could poison his wife and marry one of his mistresses. None of this was in the record. Nor, of course, was the story that the jurors were bribed, which included the sums paid to each one.

The jurors, bribed or blameless, took only a few hours to return the verdict: McDow was not guilty of murder. He had been attacked in his home. He had stood his ground.

41.

SARAH DID NOT attend the trial.

On that first rainy day she sat upstairs in her room by the window, in her small striped chair. It felt almost normal, as though she were mending and he were writing beside her. But there was nothing.

She watched the rain lashing the trees, the heavy boughs tossing slowly in the wind. The translucent drops sluiced down the pane, meeting and separating, blurring her view. The thought came to her over and over: he would not come back. It was a recurring revelation. Endlessly she forgot, endlessly she was reminded. They'd had tickets to the opera. She'd have to do something with the tickets. The idea of going without him repelled her. He was gone. Each time she was reminded.

That morning she'd woken up thinking she heard him in the next room. She lifted her head from the deep hollow of the pillow to hear him—what had he said? She waited for him to repeat it—then, waiting, she remembered, and emptiness flooded around her like a black tide.

He would not call to her again in the morning. She would not hear his voice, intimate, rough with sleep, coming through the dimness of the room, still dark before the curtains were drawn. Each time it was like a bargain that somehow she had lost. She was willing to accept the big thing, she knew he was gone. Only it was hard to lose this small thing, the sound of his voice in the dimness of her room. His appearance in the doorway, big and tousled in his nightshirt, his rumpled face, the strong rich smell of his body after sleep. Why must she lose that as well?

The sky outside was dark and lowering with rain. Sarah stood to find a shawl; the chill was coming through the glass. She started toward the armoire and stumbled over the huge dog, sprawled motionless beside her chair.

"Bruno," she whispered.

He lay flat, his nose between his paws. At his name he rolled his eyes up at her but did not lift his head.

"He's not coming back," Sarah said. "He's gone."

Bruno watched her, not moving, his tail tucked along his body. Sarah kneeled beside him. She put her hand on his broad head, hard and silky. His eyes followed her. His tail didn't move.

"But you know that," Sarah whispered. "Don't you." She stroked his head, then laid her own against it. She put her arm around him. He was warm and solid. She began to weep.

Later she sat in the big red plush chair. Her body felt heavy, as though it were filled with sand. She thought of McDow holding forth in court, telling lies. She leaned back, pressing herself against its rounded tufts. She thought of the piano downstairs. He wouldn't sit at it playing for the children, his head thrown back, that silly song about the duck. And Mozart. It seemed impossible that she couldn't find him somehow, return to the moment of him singing. He wasn't here in the room, she knew that, but wasn't he somewhere? It was impossible to think that he was nowhere in the world.

She lay her head down on his desk, on the blotting paper where he'd leaned his arm while he wrote. She could still smell him faintly, his hand, his wrist. Sometimes she went to his armoire and pressed her head into his lovely clothes, the good tweeds, the melton-cloth coats. They still smelled of him, her husband.

That day she walked from window to window in his room, then back into her own. She stood behind the thin curtain and looked down over Bull

Street. The rain was lessening; people were driving past as though it were a normal day. A Negro man came by, leading a goat and cart. The man was lame, and walked slowly, one ankle twisting with each step. He held the goat by the halter. The goat's ears flopped. She watched until he was out of sight. It was remarkable: the man acted as though nothing had happened, as if the earth had not suddenly quit its revolutions, as if Frank were still alive.

That night they had brought him back and laid him on the dining room table. The doctors had been at him. He was swathed in a sheet to his neck, but his head was untouched. They left her alone with him. His face was gray, and she could not bear to look at him. She could not look away. Inside one nostril was a smear of dark blood. He had bled from the nose and the mouth, and the skin was stained. She thought of the blood moving through his body, the exquisite network of arteries and veins, the subtle pulsing movement from heart to lungs to fingertips. He had bled from within. She could not bring herself to touch the intimate cavity, his nostril. His body had been breached from within.

She thought of McDow firing the single shot. She imagined him raising the pistol, taking aim. He'd shot Frank from the side and back. Not from the front. He had shot Frank when he had turned, when he was opening the door to leave.

She couldn't bear to think of Frank putting his hand to his side, saying the words "You have killed me." She closed her eyes when she thought of those words.

———————

THAT NIGHT SHE had sent the children to the Lafittes'. She hadn't told them what had happened. In the morning she went to fetch them. She held their hands as they walked back home, just around the corner. She took them upstairs past the niches in the stairwell. In her room she sat down on her bed and held out her arms. Frightened, they sat down on either side of her.

"Mes pauvres chéris, vos père est mort," she said. *My poor darlings, your father is dead.* She couldn't bring herself to say it in English. They looked up at her, their faces strange with shock. They didn't believe her. But it was true, and she said it again. It seemed terrible that she should have to insist.

Warrington looked down and clapped his legs together tightly and crossed them at the ankle. Ethel stared up at Sarah.

"Il est parti?" she said. *He's gone?* "I never said goodbye. I never said I was sorry."

Then they all cried, huddled together on the bed, the mourning doves trilling quietly in the branches outside. Sarah rubbed Ethel's back, her fingers getting tangled in the long hair. The two things seemed joined, incomprehensible: the tangled fingers, his death.

⸻

DURING THE TRIAL Hemphill came to see her at the end of every day, to tell her what had happened in court. They sat in the parlor with a tea tray. Hemphill passed his handkerchief over his forehead. He was a burly, kindly man. She could see that it was distressing him.

"How was it today?" she asked.

"They deposed one of the jurors," he said. "They asked if he'd told an official of the court that if McDow chose him for the jury, 'It would be all right for McDow.'"

"So bald," she said. "What did he say?"

"He more or less admitted it," Hemphill said.

She knew they'd all read Frank's last editorial. But she expected them to remember his long record of support. She expected them to find Thomas McDow guilty of murdering her husband.

They did not.

⸻

AFTERWARD SARAH AND HÉLÈNE were the only grown-ups in the household. Hélène was mournful, and wept while she sat sewing in the window. She wrote a long poem about the captain, which she gave to Sarah: we will never see his like again, she grieved. She confessed about meeting McDow; she wept and begged forgiveness. Sarah forgave her: Hélène was young, and without a mother, and far from home. To silence the gossip she had a doctor examine Hélène to be sure that she was still *intacta*. Which he said she was.

Hélène pitied Madame, who was now a figure of failure and loss, a widow. She had lost her patron. The captain had had the power, the stature. Now Madame had become powerless and old. Hélène felt, privately, that they were now equals; Madame had been brought low. She, Hélène, still had a future; Madame had none. She offered solace to Madame; that was her obligation now. She recited sayings to make her feel better: En tout pays, il y a une lieue de mauvais chemin; *in every countryside, there's a bad road*. It was comforting to know this happened to everyone.

Sarah pitied Hélène, the center of such a public scandal. That summer she took Hélène and the children up into the mountains. They changed trains in Columbia, and as they walked across the platform Sarah heard a woman whisper. People were looking at them. Someone said, "The French maid!" People gathered, avid. Sarah took Hélène's arm and looked straight ahead as they walked into the ladies' waiting room. "Ignore them," Sarah said.

Sarah made a scrapbook of the trial for Hélène. She pitied Hélène and was grateful for her company, but they were not friends. They were companions of a sort, nothing more. Each time Hélène recited a proverb Sarah thought of the intimacy she'd lost, with someone with whom she'd seemed to share a mind. Now she was reduced to a deadly dailiness with someone who spouted clichés. They were yoked together by the dreadful burden of the death, but they were not a pair.

"Après la pluie, le beau temps," Hélène reminded her. *After the rain comes good weather.*

Yes, Sarah said.

One afternoon they were in Sarah's room. They were brushing her clothes against moths before putting them away for the summer. Sarah held up a blue georgette dress by the shoulders; Hélène crouched before her, wielding the stiff-bristled brush. She held the skirt wide with one hand.

"Brush hard, Hélène," Sarah said. "Along the seams. Make sure to get the eggs."

"The eggs," Hélène repeated.

"Small and white," Sarah said. "They look like specks. Inside them are the moth larvae. Little worms. They eat their way out through the clothes."

"Yes," said Hélène. She didn't believe any of this. Eggs, worms. It wasn't likely. "It's a beautiful dress, Madame. You don't wear it." Madame hadn't worn colors since the funeral. She thought of wearing it herself. It would suit her. She wondered if Sarah would think of giving it to her.

Sarah shook her head. She couldn't imagine wearing blue. Her heart had become dark.

"Time heals," Hélène offered, brushing hard.

Sarah's arms were tiring, holding up the dress. She felt she was waiting for something, something was gathering around her, some great breath was being held, but what was it? Frank was not coming back. But she was waiting for something: for her life to start again.

"And in the end," Hélène said, under her breath, "the ocean will wash away the guilt." She turned up the hem, scrubbing along the edge.

Sarah looked at her. "Wash away the guilt?"

Hélène looked up. She was kneeling now, leaning back on her heels.

"Whose guilt will be washed away?" asked Sarah. "The doctor's?" She wouldn't speak his name. "Are you saying his guilt will be washed away? It will never be washed away. What are you talking about, Hélène?"

But Hélène plucked at the stiff bristles of the brush and said nothing.

"Whose guilt?" Sarah asked again.

Hélène shook her head and looked down at the dress. "It was a manner of speaking," she said. She began brushing, hard.

Sarah looked down at her, frowning. Whose guilt?

———·———

ONE AFTERNOON in the following spring, Sarah was in her room, reading an article in *The Century*. She heard Warrington's voice rise, suddenly high and outraged. She went on reading, waiting for it to lower. Now another voice was raised: Hélène answered him angrily. Hélène had no dignity. She quarreled with them as though she were a third child of the house. Sarah put down the magazine and went into his room.

They were grappling in front of his little fireplace. Hélène held Warrington by the wrists, he was pushing at her.

"Laisses-moi!" he cried, furious. *Let me go!*

"Non," she said, in a sort of hiss.

"What's going on?"

Warrington turned, red-faced. "She took my diary! She threw it in the fire!"

In the grate something was burning, white pages curling and blackening, smoke rising dark and twisting.

"Is that his diary?" Sarah asked Hélène.

Hélène thrust Warrington's wrists away and he staggered backward. "He wrote that I was the French maid," she said. "It's insupportable. I am not French and I am not a maid."

Sarah leaped to the fireplace. She took the iron tongs, lifted the little blaze, and dropped it on the hearth: a small notebook with a caramel-colored cover. The cover was charred, the pages lifting. Smoke rose from it in a dark twisting skein.

"How *dare* you take his diary," Sarah said. "How *dare* you destroy his property."

"It's only a child's book," Hélène said. "I saw what he wrote. He may not call me that."

"It's what they call her," Warrington said, his voice high and quavering.

"It's *wrong*," hissed Hélène. "It's wrong. You may not say it."

"And you may *not* take his belongings," Sarah said, furious. "That is his book. That is his writing. You have destroyed it."

Hélène lifted her chin.

"Do you understand me, Hélène?" Sarah said, raising her voice. "What you've done is very serious."

Maybe she'd fire her right now, this minute. Rage had been building in her for a year, rising like black smoke in a chimney. She would not put up with this.

"And he has done something very serious," Hélène said. She shifted her shoulders, almost shrugging, rude as a terrier.

"Don't speak to me like that, Hélène," Sarah said. Now she had lowered her voice. "Remember your place."

"I know my place, Madame," Hélène said. She felt something boiling up inside her. She thought of Joan. "I have always known my place in this house. I know who I am, and who you are." She could feel her true self appearing. "I knew the captain would be murdered that day. The doctor told me and I was glad. The captain was interfering with my life. He could not tell me how to behave." She set her hand on her hip. "The doctor told me what he was going to do." She held her head high. Like Joan she would never yield.

There was a long silence. Hélène's insolence, her vast overweening vanity, her stupidity, her ignorant malice, her recklessness and disloyalty rose and swelled, like hot choking air, filling the house, every space in it.

"Faites vos malles," Sarah said. *Pack your bags.* Heat rose into her throat, her cheeks. She was stiff with rage; she was incandescent. "I'll take you to the train in the morning."

They stared at each other.

Hélène stepped backward. Her face turned sober. She gave a half curtsy.

"Go to your room. I don't wish to see you anymore tonight," Sarah said.

Hélène gave another little bob. "The train? To?"

Sarah said nothing.

"The train to where, Madame?"

"To New York. My sister, Madame DuPres, will put you on the boat to France."

Hélène stood frozen. Her eyes were set fast on Sarah. She put her hands together at her breast.

"And will you give me a letter?" she asked.

Sarah said nothing.

"A letter of recommendation?" Hélène asked, timid.

Sarah said nothing, her pale eyes on Hélène.

"Without a letter, I have no future, Madame," she said. "No agency will take me."

Sarah looked at her levelly. "A letter of recommendation," she repeated. "As what?"

"Mama," Warrington said. He held the tongs, gripping the charred diary. "Some of it is all right." Though it was not; the blackened leaves broke off, charred and brittle, and drifted to the hearth.

———•———

SARAH LIVED FOR the next ten years beside her husband's murderer. Before that day Sarah had never seen him on the street; afterward she saw him often, his sloping shoulders, his awkward stride. Sarah always wore black, and when she saw him she stopped and raised her arm to point at him. She stood in silence, swiveling slowly to hold her aim as he moved past, like a compass set at Guilt. She pointed until he was out of sight.

Ten years. In 1898 Ethel married a lawyer and moved to New York; Sarah gave her the mahogany dining table as a wedding present. She rented the house on Bull Street and she and Warrington moved to France. Versailles, not Provence: she never lived in the stone house with blue shutters. It was a relief to be gone from Charleston, surrounded by the language of her childhood, on streets where she had never seen Frank.

In 1904 McDow committed suicide. He was living alone by then; his wife had left him for good. His body wasn't found for several days. Beside his bed was a glass of water containing traces of chloral hydrate.

On May 5, 1909, Sarah was in the apartment she shared with her son. Warrington was in Africa. He was now a journalist, and on assignment, covering President Roosevelt's safari. So he had become an explorer after all. Sarah was proud of him. She hoped he'd marry well, as Marie had foretold. She waited for his letters, long and newsy, one each week.

Sarah had been feeling poorly, and then a cough had come on. She'd felt weakened by it and had taken to her bed. The doctor had come: pneumonia had settled in her lungs. That day a nurse sat near her, knitting, and the room was quiet except for Sarah's slow, difficult breaths. She lay against the pillow, drifting in and out of sleep. She was waiting for her son to return. She could feel him somewhere, distant, but quick and alive. She closed her eyes. Her chest felt small and compressed, diminished. She took the linen sheet between her fingers, plucking. When she opened her eyes she saw the dark armoire across the room, and the tall windows with white curtains shifting in the breeze. She thought of the rainy morning in Baton Rouge. The pattering sound on the leaves, and the tall curtains belling slowly out, then collapsing. She could feel the cool damp wind, like sadness.

———————

SLAVERY IS AMERICA'S fell forefather, violence and racism its ghastly offspring. Slavery makes the body a tablet on which to write the messages of pain and death. Violence allows the human heart to express its darkest impulses; racism allows the human heart to close against itself.

———•———

IT'S NEARLY a thousand years since the Morgans moved to the Welsh mountains, to avoid enslavement by the foreign king. It no longer seems remarkable. Now it seems like what anyone would do, if only they could.

BIBLIOGRAPHY

Note: All texts in nonstandard fonts are direct quotes from the sources listed, including original errors in grammar, spelling, and so forth.

Some passages in standard font draw heavily from named sources—in particular, the various accounts of the Hamburg massacre, recorded in congressional testimony, and those of McDow's trial, which were published in various newspapers.

As a novelist I have imagined thoughts and dialogue. But as a biographer I have hewed to what is known and documented, and have knowingly changed no facts. The most preposterous things in this narrative are true.

BOOKS

Bederman, Gail. *Manliness and Civilization: A Cultural History of Gender and Race in the United States, 1880–1917.* Chicago: University of Chicago Press, 1995.

Budiansky, Stephen. *The Bloody Shirt: Terror After the Civil War.* New York: Plume, 2009.

Butterfield, Fox. *All God's Children: The Bosket Family and the American Tradition of Violence.* New York: Vintage, 2008.

Clark, E. Culpepper. *Francis Warrington Dawson and the Politics of Restoration: South Carolina, 1874–1889.* Tuscaloosa: University of Alabama Press, 1980.

Collins, Varnum Lansing. "Prospect near Princeton." *Princeton University Bulletin* 15, no. 3 (June 1904), https://babel.hathitrust.org/cgi/pt?id=njp.32101074935030.

Dawson, Francis Warrington. *Reminiscences of Confederate Service, 1861–1865.* Edited by Bell I. Wiley. Baton Rouge: Louisiana State University Press, 1980.

Dawson, Francis Warrington, Jr. *Le nègre aux États-Unis.* Paris: Librairie Orientale & Américaine, 1912.

Dawson, Francis Warrington, Jr. *Buz and Fury.* Chicago: Honest Truth Publishing, 1923.

Dawson, Sarah Morgan. *The Civil War Diary of a Southern Woman.* Edited by Charles East. Athens: University of Georgia Press, 1991.

Dawson, Sarah Morgan. *A Confederate Girl's Diary.* Boston: Houghton Mifflin, 1913.

Dew, Charles B. *The Making of a Racist: A Southerner Reflects on Family, History, and the Slave Trade.* Charlottesville: University of Virginia Press, 2016.

Fischer, David Hackett. *Albion's Seed: Four British Folkways in America.* New York: Oxford University Press, 1989.

McKinley, Carlyle. *An Appeal to Pharaoh: The Negro Problem, and Its Radical Solution.* New York: Fords, Howard and Hulbert, 1889.

The Miscellaneous Documents of the Senate of the United States for the Second Session of the Forty-Fourth Congress. Washington, DC: Government Printing Office, 1877.

Morgan, James Morris. *Recollections of a Rebel Reefer.* Boston: Houghton Mifflin, 1917.

Poston, Jonathan H. *The Buildings of Charleston: A Guide to the City.* Columbia: University of South Carolina Press, 1997.

Roberts, Giselle. *The Correspondence of Sarah Morgan and Francis Warrington Dawson.* Athens: University of Georgia Press, 2004.

Sass, Herbert Ravenel. *Outspoken: 150 Years of* The News and Courier. Columbia: University of South Carolina Press, 1953.

Savelle, Max. *George Morgan, Colony Builder.* New York: Columbia University Press, 1932. Reprinted 1967.

Townsend, Belton O'Neall. *When South Carolina Was an Armed Camp.* Edited by John Hammond Moore. Charleston, SC: Home House Press, 2013.

Williams, Susan Millar, and Steven G. Hoffius. *Upheaval in Charleston: Earthquake and Murder on the Eve of Jim Crow.* Athens: University of Georgia Press, 2011.

OTHER SOURCES

Barry, Ethel Morgan Dawson. *Reminiscences.* Undated.

Barry, Stuyvesant. "Francis Warrington Dawson." Thesis, Harvard University, 1931.

Charleston, SC, *News and Courier,* historical archives.

Charleston History Before 1945, Facebook group.

Francis Warrington Dawson Papers, Rubenstein Rare Book and Manuscript Library, Duke University.

ACKNOWLEDGMENTS

My thanks go first to the Rubenstein Rare Book and Manuscript Library at Duke University, where I was deeply honored to receive the inaugural Rudoph William Rosati Visiting Writer Fellowship. This provided me with a scholar's feast: the run of their beautifully maintained archives, which house the Dawson family papers. My thanks to the friendly, helpful, and superbly capable staff there, especially Sara Seten Berghausen, associate curator of collections, and the phenomenal Elizabeth Dunn, research librarian extraordinaire. I could not have imagined a more fruitful or productive opportunity for a scholar. And thanks to Christina Askounis, novelist and Duke professor, who alerted me to this opportunity. Thanks to Sarah Virginia Halman and Karen Halman, descendants of the Raines family, of Oakland, for sharing family information. Thanks to James Cummins Bookseller for providing the only known photograph of Marie-Hélène Burdayron and the Dawson family.

Thanks to my diligent and thoughtful research assistant, Abigail Struhl, who transcribed handwritten manuscripts, tracked down sources and information, and did a hundred finicky and necessary tasks. Many, many thanks to Susan Millar Williams and Stephen G. Hoffius, esteemed scholars of the period, the place, and the Dawson family, who have been generous with their thoughts and knowledge; Harlan Greene, another scholar of this subject, who has been endlessly generous and helpful; Culpepper Clark, Dawson's biographer, also generous with his thoughts and his unpublished materials; and thanks to Kevin Levin, T. J. Stiles, and Nicholas Lemann, distinguished scholars, for their prompt and informed responses to my queries. Thanks, too, to Charles East, for his meticulous scholarship on Sarah Morgan Dawson's diaries. To Allan Gurganus, Lee Smith, and Frances Mayes, who offered writerly support in North Carolina. Thanks to Josephine Humphreys, who gave me advice and encouragement, a tour of her Charleston, and an introduction to the lively and knowledgeable Facebook group *Charleston History Before 1945*. Beth Cambell Stoney, for her long and thoughtful description of 99 Bull Street when she lived there; also Sister Buchanan, for the story of her grandmother's graduation in Due West; and Kristy Nobles, for her helpful information about the Dawson house. Thanks to Mary Rasenberger, Sandy Long, and everyone at the Authors Guild, who allowed me to take time out to finish this manuscript while I was engaged by Guild matters.

My profound thanks to Sarah Crichton, for her vision and enthusiasm and her belief in this project. Thanks, too, to Jonathan Galassi, and the brilliant FSG team: Rebecca Caine, Ben Rosenstock, Richard Oriolo, and Lottchen Shivers. And thanks to my matchless agent, Lynn Nesbit.

Thanks most of all to my husband, for putting up with someone who spends half her time somewhere else, with people he doesn't know.

A NOTE ABOUT THE AUTHOR

Roxana Robinson is the author of five previous novels, three collections of short stories, and the biography *Georgia O'Keeffe: A Life*. Her work has appeared in *The Atlantic*, *The New Yorker*, *The New York Times*, *Harper's Magazine*, *The Nation*, *The Washington Post*, *The Wall Street Journal*, *Tin House*, *The American Scholar*, and *Vogue*, among other publications. She has received fellowships from Duke University, the MacDowell Colony, the National Endowment for the Arts, and the Guggenheim Foundation. She is a former president of the Authors Guild, and she teaches in the MFA program at Hunter College. She spends her time in New York, Connecticut, and Maine.